COWBOY JUSTICE AT WHISKEY GULCH

ELLE JAMES

THE LOST HART TRIPLET

NICOLE HELM

MILLS & BOON

First Published in Great Britain 2022
by Mills & Boon, an imprint of HarperCollins*Publishers* Ltd
1 London Bridge Street, London, SE1 9GF

www.harpercollins.co.uk

HarperCollins*Publishers*
1st Floor, Watermarque Building,
Ringsend Road, Dublin 4, Ireland

Cowboy Justice at Whiskey Gulch © 2022 Mary Jernigan
The Lost Hart Triplet © 2022 Nicole Helm

ISBN: 978-0-263-30357-5

0922

COWBOY JUSTICE
AT WHISKEY GULCH

ELLE JAMES

For my father, who had the heart and morals of a hero and the work ethic of a cowboy. He was the man who set the bar for all other men in my life. He was a quiet guy who loved his family and would do anything for us. I love and miss you, Dad.

Prologue

Parker Shaw was greeted with silence as he swam up out of the darkness. He stared at the stars in a clear night sky and wondered where the hell he was.

When he tried to move, pain radiated throughout his body. He lay back panting, his head swimming, his vision fogged by a gray haze.

A breeze swept over him, carrying the scent of smoke and aviation fuel, sending a rush of images through his confused mind.

Afghanistan.

The mission…kill…who?

Lying as still as possible was the only way to keep the pain at bay.

Kill who?

Taliban leader Abdul Akhund.

Memories rushed in.

They'd gone into the town, made their kill and were on their way out to their extraction point when all hell broke loose.

The alarm went out and a dozen Taliban came out of the woodwork.

They'd barely made it to the field where the helicopter was to pick them up. Once all six Deltas were on board, the pilot lifted off the ground.

The rest was a little fuzzy.

There was a loud bang…the aircraft shuttered…and dropped from the sky.

Parker lifted his head enough to see the wreckage of the helicopter a few feet away. His heart raced and he struggled again to move. Pain ripped through his leg, ribs and arm. Hell, everything hurt. But he had to get to the helicopter.

With one hand, Parker pushed to a sitting position. His other arm hung at his side, useless. His head spun, the cuts on his arms burned and the throb in his leg was excruciating.

When he tried to stand, only one leg worked, the other too injured to support his weight. The only way he could get to the chopper was to drag himself.

He dug the fingers of his good hand into the dirt and pulled himself toward the mangled wreckage, the knot in his gut nothing to do with his injuries. He knew before he reached the mass of twisted metal what he'd find.

Amid the crushed fuselage lay his friends, his team, the men he considered brothers.

No sounds rose from the wreckage. No moans of the dying. Those trapped inside had died instantly upon impact. The only reason he'd survived was because he'd been thrown.

Shouts and an engine's rumble disturbed the silence.

Unable to walk, much less run, Parker turned away from the destruction and dragged himself away.

Headlights pierced the darkness. A truck rolled to a stop beside the helicopter. Men with AK-47s dropped out of the back and surrounded what remained of the chopper, with Parker having made it a mere twenty feet away.

With the Taliban surrounding the downed Black Hawk, it was only a matter of time before they discovered him.

He lay still, facedown, and played possum.

With his injuries, he'd just as soon be dead.

A shout sounded and footsteps pounded the earth, heading toward him.

He couldn't fight back. He didn't have a gun. His knife was still in the sheath around his waist, but he couldn't fight off at least half a dozen armed Taliban. If he wanted to survive, he had to remain "dead."

Peering through his eyelashes, he watched as each of the men gathered around him, all talking at once.

Parker's Pashto was sketchy at best. From what little he understood, they were wondering if he could be alive.

One man poked his side with the barrel of his rifle, hitting one of Parker's injured ribs.

With every ounce of control, Parker fought to keep from making a sound or from flinching.

As if still unsure, the guy nudged him with the toe of his boot. Then pushed harder until Parker was rolled onto his back.

In Pashto the man said, "These are the men who killed Akhund."

One of the Taliban terrorists dropped to his haunches and pulled at the buckles on Parker's body armor, then jerked it off his body.

Bolts of pain ripped through Parker, driving him to the edge of a blackout. He must have moaned.

The Taliban fighter jumped back, holding the bullet-proof body armor to his chest and called out in Pashto, "He is alive!"

A taller guy gave the order. "Take him."

Too injured and broken to fight back, Parker continued to feign unconsciousness, hoping his deadweight would deter them from carrying him to wherever they had in mind. He needed to stay with the chopper. Eventually, a team would be sent out to recover the bodies.

If taken by the Taliban, they might never find his body. He had no doubt they'd end up killing him.

Two men hooked their hands beneath Parker's shoulders and hauled him to his feet.

The pain shooting through his arm and injured leg made him pass out, only to come to while being dragged toward the truck.

Parker was in big trouble. His team had taken out Akhund to rid Afghanistan of one of the most ruthless terrorists the Taliban boasted of. Akhund's MO had been to torture, drag his prisoner in front of a camera and then behead him.

Parker couldn't run. His leg was most likely broken. He couldn't fight, his shoulder seemed to be dislocated, and his ribs felt like someone was piercing him with a hot poker.

If they were going to behead him, he hoped it would be soon. It couldn't be any worse than the torture he was already facing.

The pain sent him in and out of consciousness.

He came to again when they dropped him in the dirt in front of the pickup's tailgate.

The largest, meanest looking man in the group

grabbed his hair, yanked his head up and said in Pashto, "You are one of the infidels who killed Abdul Akhund."

Yeah, you moron, Parker thought. He closed his eyes and pretended to pass out.

The man holding his hair backhanded him across the cheekbone and released his grip on Parker's hair.

Parker crashed to the ground and lay there, hoping they'd think he was dead and leave him alone.

That wasn't to be.

A booted foot kicked Parker in the ribs. If they weren't already broken, they would be now.

Once wasn't enough. The man kicked him again.

After the fourth kick, Parker grabbed the man's foot with his good hand and pulled it out from under him.

The man came down hard on his backside.

The other men surrounded him, kicking wherever they could get a foot in.

Parker balled into the fetal position, covering his head the best he could with his one good arm, the other lying uselessly beneath him. Agony racked his body to the point he had to disassociate himself from what was happening.

His vision blurred as he teetered on the verge of blacking out, yet again.

The big guy shouted, and the kicking ceased.

Parker sucked in a labored breath, pain knifing through his chest with even the slightest movement.

He was grabbed again beneath the arms and hauled to an upright position, dangling between the men holding him.

The big guy punched him in the face several times and then in the gut.

Blood dripped from a cut above his eyebrow, blinding one of Parker's eyes. The other had been hit enough it had begun to swell, making it difficult to see.

If not for the sound of a helicopter, the men would have continued to hit him. Instead, the one who was apparently in charge shouted orders to the terrorists holding him.

They tossed him into the back of the truck, jumped in with him and took off, headed away from the crashed chopper and the village where the Delta Force team had met their mission objectives.

Parker needed to stay at the crash site. It was the only way a rescue team would be able to find him. However, with two men holding on to him, Parker had no way of escaping.

Through the slit of his swollen eyelid, he watched as the dark silhouette of a Black Hawk helicopter appeared on the horizon, heading toward them.

The Taliban driver hit the accelerator, picking up speed, taking Parker farther away from his chance of rescue. His only hope disappeared in the cloud of dust the truck kicked up behind them.

If he survived whatever the terrorists had in store for him, he was on his own to get back to friendly forces.

The truck headed into the hills on a dirt road that curved through a narrow valley. Every rut, bump and swerve hit Parker with a fresh jolt of torment.

When the vehicle finally stopped, the leader appeared at the end of the truck bed, carrying a machete. He waved it at the men and ordered them to take their prisoner to the top of a hill.

This was it. The point at which he'd be beheaded.

They dragged him out of the vehicle. When his legs

hit the ground, the jolt of pain made him black out. Not for long enough.

At the top of the hill, they dropped him in the dirt.

The big guy chopped limbs from a scrubby tree with a machete and created four stakes. He handed them to the men with instructions to pound them into the ground. Then they tore off Parker's uniform jacket, ripped it into long strips, and tied them to the stakes.

Parker fought the best he could with one arm and one leg. It took four men to hold him down, while two more tied his wrists and ankles to the stakes.

Their leader stood over him with the machete, his eyes narrowing, his lip curling into a feral sneer as he leaned over and slid the machete across Parker's side and then over his broken leg, leaving two lines of blood. "He will die a slow death as the birds feast on his flesh."

Then he spat on Parker, turned and left. His men followed. The sound of the truck engine echoed off the hills, slowly fading away.

Parker lay in the silence, the cool night air biting his exposed flesh. Blood seeped from the wounds in his side and thigh and he thanked the Lord for sparing him the beheading.

He wouldn't give up. No, sir. Not while there was fight still left in him.

For thirty minutes, maybe an hour, he lay still, gathering strength, working at the bindings around his wrist. He pulled and tugged, slowly trying to wiggle the stake loose in the ground, until the stake finally pulled free.

Fueled by that little bit of success, he pressed his hand to the wound in his side. The blood had congealed. He could do little until he freed his other wrist and ankles. Beyond that, he didn't dare think. A man with a broken leg, left alone in the hills, had little chance of survival.

Parker rolled to his side, the broken ribs shooting a fresh kind of hell through his body. He reached for his other wrist and yanked at the bindings. The stake came free quicker than the last.

He lay back in the dirt, breathing raggedly. For a long moment, he considered how much easier it would have been had the Taliban cut off his head. But that would mean they'd won. When he survived and made it back to friendly forces, he would thumb his nose at the men who'd left him to die.

Pressing his good arm to his chest and side, he struggled to sit up, failing twice before succeeding. He bent his knees and scooted on his buttocks toward the stakes holding down his ankles. Then he leaned over and reached for the one holding his broken left leg.

Because his legs were spread wide and bending over hurt his ribs, he had a difficult time reaching with his right hand. Eventually, he snagged the binding and jerked hard, leaning back as he did.

Sweat popped out on his forehead. Through the stabbing pain in his ribs and leg, he persevered until the stake slid free of the hard-packed ground.

Not taking a break from the pain, he worked the other leg free. With only one functional hand, he didn't bother to untie the bindings from around his wrists and ankles. However, he was able to slip the stakes free at the other end.

A broken leg and a dislocated arm would make it impossible for him to get far. The rescue team would have located the crashed helicopter. Hopefully, they would have extracted his fallen brothers and realized they were one short.

His throat tightened as images of his teammates' bodies, trapped in the wreckage of the Black Hawk, flooded his mind. He should have died with them. But he hadn't. Eyes burning, he vowed to live because his fallen comrades would have expected that of him. To honor their deaths by living the life he'd been spared.

Maybe walking out of the hills and all the way to the forward operating base wasn't reasonable. But if he could let them know where he was without alerting the Taliban, he might have a chance.

Over the next twenty-four hours, he put his plan in place, dragging his broken body over the rocky hilltop inch by inch, gathering, arranging and creating a message his country would see, but not the Taliban. If they were looking.

When he was done, he found a spot in the middle, lay down and covered his body in dirt to help combat the chill of the night air and slept.

Morning dawned, waking him with the bright light of the sun rising on the eastern horizon. His leg throbbed and his ribs burned with every breath he took. What he wouldn't give for a drink of water. With the daylight, he started to second-guess his decision to send a message.

How long should he wait for help to arrive? Should he find a way to get himself out of the hills and back to the FOB? Or was it like getting lost in the forest? Should he stay in one place and let the search party have a better chance of finding him? When they didn't find his body in the wreckage, they'd either assume he'd escaped. Or they'd assume he'd been taken to an unknown location in a Taliban-held village.

He'd give his message another day and then try to get himself out of the hills.

With the pain of his injuries slowing his progress, he used his one semi-functional arm to drag himself around the top of the hill, searching for anything he could use to splint his broken leg.

The area was dotted with sparse vegetation consisting of a few short bushes and one gnarled tree— about four feet high with crooked branches—leaning toward the southeast side.

At the edge of the hill, Parker looked down into the valley below. A few taller trees reached for the sun. If he made it to the bottom, he'd have to climb back up to wave down any helicopter or airplane that might fly over.

If a friendly aircraft didn't fly over in another day, he'd drag himself to the valley for straight sticks to use as splints and a crutch. In the meantime, the crooked limbs would have to do. They'd be hard enough to acquire as it was.

He spent the next hour pulling himself up the side of the gnarled tree and breaking off limbs. Then he worked the knots loose on the ties around his ankles and used those strips of cloth to wrap around the limbs he'd pulled from the tree.

His dislocated arm hung useless throughout.

When he had his leg sufficiently splinted, he pulled himself up to stand by the tree. Then he wedged the knotted end of the fabric around the wrist of his bad arm into a fork between low branches near his knees.

He gritted his teeth, held his breath and leaned back. Pain shot through his arm into his shoulder. By leaning back, he could pull the dislocated arm downward. It wasn't enough. Parker pushed up onto the ball of his good foot, raising his shoulder higher, the knot in the fork of the tree pulling his arm further down.

The joint slid back into the socket.

The searing pain was replaced by a dull ache. Parker eased off the tension and disengaged the knot from the fork. He raised the injured arm and flexed his elbow, finally able to use the arm and hand again.

His success lifted his spirits and hardened his determination to survive.

As the sun set on the day, he lay down in the hollow he'd dug in the middle of his message and covered his body with dirt, using both hands.

Hungry, thirsty, exhausted, his splinted leg aching, he lay for a long time staring up at the sky blanketed by stars. He told himself that the hunger and pain were a reminder that he was still alive.

When morning came, he'd start his crawl down to the valley, where he'd find a long stick to use as a crutch. Then he'd walk back to the FOB.

He felt as if he'd just closed his eyes when the distant thump of rotor blades echoed against the hillsides.

Parker's eyes popped open, and he sat up.

The dark silhouette of a helicopter appeared over the top of a hill headed his way.

His pulse quickened and he scrambled to brush the dirt away from his body. Then he staggered to his feet, the pain in his leg nearly bringing him back down. Fighting back dizziness, he managed to remain standing. If only he had a flashlight or flare. Were they headed to another mission, or were they looking for him?

The helicopter flew over the top of his hill and disappeared over the next one.

Parker's heart sank to the pit of his belly.

Okay, Plan B was to start the long trek back in the morning. Maybe he should start at night. The sooner he made it back, the better. He wouldn't last very long without food. Even less time without water.

He squared his shoulders, pressed his hand to his broken ribs and took a step toward the edge of the hill.

Pain shot up his leg as he placed even the smallest amount of weight on it and hopped back onto his good leg.

Poised to repeat the effort, he paused.

The Black Hawk reappeared, heading straight for his hilltop.

Parker stood still. His breath caught and held in his lungs as he watched.

The chopper didn't slow until it was within five hundred feet of his position. Then it hovered and sank slowly to the ground.

The gunner aimed his machine gun out the side door.

Parker raised his hands.

Several soldiers leaped to the ground, weapons ready, and established a quick perimeter. Two more jumped out and ran toward him.

Parker remained upright.

"Sergeant Shaw?" one of the men asked in a distinct Southern drawl.

"Yes, sir," Parker croaked.

The man grinned and draped one of Parker's arms over his shoulder. "Thank God. I'm Grove, the flight medic. That's Skeeter. We're gonna get you back to the FOB."

The other man slipped Parker's other arm over his shoulder.

He winced and bit down hard to keep from moaning.

Together, they carried Parker between them back to the helicopter.

"When we didn't find you in the crashed helicopter, we thought we never would," Grove said. "Then we got coordinates leading to your SOS and were told we might find our missing Delta here."

Skeeter chuckled. "Smart move, man."

"How you managed to make that big a sign was amazing. Given your injuries, even more so," Grove said.

They eased him down onto the floor of the helicopter. "Lie down. We're going to get you started on an IV," Grove said as the perimeter guards climbed aboard, and the helicopter lifted into the air.

"Wait." Parker held onto Grove's arm and leaned toward the open door of the helicopter for one last look at the hill where the Taliban had left him to die.

As the Black Hawk rose higher, he could see the message he'd written in the large rocks he'd found an abundance of on that hill.

Grove shook his head, grinning. "I don't know how you did it."

Parker wasn't sure, either. But it had worked.

Skeeter nodded. "That's the biggest damned SOS I've ever seen."

"And the first time I've seen an SOS actually save a life," Grove said as he eased Parker onto his back.

"Don't worry. We've got you now. You're going to be all right."

Parker had fought so hard to make it to that point, pushing through the pain. Surrounded by US soldiers, he finally gave in.

His last thought as he faded into unconsciousness was, *I lived for them.*

Chapter One

Six months later

Parker pulled his truck and horse trailer to a stop at the side of the ranch house and shifted into Park. Tired, sore from sitting for so long on the three-day trip from Virginia to Whiskey Gulch, Texas, he dreaded stepping out of the truck. When he'd stopped the day before, his leg had given him hell. Hopefully, it wouldn't this time.

Not in front of his old friend and new boss. He could show no weakness.

A nervous whine reminded him that Brutus needed to stretch as well. It had been several hours since their last rest stop. The sleek silver pit bull stood in the passenger seat, his entire body wagging since he didn't have a tail to do the job.

Parker opened the door and slid to the ground, careful to hold on to the door until he was sure his leg wasn't going to buckle.

It held and he opened the door wider.

"Brutus, come," he commanded.

The dog leaped across the console and stood in the driver's seat, his mouth open, tongue lolling, happy to be there. Happy to be anywhere Parker was.

Ever since Parker had rescued him from his previous owner, Brutus had been glued to his side, a constant companion and eager to please him in every way.

Parker wasn't sure who'd rescued whom. When he'd found Brutus tied to that tree outside a run-down mobile home, starving, without water and in the heat of the summer, he'd known he couldn't leave the animal. He'd stopped his truck, climbed down and limped toward the dog, hoping he wouldn't turn on him and rip him apart.

Brutus had hunkered low to the ground, his head down, his eyes wary. He had scars on his face and body, probably from being beaten. A couple of the scars were round, like someone had pressed a lit cigarette into his skin.

Parker had been sick to find the dog so abused. He'd unclipped the chain from Brutus's neck. Holding on to his collar, he'd limped with the dog back to the truck.

Brutus's owner had yelled from the door. "Hey! Thass my dog."

Parker had helped Brutus into the truck. The animal could barely make it up. He was too light for his breed and all skin and bones.

The owner had come down from the trailer and stalked toward Parker, barefoot, wearing a grimy wife-beater and equally dirty, worn jeans.

Parker had shut the truck door and faced the man.

The guy reeked of alcohol as he stopped in front of Parker and pointed at the truck. "I said thass my dog."

"Not anymore." Parker leveled a hard look at the man. "He's coming with me."

"The hell he is." The drunk had lunged for the door.

Parker grabbed his arm, yanked it hard and twisted it up between the man's shoulder blades.

"What the—" the man had whimpered, standing on his toes to ease the pain. "You got no right to steal a man's dog."

"You had no right to abuse him. Now, I'm taking him, or I'm calling the sheriff to have you arrested for animal cruelty." He ratcheted the arm up a little higher. "Which is it to be?"

The drunk danced on his tiptoes. "All right. Take the damned dog. Can't afford to feed him anyway."

Parker shoved the man as he released his arm.

The drunk spat on the ground at Parker's feet. "Mutt has no fight in him. The only thing he was good for was a bait dog. He never earned the name Brutus."

Rage burned through Parker. He'd swung hard, catching the drunk in the gut.

The man bent over and fell to his knees.

Parker had fought the urge to pummel the man into the dirt. He had to tell himself he wasn't worth going to jail over. And that would leave Brutus homeless.

"Touch another dog and I'll be back to finish the job," Parker warned.

The drunk had vomited and remained on his knees in the dirt as Parker climbed into the truck and drove away.

Brutus had lain on the passenger seat, staring at him all the way to the veterinarian's office, unsure of Parker, probably wondering if this human would beat him as well.

That had been three months ago, shortly after the removal of Parker's leg cast and his move to the Hearts and Heroes Rehabilitation Ranch.

The therapists at the ranch had been hesitant to bring Brutus on board. They'd eventually allowed him to move into Parker's cabin after he'd spent a three-week quarantine period with the veterinarian, taken all his vaccinations and worm meds, and was declared free of fleas.

Parker reached out and scratched Brutus behind the ears. In the three months since he'd rescued the pit bull, the dog had gained twenty pounds, learned to sit, stay, roll over and shake.

More than the tricks, Brutus had helped Parker through therapy. Their walks got longer and longer as both veteran and dog recovered their strength.

Parker stepped back from the truck and tapped his leg, the signal for Brutus to heel.

The dog jumped down from the driver's seat and sat at Parker's feet, looking up at him, eager to please.

"Parker Shaw," a voice called out from the porch of the ranch house.

Parker looked up as Trace Travis stepped down and closed the distance between them.

The former Delta Force operator held out his hand. "I'm so glad you finally arrived. I was beginning to worry you had truck or trailer troubles."

Parker gripped his hand. "Not at all. We made a couple of extra stops along the way to exercise our legs."

Trace pulled him into a quick hug. "It's been a long time."

"Yes, it has," Parker said. Memories of the last time he'd seen Trace surfaced. "We were a good team in Syria."

Trace nodded. "Yes, we were. I miss the guys. I didn't want to take the transfer."

"We missed you, too." Parker's heart constricted in his chest.

"I was sorry to hear about Patch, Griz and Mort."

Trace stepped backward. "I'm glad you're still among the living."

Patch, Griz and Mort were three of the men who hadn't made it out of the crash that had damaged Parker's leg and earned him a medical discharge from the army.

Trace nodded toward the trailer. "I have to admit, I never knew you rode horses."

Parker snorted. "I didn't, until three months ago. The rehab ranch the VA sent me to also rehabilitates horses. I learned there."

"Horses have a way of getting into your blood, heart and soul." Trace grinned. "And I guess you liked it well enough to get one of your own."

Parker shook his head. "I didn't like it at first. Too painful." He tapped his bum leg. "Then I met Jasper. Half-starved, when he came to the ranch shortly after I arrived. He wouldn't let anyone touch him. My therapist challenged me to work with him." Parker reached down to scratch Brutus's ears. "Like the dog, Jasper just needed someone to give a damn. He still won't let anyone else touch him. But he lets me."

"It takes an incredible amount of time and patience to gain a horse's trust," Trace said.

Parker snorted. "I had plenty of time. I learned the patience." The pounding of a horse's hoof against the floor of the trailer made Parker turn toward the trailer. "Speak of the devil. I need to let him out and get him some food and water. He's had it rough the past few days, cooped up in that trailer."

Trace tipped his head to the side. "Bring him to the barn. He can have a stall while you feed him and there's a pasture you can let him run in afterward."

Parker backed Jasper out of the trailer and walked with him, Brutus and Trace to the barn.

Trace chuckled. "I've never hired anyone who accepted my offer on the condition I accept his horse and dog as part of the bargain."

"We appreciated it," Parker said. "These two beasts have been through a lot. I wouldn't have deserted them."

Trace opened the barn door and held it for Parker as he led the dun gelding inside. "Your devotion to your animals made me want you here even more. When you're not working a case, you'll be working the ranch." He followed them in and hurried to open a stall door. "We all do."

"Good." Parker said. He led Jasper into the stall and unclipped his lead, grabbed the water bucket from a hook on the wall and left the stall, closing the door behind him. "I like to keep busy. It helps keep my mind off…things."

"I get that." Trace nodded toward a spicket over a large sink against the wall. "Water's over there. You give Jasper sweet feed and hay?"

Parker nodded. "Half a bucket of feed, two sections of hay." He filled the water bucket and returned to the stall, hanging the bucket on a hook in the wall.

Jasper went to it immediately.

Parker rubbed the side of the gelding's neck and scratched behind his ears. "You're going to like your new home."

"Sweet feed first." Trace handed the bucket of feed over the stall door.

Parker poured the bucket of feed into a small trough nailed to the wall.

The gelding nudged him aside in his impatience to get to his dinner.

Parker laughed. "Greedy, are we?"

"Here's the hay." Trace handed the two sections of hay over to him.

Parker stuffed the sections of hay into the corner hay rack and stood for a few minutes, watching Jasper finish the sweet feed and move on to the hay. Parker enjoyed the earthy scent of horses and hay. "Have you already got an assignment for me?"

Trace leaned over the stall door. "Not yet. I wasn't exactly sure when you'd be ready to work. I figured you'd need a couple of days to get settled in and meet the others."

"I'm ready as soon as you have work for me. I don't need time to settle." He didn't need time to ruminate on his losses. The dead weren't coming back. However, the nightmares did. The less he thought about the past, the fewer bad dreams.

"I have plenty of ranch work to do, if staying busy is your goal. In fact, tomorrow morning, I was going to have Irish ride the fences to the south to make sure they're still intact. We've had feral hogs plowing through some of them. They tear them up and then they come in, destroy the land and kill the smaller live-stock like goats and calves."

"I could get started riding the fences today," Parker said.

Trace shook his head. "It's already late afternoon. Jasper needs to run free after being on the road for so long. And my mother and Lily have dinner on the table. I want you to meet some of the members of the

Outriders. Most of them are from my former Delta Force team."

"Are there any Deltas left in the army?" Parker gave Trace a crooked grin. "Are you hiring all of them?"

"I promise," Trace held up a hand. "I didn't take all of them, though I'm sure I could keep quite a few busy."

"That much business?" Parker asked.

"Yes. We can come back out after dinner to let Jasper out in the pasture." Trace led the way back to the house.

Parker followed him to the back porch and hesitated on the bottom step. "I'm not real good company lately. I've spoken more to Brutus and Jasper than people." His therapist had called him out on that during his last session.

"You don't have to stay at the table. If you want, after a quick introduction, you can excuse yourself. I can have Lily prepare a plate for you if you prefer to eat alone."

"That won't be necessary." Parker didn't like being treated differently. His issues dealing with others had more to do with the grief he still felt for the loss of his brothers. And guilt for not having died with them in the crash.

His physical injuries had healed over the past six months, but Parker had a way to go with the mental and emotional ones.

Other than getting stiff from the long drive, he was almost back to his normal self. Although he wouldn't say he was happy, he was no longer sad or angry all the time.

Brutus and Jasper helped him focus on something else besides his last mission with Delta Force. Sometimes even the animals didn't relieve him of the grief.

Both the dog and the horse could sense when depression threatened to take him to a dark place.

Trace waited at the door without saying a word, allowing Parker to make up his own mind.

Squaring his shoulders, Parker climbed the steps and passed through the back door into the kitchen.

Voices sounded from deeper in the house. Someone laughed and others joined in.

A surge of longing built inside Parker. He hadn't laughed since the crash. He hadn't realized how much he missed it until now. Wanting to see the source, he followed Trace through the kitchen and into a formal dining room with a long narrow table down the center.

At the far end sat a woman with salt-and-pepper hair and blue eyes. She stood and waved him into the room. "You must be Parker," she said, coming around the others at the table to take his hand. "So nice to meet you."

"Parker Shaw," Trace said, "This is Rosalyn Trace. My mother."

"Parker, has Trace shown you around the house yet?" she asked.

Parker shook his head. "I just walked through the door."

"That's fine. After dinner, I'd love to show you around and take you up to your room where you can unpack and get comfortable."

"Thank you, ma'am," he said.

She smiled up at him. "You don't have to call me ma'am. You may call me Rosalyn." She turned to a petite blonde with big blue eyes. "Parker, this lovely lady is my soon-to-be-daughter-in-law, the only woman who could possibly handle my son." She smiled at the blonde. "Lily."

Parker shook hands with Trace's woman. "Pleasure to meet you."

She grinned up at him. "I hear you brought your own horse." She glanced down at his feet. "And dog."

Parker glance down at Brutus. "I'm sorry. I didn't realize he'd come in with me. He sticks to me like a fly to honey. I'll take him back outside."

Mrs. Trace waved toward Parker. "It's okay. As long as he's housebroken, he can stay."

"He is," Parker assured her.

Trace went around the room, introducing the others. "I'm not sure if you've met Joseph Monahan. He's former Delta Force."

The man grinned. "Call me Irish."

"I don't recall meeting you, but it's nice to meet you now." Parker and Irish met halfway and exchanged a greeting and a handshake.

Irish turned to the woman beside him. "This is Tessa, my fiancée."

Parker dipped his head. "Nice to meet you, ma'am."

Trace waved to a man with black hair and brown eyes. "Levi Warren, another member of my team and former Delta, meet Parker Shaw."

The two men exchanged a handshake.

"My woman isn't here because she's sleeping. She has the graveyard shift tonight with the sheriff's department," Levi said. "You'll meet her soon enough. Look for Deputy Dallas Jones."

"I will," Parker promised.

Trace pointed to a man with sandy-blond hair who raised a hand from the other side of the table. "Becker Jackson, former Delta, and his better half, Olivia Swann."

"She's definitely my better half." Becker smiled

down at the dark-haired woman beside him and turned to raise a hand. "Welcome aboard, Shaw."

Finally, Trace turned to the man at his side who resembled Trace with his dark brown hair and green eyes. "And this is my brother, Matt Hennessey."

Matt held out his hand. "Glad you've joined us." He slid his arm around the redhead beside him. "And this is Aubrey, my girl."

Aubrey smiled and shook Parker's hand.

"Now that the introductions have been made, please, have a seat." Rosalyn waved toward an empty chair.

Trace held Lily's chair as she settled back in.

"We weren't sure when you'd make it, so we started without you," she said and passed a platter of grilled steaks his way.

"I'm glad you did." Parker selected a steak, the scent making his stomach rumble. "I wasn't sure when I'd make it, either. The wind was playing havoc with the trailer. I had to take it slow."

"Right decision," Lily said. "And the three of you made it intact as a result."

"Lily is a great help. She and my mother have managed the ranch by themselves."

His mother's mouth twisted. "Barely. Thankfully, you're home now and we have more help." She frowned and waved a hand at Trace. "Make sure Parker gets a potato and some of those green beans."

Trace stabbed a fork in a baked potato and dropped it onto Parker's plate. Then he passed the bowl of green beans. "The point is, if you have any questions about the ranch, they can answer it better than I can."

Lily stood, grabbed a pitcher of iced tea and came around to fill Parker's glass. "That's not entirely true."

She went around the table filling the glasses of others at the table before taking her seat again. "Trace has stepped right back into ranch life since he left active duty."

"Maybe so," Trace said. "However, I spend a lot more time managing my team of Outriders, which leaves much of the ranch management to you two."

Lily exchanged a nod of acknowledgement with her mother-in-law. "True. But it's nice to have help."

Trace cut into the steak on his plate and pointed his fork at Irish. "Irish, about riding the southern fence tomorrow—"

"Yeah, about that," Irish said. "It'll have to wait until I get back from the ranch supply store. We need more field fence and barbed wire."

Trace leaned his head toward Parker. "I think it would be a good opportunity for Parker to get out and stretch his horse's legs. He can ride the southern fence line and identify where we need to mend and what we'll need."

"Rosalyn and I are going with Irish to the supply store and stopping for groceries on the way back," Lily said. "Otherwise, I'd show Parker around."

"And I have a truck engine to reassemble for a customer," Matt said.

Parker frowned. "Truck engine?"

Matt gave him a crooked grin. "Before I became a part of the Trace family, I owned an auto repair shop. I still dabble in it when I'm not on an Outrider mission."

Rosalyn smiled. "Matt isn't just a mechanic."

"He's prior military," Trace said.

Parker cocked an eyebrow. "Branch?"

"Marine," Matt said.

"Marine Force Recon," Irish corrected. "He's just as spec ops as the rest of us Deltas."

Levi lifted a hand. "I can ride with Parker part of the way, but I'll have to come back early. I meet with my new client tomorrow afternoon."

"Good," Trace said. "I have a meeting with the sheriff in the morning. I can postpone it, but I'd rather not."

"Is the ranch completely fenced?" Parker didn't like feeling like someone had to babysit him. "If so, I would rather find my way around by myself. No one needs to walk me through."

"There are several gates to go through," Rosalyn said. "I can draw a rough sketch of them."

"That's all I need. If I get turned around, I can use the GPS on my cell phone to find my way back."

"If you get hurt, don't count on placing a phone call," Trace said. "Cell reception is spotty, the further you get away from the house."

"Noted," Parker said. He spent the rest of the meal eating quietly and listening to the conversations around him.

Tessa was a nurse at the local hospital. Aubrey was a home health care nurse. The two women spoke of some of the challenges they faced and how they handled them.

Matt and Trace discussed the feral hogs and the damage they'd done to a neighbor's fences and his boar goat herd.

"I saw one of the hogs last night on my drive back from town," Matt said. "It was as big as a cow."

"And meaner," Trace said. "You don't want to run across one on foot. They're fast and they're carnivores."

"And they're not picky about what kind of flesh

they eat." Lily caught Trace's attention. "You remember Fred Sarley."

"Who's Fred Sarley?" asked Parker. He hadn't meant to intrude on the conversation, but he couldn't deny his curiosity. Besides, he needed to know what he was up against.

Trace frowned. "A farmer on the south side of town. Had a lot of pigs."

"Had?" asked Parker.

Lily nodded.

"Do I even want to know?" asked Parker.

Lily exchanged a glance with Rosalyn. "No. He disappeared. The sheriff and half the town searched for him, but all they found was a single dingo boot next to his hog pen." She shook her head. "When they gave up looking, they turned to the hogs in the pen. They examined the contents of the boars' bellies and found bits of clothing and human flesh. They ran the DNA and found Fred." Lily looked around the table and grimaced. "Sorry. Not the best topic at the dinner table."

"Old man Hersh said the hogs have put a big dent in his herd of boar goats. He's lost at least ten kids and four does. He's setting out traps to catch them before they do more damage."

Finishing his meal before the others, Parker laid his fork and knife on his plate and looked around. "If you'll excuse me, I'd like to check on my horse and let him out into the pasture."

"I'm done here," Irish said. "I'll go with you. I want to check on one of the horses."

"Just leave your plates in the sink," Trace said. "It's my night to pull kitchen patrol duty."

Parker and Irish carried their plates to the sink, rinsed them and set them to the side.

Together, they walked out the back door, Brutus at their heels.

"I'm surprised we didn't run into each other on active duty," Irish said. "I haven't been out for long."

Parker shot a glance toward the other man. "I remember your call sign being mentioned, but I never forget a face. We haven't actually met before today."

"Trace says you were medically discharged."

Parker's lips pressed together. He tapped his left leg. "Helicopter crash did a number on my leg. The army has no use for a Delta who can't pass an army physical fitness test."

"You're getting around pretty well. I don't even notice a limp."

"Physical therapy, riding Jasper, and walking Brutus helped."

"Got family?" Irish asked.

Parker shook his head.

"Mom died of breast cancer when I was in high school. Dad had a heart attack two years ago."

"No wife...kids?" Irish chuckled. "Tell me to shut up if I'm being too nosy."

"Shut up." Parker grinned. "Seriously, I never married. Never had time, with the army. As far as I know, no kids. I have two younger sisters, though." He glanced toward Irish. "What about you? Were you forced out, too?"

Irish shook his head. "No way. I got out on my own terms before I took too many hits, or some terrorist tagged me." He looked out across the pasture. "I wanted to start living the rest of my life."

"And is working with Trace and the Outriders helping you get there?" Parker asked.

Irish's face split into a huge grin. "Absolutely. I wouldn't have met Tessa had I not come to Whiskey Gulch. I never knew I could love someone as much as I love her. She was actually my first assignment as an Outrider."

Parker's eyebrows dipped. "No kidding?"

"Yeah." His grin faded. "She was the target of a serial killer. She managed to escape him but didn't see his face. It was my job to protect her and help find out who the killer was."

"I take it you caught him?"

Irish nodded, his jaw tightening. "He almost killed Tessa. He's not going to hurt another woman, ever again."

"Your first assignment was a success." Parker shook his head. "Are all the assignments that intense?"

Irish's shoulders relaxed. "No. But there have been some close calls. For a small town, Whiskey Gulch has had its share of drama. Now, Becker recently took a job that started here in Whiskey Gulch. He went undercover in Dallas with Olivia to take down an art thief and kidnapper."

"I guess our training will come in handy after all."

"Exactly." Irish opened the barn door and held it for Parker.

Irish crossed the barn to the stall where Jasper pawed the ground with his hoof, eager to get outside to run. He snapped the lead onto the animal's halter and opened the gate.

Jasper pushed through and headed for the open barn door.

Parker pulled him up short. "Which pasture should I release Jasper in?"

"If you'll hold up a minute, I'll show you." Irish opened a stall door across from the one Jasper had been in and stood beside a bay horse. He bent, lifted the right front hoof and studied it carefully. He let go, straightened and snapped a lead on the horse's halter. "Sweetheart, you get to run."

He joined Parker in the middle of the barn, leading the mare. "She stepped on a nail a week ago. It had gotten infected. She needed time for it to heal where I could check on it daily. Poor girl's been in the barn since." He patted the mare's neck. "Thankfully, it appears to have healed nicely."

He led the mare out. "I'll let her loose with the other ranch horses. You can put your horse in the empty pasture until he acclimates and familiarizes with the others across the fence."

Parker opened the gate Irish indicated and led Jasper through. Once inside, he closed the gate and unclipped the lead. For a moment, he rested his forehead against Jasper's. "You're going to like it here. You'll have all you can eat and room to run. And I'll be here to take care of you. We're going to be all right."

No rocket-propelled grenades would be aimed at them. No Taliban terrorist would take them captive and leave them to die. They were on American soil. The land of the free and the home of the brave, where people could live in peace.

Except when serial killers attacked women.

Parker wasn't quite sure what he'd signed up for. Trace had mentioned he was being hired because of all the training he'd received in the army. Outriders were men with unique combat skills who wouldn't hesitate to defend, rescue or extract people from threats or violence.

But serial killers? Wow.

He rubbed his hand along Jasper's neck and then stepped back.

The horse nudged him once, turned and trotted out into the middle of the field, tossing his head. Free from the trailer and loving his new home.

Parker slipped through the gate and secured the latch.

Irish joined him and lifted his chin toward the horse galloping along the fence. "He's going to like it here." He turned to Parker. "You will, too. What better place to use our skills? And we have put those skills to use and will again. We never know who we'll be up against. We're in south Texas. We could run into drug cartels, mafia, human traffickers, serial killers, you name it."

"How soon do you think I'll get my first assignment?" Parker asked as they walked back to the house.

"Soon, I'm sure." Irish laughed. "Sometimes the jobs fall into our laps. In Matt's case, his ran out in front of him on the highway. He almost ran her over. Don't worry. You'll get yours soon enough."

Parker hoped so. He'd been away from the action long enough.

Irish glanced at the clouds building in the western sky. "Looks like we might get some rain. We sure can use some. But don't hold your breath. The weather around here is a big tease. Big clouds, dump in the next county and leave us dry here." Irish climbed the stairs.

Parker looked to the west in time to catch the flash of lightning on the edge of a thunderhead growing in size and intensity.

It would be a rough night for Brutus. The poor guy shook uncontrollably when there was a thunderstorm.

Thunder rumbled in the distance.

Brutus whined and leaned his stout body into Parker's legs.

Parker reached down and patted the dog's head. "Come on, old man. Let's get some rest. Tomorrow's the beginning of our new life here in Texas."

Chapter Two

"Abby?" A shaky voice called out in the darkness. "You awake?"

Abby lay curled in the wire cage on the threadbare, dirty blanket, shivering in the drafty air of the attic. "I am," she whispered. "You hanging in there, Rachel?"

The young mother sniffled. "Barely."

"Thinking about Tommy and Allissa?" Abby asked.

"Yes. I can't stop thinking about them." The woman's voice broke on a sob. "I shouldn't have stopped to change the flat tire. I should have driven it all the way to a town. And my babies… My poor, sweet babies…" Rachel sobbed, the sound weak after days of being held captive in a cage, in the drafty old house that smelled of dust and mildew.

"Rachel, you can't beat yourself up," Abby insisted. "You didn't ask for this. The people who did this own the blame."

"God, I hope someone found my babies and got them home to my husband. They must have been terrified. And Tommy… I hope he stayed in the car. He's so little and yet so mature for a four-year-old. If he wandered out onto the road…"

"He's okay, Rachel," Abby tried to assure her. "You

have to believe that and focus on staying alive and well for when we're rescued."

"Rescued?" Cara Jo snorted from the cage on the other side of Rachel's. "Like that's gonna happen. No one knows we're here. No one is even looking for me. No one cares." The seventeen-year-old had been a runaway living on the streets of San Antonio when she'd been snatched.

"Cara Jo," Rachel said, "your family loves you. They have to be wild with worry."

"No. I was just a stupid kid to them. And I proved them right. I ran away with Marty, my boyfriend. Too dumb to know how good I had it at home."

"What happened to Marty?" Abby asked.

Cara Jo laughed without humor. "He got smart and went home."

"Why didn't you?" Rachel asked.

"Remember the part about me being a stupid kid?" Cara Jo sighed. "I was too stubborn. I didn't want to admit I was wrong and they were right."

"And now?" Abby asked.

"I'd give anything to see my parents again." The teen spoke so softly Abby almost didn't hear her words. "I had come to that conclusion and had just reached the highway to hitch a ride home when I was taken."

"We're going to be rescued, aren't we?" Laura, the college coed, asked. "Someone has to find us. Surely they'll find my car and look for me."

"If someone didn't steal it and drive it down to Mexico to be sold there," Cara Jo said. "Were your keys still in it when you stopped for gas?"

"Yes," Laura said. "Along with my purse, laptop and all of my schoolbooks. I had midterms coming up. I shouldn't have gone home for the weekend. I'd still be in San Angelo. Not…here."

"*Mi madre* must be heartbroken," Valentina whispered. "We love each other so much. She will have searched the road between the bus stop and *mi casa*, looking for me. I knew better than to talk to a stranger." She paused. "He was so handsome and looked like a nice man. I believed him when he said he was lost and needed help with directions."

"I got caught with the same tactic," Cara Jo said. "Was the guy who snatched you blond with blue-gray eyes?"

"Yes," Valentina said. "He was."

"The guy who stopped to help me wore a ball cap," Rachel said. "I didn't notice what color his eyes or hair was. I was more worried about getting my tire changed and my kids home before dark. We still had another couple of hours to go before we reached New Braunfels. I was pulling stuff out of my trunk when he slipped a bag over my head and threw me in the trunk of his car."

"I was pumping gas at a truck stop," Laura said. "A white van pulled up close to my car. I was putting the pump handle back when someone grabbed me from behind and threw me in the van. They put a bag over my head. I never saw their faces."

"What about you, Abby," Rachel asked. "Did you see who grabbed you?"

"No," she said. "We'd taken two classes of fifth graders to visit the cowboy museum in Kerrville. We'd stopped at a rest area on the way back to eat our sack lunches and use the restrooms. I was waiting outside the boys' restroom for two of our children. The others had all loaded onto the bus. I was approached from behind. He slipped a cloth over my mouth. I tried to fight him, but whatever was on the cloth knocked me out. I woke up in this cage. Never saw who took me. And, like Rachel, I haven't stopped worrying about the children that were still in the bathroom."

"Why are they keeping us?" Valentina asked in the darkness.

"Haven't you heard of human trafficking?" Cara Jo said. "They're either going to sell us or pimp us out. The question isn't what they're going to do to us. It's when."

A flash of muted light made it through the sheet hung over the only window in the attic. Seconds later, thunder rumbled in the distance.

Abby had spent the days staring at the window, imagining herself breaking free of the cage, throwing open the window and sliding down the roof to the ground below.

If she could just get to that window, she'd find a way out of the attic.

The only time the women were released from their cages was to relieve themselves once a day. Their jailer would be up soon to take them, one at a time, down to the only bathroom in the house. A bathroom with no windows. They'd been stripped of their warm clothes and shoes, only allowed to keep the shirts and underwear they'd been wearing when they were taken. Abby wore the bright blue school T-shirt each of the teachers and children had worn for the field trip. Her shirt hung down just below her hips.

Abby had thought they'd be found within the first couple of days. After the third day came and went with no law enforcement officers breaking down the doors, she realized help wasn't coming. She'd only been there for three days. Some of the others had been there longer.

Three days? A week? She couldn't wait to be saved. She had to do something to save herself.

Her wrists were zip-tied in front of her, the plastic straps digging into her skin, chafing it raw. She'd scraped the plastic along the metal the cage was made of, hoping to weaken the plastic. If she could get her hands free, she might find a way to work the lock loose on the front of her cage.

If she made it out of the house, she'd be running barefoot in a T-shirt. Hopefully, she wouldn't have to go far to find a house and someone with a telephone she could use to call 911.

More light flashed through the sheet. Abby could see the other women, each trapped in the kind of cage in which people kenneled their dogs. Each of the cages had padlocks on the front to keep the doors secure.

With the storm moving closer, the lightning flashed more frequently, thunder following.

Footsteps sounded on the wooden staircase leading up to the attic.

Abby braced herself. So far, the men who'd captured them hadn't hurt them. But how long would that last? If Cara Jo was right, they were collecting women for human trafficking or the sex trade.

A shiver rippled through her. The nights were the worst. Fall had come to Texas and with it, cooler temperatures. The T-shirt did little to keep her warm. She pulled her legs up to her chest, tucked her knees under the shirt and waited for the door to open.

A key scraped in the lock on the door and the old handle squeaked as it turned.

The man in the ski mask appeared in the doorway, carrying a flashlight. He shined the light into each of the cages.

The women blinked as the beam blinded them.

He crossed to the cage closest to him.

Abby's.

As he squatted in front of the gate to remove the padlock, Abby pulled her legs in tighter, getting ready.

As soon as he lifted the lock off the hasp and swung the latch to the side, Abby slammed her feet into the gate.

The wire door hit the jailer in the head, the motion tipping him over. He lost his balance and fell backward.

Abby lunged through the opening, scrambled to her feet and raced for the door.

"Run, Abby!" Cara Jo yelled.

Through the door and down the stairs, Abby flew, gaining momentum she'd need to get her out of the house and away.

At the bottom of the stairs, she passed the door to the bathroom and kept going. Even before she reached the front door, she skidded to a stop. The door had boards nailed over it on the inside.

Abby spun and raced toward the back of the house, passing through what must have been the living room. The only light shining on the first floor came from a portable, battery-powered lantern sitting on a flimsy table next to a folding lounge chair, like the ones her grandmother used to have in her backyard. Pizza boxes and beer cans littered the floor.

Footsteps pounded down the stairs.

Her heart in her throat, Abby ran through an ancient kitchen to the back door. Grabbing the handle in her bound hands, she yanked it open and ran into a wall of muscles and flesh.

Thick arms clamped around her and lifted her off her feet.

She kicked and screamed, fighting her hardest. Lightning flashed and thunder drowned her screams as the man carried her back into the house and set her on her feet. He wore a black ski mask like the man who'd dealt with them for the past few days.

The captor rushed forward and grabbed her from behind. He wrapped one arm around her middle and clamped a hand over her mouth.

"We only offer the best and healthiest. Look for yourself." The man who'd stopped her at the door spoke in a deep, gravelly voice. He stepped aside and another man moved closer, this one wearing a white Halloween mask like that of a serial killer from a horror film. He wasn't as tall as the other two, but he was big and barrel-chested. A fringe of salt-and-pepper gray hair peeked out around the mask.

Abby tried to wriggle free of the arm around her.

The man lifted her off the ground, dangling her in the air.

When the man in the white mask came closer, Abby kicked out, catching him in the face.

He staggered backward and fell on his backside, his hand scraping against the doorframe.

The man who'd been talking about her reached down and pulled the white-masked man to his feet. "Sorry. She's a wild one. But don't worry, we'll provide sedative for transport."

White-mask guy stood stiffly, brushing his hands over his tailored suit and rubbing a scratch on the back of one of his hands. "She'll do," he said. "We promised five. What else have you got?" His voice boomed through the old house.

Doorstop guy jerked his head toward the stairs. "Take her up and bring down another."

The jailer spun her around, flung her over his shoulder and carried her back up the stairs. He dumped her on the floor and reached for a long metal rod that had been hung on the wall.

"In the cage," he commanded.

When Abby refused, he touched the wand to her skin, sending a jolt of electricity burning through her body. She jerked and leaped back.

He stepped toward her and held up the rod. "In the cage."

Still tingling, the pain fresh on her mind and skin, Abby backed another step, then turned and crawled back into the cage. Angry tears slipped down her cheeks as he fit the lock in place, sealing her inside.

Lightning flashed as he unlocked Laura's cage and motioned for her to proceed down the stairs ahead of him.

"Are you okay?" Rachel whispered.

"Yeah." Abby rubbed the sore spot on her arm.

"What happened?" Cara Jo asked.

"I ran out the back door and was stopped by a second guy who was followed by another." She pressed her lips together. "You're right, Cara Jo. They have a potential buyer downstairs."

Cara Jo cursed, Rachel gasped and Valentina sobbed.

"I'm not giving up," Abby vowed.

The man took each of the women down to the buyer

one at a time and brought them back to the attic. Valentina was last, crying all the way.

By the time they'd all been paraded in front of the three men, the storm was on them in full force.

Thunder boomed so loudly it shook the rafters. Abby fully expected the lightning to rip through the roof of the old house at any moment. She'd use the clash of the thunder to her advantage.

As soon as the idea entered her head, another took its place. Abby bunched her legs close to her chest and waited for the next bolt of lightning.

Light flashed.

Abby kicked the front of her cage as hard as she could.

"What are you doing?" Rachel demanded.

"Getting out of here." Abby tugged the ragged blanket out from under her and wrapped it around her feet. She pulled back her legs and waited.

Lightning flashed.

She kicked.

As the storm raged, Abby kicked.

Just when her feet had reached their limit and she was about to give up, she forced herself to kick one last time.

Lightning struck close by, followed immediately by a long rumble of thunder that rattled the timbers of the old house.

As the thunder boomed, Abby kicked.

The front of the enclosure crashed to the floor.

She scrambled out of the cage. Using a technique she'd seen on the internet, she slammed her wrists down, pulling her hands apart at the same time, and snapped the zip tie free.

Then she ran to Laura's cage.

"You can't unlock them," Cara Jo said. "You have to get out and bring back help."

"I can't leave you." A heavy weight settled on Abby's chest as she pulled at the padlock on Laura's cage, knowing Cara Jo was right.

The college student touched her fingers through the wire. "Go. Get help."

Abby pushed to her feet. In the flashes of lightning, she ran toward the attic window and yanked off the sheet. She struggled to lift the window. It moved a little but not enough. Abby ran back to her broken cage, grabbed the blanket, wrapped it around her arm and rushed back to the window.

In the next flash of lightning and boom of thunder, she slammed her arm through the glass and wiped the shards clear of the windowsill.

When she leaned out, her stomach roiled.

The constant flashes of lightning revealed a steep roof that only took her part way to the ground. She'd have to free-fall the last ten feet.

"Hurry," Rachel urged. "He's coming."

Footsteps sounded on the stairs as thunder crashed around them.

Abby tried again to raise the window. She managed to get it up a couple of inches. She quickly fed the blanket through the gap between the window frame and the windowsill and then brought the empty window frame down on the blanket. Hopefully, it would hold the blanket long enough for Abby to climb down the steep roof.

"Go, Abby," Cara Jo whispered.

"Go," Laura entreated.

Abby climbed through the broken window, lowered

herself slowly, grabbed the blanket and slid downward, using the blanket like a rope. Rain poured down, soaking her, blowing into her face and dripping from her hair into her eyes.

She ran out of fabric a few feet short of the roof's edge.

In another flash of lightning, she looked up and blinked the rain from her eyes. Her heart stalled in her chest.

The captor leaned through the window and grabbed for the blanket.

Abby released her hold on the blanket and slipped the last couple of feet down the roof and over the edge, falling ten feet to the ground.

When she landed, her feet sank into mud, her legs buckling beneath her. Abby fell backward, landing hard, the air knocked from her lungs.

Rain pounded her face and body, the cold seeping through her skin to her bones.

For a long, precious second, she lay there, trying to force air back to her lungs.

She gasped, rolled over, pushed to her feet and took off. A quick glance over her shoulder showed her what she already knew. The man was no longer hanging out the window. He'd be running down the stairs and bursting through the back door any minute.

With only the lightning to illuminate her way, she ran, ignoring the pain in her bare feet. Every rock and stick took a toll. All she could hope was for the soles of her feet to go numb. She couldn't stop until she had enough distance between her and the men who'd kidnapped her and the other women.

Her lungs burned as she ran. No matter which direction she looked, she couldn't find any lights. The old house must have been isolated.

Abby climbed hills and slid down into valleys. She trudged on, hoping to find any sign of life. As exhaustion took hold, she started to fear she was walking in circles and would wind up back where she'd started.

She stumbled through a broken fence and staggered several more feet before she dropped to her knees too exhausted to take another step.

The rain had moved on. The clouds were breaking up, allowing some stars to shine through.

Abby looked around. She couldn't stop now. She had to hide, or risk being found. When the sun came up, she'd move on and find a house, make that call and send people to rescue the others.

Abby moaned as she stood, putting pressure back on her ravaged feet. Every step was excruciating. She made it as far as a slight crevice in the ground where a tree had been blown over, roots and all. She lay in the hollow where the roots had once been and scraped leaves and dirt over her, covering her body and face. As she positioned the last leaves over her face and then her hands, her world faded to black.

Chapter Three

Having napped cramped in his truck two nights straight, Parker found it almost heaven to sleep stretched out on a comfortable bed that fit the entire length of his big frame.

After reassuring Brutus through a nasty thunderstorm, he'd slept so soundly that the rattle of Brutus snoring on a rug beside the bed hadn't disturbed him. He woke as the gray light of predawn chased away the darkness in the room he'd been assigned in Trace's home.

With a sense of purpose, he eased his legs over the side of the bed and sat up. Even his leg felt better after elevating it for seven hours.

Parker pushed to his feet, stretched his arms toward the ceiling and performed his morning physical therapy exercises to keep his muscles flexible. With Brutus at his side, he'd gotten to the point he could walk five miles easily and he could ride for hours on Jasper. Running was taking a little longer. He could go for up to two miles before the pain became unbearable.

His doctor had told him his running days were over. Parker refused to accept the diagnosis. In the back of his mind, he harbored a—perhaps delusional—belief that if he could pass the army physical fitness test, they'd let him back in.

Logic told him it wasn't possible. Not only had he sustained a leg injury, but the traumatic brain injury from the crash also continued to plague him. No. He wouldn't be invited back into the Delta Forces or the army.

While at the rehab ranch, he'd applied for a number of jobs all over the country…he and a hundred other candidates. Not one interview had come of it. Who needed a man whose only skill sets were centered around combat? Because of his injuries, he couldn't even go into city or state law enforcement.

Parker pulled on his jeans, walked to the French doors, pushed them open and stepped out onto an upper deck that wrapped around the back of the house. From where he stood, the view spread before him, past the barn and out across a pasture. The hills beyond were shrouded in fog.

Jasper grazed contentedly, keeping close to the gate Parker had led him through the day before. The overnight thunderstorm had delivered much-needed rain, leaving residual moisture in the air. Thus, the low-level fog that would burn off after sunrise.

Refreshed and ready to start his new job, Parker shaved, brushed his teeth and combed his hair. After dressing in a faded denim shirt, jeans and his army boots, he slung a leather shoulder holster carrying his 9 mm pistol over his arms and buckled it across his chest. He might need to borrow a rifle scabbard he could attach to his saddle in case he ran across the feral hogs Trace and Lily had discussed at the dinner table the night before.

When he was ready, he grabbed a light jacket and descended the stairs with Brutus at his side. Parker made it his first mission of the day to find coffee. He could go without breakfast, but coffee was a necessity.

The fragrant aroma of fresh-brewed java led him to the kitchen where Rosalyn leaned against the counter, sipping from a mug, her eyes closed.

He paused at the entrance, not wanting to intrude on her quiet time.

She opened her eyes and smile. "Good morning, Parker."

He dipped his head. "Morning, ma'am."

"Fresh coffee. Nothing like it. If you want some, you can help yourself. The mugs are in the cabinet above the coffee maker. For that matter, whenever you're hungry, you can help yourself to anything in the kitchen. Make yourself at home."

"Thank you." Parker strode across the floor, found a mug and poured a full cup. His first sip warmed his insides all the way down to his empty belly. Best way to start a new day, a new job and a new life. He could handle anything as long as he started the day with a cup of joe.

"I'm about to cook breakfast for everyone." Rosalyn said. "You will join us, won't you?"

"No, ma'am. I'm good with just coffee."

"Might be a long day. A good breakfast can take you all the way to dinner."

He nodded. "Yes, ma'am. I know."

Her lips twisted in a wry grin. "Look at me, trying to mother the new guy when he's a grown man." She set her mug on the counter. "Ignore me. Old habits die hard."

He liked Mrs. Travis. She seemed nice and obviously cared about others. "Thank you. I'll take you up on breakfast another day. I want to check on my horse and get an early start to the day. Might take me a while to find my way around."

Rosalyn straightened. "That reminds me, I made a layout of the land, the fences and gates. You won't miss the gates. There are tire ruts leading up to all of them. But you'll need to know which ones lead off the ranch, so you don't get lost on someone else's property."

She crossed to a far counter, retrieved a sheet of paper and returned to where Parker stood, sipping the hot coffee. Laying it on the counter, she oriented the drawing to the north. "You'll want to go through these gates to get to the southern border fence. Irish thinks the hogs are getting across in a low-lying area around here."

She drew her finger along the line about two thirds of the way to the back of the property. "I'm sure you won't have difficulty finding the breach or navigating your way back to the ranch house." She left the paper on the counter and reached into a lower cabinet for a large, cast-iron skillet. "I'll have scrambled eggs ready in fifteen minutes if you change your mind. You can saddle your horse and come back for sustenance."

"Thank you, but I'll head out as soon my horse is ready."

"We might still be in town when you get back, though we're aiming to be home by noon. I have a ham in the fridge for sandwiches. The bread is in the pantry and condiments in the fridge."

"Thank you," he said and finished the last drop of coffee. Parker carried the mug to the sink, rinsed it and placed it in the dishwasher. "I'll see you later, ma'am."

She smiled. "Please, call me Rosalyn. *Ma'am* sounds so formal and we're anything but formal around here."

"Yes, ma'am—Rosalyn." He settled his cowboy hat on his head and headed for the back door. As soon as he pulled open the door, Brutus was out and running across the yard toward the barn. He didn't stop until he stood at the fence surrounding the pasture where Jasper had spent the night.

The horse trotted over and lowered his head, sniffing at the dog.

Brutus's entire body wagged as he greeted the horse. The two had become friends at the rehab ranch, establishing a special bond.

Parker bypassed the horse and dog and headed into the barn.

Someone was already there, cleaning a stall. He couldn't see who.

Curious, he headed over to see if whoever it was needed help.

He found Lily, wearing scuffed dingo boots, jeans and a T-shirt. She scooped up soiled straw with a hay fork and tossed it into the wheelbarrow close to where Parker stood. Her eyes rounded when she spotted him. "Sorry. I didn't know you were standing there."

"You need help?"

Lily shook her head. "This was the last stall. If you want to push the wheelbarrow out to the compost pile behind the barn, I'd appreciate it. I've already fed the animals and filled the water troughs." She exited the stall, hung the hay fork on the wall and dusted straw from her jeans. "I was just about to head for the house, a shower and breakfast. Will you be joining us?"

He shook his head. "I had coffee with Ms.—Rosalyn. I want to get a start finding my way around."

Lily nodded. "Don't get lost." She left the barn.

Parker grabbed the handles of the wheelbarrow and pushed it through the barn door and around to the back where he dumped the contents onto a pile of soiled straw. After rinsing the barrel using a hose outside the barn, he leaned it up against the barn to dry.

Jasper whinnied.

Parker glanced across at the horse with the dog sitting patiently at its feet. He ducked into the barn, scooped feed into a bucket and poured it into the trough in the stall. Then he grabbed a lead rope off a hook and returned to Jasper.

"How about a bite of sweet feed before we get started?" He clipped the lead on the horse's halter and led him into the barn.

Brutus kept pace, careful not to get under the horse's hooves.

Parker released Jasper into the stall he'd occupied the previous afternoon and closed the gate. While the horse consumed the feed, Parker went out to his trailer for his bridle, saddle and blanket and carried them into the barn.

By then Jasper had finished his snack.

Parker snapped the lead on his halter, led him out of the stall and tied him to a post.

He found a brush in the tack room and went to work grooming the horse. Jasper stood patiently, swishing his tail occasionally.

When he was finished brushing Jasper, Parker tossed the saddle blanket over the animal's back, followed by the saddle. He cinched the girth and let the stirrup fall into place.

Jasper shifted from hoof to hoof in anticipation of going for a ride.

Parker unhooked the lead, slipped the bridle over the animal's nose, fitting the bit between his teeth, then slid the straps over Jasper's ears and fastened the buckles.

Brutus turned circles beside Jasper, eager to get out and run.

Parker would make sure he stopped often enough to let him rest. On a couple of occasions, he'd hoisted the pit bull up into the saddle with him. The dog would be fine. Parker would make sure of that.

He led Jasper out into the barnyard and over to the gate Rosalyn had indicated he should go through on his way to the southern edge of the property. Once through the gate, he mounted Jasper and nudged the horse into a trot.

The fog hung low over the field, making it difficult for him to see the gate at the other end. Old tracks in the ground indicated vehicles had probably been driven through the field on the same path over the years. Figuring it was probably the path leading to the next gate, Parker followed it.

Brutus ran alongside, darting off every once in a while to chase a moth or a bird.

Eventually, the path led to a gate.

Parker took the opportunity to dismount and stretch his sore leg as he opened the gate and led Jasper through.

Back in the saddle, he followed the path, wondering if he should have waited at the ranch house until the fog lifted. He'd wanted to explore the ranch. Unfortunately, he wasn't seeing much of it as it was blanketed in misty fog.

Based on Rosalyn's directions, he had one more gate to pass through and an open expanse of fields and hills before he reached the southern end of the ranch. When he reached it, he leaned over without dismounting and unlatched the gate. He rode through and leaned down to close the gate. It was a new task for Jasper. He danced sideways several times and then settled, allowing Parker to close and latch the gate without dismounting.

Parker had been riding for almost an hour when Brutus bolted and raced ahead.

"Brutus!" Parker yelled. "Heel!"

The dog either ignored Parker's command or didn't hear it. He disappeared into the fog.

Parker, worried Brutus would get lost on the vast ranch, urged Jasper to pick up the pace.

Ahead, Brutus's silvery form materialized out of the fog. He stood beside a fallen tree, his body tense, the hackles raised on the back of his neck.

Parker squinted into the fog, trying to catch a glimpse of whatever had Brutus riled.

Brutus held his position even as Parker rode Jasper up to where the dog stood.

The pit bull snarled, staring into the fog, his growl more menacing than anything Parker had heard since he'd adopted him.

Shadowy figures moved in the fog. They were big, hulking creatures.

Parker tensed and slipped his hands beneath his jacket, his fingers curling around the handle of his Glock. He pulled it free and held it out.

A herd of feral hogs emerged from the fog, headed toward Parker, Brutus and Jasper.

FIERCE GROWLING INTERRUPTED her nightmare of waking up in an animal cage, cold, hungry and scared. Or was she still asleep and the animal wanted his crate back?

Abby cracked an eye open and looked up through a veil of leaves. Where was she? Why was she covered in leaves?

The growling persisted. Too loud to be her stomach. A shiver shook her body, dislodging some of the leaves over her face, and she stared up at the razor-sharp teeth of a snarling dog.

Her heart slammed against her ribs and adrenaline shot through her veins. Fear gripped her, robbing the air from her lungs. Every instinct told her to run.

Logic followed, urging her to think before she acted. If she lay perfectly still, maybe the rabid dog would go away and leave her to live another day.

Another shiver consumed her as the damp earth beneath her and the cool morning air sank into her bones.

Though the dog stood over her, it looked in another direction, not toward her. It took a step forward, snarling viciously.

When it moved, another animal's face hovered over her. This one didn't snarl, but it was huge and could crush her if it chose.

Its nostrils twitched as it leaned closer and sniffed her face with a velvety nose.

A horse.

The beast ducked its head lower. Abby stared past the horse's head to the man seated in the saddle holding a gun.

They'd found her. The evil monsters from her nightmare had found her.

She couldn't let them take her again. The others were counting on her to get help. She had to get help to free them.

The dog growled low and wicked. A moment later it darted away, barking as viciously as it growled.

Abby rolled out of the shallow hollow up onto her hands and knees and then launched herself away from the dog, the horse and the armed man.

She stumbled, righted herself and kept running toward a low bank of fog. If she put enough distance between her and the man on the horse, she might lose herself in the hazy mist.

Again, she stumbled, went down on a knee and started back up when something hit her in the middle of her back, knocking her to the ground.

Over her shoulder she heard the menacing rumble of the dog's growl.

Abby froze, afraid to move lest the dog rip into her with those razor-sharp teeth.

He continued to snarl and then broke into a fearsome combination of barking and growling, his paws firmly planted in the middle of her back.

The clip-clop of a horse's hooves moved closer.

Bang! Bang! Bang!

The three shots rang out so close the sound reverberated in Abby's head. She held her breath, waiting for the pain that would surely follow.

It didn't.

The dog on her back leaped off and raced into the fog barking furiously.

Cold, scared and exhausted, Abby pushed to her feet and spun to face the man on the horse.

He swooped in, grabbed her arm and pulled her up and across the saddle in front of him. Then he spun the horse around and shouted, "Brutus, come!" He nudged the horse and it shot forward.

Abby hung on as the horse raced across a field, up a hill and down into a valley.

She lay across muscular thighs, her head bouncing against a rock-solid calf.

When the horse finally slowed, Abby pushed against the man's leg and fought to be free.

He held onto her with a hand pressed against the middle of her back. "Stay still, woman."

Abby continued to kick and twist until the man lifted her, flipped her around. He sat her in his lap and clamped his arms around her, trapping her arms against her sides. "Are you just *trying* to get yourself killed?" he demanded, a frown creasing his brow.

"Let me go! I won't go back," she vowed.

"Damn right you're not going back. That herd of hogs would have had you for dinner. Why the hell are you out here, alone and half naked anyway?"

She stopped struggling and stared into the man's face. "You're not taking me back?"

"No. Besides the hogs, you're not dressed for wandering around the ranch. Where are your shoes and clothes?"

"You don't know?" She shook her head. "You're not one of them?" Her head spun and the little bit of control she'd held on to slipped. Tears welled in her eyes. "I'm safe?" she whispered.

The man frowned. "Of course, you're safe. But if

Brutus hadn't found you first…" His frown deepened. "Those hogs would have."

She shuddered. The shudder turned to shivers and ended in her entire body trembling so uncontrollably that her teeth rattled in her head.

"Oh, hell," the man muttered and set her away from his chest. "Hold on to the saddle horn," he commanded.

Her hands shook as she wrapped them around the saddle horn.

The man shrugged out of his jacket and wrapped it around her body. Then pressed her against his chest, holding her in the circle of one arm. With his other hand, he gripped the reins and nudged the horse into a swift walk.

The jacket, warm from his body heat, helped, but not enough to stop the shakes. Her captivity, the escape, and lying cold in an earthen hollow through the night had taken their toll.

A gray haze closed in around her. The man, horse and fog blended together in the haze, and Abby gave in to the power of the darkness.

Chapter Four

When the woman went limp in his arms, Parker tightened his hold to keep her from sliding out of his lap onto the ground.

Her entire body was covered in mud. He couldn't begin to assess her injuries until some, or all, of the dirt was washed away.

Her skin was cold. At the very least, she was probably suffering from hypothermia.

His arm tightened around her even more in an effort to warm her cold body. He had to get her to the ranch house and into warm blankets or a warm bath to bring her body temperature up to normal.

He couldn't make the horse go any faster. The jolting motion of trotting or galloping might exacerbate the extent of her injuries. The ride back was excruciatingly slow. Several times, he wondered if it wouldn't be better to stop, build a fire and warm her there. What if she succumbed to hypothermia before they reached the Travises' residence?

Building a fire would only be a short-term solution. And there was the chance the hogs would find them. He needed to get her somewhere safe and warm where she could also be clean and dry. He could call for an ambulance from the ranch house. Based on the scrapes, cuts and bruises he could see, and how cool her skin was, she might need medical attention.

Juggling the woman in his arms, he struggled with the gates, managing to open and close them without dropping her in the process.

By the time he reached the ranch, his arm ached as much as his bad leg.

He tried to wake her long enough to get down from the horse, but she was completely out. It worried him. He slipped backward on Jasper, off the saddle and onto the horse's rump. Then he laid her across the saddle on her belly.

Once he was sure she wouldn't fall, he slid down Jasper's rump to the ground.

His bad leg buckled, pain shooting into his hip. Holding onto the horse's tail, he managed to remain upright until the feeling returned to his leg and he could walk almost normally.

He rounded to the side of the horse as the woman lying over the saddle moved. The movement caused her to slip. She fell backward into his arms. He scooped her up and carried her across the barnyard and up to the back porch.

Brutus followed, maintaining his vigil to protect Parker and the woman from the feral hogs.

Parker managed the door handle and pushed the door open with his foot.

"Hello," he called out.

No one answered.

He carried her into the huge living room and laid her out on one of the leather couches.

As he slipped his arms from beneath the woman, her

eyelids fluttered open, and she stared up into his gaze. "Where...am I?"

"You're at the Whiskey Gulch Ranch. I'm going to call for an ambulance."

She shook her head. "No."

"Yes," he insisted. "You're not well. You could be suffering from hypothermia, dehydration or any number of things I'm not qualified to treat. I'm calling for an ambulance." When he started to straighten, her hand grabbed his arm in a surprisingly strong grip.

"You can't," she said, her hand still gripping his arm, refusing to let go. She closed her eyes and lay still. "I need to be dead," she whispered.

"What?" He eased down beside her and sat on the floor. "I don't understand. Why do you need to die?"

"So they won't know I'm looking for them," she shivered in his jacket, her body starting to tremble again. "Cold," she murmured.

"At the very least, let's get you cleaned up and warmed up. Then you can explain to me what you're talking about."

"Warm sounds good," she said. "Never b-been so c-cold."

He stood, lifted her in his arms and carried her up the stairs. Though his bad leg protested, he made it to the top and into his bedroom. He didn't stop until he was in the bathroom. "Can you sit up on your own?" he asked.

She frowned. "I think so."

He sat her on the toilet lid and waited to see if she would pass out.

When she didn't, he turned to the tub, plugged the drain and turned on the faucet. After adjusting the water temperature, he faced her and lowered himself to sit on the edge of the tub. "Are you hanging in there?"

She'd wrapped her arms around her middle, still shivering. "I'm alive. That's what matters."

His lips twisted. "First you wanted to be dead. Now you say alive is what matters."

"If they think I'm alive, they might kill the others. I can't let that happen."

Parker tensed. "Others?"

The woman nodded. "Four others. Two teenage girls and two young women." Her body shook so hard she nearly fell off the toilet seat.

Parker steadied her, then checked the water in the tub. "Look, we need to get you warmed up. You can tell me the rest when you're feeling better." He was thinking the sheriff might be interested in her story and he wanted to have it straight before he got the law involved.

"Can you get undressed and into the tub on your own?"

She raised her hands to pull at the jacket. They shook so badly she couldn't get it off.

"Here," he said. "Let me." Parker removed the jacket.

Her eyes widened when he reached for her again.

"Don't worry. You can keep the rest. I'm just going to help you into the water."

He scooped her into his arms and eased her into the warm water. "Too hot?"

She shook her head and smiled. "It's perfect." Her shivering slowed and finally stopped.

He turned to the cabinet, found a washcloth and sat again on the edge of the tub. He couldn't leave her for fear she'd pass out again and drown.

Parker dipped the cloth into the water and squirted

bodywash onto it. "Mind if I clean off the dirt from your feet? Since you won't go to the hospital, we need to treat your cuts to keep them from getting infected."

"I should be able to do it myself." The woman bent her knees and tried to sit up. The effort appeared to be too much. She lay back in defeat, sending water sloshing over the edge of the tub.

He cocked an eyebrow. "I'd get one of the ladies of the house to do it, but they've all gone to town for supplies, and I have no idea when they'll return. You could wait for them, but the water might get cold. Or we can go with the assumption a little dirt never hurt anyone."

She rolled her head from side to side. "No. I can't risk infection. I have to be well enough to find them."

"Is that a *yes, I'll accept a little help*? Or *no, I have no idea who you are, why should I trust you*?"

Brutus entered the bathroom and laid his chin on the rim of the tub, staring at the woman in the water.

She laughed, the sound catching on a sob. "I thought this guy was going to eat me alive." She reached out a tentative hand. "Does he bite?"

Parker's lips pressed into a tight line. "His previous owner thought he was useless as a fighting dog. He said he didn't have any fight in him." He laid a hand on the animal's back. "He was wrong. Brutus just needed a reason to fight. When he found you in the dirt, he held off a herd of wild hogs to protect you."

She frowned. "The three shots?"

Parker nodded. "To scare them off. They weren't as impressed with gunfire as they were with Brutus."

She extended her hand and let the dog sniff her fingers. "Brutus, huh? At least I know your name."

Parker shook his head. "I guess we've been a little

busy getting you to this point. He held out his empty hand. "Parker Shaw."

Her brow furrowed as she placed her hand in his. "Abby Gibson." As quickly as she shook his hand, she drew hers back into the warm water and wrapped her arms around herself.

He held up the washcloth with the soap. "I'll understand if you're not comfortable with me washing your feet."

"It's just…" Abby looked away. "They were going to sell us." She pressed her fists to her lips and curled into a ball. "We were kept in cages the size of dog kennels." Her eyes filled with tears and her body shook with the force of retching sobs.

His jaw clenched and his chest tightened. Bastards. What made men so morally corrupt?

Her sobs continued.

Parker could take a beating or a bullet, but tears? He reached into the tub and pulled Abby out and onto his lap. Water went everywhere.

He didn't care.

This woman had been through trauma no human should have to endure. If he could, he'd take it all away. But the damage was done. All he could do was hold her and help her weather the storm of her memories.

The sobs slowly subsided. Her body cooled where it wasn't pressed to his and soon, she was shivering again.

He leaned her way from him and bushed a thumb over the tears on her cheeks. "You're okay now. I won't let them hurt you." Whoever they were. "Right now, you need to be warm." He helped her back into the tub.

She handed him the washcloth and looked up at him through red-rimmed eyes. "I'm sorry I've been such a burden." More tears welled and slipped down her cheeks. "But if you would… I would appreciate your help."

He took the cloth from her.

She leaned back in the warm water and closed her eyes, more tears slipping down her cheeks.

Parker reached into the tub and lifted one foot out and carefully washed her foot. With the dirt gone, the cuts and bruises were obvious. Some were already red and angry-looking. He worked the cloth up to her knees, identifying more abrasions that would need antibiotic ointment. Some needed bandages.

He stopped at the knee and laid her leg back in the warm water and lifted the next one.

The bottoms of her feet were ravaged from running barefoot through the Texas hill country. Sharp rocks, cactus and sticks had torn or bruised the uncalloused skin.

When he'd cleaned up to that knee, he rinsed the cloth, applied fresh bodywash and reached for the arm closest to him. As gently as before, he washed away the dirt and mud.

Her arms, like her legs, were covered in scrapes and cuts. When he put that arm back in the water, she offered the other.

He smiled and cleaned that one as well. By then, the water had cooled a little. It wouldn't be long before it got too cold. He rinsed the cloth again and pressed it into her palm. "Can you manage the rest?"

She nodded and struggled to sit up straight.

He stood. "Do you want me to leave you alone so you can finish?"

Her brow furrowed and a look of panic crossed her

face. "No. If you don't mind, I'd rather you stayed." Her gaze went to the pit bull lapping up water from the floor. "And Brutus."

The dog looked up at the sound of his name.

"Okay. We'll stay."

Abby pressed the damp cloth to her face and washed away the dirt, grime and tears. Then she leaned back and sank all the way into the water until only her face remained above. She reached up and worked her fingers through her hair, stopping to let her arms rest.

Parker squirted shampoo into his hands and leaned over the tub. He worked the shampoo into her hair and massaged her scalp.

"I swear I'm not always this useless," she said, staring up at him with her face surrounded by shampoo bubbles.

"From what you've been through, I'll give you a pass." He winked. "Now tip your head back and let me work the suds out."

She leaned her head back in the water. Her long hair fanned out in the water as he rinsed her hair.

"There," he said. "You're on your own for the rest."

She reached out a hand and he helped her into a sitting position.

Abby stared down at the damp T-shirt clinging to her body. "I don't have any clothes to wear. They took them."

Another surge of anger ripped through Parker. When she was up to it, he'd get the full story from her. Then he'd go after the men who'd done this to her.

"I have some things you can wear." He reached into the cabinet with the bath towels, extracted a large, fluffy white one and laid it on the closed toilet seat.

He backed toward the door. "I'll get the clothes." Pausing at the door, he studied her face. "You sure you'll be all right on your own?"

She bit on her bottom lip for a moment and then gave him a weak smile. "I'll manage."

"Let me know when you want my help. I'll just be a few steps away." He looked down at Brutus. "Stay."

The dog sat on his haunches and stared up at him, waiting for his next command. "Good boy," Parker said and turned and walked toward the bathroom door.

"Parker?" Abby called out softly.

He looked over his shoulder.

"Could you leave the door open a little?" she asked.

"You bet." He stepped out of the bathroom and closed the door halfway. For a long moment, he stood there worrying that he'd come back in to find her passed out in the water.

The sound of her moving in the water reassured him that she was still conscious. And Brutus would alert him if she was in trouble. He left the door and crossed to the duffel bag he'd brought with him. That and a backpack contained all his worldly possessions. Everything else from his apartment outside of Fort Bragg had been donated to a homeless shelter. His move to Whiskey Gulch had been a chance to start over. To reinvent himself, to leave behind the only life he'd known since graduating high school.

Parker selected a clean black T-shirt and running shorts, figuring they might be the only things that might fit Abby. The shirt would hang down to her knees and the shorts would swamp her, but it was the best he could do.

"Uh… Parker?" Abby called out from the other room.

He hurried into the bathroom.

"I should be embarrassed," she murmured. "But I've never cared less about modesty than I do at this moment. Help." Abby still sat in the tub, only the T-shirt she'd been wearing was halfway over her head and stuck to her arms. Beneath it all was a matching bra and bikini panties in a soft shade of purple.

Parker gulped, his groin tightening automatically.

"I tried," she said from inside the fabric wrapped around her arms and head. "I. Just. Can't."

He dropped the shirt and shorts on the counter, gripped the hem of the T-shirt and dragged it up her arms and off.

Immediately, she dropped her arms to cover herself, her cheeks flaming red. "Thanks."

He shook his head. "It's too late to be embarrassed. Let me help."

She nodded and reached out.

With his assistance, she stood and stepped out onto the bathmat. He wrapped her in the towel and helped to dry her off.

Once again, he scooped her up in his arms, towel and all, and carried her into the bedroom, settling her on the bed.

"Stay," he said to Brutus, who had followed them into the bedroom.

The dog sat beside the bed and waited for Parker to return from the bathroom, carrying the shirt and shorts.

Parker also brought another towel. He used it to pat the moisture out of Abby's hair. Then he fit the T-shirt over her head.

"Wait." Abby stopped him from pulling the shirt down over her body. "Turn around."

He frowned.

"I want to remove this wet bra," she said.

"Right." He performed an about-face.

A moment later, she said, "Okay. I'm decent."

When he faced her, she wore the T-shirt and held out the bra. "If you could hang this in the bathroom, I'd appreciate it."

Again, his groin tightened as he took the bra into the bathroom and hung it on a hook.

When he returned to the bedroom, she'd shimmied out of her panties and into the shorts. She was in the process of sliding between the sheets of the bed when he walked back into the room.

"Is it me or is it cold in here?" she said, her teeth clattering together.

"It's you." He helped her adjust the sheets and comforter around her, tucking it around her shoulders. Then he lifted her head, laid the driest towel on the pillow lowered her head and wrapped the towel like a turban around her damp hair. He laid the brush on the nightstand. "We'll tackle tangles later."

When she was covered from her toes to her chin, she looked up at him. "Thank you, Parker Shaw." She glanced down at the floor where Brutus sat patiently. "And thank you, Brutus."

Brutus took her mention of his name as an invitation for him to join her on the bed. He jumped up and settled beside her on the comforter.

Abby laughed and rested her hand on the dog.

"I'd be annoyed with him being on the bed, but I know how warm he can be," Parker said.

"He is warm." Abby blinked up at Parker, her eyelids drooping. "I need to find the others," she said.

"You need to rest," he said and sat on the edge of the bed. "When you're up to it, you can tell me everything. I'll help you find them."

Abby reached for his hand. "Promise?"

He nodded and gently squeezed her fingers. "I promise."

She brought his hand up to her cheek and closed her eyes. "Why should I trust you?" she whispered.

He chuckled. "I don't know. Why should you?"

Her lips curled in a smile. "You and Brutus saved my life."

"That was all Brutus," he said, liking the way her fingers curled around his.

She opened her eyes long enough to connect with his gaze. "Brutus didn't carry me back."

He smiled. "No, he didn't."

"You don't have to help me—" she looked up into his eyes "—but thank you."

"They say when a person saves another person's life, he's responsible for that person forever."

"Lucky me," she said with a crooked smile. Her smile faded. "For your sake, I hope it's not forever."

Parker stared down at the woman in his bed. He wasn't sure if she had fallen asleep or passed out again. Either way, she needed warmth and rest.

In the meantime, she was safe from whoever had kept her captive. He'd make sure she stayed that way.

Chapter Five

Abby lay scrunched in a fetal position, trapped in a cage while a storm raged around her. Footsteps pounded up the staircase leading to the attic where she and the other women were held hostage.

She had to get out of the cage and run before the kidnappers made it to the top. Abby pounded her feet against the cage door. Thunder boomed. The footsteps came louder as they neared the top of the stairs. With only seconds to spare, she kicked again, and the cage door broke free.

Abby scrambled out of the enclosure and pushed to her feet.

The door burst open, slamming against the wall.

One of the kidnappers in his black ski mask advanced toward her.

"No," she said inching away from the man. Her back bumped against the wall. Out of the corner of her eye she saw the window beside her.

Abby cocked her arm and knocked her elbow through the glass.

The man lunged for her, hitting her in the belly. Abby staggered backward and fell through the breached win-

dow, landing with a hard thump on her back, knocking the air from her lungs.

She blinked her eyes open to sunlight.

Hands slipped beneath her back and legs. "Hey, are you okay?" a deep, familiar voice spoke softly against her ear as she was lifted off the cool hardwood floor and deposited on the warm, soft comforter. Her body shook. Not from the cold, but from the panic of being confronted by one of the men who'd held her captive, by the nightmare of being held in a cage in the dark, the hope of rescue fading with each passing day.

Abby looked up into the eyes of the man who'd saved her. When he started to straighten, she gripped his arm.

He paused. "I take it you had a bad dream."

She nodded. "I was back in that attic. He was coming for me. I—I had to get away. Then I fell through the window and landed…"

"On the floor." Parker sighed. "Scoot."

She frowned.

He waved a hand indicating she should move over on the bed.

Abby eased across the mattress and slipped her legs between the sheets.

Parker kicked off his shoes, sat on the edge of the bed and swung his legs up onto the comforter. "Better?"

She stared up at him, frowning and unsure of this man or his intentions. "A little."

He opened his arms. "Come here."

Abby sat up and moved into his arms. As he wrapped them around her, she rested her cheek against his chest.

"Think you can tell me everything now?" he asked, his voice rumbling through his chest into her ear.

She nodded and started talking. As she explained

about the field trip and abduction at the rest area, her fingers curled into his shirt.

His arms tightened around her reassuringly, giving her the courage to go on.

By the time she got through the part where she had escaped, her pulse pounded, and her gut knotted. "Then I ran until I could run no more."

"You're lucky you didn't break something in your fall from the roof," Parker said, stroking her drying hair. "And you're wrong."

"Wrong?" She tilted her head back and frowned up at him. "Why?"

"Brutus and I didn't save you." He touched a finger beneath her chin. "You saved yourself."

"I wouldn't be alive right now if you and Brutus hadn't shown up when you did." She laid her cheek back on his chest. "Now help me save the others."

"We're going to need help," he said.

Her heart beat faster. "No one can know I'm still alive. They'll move the others, hurry their sell or kill them." She looked up at him. "I couldn't get them out fast enough and had to leave them behind with the promise that I'd bring help." She shook her head. "I can't break that promise. None of them deserve what's happening to them."

Parker nodded. "I understand. But we're going to need help. You and I alone can't find them fast enough." When she started to protest again, he held up a hand. "Hear me out, will ya?"

She bit down hard on her bottom lip and nodded.

"I'm an Outrider. We're former military who help people, without all the rules and regulations that come along with government-run law enforcement." He smiled. "People like you and the women you want to save."

Her brow puckered. "What do you mean? Like vigilantes?"

He shook his head. "Security specialists. All with military training."

She laid her hand across his heart. "Do you trust them to keep my existence silent?"

He nodded. "These men are former Special Forces. We've had top-secret clearances and performed missions we can't talk about. Ever." He grinned. "I think we can keep a secret."

Abby drew in a ragged breath. "Okay. We could use all the help we can get."

The sound of doors opening and closing in the house below alerted Abby to the fact they no longer were alone in the house. "What will you tell them?"

"Exactly what you told me. They'll need as much information as possible."

Abby laid her cheek against his chest again, a shiver rippling through her body. "We have to hurry. I don't know how much time we have. Some of them had already been there a week. I was the last to arrive four days ago. Now that I've escaped, they'll probably move quick to keep from getting caught."

"Look, if you're okay on your own for a few minutes, I'd like to pull my boss aside and bring him up to speed on what happened." He tipped her chin up. "Will you be okay?"

She nodded.

"You'll be here when I get back?"

She frowned. "I'll be here. I have nowhere else to go."

"I just don't want you to go off and try to do this on your own."

She caught his arm. "No law enforcement?"

He shook his head. "No sheriff departments, police or FBI. We'll keep this operation on the down low."

"Thank you," she said. "I don't know what I'd have done if Brutus hadn't found me."

"I imagine you'd have found a way." He winked. "Rest and get your strength back. I'll be back shortly."

Parker left the room.

As soon as the door closed, the walls seemed to close in around her. Abby's breath caught and her pulse ratcheted up with the beginning of a panic attack. She pulled her hands out from beneath the comforter, knowing they were free of restraints, but she had to see them for herself.

She got out of the bed, her legs wobbling, sore and tired from her midnight run. For a long moment, she stood, letting her muscles adapt and legs steady before she crossed to the French doors. She reached for the handles, her heart racing, fully expecting the doors to be locked from the outside. When the handles turned, she let go of the breath she'd been holding and opened the doors, letting more sunlight stream into the room. She stood for a long time as the rays warmed her skin.

A cool breeze touched the bare skin of her legs, making her shiver.

Leaving the doors open, Abby returned to the bed and crawled beneath the comforter, her gaze on the open door and freedom.

Abby never wanted to be trapped in a cage, in the dark again. She'd rather die than live through that again.

She lay staring out at the sunshine, her arm hanging over the side of the bed to rest on Brutus's smooth back. Her last conscious thought before dreamless sleep claimed her was of the cowboy who'd swept her off her feet and carried her away from danger. The man was what heroes were made of.

PARKER DESCENDED THE stairs and went in search of whoever had returned from town, hoping it was Trace. He desperately needed to talk to the man. Time was ticking by on the fate of four women.

He found Rosalyn in the kitchen unloading bags of groceries.

When he walked into the kitchen, she smiled. "Oh, Parker, back from riding the fence line already?"

He nodded. "Do you know when Trace will be back?"

"We ran into him in town. He said he'd be right behind us. He wanted to stop by Matt's shop for a minute about something the sheriff had told him. I expect he'll be coming through the door any moment."

"Thank you, ma'am."

She shook her head, her lips pinching. "Rosalyn."

"Rosalyn," he corrected. "Could you point me to the cabinet with the cups?"

She tipped her head toward one she passed as she carried a carton of milk to the refrigerator. "I was just about to make ham and cheese sandwiches for lunch. Would you care for one?"

"Yes, please," he said. "Could I get two?"

She laughed. "Absolutely. A man can work up an appetite riding fences."

He didn't want to tell her the other sandwich was for an unexpected guest. Not until he briefed Trace on the woman in his bedroom.

The sound of a truck's engine caught his attention.

"That's probably Trace now," Rosalyn said. "I'll start on those sandwiches as soon as I finish putting away all the groceries. Irish and Lily are unloading feed and fencing supplies in the barn."

Parker left through the back door and stepped out on the porch as Trace Travis drove by in a Whiskey Gulch Ranch truck and parked in the barnyard next to another truck with a pallet of feed sacks in the bed.

Parker went down the porch steps and started across the yard toward his boss.

As Trace climbed out of the truck, Lily emerged from the barn with a smile. "You're just in time to lend a hand."

Trace nodded, opened his arms and engulfed her in a big hug. Then he kissed her, long and hard.

Finally, he set her on the ground, his arms around her waist.

"Wow," she said. "What was all that about?"

"Nothing. Everything." He smiled down at her. "I love you, Lily. I don't think I say it often enough."

She leaned up and kissed his lips. "You do. But I don't get tired of hearing it. I love you, too."

Parker stopped several yards from the tender scene, not comfortable interrupting, but anxious to speak with Trace.

Irish came out of the barn about that time and raised a hand. "Parker, is everything all right? I found your horse in his stall still saddled. I was just about to go looking for you."

Trace and Lily glanced from Irish to where Parker stood.

He'd completely forgotten Jasper in his hurry to get Abby warmed up.

"I had an issue come up and got sidetracked. I'll take care of my horse in a little bit."

Irish shook his head. "No worries. I already took care of him. Your tack is in the tack room, the horse has been brushed and is currently eating oats and hay. I'll turn him out to pasture when we're done unloading the truck."

"Thanks." Parker turned to Trace. "If you can spare a minute, I need to talk to you."

Lily stepped out of Trace's arms.

"Certainly. Here or in my office?" Trace strode toward him.

"In your office," Parker said and turned to walk alongside Trace toward the house.

"Did you find the break in the fence?" Trace asked as they climbed the porch steps together.

"No," Parker said. "I didn't make it that far."

Trace frowned as he led the way inside and down the hallway to his office. "What happened?" he asked as he held the door for Parker to enter.

Once Parker was inside and Trace closed the door, he started. "Brutus found a woman."

Trace's eyebrows shot up. "A woman? Where?"

"On the ranch, near the southern fence you wanted me to inspect," Parker said.

He gave Parker a crooked smile. "By woman, you

mean human, not dog, right?" He settled in the chair behind his desk.

"Human."

Trace's smile faded. "Dead or alive?"

"Alive." Parker took a deep breath and launched into what had happened, pacing across the floor as he spoke. Minutes later, he stopped and faced Trace.

Trace whistled. "Hell of a first day on the job, huh?"

Parker nodded. "Not exactly what I was expecting to find on my first day."

"Why didn't you take her to the hospital? She could be suffering from hypothermia and hallucinations."

Parker still wanted to take her, but he'd promised her that he wouldn't. "She doesn't want anyone to know she's alive. Since none of the women knew who abducted them, Abby's afraid they would be able to identify her before she could identify them. She's also afraid that if she turns up alive, they'll hurry to get rid of the evidence and either make a hurried sale of the women, move them or kill them and hide the bodies."

Trace pushed hand through his hair. "They might have moved them already."

"I thought the same," Parker said. "Abby said she ran a long way without seeing any other lights. She also said it was raining hard when she left the house. It's possible she didn't see any other lights through the downpour."

"Yet, she ended up on Whiskey Gulch Ranch."

"Running barefoot all the way." Parker's jaw clenched. The bastards who'd abducted her needed to die.

"I'll call the team to have dinner with us tonight. And, so you know, I had a meeting with the sheriff today. He asked for any help we could give him in finding a missing teen from a neighboring town."

"Abby said two of the women were teenagers."

Trace's eyes narrowed. "I'd like to get the sheriff involved."

"You can't. Abby couldn't have run through the entire county. Not at night, in the dark and rain. Which means the house where she and the other women were held could be fairly close. The men who abducted those women could live in the county. They could live in the town of Whiskey Gulch."

"From what you said, the women weren't all from around here."

"No. The teenage runaway was picked up in San Antonio. The college student was taken from a truck stop along the interstate between Whiskey Gulch and San Antonio. A young mother was picked up on the interstate when she stopped to change a flat tire. She even had children in the vehicle. They took her and left the children. The other teenager was taken after she got off a school bus a quarter mile from her house."

"Damn," Trace said. "Their families have to be worried sick."

"We can't let them know their loved ones are still alive," Parker said.

Trace's mouth set in a firm like. "Especially since we're not sure they are still alive, nor do we know where they are. All the more reason to get started on our search right away."

Parker nodded. "My thoughts exactly."

Trace picked up his cell phone. "I'll get the team together. We'll meet here, in my office, in forty-five minutes."

Parker nodded. "I want to go check on her again. She needs food and water."

"I'm sure my mother will fix her up." Trace selected a number and hit Send.

"I'd rather not announce her presence until everyone understands the implications of disclosing that she's here."

"Okay. But my mother and Lily know this house. It won't be long before they discover the extra guest." His attention focused on his phone. "Matt, I'm calling an emergency meeting in my office…as soon as possible. If you could contact Levi, I'll inform Becker… Roger. Out."

Parker left Trace's office and returned to the kitchen.

Rosalyn had finished putting away the groceries and had a stack of ham and cheese sandwiches on a platter on the counter.

"There you are," she said with a smile. "Help yourself to the sandwiches. There's a cup on the counter. I have tea and lemonade in the refrigerator, or I can make coffee."

"Water will be fine." He wasn't sure what Abby had been given to eat and drink during her incarceration. At this point, anything was better than nothing.

He wrapped two sandwiches in paper towels, filled the cup with water from the tap and left the kitchen.

He hurried up the stairs almost afraid he'd get to his room and find the bed empty and Abby Gibson nothing but a figment of his imagination.

Balancing the sandwiches on top of the cup, he reached for the door handle, took a deep breath and held it as he pushed the door open.

His gaze went right to the bed and he exhaled in relief.

Abby lay on her side, her arm draping over the side of the bed resting on Brutus's back.

Brutus rose, stretched and trotted over to Parker, sniffing the air, his gaze on the sandwiches.

"Don't worry, I'll give you some of mine." He closed the door and carried the cup and sandwiches to the bed and set them on the nightstand.

A cool breeze swept through the room.

Parker crossed to the French doors and closed them. He hadn't opened them before he left. Abby must have done it. After being locked in a cage in a dark attic for days, she probably needed to know she could open the doors and leave whenever she wanted. Still, the air in the room was too cool. If she wanted the doors opened again, he would do it for her.

When Parker turned back to the bed, Abby's eyes were open.

"Hey," he said. "Feel like eating something?"

She nodded, stretched and pushed to a sitting position. A shiver shook her frame. Abby pulled the comforter up over her chest.

Parker handed her a sandwich and moved the cup of water closer to her.

"Thank you," she said as she unwrapped the paper towel.

"You're welcome," he said as he took out the other sandwich and tore off a piece of bread for Brutus.

The dog sat three feet away, salivating.

"You'd think I never feed you." He tossed the bread into the air.

Brutus caught it before it hit the ground and swallowed it whole.

"You might try chewing next time." Parker tore off another piece and Brutus easily caught the offering again and chewed it before swallowing.

"That's more like it." Parker reached out and scratched behind Brutus's ear.

"You two have a special bond, don't you?" Abby took a small bite of her sandwich.

Parker nodded. "He and I helped each other through some dark times. Together, we help Jasper, as well."

"Jasper?" Abby asked over the sandwich in her hands.

"My horse."

"They mean a lot to you," she observed.

Parker nodded. "They do."

"Did you talk to your boss?"

"I did," Parker said and bit into his sandwich.

Abby captured his gazed and held it. "Well?"

Parker chewed the bite and swallowed before answering. "He's calling in the rest of the team."

She sighed. "I worry that the more people who know I'm alive and here, the more chance of it slipping out."

"The people on this ranch can be trusted."

"So you say." She stared down at the sandwich. "People can slip up and not even realize what they've done."

"In a perfect world, we'd enlist the help of everyone in the county to look for the women. But it's not a perfect world. And we need more eyes on the ground and in the air."

She set the food on the nightstand and picked up the cup of water and sipped. "When will they be here?"

Parker glanced at his watch. "Thirty minutes or less."

"I want to talk to them." Abby swung her legs over the side of the bed and reached for the brush next to the lamp on the nightstand. She dragged the brush through her hair, working the tangles. She stopped several times to rest.

Parker held out his hand.

Abby handed the brush to him.

"Turn around," he said.

She did, sitting cross-legged on the bed.

He eased the brush over her long blond hair, gently teasing the tangles loose.

"You know that if you go downstairs, the other members of the household will notice you," he reminded her.

"Then we'll have to make sure they're on board for keeping my secret." Her mouth pressed into a thin line. "It's all risky."

"We'll do our best." Parker smoothed the tangles and brushed Abby's hair straight back.

"Where did you learn to brush long hair?"

"Would it bother you if I said I once had long hair?" He grinned.

Abby's eyes rounded. "Of course not."

"Back as a freshman in high school, I was a bit of a rebel."

"And now?" she asked.

He chuckled. "The army worked it out of me and let me use it at the same time. It takes a rebel to pull off some of the missions we've been tasked with."

"Once a rebel, always a rebel?"

"Yes. But I can only go by my experience."

"And where did you learn to brush a woman's hair?"

"Like that?" he asked.

"Oh, yes," Abby said.

"I have two younger sisters. I helped get them ready for school in the mornings." Though all the tangles were gone, Parker continued to brush Abby's hair. "I even learned to French-braid. Mom never could get the hang of it. A friend of mine showed me how to do it. I practiced on my sisters until I got it right."

"You're an amazing man," Abby said. "And you can bush my hair as long as you like."

He continued for a few more minutes.

Her hair had dried and lay soft and straight around her shoulders, the light blond color a distinct contrast with the black T-shirt.

"I didn't know what I had when Brutus found you in the dirt."

"Yeah?" She turned to face him, her face clean of dirt and makeup, her lips a dusty rose and eyes light blue like a fresh spring sky. "I must have been a mess."

He frowned, far too aware of her in his T-shirt and shorts, so much of her legs bare. He needed to maintain focus on the issue, not how beautiful she was. "I never would have seen you if not for Brutus."

Abby reached down to scratch behind the pit bull's ears. "I'm lucky you both found me. Now, if only Brutus could sniff out the others, we'd make this go a whole lot faster."

"If anyone can find them, it's the Outriders."

She sighed. "I hope so. They're desperate to get home to their loved ones."

"And you?" he asked. "Are you desperate to get home to your loved ones?" This was the first time he'd considered that Abby might have someone else in her life. A husband, fiancé or significant other waiting for her to return.

"If you count my twenty-four fifth graders, I have twenty-four loved ones waiting for my return."

"No boyfriend?"

She snorted. "I teach fifth graders. I barely have time to grade all the students' papers."

Parker didn't want to admit to himself the relief he felt that she was single.

His gaze captured hers. "It takes a special person to teach. My mother was a teacher."

"Then you know how much work it is."

He nodded. "I do."

A knock sounded on the door.

Abby jumped, her eyes rounding.

Parker reached out to touch her leg. "It's okay."

"Parker," Irish's voice sounded on the other side of the door.

"Yeah?" Parker responded.

"Team's gathered," he said. "Trace wants us to meet in his office."

"Roger," Parker said. "I'll be right down." He stood and looked down at Abby seated on the side of the bed. He held out his hand. "Coming?"

She sighed and placed her hand in his.

He pulled her to her feet and into his arms.

She rested a hand against his chest and stared up into his eyes.

"Why is it that I've only just met you and already I want to kiss you."

A smile spread across her face. "What are you waiting for?"

"I don't want to take advantage. You've been through a lot."

She laughed. "Seriously?" Abby cupped both of his cheeks between her palms. "My feet hurt, I'm physically and emotionally exhausted, and afraid for the others I left behind. A kiss could only improve the day." She pressed her lips to his. "If you're the one doing the kissing. Please." Her lips took his, her tongue sweeping across his mouth.

He opened to her, his tongue caressing the length of hers.

When he finally broke away, he held her at arm's length and stared down into her eyes. "I don't know what that was all about, but damned if I don't want to do it again."

Chapter Six

Trace's entire team had gathered in his office. Trace sat behind the massive mahogany desk. Levi and Becker had each claimed one of the leather chairs. Irish perched on the edge of Trace's desk and Matt stood looking out the French doors.

Parker stood on the threshold, holding Abby's hand. He'd given her a pair of his sweatpants and socks. Everything she wore swamped her small frame. She'd walked gingerly on her bruised and damaged feet. With her shoulders back and her head held high, she entered the room, ready to go to work finding the women, her tight grip on Parker's hand due to determination, not fear.

"Gentlemen, this is Abby Gibson," Parker said. "Brutus discovered her this morning on the south end of the ranch."

The men rose from their seats as Abby entered the room.

Trace rounded the corner of his desk and took her hand. "Ms. Gibson, please, have a seat."

He led her to his office chair and held it while she eased onto the leather. Then he turned to the others. "Ms. Gibson needs our help. Our mission is time-sensitive and the lives of four women are at stake." He glanced down at Abby. "Do you want to tell them what's happened?"

She caught Parker's gaze and held it as she spoke. "For me, it started four days ago."

She detailed her abduction, holding herself together throughout the narrative all the way to her escape and subsequent race to freedom. "I managed to get out, but there are four other women being held against their will. I promised to get help." Abby looked around the room. "Parker said your group could help. I pray that's the case. Those women, two of whom are teens, have no other hope of being found. They'd been there longer than I had."

Trace nodded toward Abby. "The answer is yes. We will help." He faced his team.

Parker barely knew these men. Based on Trace's faith in them and the fact most of them had fought as Delta Force operatives, Parker would put his life in their hands and trust that they would do their best to find and free the women and bring their captors to justice.

"Time is critical," Trace said. "If they haven't already moved them, it's a high possibility they will…soon, unless they're convinced—" he waved a hand toward Abby "—that Ms. Gibson succumbed to her injuries before she had a chance to reveal their whereabouts. The women's lives and freedom depend on us keeping a lid on this. Y'all know the drill. Let's get to it."

"Yes, sir!" the men replied as one.

"Ms. Gibson," Trace started.

"Please," Abby stopped him. "Call me Abby. Only my fifth graders call me Ms. Gibson. Y'all don't look anything like fifth graders and it's throwing me off." She gave a crooked grin.

Trace nodded. "Abby escaped last night right about the time it started raining. She found her hiding space shortly after the rain stopped. Given she ended up on the south end of the ranch, she must've come through the break in the fence. She couldn't have traveled too far in her condition and under the circumstances, even with adrenaline pumping. We can create a grid of the area and start our search within a five-mile radius."

"We need to get a drone in the sky," Irish said.

Trace nodded. "You're right. We're on borrowed time. A ground search will take too long."

"I'll get it ready," said Matt.

"Parker and Abby, you'll need to work closely with Matt and Irish," Trace said.

Parker nodded.

"I'd like to get Dallas involved. She can research the names of the women abducted and see if there's a pattern that would help reveal the identities of their abductors."

"Who's Dallas?" Abby asked.

Trace's gaze met Parker's and then connected with Abby's. "Dallas is Levi's fiancée. She's a deputy sheriff in this county."

Abby shook her head. "No law enforcement. If word gets out—"

Levi held up his hand, stopping her words. "Dallas won't let that happen. None of us will."

Abby chewed on her lip as she glanced around the room at the men. "I'm not even comfortable with the number of people in this room, and you're asking me to let someone else in on it?" Her gaze landed on Parker.

He gave her a single nod. "They can be trusted," he said.

"And what about the deputy?" She held his gaze. "Do you know him?"

"Her," Levi corrected. "She's also prior military and knows the importance of keeping secrets."

"Those women are counting on me."

"And finding and rescuing them and taking down those responsible will be impossible by yourself," Trace said. "Let us help in the best manner we know how."

For a long moment, Abby stared around the room, a crease across her forehead. Finally, she sighed. "You're right. I can't do this by myself."

"And if they've moved them, it will be even more difficult to find them," Parker squeezed the hand he still held. He hated that she was so afraid and desperate. In his gut, he knew this team was her best bet.

"Okay," she finally said. "We need to hurry."

Trace turned to Matt. "Go get the drone."

Matt was already halfway across the room. "I'll be back in less than thirty minutes."

"Levi—" Trace started.

"I'll give Dallas a heads-up we need her to pay a visit to the ranch. She's on graveyard shift and sleeping right now. She could be out here later this evening to talk with Abby before she heads to work at midnight."

Trace glanced at his watch. "In the meantime, while we're waiting for Matt, the rest of us can pull up a satellite map for the surrounding area and see if we can narrow down the possibilities."

Trace turned back to Abby. "You realize my fiancée and mother live in this house. They'll have to know you're here."

She nodded.

"Could I bring them in and introduce them to you?" Trace asked.

"Okay," she said, holding onto Parker's hand.

He gave her a reassuring smile.

Trace left the room and returned a couple minutes later with three women.

Irish leaped to his feet and crossed to Tessa and pulled her into his arms. "Hey, babe."

She looked around the room, her gaze landing on Abby.

Rosalyn and Lily also looked to Abby.

"We have a guest?" Rosalyn asked.

Trace nodded. "Mom, Lily, Tessa, this is Abby Gibson. She needs our help and will be staying with us for a few days. No one else can know she's here. No one but the people in this room." He stared hard at the women. Then he explained what had happened. "So, we need to keep this to ourselves until we find those women."

"Why don't you call the sheriff and state police in to help?" Rosalyn asked. "Surely the more people you have looking, the quicker you'll find them?"

"Or they could move them or kill them and hide the bodies," Trace said. "We need to find them before that happens."

Rosalyn nodded. "Okay. My lips are sealed."

"And mine," Lily said.

"That goes for me, too," Tessa said. Her eyes narrowed as she studied Abby. "Are you sure you're all right? After what you've been through, a visit to a doctor would be a good idea."

Abby shook her head. "I'll be okay and even better when we find the others."

"At the very least, you should have Tessa look at the wounds on your feet and legs," Parker said. "She's a licensed nurse."

"Okay," she said. "If it's not too much trouble."

Tessa shook her head. "No trouble at all."

Rosalyn reached out a hand. "Come. I have a first aid kit in the master bathroom."

"And I'll find some clothes that fit you better," Lily said.

The women gathered around Abby and led her out of the office and down to the end of the hallway.

Parker stood in the doorway and watched them until they disappeared around a corner. He'd been with Abby since he'd found her in the dirt. That sense of responsibility for her welfare stuck with him, making him want to follow.

Trace clapped a hand on his shoulder. "They'll take good care of her."

"I know." Parker turned back to the room. "Let's look at those satellite maps. We need to find that house."

Trace nodded. "They could be targeting other women, looking for an opportunity to strike."

"Like Lily or Tessa." Parker's hands tightened into fists. "And no doubt they'll come after Abby if they find out she's still alive."

"We can't let any of that happen," Trace said. "Let's get to work."

As ROSALYN AND TESSA led Abby away from Parker, her anxiety levels spiked. She almost stopped in her tracks and ran back.

When they turned the corner in the hallway, Abby glanced back.

Parker stood in the doorway of the office, his gaze on her.

Seeing him there, watching her, helped to calm her anxieties enough to allow her to continue with the women into the massive master suite.

"Those men need to pay for what they did to you," Rosalyn said. "I can't imagine how awful it must have been to be caged like an animal and then to have to run barefoot and half-naked." The older woman held her arm, walking her through the bedroom into the adjoining bathroom.

"I imagine your feet are like hamburger meat," Tessa said. "Texas hill country isn't kind on tender, bare feet."

Rosalyn pulled a white, tufted velvet stool from beneath a counter. "Sit here while I find the first aid kit." She gently pressed Abby onto the stool.

Tessa knelt on the floor in front of her.

Abby's cheeks heated. "You really don't have to do this."

"Yes, we do," Tessa said. "What kind of nurse would I be if I didn't?" She removed the big socks from Abby's feet and brought one up onto her knee and then the other, inspecting both carefully. "You did a good job cleaning them. Some antibiotic ointment wouldn't hurt and bandages for the deeper cuts when you're walking on them. Other than that, it'll take time for the wounds to heal and the bruises to fade."

Rosalyn opened a first aid kit and laid it on the floor beside Abby.

Tessa reached for an alcohol pad. "This will sting a little." She wiped the bottom of Abby's foot.

Abby sucked in a sharp breath at the burning sensation.

Rosalyn shook her head. "How on earth did you walk so far on bare feet?"

"I ran as long as I could. I guess my feet went numb and I kept going. I was looking for lights from a house or business. Anywhere I could get help or use a phone."

"The south side of the ranch borders on several large tracts of land. I'm surprised you didn't run into any fences, but then some of those hills are rugged with little useful vegetation, usually dotted with cedar, cactus, scrubby live oak trees and very little grass," Rosalyn said.

Tessa applied antibiotic ointment and a large bandage to Abby's heels and the balls of her feet. "It would help if you slipped out of the sweatpants. I'm sure there are other wounds needing attention."

Abby stepped out of the sweats and shivered. She rubbed her hands up and down her arms, trying to get warm.

"Oh, sweetie, here." Rosalyn grabbed a fluffy white bathrobe off a hook behind the door and held it out to Abby.

She slipped her arms into the garment and wrapped it around her body. "I've never been so cold as I was last night, lying on the damp ground covered in wet leaves." Abby's teeth chattered from a combination of a chill and nervousness in front of the two women.

Tessa checked all the cuts and bruises, applied ointment and bandages where needed. She examined the raw skin around Abby's wrists and looked into Abby's eyes.

"Zip ties," Abby said.

Tessa shook her head. "We definitely need to find

the men who did this and make sure they don't harm anyone else." She closed the kit and set it on the counter.

Lily sailed through the door carrying an armload of clothes. "Since I didn't know how long to plan for, I brought enough clothing for a week."

Abby shook her head. "I have my own clothes in my apartment in Boerne."

"I'm sure you do," Lily said. "But you're not going there until you're safe and those other women are safe as well. So you'll have to put up with my boring taste in clothes."

Abby's heart swelled at the outpouring of concern from Rosalyn, Tessa and Lily. Tears welled in her eyes. "Thank you. I don't know what I would have done if Parker and Brutus hadn't found me."

"You got out of a locked cage," Tessa said. "You'd have found a way to make things happen."

Like the men, the women had confidence in Abby's resilience. Abby believed everything she'd done so far had been performed out of pure desperation and a will to live.

Lily held up a pair of black leggings and a cream, cable-knit sweater. "This should keep you warm."

Abby reluctantly shed the robe and the black T-shirt. The robe for its warmth. The T-shirt because it was Parker's and smelled like him.

She quickly pulled the sweater over her head, wishing her bra was already dry.

The ladies gave her the courtesy of turning their backs while Abby changed out of the T-shirt into the sweater.

She slipped out of the shorts and into the leggings. They weren't as warm as the sweats, but they fit her nicely and made her appear less like a vagabond. Still, she slipped the robe over the leggings and the sweater, basking in the warmth.

Rosalyn sat her back down on the stool and used her own brush to smooth Abby's hair.

When she was done, she stepped out of the way of the mirror and smiled at Abby's reflection. "There, that's better," Lily said. She leaned in and hugged Abby. "Don't worry. We'll get through this," she said. When she straightened, she held out a hand to Abby and pulled her to her feet.

Abby winced when her full weight came down on her damaged feel.

Tessa took her arm on one side. "You really need to stay off your feet until the wounds can heal." She looked at Abby, her eyebrows cocked. "You're not going to do that, are you?"

With a chuckle, Abby shook her head. "No. I can't sit around with my feet up when there are four women out there caged like animals. I'm ready to get started." And to get back to Parker. She only felt safe in his arms.

Chapter Seven

Parker, Trace, Irish and Becker skimmed through satellite images of the hill country south of the ranch, searching through the blurry images of tree crowns for the straight lines of rooftops.

Many of the places they found were so far from the ranch that they couldn't be from where Abby had originally escaped.

They also identified state highways and county roads they would need to use when they went in search of whatever house they found.

The sound of a truck engine made them all look up.

"That's Matt." Irish left his seat at the computer, unplugged the laptop from its docking station and carried it out of the office.

Trace, Becker and Parker followed.

Parker paused in the hallway.

At that moment, Abby, Rosalyn, Tessa and Lily came through the doorway.

Abby wore black leggings and a cream-colored sweater with a fluffy white bathrobe over it all.

He held out his hand.

She went to him, a smile curling the corners of her lips.

"Love the robe," he said. "Goes great with the rest of the outfit. Are you staying here, or coming with us?"

"With you," she said.

"I'll get Abby a coat." Lily hurried for the closet by the front door and returned with a Sherpa-lined jacket. "This should keep you warmer than the bathrobe."

Abby surrendered the robe and slipped her arms into the jacket. "Thank you for everything."

"I'm not sure we're going anywhere," Trace said, "but it'll be dark in less than an hour. We'll be less conspicuous then."

In the meantime, they recapped everything Abby had told them to make sure they hadn't missed anything. When the time came, everyone stepped out onto the porch as Matt climbed down from his truck. He reached into the back seat and withdrew a black drone and the handheld controls.

Irish joined Matt, laying the laptop on the hood of the truck.

"Battery fully charged?" Irish asked.

"Roger," Matt responded and laid the drone on the ground.

Trace stood nearby as Matt turned on the control box and the drone and lifted the device into the air. After a few wobbly starts, Matt got the drone off the ground. He flew it up to ten feet and practiced moving side to side and forward and backward. Then he worked moving the drone up and down, landing it five times before finally going up to thirty feet in the air.

Matt directed the drone in a circle over the house, making a clockwise and then counterclockwise rotation. He did this three times around the house before sending the drone to circle the barn. Moving a little too fast, it almost crashed into the roof.

At the last moment, Matt made the drone climb higher, avoiding hitting the barn.

A collective gasp sounded from the spectators.

Parker shook his head. He reached for Abby's hand and squeezed it gently.

"The controls are very sensitive," Matt remarked.

Trace leaned over Matt's shoulder to view the screen and joysticks on the control box.

Matt circled the barn several times before bringing the drone back to land near their feet.

When it was on the ground, Matt wiped the sweat from his brow. "I need more practice."

Irish clicked the laptop keyboard and set up a livestream channel on his video app. He held out his hand. "Let me see the controls."

Matt handed over the control unit. Irish entered the URL website link on the control box, hit Enter and then looked to the laptop screen.

Irish swore, set the controls aside and keyed information on the laptop.

Once again, he played with the control box, entering data and clicking the enter key. This time an image of the gravel parking lot came into view. "Bingo! We're livestreaming."

Abby and the other women clapped their hands.

Matt reclaimed the control unit. "I need more practice here before I launch this over the hill country."

"And we need time with the drone in the air to understand what we're viewing," Irish said.

"Do all the practice you can this evening." Trace glanced at the sky. "Looks like we're in for some more rain. We'll have to wait until morning to fly it any distance." He glanced at his watch. "By the time we get to the south fence line, the sun will be setting. It'll be dark even sooner, with the clouds moving in. We can't risk losing the drone in the dark or the rain."

Abby's fingers tightened around Parker's. "That's another night those women will be held in captivity. Another night the men could use to move them."

"Hopefully, by keeping your whereabouts secret, they won't feel the need to do anything," Parker said.

"We can't do anything this late," Trace said. "Even if we rode out now on four-wheelers or horseback, we wouldn't cover enough ground to find anything. We'd barely get to the south fence line. We'll start out early tomorrow morning and be at the point where Parker found you by the time the sun comes up."

Abby's shoulders slumped. "I don't like it, but I understand." A cool breeze lifted her hair. She leaned against Parker, a shiver shaking her body.

Parker slipped an arm around her, sharing his own body warmth.

"I have a roast in the slow cooker," Rosalyn announced. "We can have supper on the table in thirty minutes with a little help."

"I can help." Parker glanced down at Abby. "Want to join me?"

She nodded "Anything to keep my mind off what those women are going through."

"Good," Parker said. "I can peel a mean potato and make chili, but that's about the extent of my culinary skills."

"Can you wield a knife?" Lily asked.

"In a fight, filleting fish and peeling potatoes, yes," Parker said.

"You two can cut the veggies for the salad," Lily said.

"I can help set the table," Becker volunteered.

"You're hired," Rosalyn said with a smile.

While Matt, Irish, Trace and Levi worked with the drone, the others entered the house.

In the kitchen, Rosalyn pulled out lettuce, tomatoes, carrots, purple onions and black olives from the refrigerator and pantry and set them out on the counter along with a large bowl, two cutting boards and a couple of sharp knives. "It's all yours."

Abby shed her jacket and hung it on a hook by the back door.

Parker grabbed the head of lettuce and started chopping.

Abby sliced the tomatoes.

They had the salad finished in ten minutes and set on the dining table with several bottles of various dressing options.

Abby filled glasses with ice from the ice maker on the refrigerator door. Parker carried them to the table and helped Becker finish setting out plates, cutlery and napkins.

Lily made iced tea and lemonade and set the pitchers on the table.

By the time Rosalyn carried the platter of roast beef, potatoes and carrots to the table, the sun had set.

Matt, Irish, Trace and Levi entered through the back door.

"Perfect timing," Rosalyn said. "We'll eat as soon as you boys wash up."

Everyone convened around the dining table.

Parker held Abby's chair and waited until she and the other women were seated before he claimed his seat next to Abby.

Lily, on the other side of Parker, handed him the platter of roast.

Parker scooped potatoes and carrots onto his plate and added a slice of roast beef. As he held the platter for Abby, he asked, "How are you holding up?"

She shrugged and took a small portion of the beef, a chunk of potato and a couple of carrots. Barely enough to call dinner. "I'm eating hot food while the other women are still captive and lucky if they get cold sandwiches once a day. They barely gave us food and water. I was so hungry, but the thought of eating while they're still suffering…"

"Think of it this way," Parker said. "You need to keep up your strength. Food is fuel for your body. Without it, you won't be of much use in finding them."

She nodded. "I know. I just feel like I wasted today. I should have been out looking for them, not sleeping."

He reached for her hand. "You needed the rest. After you raced through the storm last night and slept on the cold, wet ground, you're lucky to be alive."

She didn't look convinced.

Her melancholy made Parker want to hold her close and reassure her even more.

"Yoo-hoo!" A female voice called out from the front of the house. "Where is everyone?"

"That'll be Dallas." Levi rose from the table with a smile and called out, "We're in the dining room."

A woman wearing the tan-shirt-and-black-trouser uniform of the county sheriff's department stepped into the dining room with a grin. "Something smells really good," she said.

"Dallas," Rosalyn said with a welcoming smile. "So glad you could join us."

"I was getting ready for my shift when Levi texted saying you had one of your pot roasts cooking. I couldn't miss out." She glanced around the table, an eyebrow cocked. "That is, if there's enough for everyone."

Rosalyn waved a hand toward the empty chair beside Levi. "There's always enough. I always cook more than we'll need so we can snack on it later. Take a seat."

Levi held a chair for her. Once Dallas had taken her seat, Levi rested a hand on her shoulder, leaned forward and pressed a kiss to her temple. "Hey."

She covered his hand on her shoulder and looked up at him. "Hey."

Levi sat beside her and handed her the platter of food.

Dallas scooped a generous portion onto her plate and looked around the table. "Levi tells me I need to talk with the new guy and his gal." Her gaze landed on Parker and moved to Abby.

"Dallas," Trace said, waving toward Parker. "This is my newest Outrider, Parker Shaw."

Dallas nodded toward Parker. "Prior military?"

Parker nodded. "Army Delta Force."

"Thank you for your service," Dallas said.

"Dallas is prior army as well."

"What MOS?" Parker asked.

"31Bravo, Military Police." Dallas glanced down at her law enforcement uniform and shrugged. "Surprised?"

"Thank you for your service." Parker turned to Abby. "This is Abby Gibson."

Dallas nodded. "Are you prior service as well?"

Abby shook her head. "I'm a fifth grade teacher in Boerne."

Dallas's brow puckered. "Visiting here in Whiskey Gulch?"

"Not exactly," Abby said.

Dallas's frown deepened. "Abby Gibson. The name sounds familiar."

Levi leaned close to Dallas. "Abby's the reason why I wanted you to stop by the ranch before you went on duty tonight."

Dallas's gaze met Abby's. "What's the story?" She speared a bite of roast and popped it into her mouth as she listened to Abby's recounting of her abduction, the others in captivity and her subsequent escape.

Dallas's frown cleared. "That's where I heard your name. We had a BOLO come across from Kerrville PD about a late model silver Toyota Prius, the vehicle of a missing woman believed to have been abducted from a rest area near there."

"That would be me." Abby sighed.

Dallas pulled a pad and pen from her front pocket. "I'll need the names of the others."

Abby gave her what she knew. "Cara Jo Noble, Valentina Ramirez, Laura Owens and Rachel Pratt. From what I could gather, they planned to sell us."

Dallas frowned. "I recognize a few of those names from Amber alerts. Can you describe any of the men involved?"

Abby shook her head. "No. They all wore ski masks. Cara Jo and Valentina described the man who abducted them as young, blond, nice-looking and approachable. He lured them in, asking for directions, then snatched them."

"I work the graveyard shift," Dallas said. "I usually patrol. I might be able to get some information from the computer on my unit, but I'll take my breaks at the office and do some more snooping on the main computers and databases." She glanced at Levi. "The Rangers should have pulled the cameras at the truck stop where Laura Owens was abducted. I'll see if I can get more info. I have a friend who might be able to help."

Abby leaned forward. "Dallas, I don't want anyone to know I'm here. I'd rather the men who kidnapped me think I died in that storm. It might buy some time before they move the other women."

"If I were them and one of my prisoners escaped," Dallas said, "I'd have moved the others immediately."

Parker agreed with Dallas but didn't voice his agreement. "At the very least, if we find the house they were held in, we might find some clues as to who is orchestrating these abductions and human trafficking."

Dallas nodded. "If they have moved, perhaps they were in such a rush they left behind clues or evidence as to who they are or where they're heading. I'm not sure how much I can delve into the case without letting my department know I'm accessing the information. But I'll do the best I can."

Abby gave her a weak smile. "Thank you."

Parker drew in a deep breath. "Since Abby ended up here on the ranch, we have to assume the men who did this are from around here or are staying close by. We don't know who they are. They could be anyone. We can't be too careful."

"Although my instinct is to remain hidden, it might help for me to be out in the nearby community." Abby wrapped her arms around her middle. "I might recognize one of them by voice."

"They would want to do away with the escapee." Dallas leveled a glance at Abby. "If you're out and about in Whiskey Gulch, you will want to wear some kind of disguise."

"I can fix you up with a disguise," Lily said. "My mother left me all her costumes. I'm sure I have a wig or two you could use. Add some big sunglasses, we can make you look completely different from the fifth grade teacher they snatched."

Parker gave her a puzzled look.

Lily shrugged. "My mother was a stripper. A story for another time. She had a whole trove of wigs and costumes. At least you won't have to hole up at the ranch if you can get out and about as Sissy Bling, or Lala Swoon." She grimaced. "Again, my mother went by a number of different stage names over the years."

"Lala Swoon?" Abby smiled. "I like it. And I've always wanted dark hair."

"I have the prettiest long, black wig," Lily said. "You'll look amazing in it."

"I thought you'd gotten rid of most of those old costumes," Trace said.

Lily gave him a sexy side-eye. "I kept a few of my favorites. You never know when I might take up the trade."

Trace's eyebrows dipped low. "The hell you will."

"I could give a private performance," Lily said, batting her eyelashes.

Trace's frown deepened.

Lily laughed. "Oh, don't be so stuffy." She turned

to Abby. "We'll get you fixed up in case you want to go to town."

"Right now, I want to go back out to where Parker found me and retrace my footsteps."

"You were running in the dark, in a rainstorm," Parker said. "Your footsteps will have been washed away."

"And you might not have run in a straight line," Trace said. "It's highly unlikely. The drone is going to be our best bet. I'm also checking with a friend of mine to see if we can get a helicopter in the air if the drone doesn't work out."

"Wouldn't the noise warn them?" Abby asked, her brow furrowing.

"We need a backup plan if the drone doesn't help us find the house," Trace said.

Dallas shook her head. "If we could get the DPS in on this, we might find them sooner. They're already looking for you and the other missing women."

"They'll move them," Abby said, shaking her head. "Or kill them and hide the bodies."

"I feel like I'm concealing key information." Dallas held up a hand. "Then again, we don't know where they are, so we aren't really." She finished her meal and pushed back from the table, collected her plate and glass and carried them into the kitchen.

One by one, the others followed, until the table was clear.

Dallas hugged Trace's mother. "Rosalyn, thank you for a wonderful meal. I think I'll get to work early and do some digging around for information about the abductions and also see if there are any felons living in the area we should be watching."

"Thank you, Dallas," Abby said. "For helping us find them, and for keeping quiet about me."

Dallas gave her a crooked smile. "I'll work through some of my contacts to keep this on the down low. I'll do the best I can." She pointed at Abby. "Stay safe."

"I'll make sure she does," Parker said.

Dallas nodded. "Nice to meet the new Outrider. Welcome to Whiskey Gulch. I promise we're not all bad here."

"I'm going to follow Dallas into town and head to our place for the night," Levi said. "Do you need me here in the morning?"

"No," Trace said. "But be on standby in case we find the house. We might need you for backup."

"Roger." Levi lifted his chin toward Rosalyn. "Thanks for supper, ma'am." He walked Dallas out to her vehicle. A few minutes later, Parker heard the sound of their engines as they left the yard and headed to town.

"Do you need help cleaning up?" Tessa asked.

Rosalyn shook her head. "We can manage."

"Okay, then. We need to get going," Tessa said. "I have to be up for an early shift in the morning."

Irish slipped an arm around Tessa's waist. "I'll be back before dawn." He caught Abby's glance. "We'll find them."

"Thank you for your help," Abby said.

Irish and Tessa left.

Abby looked around at the dishes on the counter in the kitchen. "I'll do the dishes," she said.

"Don't be silly." Rosalyn waved her hand. "You're a guest."

Abby shook her head. "An uninvited guest. It's the least I can do to repay your kindness."

Parker piled plates together and stacked them by the sink. "If you wash, I'll dry."

"Deal," she said and filled one side of the sink with soapy water.

"You know, we're pretty modern here," Rosalyn said. "We have a dishwasher."

"And I plan to use it," Abby said with a grin. "I'll wash the dishes by hand."

"Then I'm going to grab a beer and step outside to enjoy the evening," Rosalyn said. "Nothing is better than the smell of freshly washed earth after a rain." She grabbed a beer from the refrigerator, unscrewed the cap and handed it to Trace.

"Thanks," he took it and handed it to Lily. Then he got out two more bottles from the refrigerator, twisted off the caps and handed one to his mother. "Dinner was great. Thanks."

"You're welcome," Rosalyn slipped an arm around her son's waist as they walked out the back door onto the porch.

Parker liked that Trace was a man who cared about his family and cared about the men with whom he'd served.

He helped Abby rinse and load the dishes into the dishwasher. Then while she washed, he dried the dishes and the slow cooker.

Brutus found a rug to curl up on and napped while the humans worked.

Parker liked working alongside Abby. She didn't say much, and he didn't feel like he had to make conversation. They worked in a comfortable silence.

When he bumped into her on occasion, electric jolts zipped through his body, shocking him with the flame of desire quickly building. He'd found her dirty, nearly naked and desperate, climbing out of what amounted to a shallow grave. Yet, she stood beside him hours later, willing to work as repayment for her hostess's hospitality. That she was willing to go back to where she'd been held captive showed courage and a caring heart.

He liked this woman and wanted to get to know her better.

She emptied and rinsed the sink and hung the dishtowel on the oven handle.

"Are you heading to bed?" he asked.

She shook her head. "I'd like to spend some time outside, if that's all right. It's not often I get to be where city lights don't shine and hide the stars. And after being stuck inside an attic for days…"

He nodded. "You want to be in the open without walls around you."

"Exactly."

"Would you like a beer?" he asked.

She nodded. "That would be nice."

He claimed two from the refrigerator, opened them and handed her one. Then he raised his bottle and tapped hers. "To finding them quickly."

Abby nodded and tipped her bottle up, downing a long swallow. She held up her beer. "To heroes who rescue damsels in distress."

Brutus chose that moment to lean against her legs.

Abby laughed. "Yes, Brutus, that means you, too."

"He's the real hero," Parker said. "He found you and stood guard against the feral hogs."

She raised her eyebrows. "And if you hadn't swept me off my feet when you did, that herd of hogs would have overwhelmed poor Brutus and had us both for lunch." Abby touched his bottle with hers again. "To hero teams who rescue damsels in distress."

"I'll drink to that." He tipped his bottle back and swallowed. "Let's go look at some stars. I'm feeling the walls closing in around me." He grabbed her jacket from the hook by the door and helped her into it. Once she had it zipped, he held out his hand.

Abby curled her fingers around his and leaned into him as they stepped out onto the porch.

She fit nicely against his side, like she belonged there. Having saved her life really had left an impression and an obligation with him. More than an obligation or duty. He was *compelled* to continue protecting her.

Whether she liked it or not, she was stuck with him.

Chapter Eight

Cool night air felt good against Abby's cheeks. She lifted her face to the gentle breeze, glad for the jacket to keep her body warm.

Other than the light shining through the window in the kitchen, no other lights had been turned on. The stars glowed brightly enough she could see all the way past the barn to where Parker's horse, Jasper, grazed in the field.

"We were about to send a search party into the house to see what was keeping you two." Lily asked from where she perched on the porch rail with Trace beside her.

"Sorry. We got carried away talking," Abby said.

"Thank you for cleaning the kitchen," Rosalyn said from her seat on the porch swing. "We're glad you joined us. We couldn't ask for better weather after last night's storm."

"I, for one, am grateful for last night's storm," Lily said.

"Me, too," Abby murmured softly.

"We needed the rain," Trace said. "Another week without it, along with the cooler weather, and the grass would've died, and we'd have to feed the animals hay sooner."

"That little bit of rain will buy us another week or two of grazing," Lily said.

Parker led Abby down the steps and out into the yard before he stopped and looked up at the sky.

Abby tipped her head back and stared at the bright stars, thankful to be outside where she could stretch her arms and legs and breathe clear, crisp air.

"I'm sorry we didn't make any more progress toward finding the others today," Trace said.

"I am, too," Abby said. "I hope they're okay and can hold out a little longer until we can get to them."

"We all hope the same," Lily said. "I can't imagine what their families are going through. I'd be tempted to tell them you know they're alive."

"I thought the same." Abby shook her head. "But they're better off not knowing. What if we don't get there in time? If they're moved to another location or worse? We'd have given their families hope only to be crushed again."

"Good point," Rosalyn said. "It must have been horrible being trapped in cages. I'm amazed you were able to break free."

"That took a great deal of courage," Trace said.

Abby shook her head. "Desperation. By day three, I was starting to lose hope that we were ever going to be rescued. I figured it was up to us. Then the storm came and the thunder helped drown out the noise I made. So, yes, I was grateful for last night's storm. And though I can't retrace my footsteps, neither can anyone track them here."

Rosalyn pushed to her feet. "I'm headed for a shower and bed. Tomorrow will be a busy day for us all. While you guys are flying drones, I have the farrier coming to work on the horses' hooves. I would reschedule, but he's booked out two months in advance. Once I get the horses into the stalls, I'll come help however I can."

"We shouldn't need you out there," Trace said. "We're going to be looking at a computer screen and tracking against the map. When we find a building, we'll be back to the house and going around by road. My team will handle that. We don't know what we'll be up against."

Rosalyn nodded. "I'll be up early to make drinks and sandwiches to take with you. And I'll have something ready for supper at the end of the day."

"You don't have to cook for us." Trace walked over to his mother and kissed the top of her head. "We can get dinner in town."

"Whatever you decide, let me know early enough so I don't make up a big meal if no one will be here to eat it."

"Plan on us eating out. If we don't, we're old enough to make our own sandwiches." He hugged his mother. "Get some sleep. You know I love you."

She patted her son's cheek. "I know. And I love you, too." She leaned up on her toes and kissed his cheek. "Be careful tomorrow.

"Promise," Trace said. "Good night."

"Good night, everyone," Rosalyn entered the house, closing the door softly behind her.

"I'm tired as well," Lily said. "I'm calling it a night." She looked up into her fiancé's eyes. "Coming?"

He smiled down at her. "You bet." Trace turned to Parker and Abby. "If you need anything, help yourself, or don't hesitate to ask. And lock the back door behind you when you come in. I'll get the rest."

Parker nodded. "We'll lock up."

Lily took Trace's hand and led him through the back door into the kitchen.

Finally alone, Abby wrapped her arms around herself and looked out at the endless heaven of stars.

They were at once reassuring in their consistent appearance every night and frightening with the sheer vastness of their expanse. She could easily feel small and insignificant, a tiny speck in the universe.

Abby moved closer to Parker. He was her rock in the troubled flow of her existence. With him, she felt grounded and secure. Away from her, she was quickly consumed by a tsunami of emotions and fear.

Parker slipped an arm around her shoulders and pulled her close. "I'm here for you," he said softly.

"How did you know I needed you to be?" she whispered.

He shrugged. "I don't know. I just felt it."

She leaned into him. "Thank you for being here with me. I don't think I could do this without you."

He shook his head. "You could. And you did up to the point Brutus found you."

"Still, I was close to going to sleep and never waking up. I've never felt that cold inside and out." She shivered.

His arm tightened around her. "Are you ready to go in? The temp is dropping."

Abby nodded. "I guess we need to get some rest. Tomorrow is going to be stressful."

"Yes, it will be." He turned her around and headed up the stairs onto the porch.

He held the door for her as she entered.

Brutus slipped in behind her.

Parker followed, pulled the door closed behind them and twisted the lock to engage the dead bolt.

"I asked Lily to let you sleep in the room next to mine," Parker said as they climbed the stairs to the second floor.

"Thank you."

"If you have a nightmare, I'll be right next door."

"I'll try not to wake you," she said.

"That's not what I meant," he reached for her hand. "I'll be there when you need me. I'm a light sleeper. All you have to do is call out my name."

Her cheeks heated. She'd always been an independent woman who didn't let much scare her. But having been forcefully taken and held against her will with no easy way out, her confidence had taken a huge hit. "Thank you. I'll keep that in mind."

Parker passed the room he'd brought Abby to earlier that day and moved on to the next one beside it. He opened the door and stood back, waiting for Abby to enter.

She stepped through and looked around. Like the other rooms in the house, it was open and airy, with French doors leading out onto the same upper deck as the room Parker was staying in.

Knowing she could get to him through two different doors helped somewhat to alleviate her anxiety over being left alone.

Brutus slipped past her and lay on the rug at the end of the bed.

Parker stepped into the room, turned her around and stared down into her eyes. "Are you going to be all right?"

She gave him a weak smile, her brave facade slipping

as a lump formed in her throat. Unable to push words past that lump, she nodded, refusing to meet his gaze.

Parker cupped her cheeks in both hands and tipped her chin up, his gaze connecting with hers. "It's okay to be scared. And it's okay to admit it. There's no shame in it." He bent to touch his lips to her forehead.

Abby leaned into that kiss. The next thing she knew, she'd wrapped her arms around his waist and pressed her forehead to his chest. "I'm scared."

"Do you want me and Brutus to stay with you until you go to sleep?" he asked softly.

She hated her weakness but hated even more being left alone. Abby nodded. "Please."

Parker kicked the door shut behind him. "Go. Get ready for bed. I'll be right here."

She looked up into his eyes for confirmation.

He stood firm, meeting and holding her gaze.

Finally, she backed away, her arms falling to her sides.

When she turned away, her anxiety ramped up, her chest tightened, and she almost flung herself back into his arms.

Abby stood for a moment, breathing in and out until she could move forward, away from Parker.

The stack of clothes Lily had loaned her were lying on the bed. Among them was a nightgown, a hairbrush, a new toothbrush and a small tube of toothpaste. Abby gathered the nightgown and toiletries and headed into the adjoining bathroom. She glanced back at Parker before she closed the door between them.

Quickly, she stripped out of the coat, sweater, trouser and shoes and slipped the nightgown over her head.

She opened the package with the toothbrush, spread toothpaste on the bristles and ran it beneath the water.

She brushed her teeth for a long time. After three days without a brush and toothbrush, she'd never take them for granted again.

Once she'd finished brushing her teeth, she ran the brush through her hair, smoothing the tangles until it fell softly around her shoulders.

She studied her reflection in the mirror, seeing a stranger, remembering how she'd felt when she'd been forced to stand in front of a potential buyer like cattle at an auction. Even wearing the school T-shirt, she'd felt naked and dirty, and completely helpless to change a thing as long as the captor threatened her with the cattle prod.

Now, her body, hair and teeth were clean. The gown fell to the middle of her thighs, the snow-white fabric a semi-sheer material with lace embellishments along the plunging neckline.

She left the bathroom, intent on throwing herself in the bed and pulling the blanket up to her chin to hide her body.

She'd only taken two steps when she came to a halt.

Parker stood with his back to her, giving her the privacy she needed to make it to the bed without embarrassment or a panic attack.

Her heart swelled and tears welled in her eyes. She tiptoed to the bed, pulled back the comforter and slid between the sheets.

How had she been so lucky as to be rescued by a man who was not only strong and handsome, but a gentleman who obviously sensed her panic and made it easy on her by giving her the space she needed.

"You can turn around," she said softly, pulling the sheet up to her chin.

When he did, his brow puckered as he studied her face. "Feel better?"

She nodded. "I think I scrubbed a layer of enamel off my teeth."

"I know what it means to have access to a toothbrush after days in the combat." He smiled. "It makes you appreciate good dental care."

She smiled. "That's just what I was thinking."

He walked over to a high-backed, floral-patterned chair positioned close to the French doors. "Do you mind if I sit?"

She turned on her side and craned her neck to see him where he stood by the chair. "Could you bring the chair closer before you do? I can't see you easily over there."

He lifted the fancy chair and carried it over to set it down gently next to the bed. "Better?"

She smiled. "Yes, thank you."

He went to the bathroom, turned on the light and closed the door but for a crack. Then he turned off the light on the nightstand, plunging the room into shadows, with only a wedge of light from the bathroom.

"Is that enough light?" he asked.

She nodded. "Thank you for leaving the light on in the bathroom. We spent much of our time in the dark with only our voices to remind us we weren't alone."

Parker lowered himself into the flowery chair, his hands on the armrests. "You should try to sleep. Tomorrow will be a long day."

She nodded and closed her eyes. That panicky feeling spiked and her pulse took off at a gallop. She opened her eyes. When her gaze landed on the man in the chair next to her bed, her pulse slowed back to normal.

He'd closed his eyes and leaned his head back against the chair cushion. He was a handsome man with dark hair and darker eyes. One of those dark eyes opened. "You're not sleeping."

"I will. But I'd rather fall asleep with my eyes open."

He frowned. "That's hard to do."

She shrugged. "Closing them makes me anxious. I feel like I'm back in the dark attic. I'm sure I'll go to sleep eventually. But don't let me keep you awake."

His lips quirked upward. "Right." He shifted in the chair, clearly uncomfortable. It didn't even lean back or allow him to put his feet up.

Guilt tugged at Abby's belly. "You can't be comfortable in that chair."

"I've slept in worse," he said, crossing his arms over his chest and one ankle over the other, stretching his legs out in front of him. Both eyes closed.

Abby watched for a long while before she said, "You don't have to stay. I'll be okay."

"I told you I'd stay until you fell asleep," he said with his eyes closed.

"What if I don't go to sleep?" she asked. "You can't sit in that chair all night.

"I can, if I need to," he said. "Now hush and sleep."

She lay for another couple of minutes, shaking her head. "You can't sleep like that," she burst out. "You need rest for tomorrow even more than I do. Go to your room and sleep."

He chuckled and looked at her through slitted eyes. "Is that how you talk to your fifth graders?"

"No. They listen to me and do as I say." She frowned.

"Please. I can't feel right about you sleeping in that chair all night."

"I'll be fine. Besides, sleep is overrated." He smirked. "Or so my old commander tried to tell me."

"If you won't go to your room, at least lie down on the bed with me. I won't allow you to pretend to sleep in that chair for another minute. I'm already bearing the guilt of leaving those women. I won't feel right if something happens to you tomorrow because you're too exhausted to think straight."

He sat up, his brow furrowing. "I'm not going to my room."

Abby scooted to one side of the bed and patted the empty space with her hand. "Lie down on the bed."

He shook his head with a smirking half smile. "We're practically strangers," he said. "It wouldn't be right."

"I don't give a flying flip if it's right. What's wrong is you sleeping in that horrible chair." She gave him her best stern-teacher stare. "Now, get over here, or go to your own room."

His eyes narrowed. "I can't get into the bed with you."

"Why not?" Her brow twisted. "Are you married or something?"

"Something," he said.

"Oh. You have a significant other?"

"No, the something is that I'm attracted to you. Getting in a bed with you, and not touching you, will lead to a whole lot more hurt than sitting up all night in this chair." He leaned his head back again and closed his eyes. "Now, stay awake or go to sleep, but be quiet whatever you do. I'm trying to catch some z's."

Abby lay still, her pulse racing for an entirely different reason now.

"You're attracted to me?" she whispered, her heart pounding so hard she was sure he could hear it from where he sat in his chair.

"Of course, I am." His forehead creased. "But don't worry. I won't act on it. You're safe with me."

Her blood burned through her veins and swirled low in her belly, coiling around her core. "What if I want you to touch me?" she asked.

His eyes shot open and then narrowed. "You're scared and not thinking straight. Understandable after the trauma you've experienced. But I'm not going to take advantage of your vulnerable condition. You deserve better."

"What makes you think you touching me wouldn't make things better?" She drew in a deep breath and let it out. "I *want* you to touch me. I'm not confused or just trying to use you for comfort, although you do give me that."

Parker's hands tightened on the armrests of the awful chair. "What kind of jerk would I be to take advantage of you when you've been through so much over the last four days?"

"You'd be the best kind of jerk," she said with a wicked smile. The more she thought about lying naked with Parker, the better she liked the idea.

"I'm not going to do it," Parker said as if reading her mind. "Your sensitivities are heightened. You may regret it later and wind up feeling worse than you do now. I can't let that happen."

"I'm willing to take that risk," she said.

"We're strangers. Why push this?"

"Why not? I don't want to be alone."

"So, you'll sleep with a perfect stranger? What if I were a serial killer?"

"You were properly vetted before you were asked to join this expedition. I'm convinced you aren't a serial killer," she said. "And last but not least, I'm on birth control and I'm clean, no STDs. Any other concerns?" She cocked an eyebrow and challenged him with a stare.

"I don't like being coerced into doing something," he grumbled.

"Didn't you just say you were attracted to me?" she demanded.

"I might have." Ruddy red color rose up Parker's neck into his cheeks. "And believe me it's easier to stop before you get started."

Abby sat up in the bed and crossed her arms of her chest like Parker. "Are you going to get into this bed?"

He shook his head. "No."

She stared at him with her lips pressed tightly together. "Fine." Abby turned her back to him, pulled the comforter up over her shoulders and forced herself to count freaking sheep. At eighty she gave up.

As fast as her heart was beating, she wouldn't go to sleep anytime soon.

She lay staring at the other side of the room, tired beyond caring.

The man was attracted to her and she couldn't even take advantage of that.

Right then, she needed the workout, and the closeness sex would provide. Then maybe she could fall asleep.

To hell with him.

She forced her eyes closed, pushed back her desire
for the stubborn man and willed herself to calm and
ultimately sleep.

Chapter Nine

Parker sat as still as he could until Abby's breathing grew deeper and slower. Finally, she was asleep.

He stood and adjusted himself in the tight confines of his jeans.

Yes, the woman made him hot all over. No, he didn't have to act on it. Yes, he wanted to make love to her more than he wanted to breathe.

But she wasn't ready for a man to force his attentions on her. It might trigger her into a panic attack.

Parker paced across the room. Abby had been right about one thing. He could never sleep sitting up in that chair. At the other end of the room, he spun and stared at the bed and the woman in it.

All he'd had to do was agree with her, climb into the bed and make love to her. He'd be satisfied and she'd be…what? Satisfied enough to sleep? Or even more traumatized?

Parker had seen panic in her eyes several times. Mostly at the idea of being alone.

His eyes narrowed. Not at being alone so much as being without him. When she'd been led away by the women, she'd looked back for him. She hadn't been alone and wasn't going to be left alone in a room. Abby had wanted to be with him.

But was that purely a distraction so she didn't have to deal with her situation or was she genuinely attracted to him? Was it that she wanted to be with the man who'd saved her? Was it that she felt safe only with him?

He crossed the room and settled on the edge of the chair, his hands clasped between his knees. Why had he been so adamant about not lying in bed with her?

He knew the answer. Because she might have wanted him to make love to her out of some reaction to having no control over her life for the days she'd been held hostage. By making love with him, she had the control.

And when it was over, she would've regained control and would no longer need him.

Was that what he was worried about? If he made love to her, he might fall even more in love with her. And after she got over the trauma of her abduction, she'd no longer need him. By then, he'd be stupidly head over heels and left brokenhearted.

No. He'd made the right decision. He was better off not getting involved.

Abby rolled onto her back, her forehead dented in a deep frown, her eyes squeezed shut.

Parker could see the pulse at the base of her throat beating fast and furious.

Abby's fists clenched and her head moved side to side. "No," she murmured. "Lemme go."

Parker's chest squeezed tight.

She was in the middle of another nightmare.

He waited, hoping it would subside.

Her head rocked back and forth on the pillow. She

drew her knees up to her chest and whimpered, tears flowing down her cheeks.

That was it. Parker could stand a lot, but the tears were his undoing.

He kicked off his shoes, pulled back the comforter and slid between the sheets next to Abby.

Her feet kicked out, again and again.

By now, soft sobs racked her body, the tears continuing to flow.

Parker slipped an arm beneath her and pulled her close. "Abby, honey. Wake up."

She pushed against him, fighting his hold on her.

"Abby, it's me, Parker. You're having a bad dream. Please sweetheart, wake up." He stroked her cheek, tucked a damp strand of hair behind her ear and kissed away her tears. All the while, he spoke to her in deep, soothing tones. "Abby, look at me. See me. It's Parker. I'm here. You're with me. You're going to be all right. Wake up."

Brutus rose from the rug at the end of the bed and came around to the side next to Parker and laid his chin on the mattress, his eyes wide and soulful.

When Abby whimpered again, Brutus whined.

"Abby, wake up," Parker said. "Brutus is worried about you."

Brutus whined again and laid a paw on the mattress.

"It's okay, Abby. Brutus and I have your back. We won't let anything bad happen to you." He held her close, rocking her in his arms.

Her eyes fluttered open and stared up into his. "Parker?"

"Yeah, baby. I'm here."

She looked around at the room, her eyes wide, her body tensing.

"You're safe, sweetheart. You're with me and Brutus at the Whiskey Gulch Ranch."

She sagged in his arms. "I thought I was back there."

"You're not. You're here with me."

She turned on her side and rested her cheek and her hand on his chest. "I thought you didn't want to get in bed with me," she said, her voice low and sexy as hell.

"I told you I was attracted to you." He touched his lips to her forehead. "You're beautiful, smart and brave. How could I resist?"

Her fingers settled on a button on his shirt. "I don't understand."

"What don't you understand?"

"If you're so attracted to me, why are you wearing so many clothes?" She flicked the button through the hole and moved to the next one, loosening it and then moved to the next.

He started to put his hand over hers and stop her journey down that path. But he didn't. Why fight it? She wanted him. He wanted her. What was the worst that could happen?

He was falling in love with this amazing woman.

He was a man used to taking risks with his life. But not with his heart.

He wasn't on active duty. He wouldn't be deployed by the army to some hostile hot spot where he could be surrounded by the enemy. He was a civilian now. He could let down his guard and the wall around his heart and allow himself to fall in love.

Was Abby the one? He'd only just met her. How could he be sure? Was love at first sight real?

The first time he'd seen Abby, she'd been covered from head to toe in mud, sticks and leaves. But even covered in all that dirt, he'd witnessed courage, strength and vitality in her. She was a fighter. Unsurprising, considering her occupation. No doubt handling a room full of fifth graders on a day-to-day basis was no easy feat. Oh, if those kids could have seen her the way he had the first time. He chuckled.

"What's so funny?" she asked as she reached the point where his shirt tucked into his jeans. Abby looked up into his eyes.

"I was just thinking about how you looked the first time we met," he admitted.

Her brow puckered. "I'm about to undress you and that's what you think about?" She sighed. "Obviously, I need to up my game." Abby pulled his shirt free of his jeans, reached for the button at his waistband and flicked it through. She paused, pushed up on her arms and leaned over him. "If you don't want this, speak now," she said. "Because once I start, I'm not sure I can stop."

He grinned. "That should be my line."

Abby cocked an eyebrow. "You weren't forthcoming. Someone had to take the lead."

"I want this," he said, his voice deepening as desire flared, running like quicksilver through his veins.

A slow smile curved her lips as Abby bent over him and claimed his mouth with hers.

Her tongue thrust between his teeth and swept over his in a slow, sensuous glide.

Parker's hands curled around her hips and brought her over him.

Abby straddled him, the nightgown riding up her

thighs, exposing every inch of her legs up to the edge of her panties.

Parker moaned. "Yeah, I want this." His fingers tightened around her hips.

Abby's lips left his mouth and traveled across his jaw and down the length of his throat. She flicked her tongue across his rapid pulse.

Not pausing long, she seared a path across his collarbone and his chest, stopping at one hard brown nipple. Her tongue flicked him there, causing a firestorm of sensations to spread throughout his body, culminating in his groin.

He tipped his head back and drew in a shaky breath. What she was doing was going to send him over the edge far too soon.

Parker inhaled deeply, tightened his hold on her hips and rolled her onto her back, coming up over her in a front-leaning rest position.

She blinked up at him. "Did I do something wrong?"

"No. Just the opposite. It was so right. I wasn't going to make it last more than a second or two. I want you. But I want you to want me, too."

Her lips spread in a sultry smile. "I already want you."

"Not like you will soon." He kissed her, tracing his tongue across her lips. When she opened to him, he teased her with gentle thrusts, touching her tongue and pulling back several times before taking more in a long, sexy caress.

From there, his mouth traveled down her neck, following the neckline of her nightgown to the deep shadows between her breasts. Balancing on one hand, he traced the fingers of his other hand up her torso and cupped the curve of one breast through the thin fabric of her gown. He pinched the nipple between his thumb and forefinger, rolling the tip as it tightened into a hard button.

Parker leaned down and claimed the nipple through the gown, sucking it into his mouth, flicking the tip with his tongue.

Abby's back arched off the mattress, a moan reverberating from deep in her throat.

Encouraged by her response, he abandoned the breast, gripped the hem of her nightgown and slowly drew it up, exposing more flesh, inch by inch.

She raised her hands over her head as he pulled the gown upward and off her body.

Abby lay against the mattress, wearing nothing but the thin scrap of material of her panties covering the tuft of hair over her sex.

Her breasts weren't overly large, but just enough to fill the palm of his hand.

He cupped both, squeezing gently. Then he lowered and took one into his mouth, gently pulling on the flesh.

Again, Abby's back arched off the mattress. Her hands moved from his shoulders to his head, her fingers weaving into his hair, urging him lower.

He obliged, liking that she wasn't afraid to let him know what she wanted.

Parker kissed his way down to the elastic waistband of Abby's panties and slipped his hand inside. The soft hairs curled around his fingers as he edged closer to her core. He dipped a digit into her slick channel. He wanted to take her then. Though she might be ready to accept him, she wasn't nearly close enough to her release.

Yet.

But she would be soon.

ABBY WAS ALREADY having difficulties breathing. Every time she drew in a breath, he touched her in a way that made her gasp.

Moving lower, Parker rolled to the side, took charge of her panties and stripped them down her legs, removing and tossing them across the room. He turned toward her, his gaze sweeping across every inch of her.

Abby lay naked against the comforter, turned on and hesitant at the same time. What if he didn't like what he saw? What if she wasn't experienced enough to satisfy him?

"You are beautiful," he said, his tone hot with his desire, melting into her bones like chocolate on a sweltering summer day.

"You're still wearing too many clothes," she said, her voice breathy, her lungs unable to pull in enough air to do any better.

He smiled, left the bed and stripped out of his jeans, kicking them to the side.

Her heart skittered through a quick succession of beats before settling into a racing rhythm.

Parker climbed onto the bed, slid his hands up the inside of her thighs and parted her legs, spreading them wide. He settled his body between them and kissed the sensitive skin from the bend in her knee all the way up her inner thigh to her core.

By then, Abby struggled to breathe. She felt like she teetered on the edge of a cliff, ready to soar to the heavens.

He parted her folds with his thumbs and touched her there with the tip of his tongue.

Abby gasped, drew her knees up and dug her heels into the mattress.

He flicked the nubbin of tightly packed nerves again and again.

Tension built inside her with every touch until she rocketed into the stratosphere, sensations exploding and spreading throughout her body.

She dug her fingers into his scalp and held on as wave after wave engulfed her, lifting her up, carrying her along until she slowly slid back to earth.

Adjectives like *great* and *good* didn't seem to encompass what she'd felt. All she knew was that it wasn't enough.

Abby tugged on his hair.

Parker crawled up her body, leaned over to fish his wallet out of his jeans and pulled out a small packet.

She grabbed it from his fingers, tore it open and rolled its contents over his engorged shaft.

He settled between her legs and bent to kiss her in a long, hard kiss that spoke of his intense concentration on controlling his own release.

Abby guided him to her entrance.

He dipped in slowly, coating himself with her juices.

Beyond patience, Abby gripped his buttocks and pulled him close, sheathing him in her channel.

Parker leaned his head back, his lips pressed tightly together as he held still, giving her body time to adjust to his girth.

Again, Abby took control and eased him out and back in, working up speed until he took over and pumped in and out of her.

The tension built again inside her, matching the tightness of Parker's muscles and the control he clung to so precariously.

Abby quickly shot to her climax, lifting her hips to meet his thrusts with her own.

Parker slammed into her one more time, sinking deep, burying himself as far as he could go. He remained there, his shaft pulsing his release against her channel. His breathing was ragged as if he'd run a marathon and his body was coated in a fine layer of sweat.

Abby lay back, basking in the afterglow of making love with Parker, knowing she'd brought him to this level and he'd made sure she'd gotten there too. For a brief moment in time, she blocked the constant churn of all the awful scenarios the other captives might be facing and lived in the moment of making love with Parker.

"You should smile more often," Parker said as he eased down on top of her and rolled them both to the side, maintaining their intimate connection.

She draped her leg over his and laid her hand on his chest. "I will. When we free the others." She frowned. "I'm not usually so negative. I have to be upbeat to keep twenty-four students engaged every day."

He brushed a strand of her hair back behind her ear and brushed a kiss across her lips. "We'll find them. In the meantime, you need rest. You've been through a lot."

She rested her cheek against his chest, reassured by the strength of his muscles and the backing of his team. She wouldn't have to do this on her own. She had the Outriders behind her.

And he was right. She needed rest.

Tomorrow would come soon enough.

She prayed they'd find the house with the women alive and well inside.

But that would be too easy, wouldn't it?

Chapter Ten

Parker lay awake well after Abby drifted off. He couldn't believe how much she was coming to mean to him in such a short time. Frankly, it scared the hell out of him.

Not enough for him to get out of the bed and return to his room. No. He loved holding her close, feeling her warm, soft skin against his. He could get used to it. But he worried she would lose interest as soon as her world returned to normal.

He must have got to sleep shortly after midnight. When he glanced at the clock again, it was five in the morning and still dark outside with the barest of light in the predawn sky.

Abby lay on her stomach, an arm draped over his middle, her cheek resting on her pillow, blond hair hiding her face and eyes.

Parker lay still for a couple minutes memorizing every detail of the curve of her shoulder, the soft rose color of her lips and the scent of the shampoo she'd used.

Yeah. He could get used to waking up to this every day.

Today would be a challenge. One he needed to face

sooner than later. He slid from beneath her arm, rose from the bed and dressed.

Abby rolled onto her side. Her hair slid away from her face revealing her closed eyes, the crescents of her lashes dark feathers against her cheeks. She was still asleep and Parker didn't have the heart to wake her yet.

He left the room and descended the stairs in search of coffee. The scent of bacon reached him before he arrived at the kitchen door.

Rosalyn stood at the stove, spatula in hand, turning over fluffy yellow scramble eggs in one skillet while bacon fried on a griddle.

"Coffee's made. All you need is a cup," she said.

"Thank you."

"I figure everyone will want to get out to the south fence before sunup and won't take time to eat, so I thought I'd make breakfast burritos for you to carry with you." She scooped the eggs out of the pan into a bowl and flipped the bacon over to cook on the other side. "I'll have them ready in just a few minutes."

"That's really nice of you. But you know you don't have to cook for us. We don't want to be more of a burden on your busy schedule."

She smiled. "I love cooking for people. I'm one of those people who need to be needed. It's my happy place."

Parker fished a mug out of the cabinet over the coffee maker and poured a cup. "Well, I appreciate everything you do."

"I just want to make it easier for you to get out there and find those girls."

He nodded and sipped the hot coffee, needing the caffeine boost to face the day.

"Irish and Matt got here a few minutes ago. They're

outside now working with the drone, practicing with the controls and the livestreaming. I think they're getting the hang of it."

"Do you need help with the burritos?" Parker asked.

Rosalyn shook her head. "No, thank you. I have a system that works for me. I'll have them ready in no time. Lily and Trace are taking care of the animals. You might see if they need help to get done more quickly."

Parker took one more sip of the life-giving brew, set his coffee mug on the counter and stepped out onto the porch.

The whir of tiny rotor blades made him look up before descending the porch steps.

Matt and Irish stood next to Matt's truck. Irish had the laptop open on the truck's hood. Matt held the controls for the drone, maneuvering the two joysticks, a frown of concentration denting his forehead.

"How's it going?" Parker asked.

"Better," Matt responded. "I'm learning a little movement goes a long way."

"The camera on the drone is really sharp," Irish said. "Even in the semidarkness, it picks up more than I expected. And the livestreaming is working great. Let's hope it works as well away from the Wi-Fi."

"That's a good question. Will it work out there without immediate access to the internet?" Parker asked.

"I have a signal booster on my truck for my cell phone," Matt said. "It should allow us to access the internet through my hot spot."

Irish nodded. "We've tested it and it seems to work well."

"Unless you need me, I'm headed to the barn to see if Trace and Lily can use my help," Parker said.

"We've got it here," Irish said without looking up from the laptop display.

Parker continued past the two, glancing up to keep a watchful eye on the position of the drone as he crossed to the barn.

Inside, he found Lily and Trace pouring feed into buckets.

Lily looked up from the large feed bin. "We have the animals in the stalls. If you want to bring Jasper in, his stall is empty."

"He'll be all right for the day as long as he's grazing in the pasture." Parker glanced around. "Have you set out the hay?"

"Not yet," Trace said from where he was filling a bucket full of water. "We usually put two sections in each stall."

Parker hurried to the stack of hay and broke open a bale. Pulling off several sections, he carried them to the stalls with horses in them and placed the hay in the wire hayracks attached to the walls. When he finished, he looked around. "What else?"

Lily, still scooping feed into buckets, nodded toward a large trash can. "That can contains the chicken feed. Take a coffee can full out to the coop and fill the feeder. You can collect the eggs in the empty coffee can. While you're out there, make sure they have fresh water."

Parker scooped a coffee can full of chicken feed and headed for the barn door.

"Hey, Parker," Trace called out. "Watch out for the rooster. He's a master at sneak attacks. I have the scars to prove it."

"I'll be on the lookout."

"There's a fishnet on the side of the chicken coop,"

Lily said. "If he gives you any trouble, scoop him up with the net and hang it on the outside of the chicken coop until you're done inside." She grinned. "I've never been spurred using that method. You can carry the can up to Rosalyn when you're done. We're headed that way soon."

Armed with chicken feed and knowledge, Parker carried the can out to the coop. As expected, the rooster stood guard at the gate, daring him to step inside. Parker grabbed the fishnet from a hook on the outside of the coop, opened the gate and scooped up the rooster. The beast protested loudly, but didn't have much of a choice about being hung on the side of the coop.

Parker poured the chicken food into the feeder and collected the eggs from beneath the nesting chickens, only getting pecked once in the process. He filled the water trough and released the rooster back into the coop.

The offended fowl shook out his feathers and went back to his position as guard in front of the gate.

By the time he returned to the house, Rosalyn had a dozen burritos rolled into plastic wrap and two thermoses full of coffee ready to go.

Abby stood next to Rosalyn, loading the food and drinks into a backpack, along with paper coffee cups and several bottles of water.

When she looked up and met Parker's eyes as he stepped through the kitchen door, her cheeks reddened.

"I'll take those." Rosalyn relieved him of the fresh farm eggs. "You're all set with food that should last you at least halfway through the day."

"The coffee won't make it halfway through the morning." Trace followed Parker through the back door. "But it'll do for a start." He smiled at his mother. "Thank you. You're a godsend."

Rosalyn gave a knowing smile. "I know." She glanced out the window. "You better get going before the sun comes up. You'll want to make use of every minute of daylight that you can."

"Yes, ma'am." Trace popped a salute. "You could have been a drill sergeant in another life."

His mother lifted her chin. "I could have been a drill sergeant in *this* life."

He dipped his head. "Yes, you could have. And a damned good one." Trace lifted his gaze to Lily. "Are you ready?"

"I am," she said, rubbing her wet hands on her jeans.

"After I wash my hands, I'll be ready," Parker said and headed for the bathroom.

Parker emerged from the bathroom to find Trace headed down the hallway, carrying an AR15 and a duffel bag and a sniper rifle slung on a strap over his shoulder.

"I have handguns and ammunition in the bag," he said. "Matt and Irish brought their own weapons."

"Is this all?" Parker asked.

Trace nodded.

"Let me carry some of that," Parker said.

Trace held over the AR15.

Parker took it and followed Trace out the back door to where the others had gathered around the truck.

Abby stood to the side with Brutus sitting quietly at her feet.

Trace laid out the plan as he loaded the weapons and bag into the back of his pickup. "We'll take two trucks.

Parker, you and Abby will ride in my truck. Irish will ride with Matt."

Parker lowered the tailgate of Trace's pickup. "Brutus, up." The pit bull leaped into the back. "Stay."

"He won't jump out?" Abby asked.

"No." Parker scratched behind the dog's ear. "He learned how to be a ranch dog at the rehabilitation ranch."

Abby frowned. "Rehab ranch? I didn't know you'd spent time in rehab."

"How could you? We only met yesterday. We haven't had much time to get to know each other." A fact he meant to remedy soon. "Don't worry, it was for physical rehabilitation, not for drugs or alcohol." He opened the back door on the passenger side of the truck and handed Abby up into the truck. Then he rounded to the other side and slid in behind Trace, who sat in the driver's seat.

Matt stowed the drone and controls in the back seat of his truck and climbed into the driver's seat. Irish shut the laptop and climbed into the passenger seat.

Lily remained on the ground to open the gate. Once both trucks were through, she ran to climb into the lead vehicle with Trace.

They bumped along rutted tracks, across fields, down into streambeds and up over low hills.

Parker insisted on getting the next two gates, holding them open for the trailing truck.

Because Matt was familiar with the land and the direction they were headed, they covered the same amount of ground in less time than it had taken for Parker to ride Jasper to the same location.

Unlike the previous morning, the land and sky were clear of the dense fog.

The sun eased up on the horizon, a bright orange blob to the east.

"It's supposed to be a clear day with five to ten miles per hour winds," Trace said. "A perfect day for flying the drone."

Abby sat beside Parker, leaning around the back of Lily's seat to see their path ahead.

Parker spotted the uprooted tree and pointed. "See that dead tree? That's where we found Abby."

Trace brought the truck to a stop shot of the tree and the hollow where the roots had been and Abby had spent the night covered in dirt and leaves.

Parker recalled the shock he'd felt when she'd staggered to her feet like a creature born of the earth and ran from Brutus. When he realized it was a woman, he'd been even more shocked and afraid when Brutus attacked her, knocking her to the ground.

The dog had never attacked him or anyone else at the rehab ranch. Parker couldn't understand why he'd do it then. Until the shadow shapes of the feral hogs materialized through the fog.

"For the record," Parker said, "you were right…some of those hogs were as big as full-grown cows."

"Right?" Trace met Parker's gaze in the rearview mirror. "The first time I saw one standing in the middle of the highway, I thought it was a cow." He shifted into Park and opened his door. "I wouldn't want to come face-to-face with one of those beasts."

"We came face-to-face with a herd of them yesterday." Parker cast a glance toward Abby. "Did you see them?"

Her eyes narrowed. "I think so, but it was hard to tell. Brutus had me pinned to the ground."

Lily opened Abby's door, her brow wrinkling. "Big ol' cuddly Brutus pinned you to the ground?"

"Big ol' terrifying pit bull with razor-sharp teeth, growling like he would rip my head off." Abby climbed down and reached into the back of the truck to scratch the monster's ear. "That's him. He didn't want me to run right into the middle of the hog herd."

Parker smiled at how quickly Abby had recovered from her fear of the pit bull and taken a shine to the big guy. He lowered the tailgate.

Brutus jumped to the ground and ran to where he'd found Abby.

Lily chuckled. "Do you think he's looking for another person to come out of the dirt?"

The dog sniffed the ground, ran a few steps and sniffed some more.

Parker crossed to see what the dog was so interested in. Hundreds of pig tracks speckled the ground around the hollow, and the dirt had been churned as if the hogs had been rooting in the soil.

Abby came to a stop beside Parker. "Are those pig tracks?"

Parker nodded. "Yes, ma'am."

She shivered.

"You might have chosen one of their favorite places to root around for grubs and bugs," Lily said.

Abby shivered again. "I might need another shower when we get back to the house. The thought of bugs and grubs crawling all over me gives me the willies."

"Better than hogs thinking you were part of their dinner," Lily said and turned to watch as Matt got out the drone and laid it on the ground, then reached for the control box.

Irish laid the laptop on the hood of Matt's truck and brought up the livestreaming video and the satellite map of the area, toggling between the two.

Abby and Lily gathered around the laptop while Trace and Parker converged on Matt.

Parker alternated looking at where the drone hovered several feet from the ground and glancing at the control box's monitor to understand what the camera would display.

"Ready?" Matt called out.

"Ready," Irish affirmed.

"Then let's get this party started." Matt lightly thumbed the tiny joysticks.

The drone rose into the air, heading south past where the fence was down and toward a line of hills dotted with live oak and juniper trees.

"What's the range of the drone?" Parker asked.

"It's a commercial drone with a range of almost five miles," Matt said.

"The challenge is that it has a battery life of only thirty minutes," Trace said.

"Five miles as the crow flies is a pretty good distance," Matt said.

"Running barefoot in the dark with a thunderstorm raging, rain hammering down on her head and over rough and hilly terrain, I doubt Abby got much further than that." Parker glanced back at Abby as she hovered over Irish's shoulder, her gaze intent on the images the drone was sending.

As it rose higher into the sky, the camera had a broader range.

Parker joined the women watching the larger monitor.

"If we can't make out much on this screen, we can spend more time looking at it on the large video screen in Trace's office back at the ranch," Irish said.

"The main idea is to get the video in the thirty minutes we'll have before the battery dies," Trace said.

"Make that an hour," Matt corrected. "I have one backup battery. And we can plug the charger into the truck and charge the dead battery while we use the backup. There might be some downtime, but not too much. I'm not sure how long it takes to fully charge a battery."

The first thirty minutes passed too quickly. Matt chose landmarks to fly the drone between, establishing a kind of fan-shaped grid, covering a five-mile radius from the Whiskey Gulch Ranch property line.

They spotted a few straight lines that ended up being the tin roofs of deer stands, nothing as large as a two-story house.

By midmorning, Parker could see the disappointment and worry in Abby's face. He wished he could bear that burden for her. She looked tired.

Matt had grounded the drone while he waited for the battery to charge.

Irish had rewound the videos and was going over them, stopping every so often to zoom in on various areas that showed promise. With Lily, Abby and Trace looking over his shoulder, they didn't need Parker to add to the crowd.

His stomach rumbled, reminding him that none of them had eaten breakfast. He remembered the burritos Rosalyn had packed for them and went to Trace's truck in search of the bag she'd packed. He found it and the thermos of coffee, and returned to Matt's truck.

Parker handed a burrito and an empty paper cup to Matt who sat on the tailgate.

"I could skip the burrito, but the coffee is a must."

Parker unscrewed the thermos cap and poured coffee into Matt's cup. It was still hot and smelled good.

"Do I smell coffee?" Irish called from where he hovered over the laptop.

"Yes, you do," Parker said. He passed the thermos to Lily and distributed cups to Trace and Irish. When he tried to hand one to Abby, she held up her hand. "Not me. I never developed a taste for coffee."

"Good to know," Parker fished in the backpack for one of the bottles of water and handed it to Abby.

She smiled and took it. "Thank you."

Once everyone had drinks, Parker handed out the burritos.

"Eat them, even if you don't want one," Lily said. "Rosalyn went to a lot of trouble to make these for us."

"You don't have to tell me twice," Irish said. "Rosalyn makes the best breakfast burritos. She made enough for two each, right?"

"She did," Parker said.

By the time they finished their snack, one of the batteries had reached its full charge. Matt swapped out the batteries and put the dead one into the charger.

Becoming quite the expert, Matt had the drone in the air and headed down the next section of the grid.

Once again, Trace, Irish, Lily and Abby gathered around the laptop monitor.

Parker stood close to Matt, watching the smaller screen on the control box. The drone had reached the outer limit of its range and was headed back when a straight white line broke up the darker asymmetrical shapes of green, leafy live oak trees.

"Whoa," Parker said. "Can you get lower there?"

Matt brought the drone to a stop, hovering over a clump of trees.

"You see something?" Irish asked.

"Maybe." Parker leaned closer to Matt and pointed at the screen. "Can you back it up a bit?"

Matt eased the joystick and squinted down at the screen. "There?"

"Yeah. Hold steady." Parker turned and ran to where the others were studying the monitor.

"We have a slight delay in the livestreaming," Irish said.

Parker nodded. "You should see what we're seeing by now." He stepped between Lily and Abby and leaned over Irish's shoulder. It took him a moment before he found what he was looking for. "There." He pointed at the monitor. "See the white line?"

Irish leaned forward. "Yes."

"Matt, take it closer and swing around at a different angle," Trace said.

Matt eased the joysticks, sending the drone down and around the clump of trees. Approaching the trees from a different angle, the white line became the side of a white building. An old, two-story farmhouse.

Abby pointed with one hand and reached for Parker's with the other. "See that window under the A-frame roofline? Can you zoom in on it?"

Her fingers curled tightly around Parker's. He could feel her tremble.

Irish zoomed in on the window.

Abby gasped. "That has to be it."

"You said you broke the window. That window doesn't look broken," Trace said.

"They rehung the sheet over the window," Abby said. "If you notice, there isn't any glare or reflections of the sky or trees in the glass. Because there isn't any glass. And they removed the blanket I'd used to slow my slide over the roof."

"Matt, position the drone directly over the house," Trace said, "and save the coordinates. The rest of us will load up in my truck. We'll have to approach the house from the road. Matt, we need you here monitoring the location the best you can, given the battery life."

Matt nodded. "I have to bring in the drone now. The battery is getting low."

"Do it and get it back out there as soon as possible," Trace slipped into the driver's seat.

"I'm leaving Brutus with you." Parker turned to Brutus. "Come."

Brutus trotted over to where Parker stood near Matt.

Parker patted his head and then said, "Stay."

The dog maintained his position as Parker climbed into the back seat next to Abby. Lily slid in on the other side of Abby and Irish rode shotgun. Irish had the coordinates pulled up on the map on the laptop and the fastest route selected. Unfortunately, there weren't any roads nearby. They had to backtrack through the fields with Parker handling the gates. They wound up near the barnyard.

Rosalyn emerged from the barn.

Trace lowered his window and shouted as he sped past, "Found the house. Going to check it out."

"Be careful!" she shouted back.

Once Trace emerged onto the highway, he said, "Get Dallas on the phone. Tell her and Levi to meet us at the coordinates. If the house is occupied, we could use the help. If it's empty, we will want Dallas to get a crime scene unit out there."

Lily pulled out her cell phone. "Dallas, we think we found the house where Abby was held. I sent you the coordinates. We're on our way. Grab Levi and meet us there." She ended the call and slipped her phone into her pocket. "Should we have Dallas make this more official?" Lily asked.

"You mean bring in the sheriff's department?" Abby frowned. "That might take too long for them to get out there."

"We'll be there in ten minutes. It'll take Dallas and Levi at least fifteen. We'll stop half a mile short of the house and go in on foot. Lily, I'd prefer you and Abby stay in the truck until we give the all-clear."

Lily's mouth set in a tight line. "I can handle a gun."

Travis shot a quick smile in her direction. "I know how well you can. But Irish and Parker are trained Deltas. They know how to infiltrate a location, clear the rooms and when to shoot. Besides, I need you to stay with Abby and keep her safe in case the slimeballs comes up the road behind us."

Lily stared at the back of Trace's head for a long moment before she sighed. "Okay, I'll stay. I'd rather go with you, but I'll stay for Abby."

Trace smiled into the rearview mirror. "Thank you."

They turned onto a dirt road and drove for a couple of miles. Half a mile short of their destination, Trace pulled the truck off the road and parked it behind a fat juniper tree.

Trace leaped out, chose the sniper rifle and a handgun from the bag, and stuffed loaded magazines into his pockets. Parker grabbed the AR15 and a Glock 9 mm pistol and several magazines of ammunition.

It felt odd gearing up like he had prior to going into hostile enemy territory. But this wasn't Afghanistan, Iraq or any of the other foreign countries where they'd conducted special operations. This was the United States. A peaceful country. The land of the free and all that.

"You okay?" Trace asked.

Parker nodded. He shoved the magazines into his pocket and loaded one each into the rifle and the pistol. "I'm ready."

Lily selected a handgun from the bag, loaded it and stepped up to Trace. "Don't get yourself killed."

He pulled her close to him and kissed her hard. "I won't. I have too much to live for."

Abby touched Parker's arm. "You, too," she said softly. "Don't get yourself killed. I kind of like you."

"I like you, too." He cupped her cheek and bent to brush his lips across hers. "I'll be back for more of this."

Irish waited near the road with his own AR15.

Trace and Parker joined him.

"Consider this a reconnaissance mission," Trace said. "We'll observe first."

Irish and Parker nodded.

Together, they moved swiftly and silently, cutting through the woods.

Parker wasn't sure what they'd find. Hopefully, they'd find the women and their jailer, as Abby had called him. One guy would be easy to take down. Three or four? Still easy, just a little messier.

Chapter Eleven

Wearing the wig and sunglasses Lily had loaned her, Abby paced from the road to the truck and back to the road where she stopped, looked and listened, hoping to hear or see the team's progress.

Nothing.

They'd blended into the shadows and moved quickly, disappearing within the first twenty yards.

"They'll be okay." Lily stepped up beside her.

"I want to know what's happening," Abby said. "To see what they're seeing."

"I get it. I would like to have gone in with them." Lily held the gun at her side, aimed at the ground. "I do know how to handle a gun, but they're right. I don't have the training they do."

Abby wrapped her arms around her middle and rocked back on her heels. "Do you think they're up to the house yet?"

Lily laughed. "I really don't know. But we might want to step back from the road. If one of the men who kidnapped you comes along, we don't want to give him the opportunity to get you again."

"You have a gun," Abby said.

"That's right, but I'd rather not shoot someone unless I absolutely have to." She tipped her head toward the truck hidden behind the tree. "Want another one of Rosalyn's burritos?"

Abby shook her head. "I'm not hungry. But I imagine Laura, Rachel, Valentina and Cara Jo are." Abby followed Lily back to the truck. "I shouldn't have just left them."

"You didn't have time to pick the locks on their cages."

"No, but I should have stayed and fought."

Lily planted a hand on her hip and pursed her lips. "How big was he?"

"Pretty big. Maybe six feet three or four."

"Weighing around two-sixty or more?"

"Probably," Abby said. "Why?"

"Girl, unless you're highly skilled in self-defense, a man like that would easily overcome you and you'd be right back where you started from." Lily touched her arm. "You did the best thing you could do. And that was to get away as fast as possible. That way at least one of you could go for help."

Abby stared into the distance. "I hope the men find them alive."

"Me, too." Lily leaned against the truck and gave Abby a sly grin. "So, what exactly is going on between you and our newest Outrider?"

Heat climbed up Abby's neck into her cheeks. "Nothing." She continued to stare off into the distance, not willing to look Lily in the eye.

"That kiss wasn't nothing. I know it's none of my business, but Parker's bed wasn't slept in last night." She held up her hands. "I promise I wasn't snooping. I passed by his room early this morning and the door was open. And yeah, the bed hadn't been slept in." She shook her head. "Look, it's not any of my business who people sleep with. Lord knows, my family was notorious for what they did for a living. I'm just curious. You two just met, but you look at him like I look at Trace."

Her cheeks burning even hotter, Abby pressed her palms against them and glanced at Lily. "And how is that?"

A smile spread across Lily's face. "You look at him like you can't stand for him to be out of your sight. Like he hung the moon and stars and no one else exists in the world but him. That's how I feel about Trace. We had a rough start to our relationship, but now…he's my everything. I know I can live without him. I've done it before. But I'd rather live with him in my life and I'll do everything in my power to make him happy." Her smile broadened.

"And that's how I look at Parker?" Abby blinked. Not cool. "I barely know the man. Yeah, he saved my life, but that's not reason enough to fall in love with him in less than twenty-four hours." She frowned. "Is it?"

"I don't know about love at first sight. I can't remember when I haven't loved Trace. I think I was born loving him." She shrugged. "I've heard women say, when you know, you know. One day, one month, one year? Everyone is different." She pushed away from the side of the truck. "I just hope you both don't get hurt. I know how bad it can hurt when the one you love doesn't love you in return." She paused, tilted her head to the side, her eyes narrowing. "Do you hear that?"

Abby lifted her head and strained to hear what Lily was hearing.

The rumble of an engine and the crunching sound of wheels on gravel increased in volume.

Abby peered around the juniper tree.

A plume of dust rose on the road.

"What do we do?" Abby asked.

Lily frowned. "We can't let anyone drive up to the house before the men are done."

"If it's more of the men who kidnapped us, we can't let them pass. And if we stop them, they might recognize me and blow our cover and put our guys in danger." Abby looked around. "Is there another gun in that bag?"

Lily nodded, reached into the bag, extracted a pistol and loaded a magazine full of bullets into the handle. "Do you know how to use one?"

Abby shook her head. "Not actually, but how difficult can it be?"

Lily's eyes widened. "Oh, sweetheart. When we get past all this drama, I'm going to teach you how to properly use a gun." She dropped the magazine from the handle of the gun, cleared the chamber and grabbed a baseball cap out of the bag instead. "Here, put this on and stay back. That vehicle is coming fast. I have to do something to slow it down."

Before Abby could stop her, Lily stuck the pistol in the back of her blue jeans and stepped into the middle of the gravel road and waved her arms.

Abby pulled the cap down low over her forehead, reached into the bag of hardware and retrieved the handgun Lily had put back and the magazine full of bullets. She inserted the magazine into the handle and eased up to the road, hiding behind the juniper tree.

"If they don't slow down," Abby called out. "Get out of the way."

"I will," Lily said. "I know you got that gun. Do me a favor and please don't shoot me."

Abby's hand shook. They'd have to be very desperate for her to fire the gun. It was strictly a last resort.

WHEN THEY WERE within a few yards of the house, Trace held up his fist.

Parker and Irish stopped immediately.

Trace motioned Irish forward. "While Parker and I check the house, you need to scout the perimeter for outbuildings, storm shelters or any other structure big enough for people to hide or be hidden in."

Irish nodded, backed into the woods and disappeared.

Parker moved forward and squatted in the shadows beside Trace.

Keeping low and in the shadows, Parker moved close to Trace.

"The place looks deserted," Trace whispered. "No vehicles and the front door is open. Lower windows are covered from the inside with cardboard."

Parker strained to hear anything from the interior. Nothing moved and no sounds came from inside. "I'll take point," Parker said.

Trace nodded. "I'll cover." He leaned against a tree, lifted his rifle to his shoulder and aimed it at the house. "Ready when you are. I'll leap in once you make the side of the house."

Parker nodded, glanced left then right and darted out of the trees, crossed the open space between the tree trunks and the walls of the building. Once there, he knelt.

Trace raced across the open space and into the

shadow of the building. Once there, he didn't slow until he was up on the dilapidated front porch, moving quietly toward the open front door.

Parker followed.

Trace stopped short of the door.

Parker caught up to him, moved past and dove through the front door into the house. Tucking the rifle to his chest, he came up on his feet, aiming he AR15 toward the center of the room.

Not much light filtered through the overhanging branches of the giant old trees surrounding the house. Even in the dim light filtering through the door, Parker could tell the room was empty.

Trace ducked through the door and took position on the opposite side of the room.

Parker moved toward the back of the house. A hallway led past a staircase. With his foot, he pushed open the door to his right and aimed his rifle into a bathroom. Another empty room.

He continued down the hallway, emerging into a kitchen that probably hadn't been updated since the 1940s. It was empty. A couple of the cabinet doors hung off the hinges, revealing nothing inside.

Parker retraced his footsteps to the living room and covered Trace as he climbed a staircase to the second story. A door at the top of the staircase was closed with a shiny metal hasp hanging loose from the matching metal loop screwed to the door.

Trace dug a glove from his pocket, wrapped it around the door handle and turned it, pulling it toward him.

Parker lifted his rifle and covered Trace.

Trace disappeared into the room at the top of the stairs and reappeared. "Clear." He fished his cell phone out of his pocket and frowned. "Not much of a signal, but maybe enough." He tapped a text message and sent it. "I sent a text to Lily and let her know the house is empty. They can come up."

Moments later, a vehicle pulled up on the gravel drive and skidded to a stop.

Parker frowned. "That was fast."

Trace nodded. "Too fast." With his weapon in front of him, Trace eased up to the side of the window and peered out.

Parker moved up beside him.

"It's not my truck," Trace said.

Parker looked over Trace's shoulder.

The truck doors opened. Trousered legs dropped down below the driver's door. A handgun appeared first around the side of the open door. Dallas Jones stepped away from the truck and hurried toward the house.

Levi left the passenger side and followed Dallas across the yard.

Trace's shoulders relaxed and he chuckled as he moved toward the open front door. The truck was so filthy he hadn't recognized it. "Dallas, don't shoot, it's me, Trace Travis. I'm coming out."

He opened the door wider and stared into the barrel of Dallas's pistol.

"What part of don't shoot me, did you misunderstand?" Trace placed a finger on Dallas's gun and pushed it to the side, out of his face.

"When I didn't see you standing outside with no gun in your back, I wasn't going to risk it," she said and lowered her weapon.

Parker stepped up beside Trace. "We cleared the building. It's empty."

"I know. Lily told us you'd just texted her. You should have waited for us," Dallas said, lowering her weapon. "The place could just as easily have been occupied."

Levi stepped up beside Dallas. "Not here, huh?"

Trace shook his head and walked out onto the porch. "We were careful not to touch anything. Maybe you can lift prints."

Trace's truck pulled into the driveway and stopped next to Dallas's. Lily dropped down from the driver's seat. Abby got out of the passenger seat and approached the house, her eyes wide and haunted.

Parker dropped down off the porch and hurried to Abby. "I'm sorry."

She shook her head, tears slipping silently down her cheeks. "They're not here. I didn't get here fast enough."

"You can't beat yourself up about this," Trace said. "The place is clean. Most likely, they moved the others as soon as they discovered you'd escaped."

"I want to see," she said and climbed the steps to the porch.

Dallas caught her arm. "Don't touch any surfaces, especially door handles. The crime scene investigators will need to process the structure."

Abby nodded.

Parker took her hand and led her through the front door.

She stopped and stared at the empty room, a frown puckering her forehead. "There was a camp chair over there," she said, pointing to the right. "He had a bat-tery-powered lantern next to it and empty pizza boxes."

Her gaze went to the staircase and the color drained from her face.

"You don't have to go any further," Parker said.

"Yes. I do." She started up the stairs, her feet moving slowly.

Parker followed behind her.

When she reached the top, she pressed her hand to her mouth and her shoulders shook with silent sobs. "We were here."

Parker slipped his arm around her waist and pulled her close. "We will find them."

"How? We don't know who has them or where they took them? They could be halfway across the country, or across the border in Mexico. I failed them."

He turned her toward him. "You didn't fail them. We're going to find them and get them home."

She stepped into his embrace and wept.

Parker's heart hurt for her. They had to find the women safe and sound and return them to their families.

Dallas and Lily entered the room and looked around.

Parker remained where he'd been standing. He held Abby until her sobs subsided into sniffles.

"Better?" he asked.

Abby nodded. "A little."

"Parker, Abby," Lily called out from the bottom of the stairs. "We're heading back to the ranch to come up with a game plan for our next move."

"Coming," Parker responded without releasing his hold on Abby. He tipped her chin up and stared down into her red-rimmed eyes. "Ready?"

Abby stared back, her back stiffening. "I'm ready." She stepped back and squared her shoulders. "I'm not giving up. I owe it to them. Those women deserve to be saved, and I won't stop until I see that happen." She scrubbed her hand over her face, wiping away the tears. "I'm done crying. It's time for action."

Parker cupped her cheek and bushed away one of the tears she'd missed. "Let's do this." he took her hand and led her out of the house. Only Trace's truck remained in the driveway.

"We'll meet the others, including Matt and Brutus, back at the ranch," Trace said as he climbed into the truck.

"Will Dallas get any fingerprints?" Abby asked.

Lily shook her head. "The crime scene investigators will process the scene. They'll need your fingerprints to rule out yours." Lily slid into the front passenger seat and buckled her seat belt.

"I hope they find enough," Abby said.

Parker did, too. They didn't have much else to go on in their investigation.

He helped Abby up into the truck and closed her door. As he rounded the back of the vehicle, something white in the gravel caught his attention.

He bent and carefully brushed aside the dirt and lifted a piece of paper. He carried it with him as he climbed into his seat and buckled his seat belt.

"What's that?" Abby asked.

Parker shook his head. "I'm not sure."

"What did you find?" Trace asked.

Parker handed the crinkled, muddy document to Trace. "A temporary tag for a vehicle."

"Hold on to that," Trace said.

Parker nodded. "Dallas should be able to run the tag ID." He pulled out his cell phone and snapped a photo of the document.

"Send it to me. Lily can forward it to Dallas." Trace handed his cell phone to Lily.

Parker texted the photo to Trace's number.

Lily forwarded the text. "Dallas should have it now."

As Trace pulled out onto the gravel county road, he glanced in the rearview mirror at Parker. "I'll get you set up with a contact list of all the Outriders, their significant others and local law enforcement." He grimaced. "I need to set up a checklist for all new members."

"Yes, you do," Lily said. "Especially if you keep growing as fast as you have. I can be the administrative assistant, if you'd like."

Trace smirked. "In between running the ranch and keeping everybody and his brother fed?" He shook his head. "I'll hire someone else to manage the administration duties. You and Mom have enough on your plates. We still need to hire more ranch hands."

"Is there that much work?" Abby asked.

Trace nodded. "Yes, ma'am. And the more we do, the more word spreads and more jobs come our way. All by word of mouth."

Lily worked her cell phone, clicking keys and scrolling and clicking again. "There." She looked back at Parker. "I shared the phone numbers of the members of our team, Dallas, me and Rosalyn. You should be getting texts with those contacts."

Parker's phone dinged with each contact. He saved each of them to his list of contacts. "Thanks," he said.

Abby slipped her hand into Parker's and rode the rest of the way to the ranch, listening to Trace and Lily talk about different animals on the ranch and the operational issues.

When they arrived at the ranch house, Matt's and Dallas's trucks were there and empty.

Parker stepped down from the truck and was greeted

by Brutus, whose entire body was wagging in pleasure at seeing Parker.

He patted the dog and scratched his ears as he rounded the truck to the passenger side.

Abby had already climbed down and stood beside the door.

Brutus transferred his attention from Parker to Abby, leaning his entire body against her knees in his happiness to see her.

Abby knelt to give the beast a belly rub.

"Traitor," Parker muttered. He pointed at Brutus. "Yeah. You."

Brutus licked Parker's finger and remained where he stood, leaning against Abby's legs.

Trace and Lily led them into the house, passed through the massive living room and turned down the hallway to his office.

Once through the office door, Parker could see the other members of his team perched on the leather sofa, leather chairs. Matt leaned his back against the stone fireplace at the other end of the room from Trace's desk.

"Good," Trace said as he strode into the room and slid to the side a large wooden wall panel, revealing a giant magnetic whiteboard. "For lack of a better term, I want to construct a timeline of the events leading up to Abby's escape."

Dallas fished several papers out of a satchel she'd brought into the house. "I have images of the victims you named, all subjects of missing persons reports, the dates they disappeared and the locations where they were taken."

Parker took the photographs and sorted them by date. He handed them to Trace one at a time.

Trace affixed them to the whiteboard in chronological order using magnetic clips.

Dallas pointed at the first girl's image. "Cara Jo Noble disappeared from Comfort, Texas, three weeks ago. Her parents reported her missing, believing she had possibly run away with her boyfriend who was also missing. When her boyfriend returned home without her, the local police opened an investigation. They questioned the teen who said she'd refused to come with him. That was eight days ago."

Abby nodded. "Cara Jo said she'd started home shortly after her boyfriend left her. She had just made it to the interstate to hitch a ride when she was picked up by a nice-looking young man, who appeared to be kind and friendly. She said he was blond with blue-gray eyes. Valentina indicated she'd been lured by a young man of a similar description."

Parker handed Trace the next photo. "Laura Owens disappeared a week ago."

"My contact said, she left her parents' home in Hondo on her way back to San Angelo where she attends college," Dallas said. "Her car was found at a truck stop on Interstate 10 where she'd apparently stopped to get gas. There was video footage taken at the gas station, but a big RV blocked the view of Laura pumping gas. She was there and then she wasn't."

"Can we get that footage?" Trace asked.

Dallas shrugged. "I don't know, but I'll see what I can do."

Parker handed Trace the next photo. "Rachel Pratt."

"Disappeared five days ago after she got a flat tire on Interstate 10 thirty miles from the Whiskey Gulch exit," Dallas said. "They found her car with her two small children. No sign of their mom. No witnesses. At the time, our department was notified to be on the lookout for her."

"Rachel said a young man stopped to help her. He wore a ball cap, so she didn't get a good look at his hair or eye color." She was just thankful for the help changing her tire. Until he threw her in the trunk of his car." Abby pressed a hand to her chest. "She was more worried about her children than herself."

"Valentina Ramirez," Parker handed the next photo to Trace, who affixed it to the board with a magnet.

"She's only sixteen." Trace shook his head.

"And so afraid," Abby drew in a deep breath. "She was walking home from the bus stop after school when a young man with blond hair and blue-gray eyes pulled up and asked for directions. Her mother must be beside herself. She said they were very close."

Parker put the last photo on the board, his chest tight as he pinned it with a magnet. "And the most recent abduction, Abby Gibson from Boerne, Texas."

Abby stared at the board, her face pale, her eyes shining with unshed tears. "They stole our lives."

Parker slipped an arm around Abby's waist. "And we're going to get them back."

"All the abductions were along the interstate between San Antonio and here, except Valentina." Dallas stood in front of the whiteboard, tapping her chin. "Hers was in one county over." She grabbed dry-erase marker and drew a line in a diagonal and wrote San Antonio at the bottom right and Whiskey Gulch at the top and added tick marks along the line where the women had been taken and added a box and marked their last known location, the house in the country.

Levi joined Dallas in front of the board. "I noticed a For Sale sign that had fallen over at the driveway entrance to the house where the women were held. It was a WG Realty sign. I think the listing agent was Celia Mann."

"Cecilia Mann," Matt corrected. "She's one of the agents at WG Realty. Nice enough woman in her fifties."

Dallas's cell phone rang. She glanced down at the number on the display. "I need to take this." She stepped out of the room into the hallway.

"We have to assume the people holding the women are from around here," Matt said. "How else would they know where to find an empty house?"

"Or know when a teenager gets off the bus and walks home alone," Lily said, her lips tight, her face grim. "That poor kid."

Trace continued to stare at the whiteboard. "We can ask the listing agent to see who is selling it and who has had access to it."

"And why the lock box was missing," Lily added.

Dallas returned to the room. "That was a contact of mine with the state police. I sent him an image of the fingerprints and the temporary tag."

Abby frowned.

Dallas held up her hand. "Since we think someone from around here might be involved and we didn't want locals to catch wind, I figured I'd work with an acquaintance in Austin."

"Good call," Trace said.

Abby nodded.

"Anyway, only one of the prints struck pay dirt." Dallas glanced at her phone. "A Roy Felton, convicted felon, registered in this county. I have his address. He was convicted of aggravated assault, spent two and a half years in prison, and was paroled a couple of months ago. He works at Greenway Lawn Care in Whiskey Gulch."

"We'll check it out," Trace said. "What about the tag?"

"Belongs to a car registered to one Scott Wilcox, also from Whiskey Gulch," Dallas said. "He's clean. No criminal record. I have his address."

Trace clapped his hands. "The workday isn't over yet. We can hit a few of these places and ask some questions. Matt and I will check out Roy's home address. Levi and Dallas, see if you can meet with Roy's parole officer."

"Just so you know," Dallas said. "I work graveyard tonight. After we check in on Roy, I'm headed to the house for a few hours' sleep before I'm on duty."

"Noted," Trace said. "Irish and Becker, check in with the Scott." He turned to Parker.

"We'll go to the real estate company and find out who owns the house," Parker said.

"We?" Trace cocked an eyebrow, his gaze going to Abby. "Are you sure you want to be seen in Whiskey Gulch?"

Lily stepped in. "I'll get another wig and sunglasses." She left the office, passing Rosalyn in the doorway.

"Sorry to interrupt," Rosalyn called out. "I need to know how many will be having dinner here."

"We'll grab something in town. You don't need to be cooking after working with the farrier all day."

She pushed a stray strand of hair back from her forehead and gave him a tired smile. "Good. I think I'll go soak in a hot bath and call it a night." She turned to leave, calling out over her shoulder, "If you don't feel like eating in town, you can make sandwiches when you get back. There's plenty of cold cuts and cheese in the fridge."

When she was gone, Trace said to the people in the room, "Don't forget to grab dinner while you're in town. Everyone know their assignments?"

Parker nodded along with the others.

"Let's go," Trace said.

Lily appeared with the wig and glasses.

Abby thanked her and carried the items out to Parker's truck.

"Are you sure about this?" he asked as he helped her up into the passenger seat.

She met his gaze with a stubborn tilt of her chin. "Absolutely. I promised to bring help. And, dammit, I will."

Parker hurried around and climbed into the driver's seat. He hoped the information they had would lead them to the women. Seeing their photos on the board along with Abby's had brought it closer to home. They weren't just names. Those women were mothers, daughters, wives and granddaughters to someone. If he had a daughter, how would he feel if she was kidnapped and sold into the sex trade? He glanced at the woman beside him. How would he feel if his wife were kidnapped and sold?

He drove off the ranch. Once he hit the highway, he pressed hard on the accelerator. The sooner they found the women, the better.

More than that, they had to find everyone involved and put them out of commission.

Chapter Twelve

While Parker looked up the address of WG Realty, Abby pulled back her hair, secured it in a tight bun and slipped the black wig over her head. She tucked in the stray blond hairs and viewed herself in the mirror on the visor.

"It's not me, but that's the point." She added the sunglasses and applied the lipstick Lily had provided.

Parker grinned. "A complete transformation. No one will recognize you."

She sat staring at the road ahead, her thoughts miles ahead, composing what she would say to the real estate agent. "I think we should approach the agent as if we were a couple looking for a private retreat. The further off the beaten path the better."

"Agreed. This agent might not know what was happening in that house. We don't want her to inadvertently alert anyone who might be involved."

Abby nodded. "We could say we were driving around and found their sign and were interested in the property. We could ask how long it had been on the market and if she could share anything about the history of the old place and the people who lived there."

"She could also point us in the direction of other remote properties that are currently vacant," Parker said.

"Places they might have moved the women to." Abby nodded.

Parker pulled into a small parking lot in front of a building on Main Street in Whiskey Gulch. A sign over the door read WG Realty.

Abby's pulse kicked up.

A strong hand reached across the console and gripped hers. "Are you okay?"

"I've never worked an undercover operation." She laughed. "Fifth grade teachers aren't usually called on for that kind of work."

"You'll be fine," he said. "You look amazing, like a cover model incognito. The agent will think you're a celebrity or something."

"And I married my bodyguard?" She smiled. "Ha. And I'm completely opposite. Oh, and did I tell you? I'm a terrible actress in front of adults." She gave him a tight smile. "Let's get this over with."

Parker chuckled as he got down from the truck and round the hood to the other side. He helped her to the ground and offered her his elbow.

She linked her arm through his and smiled up at him like a lover. And weren't they just that? Especially after the previous night's mattress gymnastics. He'd been a gentle and considerate lover, concerned about her needs and satisfaction. What more could a woman ask for?

He held the door for her and followed her in.

A receptionist looked up from her computer screen. "Can I help you?" she asked.

"We'd like to speak with Cecilia Mann," Parker said.

The woman smiled. "Let me see if Ms. Mann is available. What name shall I give her?

"Shaw," Parker said. "Mr. and Mrs. Shaw."

A twinge of joy rippled through her. She liked the sound of that. Maybe a little too much for having just met the man.

She lifted a desk phone receiver and tapped a button. "Ms. Mann, Mr. and Mrs. Shaw would like to meet with you. Are you available?"

The woman listened and nodded. "I will. Thank you." She set the receiver back in its cradle and smiled up at Parker and Abby. "She'll be with you in a moment." She stood and waved a hand toward a glassed-in room. "If you'll follow me, you can have a seat in the conference room." She led the way into the room. "Can I get you something to drink? Coffee, water, a soda?"

"I'd like water," Abby said. Anything to keep her hands busy and prevent fidgeting.

Parker held up his hand. "Nothing for me, thank you."

The receptionist disappeared and returned with a chilled bottle of water, handed it to Abby and left.

Abby twisted off the top and drank half the bottle, thirstier than she'd thought. After three days in captivity with little food or water, she could use it.

A woman with a stock of white hair entered the room with a smile. "My apologies for keeping you waiting. I was on the phone with a client who will be closing on her new house tomorrow." She sat at the end of the table where a laptop lay closed neatly on the surface. She folded her hands in front of her and gave them her complete attention. "What can I help you with? Looking for a house, land or a builder?"

Abby glanced over at Parker.

He smiled at the woman. "Parker Shaw and this is my wife, Amy."

"Cecilia Mann," she said and shook Parker's hand and then Abby's. "Nice to meet you both."

"We're new to the area and interested in a country setting with acreage and privacy." He smiled at Abby. "My wife is a writer. She needs to limit distractions to allow her to focus on her work."

"Really?" Cecilia raised her eyebrows and directed a glance in Abby's direction. "Amy Shaw... I love to read. I wonder if I've read any of your books."

Writer? Abby fought to keep from glaring at Parker for making up the lie that she now had to propagate. She forced a tight smile. "I doubt it. There are so many books available to read. We've been driving around the county just trying to get the lay of the land and areas we'd be interested in living. We found you because there was a particular home on a gravel road in the middle of nowhere that could be perfect with some remodeling."

"Well, let me look it up," she said and opened the laptop. After it booted, she clicked on the keyboard and paused. "Address?"

Parker shrugged. "We're not quite sure. It's quite secluded and we didn't see a street number." He gave her the name of the road.

"I should be able to find it," Cecilia said with the confidence of a seasoned Realtor. She entered the road name and waited for the system to bring up a map of the properties in that area. She reached for a remote control in the middle of the table and clicked a button on it. A large monitor flickered to life on the far wall with a map of the road and the properties on either side.

"I don't see any actually for sale." She frowned. "I seem to recall listing a house on that road at one time. I don't think it actually sold. It needed too much work, if I remember correctly. I might have forgotten to pick up the sign."

"Oh, we don't mind a fixer-upper," Abby said. "And we love older homes with a history."

Cecilia clicked on a property and a picture of the house flashed up on the screen. "Is this the house you saw?"

"Yes," Abby said, her heart pounding wildly in her chest.

"I remember this one. The owners were an elderly couple unable to live on their own anymore. They moved in with their daughter in Houston. They tried to sell the house, but their daughter and her husband just didn't want to deal with it. They think the house should be bulldozed to the ground and the land sold. But they don't want to upset her parents while they're still alive. So they left it to me to list it for as long as it takes to sell it."

She waved a hand at the screen on the wall. "Would you like to look at it?"

"We'd like for you to put together several options for us to drive by before we ask to see the insides," Parker said. "We're looking for two to ten acres of land and enough room for our dogs to run where they won't disturb neighbors. The more remote the better. And since we're having to stay in a hotel right now, vacant homes would be best. The sooner we get moved in, the better."

Cecilia frowned at the laptop. "That's odd," she said. "The house you're inquiring about shows that it's been delisted." Her brow furrowed. That was my listing. I don't remember the owners calling to have me pull the listing."

"Can anyone remove a listing?" Abby asked.

"Usually, the agent who listed it is the only one who can remove it," she said. "Or someone else within her agency. I'll check into it and pull some other potential homes meeting your criteria and send you the links if you'll leave your phone number or email address." She slid a pad of paper and pen toward him.

Parker scribbled his cell phone number on a pad. "When can we expect to hear from you?"

"Oh, I'll get right on it," she said. "I'll have some options to you within the hour. Look over them and call me with the ones you'd like to tour."

Parker pushed to his feet and held Abby's chair as she rose. "Thank you for your time, Ms. Mann. We look forward to hearing from you."

The Realtor beamed. "Thank you for choosing WG Realty for your housing needs."

As they rose to leave the conference room, a barrel-chested, silver fox of a man appeared in the doorway with a smile. "Good afternoon," he said, his voice booming in the confines of the office. He held out a hand to Parker. "Brandon Marshall."

Cecilia smiled. "Brandon, this is Parker and Amy Shaw. They're new to town and looking for a home. Parker, Amy, Brandon is the owner of WG Realty."

Parker gripped the man's hand and shook.

Brandon winced and pulled his hand free quickly.

He reached for Abby's hand next, his eyes narrowing for a split second as he studied her face. The man's smile never slipped. "Nice to meet you two. Is Cecilia helping you out?"

"Yes, she is," Parker said.

"They're interested in the old Golenski place," Cecilia nodded toward the image on the big screen. "I told them it needs a lot of work, but that it's vacant and they're eager to get settled."

Brandon's eyes narrowed again. "Is it even on the market?"

"That's what's strange." Cecilia's brow wrinkled. "I listed it. When our contract expired, I called them. The owners said to leave it up. When I went online a minute ago to look at the listing, it showed as inactive. If this nice couple hadn't seen our sign out there, I might never have known it wasn't showing on the system." She smiled at Parker and Abby. "It's so good that you came in today."

"When did you go out there?" Brandon asked.

"Just a little while ago," Parker said.

"It's a lovely, peaceful location," Abby said. "We liked the big trees and the seclusion."

"It's definitely secluded," Brandon said in his big voice.

"I'm going to pull a few listings to show them tomorrow or the day after," Cecilia said.

"If you'll excuse us," Parker laid a hand on the small of Abby's back and urged her forward. "We didn't have lunch today and would like to find somewhere to have an early dinner."

"Try the diner," Cecilia said. "Their food is good no matter what time of day."

"Nice to meet you, Mr. Marshall," Abby said.

Parker steered her past the reception desk and out into the parking lot.

Neither spoke until they were inside the truck with

the windows rolled up and they were driving out of the parking lot.

"Convenient that the listing had been delisted, don't you think?" Parker said.

"Like Cecilia said…odd. The whole visit was odd." Abby couldn't quite describe the level of unease she'd felt the entire time she'd been in the realty office.

"What do you mean odd?"

"I can't put my finger on it. Maybe it was the house that leaves me with bad vibes. Or the fact that the listing had been delisted, especially for the time when five women were being held hostage in the attic." She shrugged, trying to dispel that oppressive sense of doom.

Parker shot a glance in her direction. "Think Cecilia is in on this operation?"

"No," Abby said. "But it wouldn't hurt to have Dallas run a background check on the agents who work at WG, including Brandon Marshall."

Parker handed her his cell phone. "Would you do the honors and send that text to Dallas?"

Abby took the phone, keyed the message and sent it to Dallas. "Didn't she say she works the graveyard shift again tonight?"

Parker nodded. "She did."

"Then she might have time to do some computer sleuthing if she's not out on patrol the whole night."

"We should also see if Trace has some internet contacts who can dig deeper." Parker pulled into a parking space in front of the diner, shifted into Park and turned off the truck. "Hopefully, the other guys have had more luck with their assignments."

Abby nodded. She worried they wouldn't find the women in time.

As they entered the diner, a petite waitress with silky brown hair and bright green eyes sailed by them with a smile. "Find a seat. I'll be back with a menu."

Parker steered Abby to a corner booth and sat with his back to the wall.

Abby smiled. "Do you always sit with your back to the wall?"

He nodded. "Doesn't hurt to be where you can see what's coming and going. Situational awareness at all times."

She scooted out of her seat and stood. "Move over," she said.

Instead of scooting, Parker stood.

"Don't tell me you also like to be on the outside, too." She shook her head and slid into the booth all the way over.

Parker sat beside her.

The waitress handed them laminated menus. "I'm Misty. I'll be your server. What would you like to drink?"

"Water for me," Abby said.

"Water and a cup of coffee," Parker said.

Misty disappeared and returned quickly with a tray holding two glasses of water and a cup of coffee. "Do you need more time to order? I'd go for the country fried steak. Joe makes the best. It's the special for the day."

"Sounds good," Abby said, liking the perky young woman. "I'll have that."

"Me, too," Parker said.

Misty took their order to the kitchen and was out in

the dining room seconds later, filling glasses and fetching items for other customers.

A man in a sheriff deputy's uniform stepped through the door and looked around, his gaze going to the table where Parker and Abby sat. His eyes narrowed briefly.

"Sonny!" Misty the waitress called out as she emerged from the kitchen. She hurried forward, wrapped her arms around his waist and kissed him. "What a nice surprise. Are you staying?"

"Can't," he said. "I'm on duty. Thought I'd stop and see my best girl."

She smiled. "Thanks. Nice to know the county's finest is around to protect the blue-collar residents of Whiskey Gulch." She danced away. "Don't forget we have a date this weekend."

"About that…" he started.

"Not again," Misty pouted.

Parker leaned toward Abby. "You're eavesdropping, aren't you?" he asked.

"Totally," Abby said. "They're such a cute couple. It's hard to look away. And when he smiles, I can see why Misty is so into him. He's gorgeous."

"Whoa. Wait. You're *my* wife," Parker said with a crooked grin. "Don't go making me jealous."

"Shh." Abby touched a finger to her lips. "I can't eavesdrop if you're talking at the same time."

"Yes, ma'am," he said.

The deputy had Misty in his arms again. "Sorry, babe. I'm flying down to Mexico." He ran his hand through his blond hair, making it stand on end. "You know my friend I've told you about? Well, he had a motorcycle wreck and is in the hospital. I'm leaving as soon as I get off, and won't be back until Sunday."

Misty touched his arm, a frown denting her brow. "I'm sorry to hear that. And I'm sorry you won't be here. I bought the cutest black skirt with long black fringe." She sighed and moved her hand on his chest. "I was going to wear it the first time just for you."

"I'll take a rain check on that skirt."

"You know…" Misty walked her finger up his chest. "You wouldn't have to take a rain check if you took me with you to Mexico." She looked up at him and batted her eyelashes. "I have my passport and I've never used it."

"I don't know…" he said. "I have a friend flying me down. I'd have to see if he can take another passenger."

Her face lit up. "Then ask him. I'm off in fifteen minutes. You can pick me up, take me by my place. I can pack in no time. Please say yes."

He stared at her a moment longer and finally nodded. "I'll ask. Are you sure you'll be done in fifteen minutes?"

She nodded, already untying the apron around her waist.

"Okay, then. I'll clear it with the pilot and be back." The young deputy kissed her again and flashed his engaging smile.

Abby blinked at how charismatic the man was and how his blond good looks complimented Misty's dark hair and green eyes. How fun would it be to fly off at a moment's notice to Mexico with the man you loved?

The deputy left the diner, slid into his service vehicle and drove away.

Misty snagged the coffeepot and hurried to their table, her cheeks pink. "Sorry for the delay. My boyfriend doesn't always understand that I have to work. Now, what can I get for you?"

"Your boyfriend works for the sheriff's department?" Abby asked.

The young woman's head bobbed. "What can I say, I love a man in uniform. And he always brings me presents when he comes back from Mexico." She reached up and tapped one of her earrings. "He gave me these a couple of days ago." She leaned close to Abby. "Aren't they beautiful?"

Abby nodded. "Yes, they are."

Half-moons made of silver and mother-of-pearl dangled from Misty's earlobes. "Don't you just love them?"

"I do." Abby smiled.

The waitress topped off Parker's coffee. "I'll be back with your food. Then I'm headed out. Margie will cover your table after I'm gone."

The diner door opened again. Trace and Matt entered and looked around.

Parker raised one hand.

The two men joined Parker and Abby, sitting in the booth across from them. "Anything?" Trace asked.

Parker shook his head. "Not much. Only that the house was on the market and then it wasn't. Cecilia Mann is the listing agent, but she doesn't remember delisting it. The owners are elderly and moved closer to their kids. They're not in a big hurry to sell."

"I feel like there's more to the story." Trace said.

"Obviously, but I don't think the owners are involved." Abby frowned. "Someone knew the house was empty and decided to squat."

"What did you find at Roy's place?" Parker asked.

Trace's lips pinched together. "He wasn't there. His

snoopy cat-lady neighbor said he hadn't been there for several days." Trace's cell phone rang. "That'll be Irish and Becker." Trace pushed to his feet and walked out of the diner.

"When the waitress comes around, we need to order coffee for two," Matt said.

Misty returned with Trace and Abby's food and set it on the table in front of them. She took Matt's drink and food order, stopped to talk to another waitress and headed for the kitchen.

Trace returned to the table and slid in next to Matt. "That was Dallas. She and Levi visited Roy's parole officer. The man said Roy was doing good until about a couple weeks ago and then he stopped checking in. If Roy doesn't check in soon, the officer will have him arrested. He said Roy worked for Greenway Lawn Care as a day laborer. They spoke to the manager there and found that Roy hadn't shown up for work for over a week."

"Did they have a description of Roy?" Abby asked.

"Yes. They said he was hard to miss, standing at six feet four inches."

"Sounds like our jailer." Abby hugged herself around the middle, remembering how strong Roy was and how she'd been helpless to break free of his grip.

Trace continued. "Irish and Becker went to check on the owner of the car with the temporary tag."

"Did they find the car?"

Trace nodded. "It was clean. I mean clean. Not a single fingerprint on it. Someone wiped it down. Irish got under the chassis and found the dirt. Literally. The SUV had been on a dirt road. When they'd washed it, they hadn't taken into account the amount of mud caked to the undercarriage."

"So? There are a lot of dirt roads in the county," Parker said.

"But this vehicle was on that particular dirt road the night of the storm, and whoever was driving it, went to the trouble of cleaning it and wiping away the fingerprints," Matt said.

"So, is Scott Wilcox involved?" Abby asked.

Trace shook his head. "No. Irish called him. He's been in New Jersey for three months. He'd ordered the SUV to be delivered to his house. His plan was to come and get the new vehicle this weekend from his house."

"You say Scott had the car delivered," Parker said. "Where did he purchase it?"

"At a local dealership, managed by William Dutton," Trace said. "They stopped by the car lot, but William Dutton wasn't there. I remember Will Dutton from high school."

"I do, too," Matt said, his eyes narrowing. "Wasn't he a defensive lineman on the football team a couple years ahead of us?"

Trace nodded. "A big guy."

"A bully," Matt added, his lips pressing together. "He liked to push people around on and off the field."

Trace nodded. "He must have straightened up after high school to land a job managing a car dealership."

Parker's phone dinged with an incoming text. He glanced down at the message on the screen. "Cecilia just sent some potential homes for the *wife* and I to look over." He winked at Abby and pulled up the first link on his cell phone.

"How many did she send?" Trace asked.

Parker counted the list. "Ten."

"Good grief. That would take some time to check all of them," Matt said.

"And those are the active ones," Parker pointed out. "They'd delisted the first house before moving in to make sure no one came out to show it to a potential buyer. It would be too risky to stash the women in an active listing."

Trace's phone buzzed with an incoming text. He read the message and frowned. "This from Dallas. She stopped by the sheriff's office and did some asking around about Brandon Marshall. She talked to his former girlfriend. Apparently, he's in debt up to his neck and has defaulted on a couple loans, including the loan on his personal airplane."

Parker leaned over the table to look at Trace's phone. "Did Dallas share Marshall's tail number for his plane?"

"Let me look," Trace stared down at his phone. She sent some of the documents filed with the state." He scrolled through the text and stopped. "Here."

Parker brought up an app on his cell phone and keyed in the tail number. "This app tracks the flight plans of airplanes by their tail numbers or flight numbers. That plane has made a number of flights to Mexico in the past few months."

Mexico.

Abby's gaze followed Misty as she poured coffee, settled checks and greeted each customer with a friendly smile.

Mexico.

Something wasn't sitting right with her. She felt like

she was finding pieces to the puzzle, but she hadn't figured out how to fit them together yet. She wanted to talk with Misty about her boyfriend and their proposed trip to Mexico.

Misty was waving to her coworkers and heading for the back of the restaurant.

"Why would a real estate agent whose business is in Texas go to Mexico so many times?"

"Maybe he has a vacation home there," Matt said. "Lots of Texans do."

Parker held up his phone with a picture of an airplane. "This is the model aircraft he owns. It's not just a little recreational plane. It's a turbo prop that can take eight to ten passengers and their luggage."

"No wonder he can't make the payments on it. Those cost in the millions," Trace said.

Abby's heart beat faster as the puzzle pieces started sliding into place. "What if—"

Before she could voice her thoughts, a horn blared, tires squealed and an older model tank of a car crashed into a jacked-up, four-wheel-drive pickup in the diner parking lot.

Parker, Matt and Trace leaped from their seats and ran out the door. Abby followed, stopping short of the threshold. A dozen people gathered around the car where a little, old woman sat behind the wheel, stunned and shaken.

With all the people out front helping, they didn't need Abby. But someone else might.

She turned and walked through the swinging kitchen door.

The woman Misty had called Margie stood near a

large vat of hot oil. She lifted a basket of fries out of the oil and dumped them into a bin.

"Margie?" Abby called out.

"That's me," she looked up from sprinkling salt over the hot fries.

"Which way did Misty go?" Abby asked.

Margie tipped her head toward the rear exit. "Her shift was over. She left through the door back there. Do you need me tell her something?"

"No, thank you. I can do that."

Margie snorted. "If you catch her."

Abby sprinted for the door. Hoping she wasn't too late.

Misty was about to go to Mexico with the deputy, someone people would trust because of his friendly face, easy smile and his uniform.

Abby walked faster and broke into a run down the hallway to the exit door.

Brandon Marshall owned a plane and a real estate agency. He had knowledge of and access to vacant properties. He went to Mexico often in a plane that could hold eight to ten people.

Maybe she was adding two and two and coming up with seven, but she felt compelled to warn Misty not to go to Mexico.

She burst through the back exit as Sonny climbed out of an expensive-looking black car and smiled at Misty.

"Misty," she called out.

The waitress turned back, a frown pulling her eyebrows down. "I'm sorry," she said. "Did I forget something?"

Abby couldn't think fast enough to come up with anything other than, "Don't go."

"Excuse me?" Misty's frown deepened.

Abby's gaze met Sonny's. "Don't go with him to Mexico," she said in as calm a voice as she could muster.

"Why?" Misty asked.

Behind Misty, Sonny's brows descended into a dangerous glare. "Yeah. Why?"

"It's…dangerous," she said. Now that she'd barged into their escape, she wondered if she'd read too much into the deputy's handsome face. If he wasn't the man who'd lured Cara Jo and Valentina into his vehicle, Abby would be embarrassed.

If he was one and the same, she could possibly have thwarted his attempt to kidnap Misty and sell her in Mexico with the other four women.

His lip curled back in a sneer. "Your hair is crooked," he said, pointing to her wig.

When she reached up to straighten the wig, she realized her mistake.

Sonny reached behind his back and pulled out a handgun, wrapped his arm around Misty and pointed the gun to her temple.

"Sonny, what are you doing?" Misty cried.

"Shut up," he said. His gaze on Abby, he waved the gun toward the rear of the car. "Get in the trunk."

She backed a step, shaking her head. "No way." Having been a prisoner before, she'd rather die than be one again.

"Get in the trunk or I hurt her." He pressed the tip of the barrel to Misty's temple.

"Sonny, you're scaring me," Misty whimpered.

Abby's gut clenched. "Let her go, Sonny. If you fire a shot, everyone will hear it and come running."

"What are you doing?" Misty whispered. "I thought you liked me."

"I'm taking care of business," he said. "You," he tipped his chin toward Abby. "Get in the trunk. Now." He looped his arm around Misty's throat and tightened his hold.

Misty's eyes widened and her hands rose to claw at the arm around her neck. "Sonny," she said, her voice barely a whisper. "Don't."

His gaze held Abby's. "Get in the trunk, or her death is on you."

In the back of her mind, Abby knew better. Misty's death was all on Sonny. But the fear and desperation in Misty's eyes tore at Abby's heart. "Let her go and I will," she said.

"Get in first, and I'll let her go." Still, he held her gaze, his arm unrelenting in its hold on Misty.

The woman's struggles weakened. If Abby didn't do as he said soon, she'd be dead.

Abby walked slowly toward the car, praying Parker would notice she was gone before she made it into the trunk.

"Move," the deputy ground out.

Misty's hands slipped from his arms and fell to her sides.

Abby stood at the trunk, dread filling her soul. Sonny stepped up behind her, slammed the butt of his pistol against her temple and shoved her hard.

Abby fell into the back of the car, her head spinning, darkness closing in around her. She fought the darkness, knowing she had to stay awake and alert to find another way out of this mess.

Something heavy landed on top of her and dark brown hair fell into her face.

He'd dumped Misty's limp body in the trunk with her and closed the lid.

Chapter Thirteen

When the vehicles crashed in the parking lot in front of the diner, Parker, Trace and Matt had reacted immediately, rushing out to help.

The old woman in a vintage Cadillac sat shaking behind her steering wheel, tears pouring down her cheeks. Parker tried to open her door, but it was jammed shut. When Matt yanked open the back door, a small ball of white fluff leaped out and ran.

"Sweetpea!" The old woman screamed, "Catch her! Don't let my baby get away."

Matt dove after the little dog.

It ran in the opposite direction.

Trace grabbed for her.

The little white rat of a pup evaded him as well.

Park stepped in front of it. "Sweetpea, stay," he commanded.

She dashed between his legs.

"Abby, grab her!" he yelled and spun.

Abby wasn't behind him. The white fluff ball ran under a parked car and stopped, hiding behind one of the tires.

Parker looked back at the woman in the old car.

She waved at him. "Don't worry about me, I'm not going anywhere. Catch my Sweetpea."

He dropped to the ground next to the car, reached around the tire and snagged the dog by its long hair.

She wiggled but couldn't get loose.

He rolled to his feet holding the frightened dog in his arms.

Sweetpea shook, she was so traumatized.

"Oh, thank God," the woman said and cried grateful tears.

A siren wailed in the distance as a fire truck and an ambulance raced toward them, lights flashing.

Parker handed Sweetpea to a female bystander. "Hold her. Don't let her go. Her name is Sweetpea."

The woman nodded. "I've got her."

Parker joined Matt and Trace as they stood back, watching the fire fighters pry open the Cadillac.

"Have you seen Abby?" Parker asked.

Trace looked around him. "I thought she was with you."

"No," Parker said. "I haven't seen her since we left the diner. I'll go see if she's there." He hurried toward the front door of the diner looking all around him as he did. All the while, a sense of impending doom filled his chest.

"Abby!" he called out. "Abby!"

Parker pushed through the door, his gaze shooting to the booth he'd shared with her.

It was empty and clean, as if they'd never sat side by side on the bench.

"Abby," he called out softly. Then louder. "Abby!" He ran down the short hallway to the ladies' room, pushed the door open slightly and called out her name again.

No one answered. He went in and checked the stalls. Empty. No Abby. Hurrying back out into the dining room, he yelled, "Abby!"

"Can I help you?" the waitress named Margie emerged from the kitchen, carrying a tray loaded with plates full of food.

"I'm looking for the woman who came in with me. She has blond-black hair."

Margie nodded. "She went out the back through the kitchen, trying to catch Misty before she left with Deputy Tackett. That was a few minutes ago. I don't think she came back in."

Parker pushed through the swinging door into the kitchen and ran for the back door.

He burst through into an alley where a large trash bin stood. There was no sign of Abby.

Parker checked behind the trash bin and ran around the side of the building back to the front, where the emergency medical personnel were loading the old woman into the ambulance with her little white dog.

Still, he couldn't find Abby.

He hurried toward Trace and Matt, who stood with the firefighters.

Trace turned as Parker joined them. "What's wrong?"

"Abby," Parker said. "I can't find her."

Matt turned with Trace and searched the faces of the people standing around the wreck. "When was the last time you saw her?"

"Right before we ran out of the diner."

"Have you checked inside?" Matt asked.

"She's not in the diner. One of the waitresses said she went out through the kitchen trying to catch up with the waitress named Misty before she left with her deputy boyfriend."

Trace frowned. "Did she tell you she was going to talk to Misty?"

Parker shook his head. "I thought she was right behind me when we came out. Then the dog. Now she's gone."

"Why would she try to catch Misty before she left?"

Parker shook his head, thinking back to their conversations with the waitress. Then he remembered. "Misty was ending her shift. Her boyfriend, Deputy Tackett, mentioned he was going to Mexico. Misty was going with him." He smacked his forehead and shook his head. "He said he had a friend who was going to fly him down."

Matt nodded. "And right now, you're thinking Brandon Marshall is the friend."

"Think about it. It makes sense," Parker said. "Marshall knows the places to hide the women and he has a plane to transport them. The runaway teen and the girl walking home from her bus stop both said the man who abducted them was nice-looking, open, friendly and trustworthy, with light-colored hair and blue-gray eyes. Like Deputy Tackett," Parker said. "Abby might have come to that conclusion and was going to warn Misty."

"We don't know that for certain," Trace said.

"Do we know where Marshall keeps his plane?" Matt asked.

"We have a small general aviation airport just outside of town with a 3600-foot runway," Trace said. "He might take off from there."

"Are there private hangars out there?" Parker asked, his pulse picking up.

"Yes," Matt said. "A perfect place to hide women and stage them for a flight to Mexico."

The three men moved at the same time, racing for their vehicles.

"I'll tell Levi and Becker to meet us out at the airport."

"What about the sheriff's department?" Matt asked.

Trace shook his head. "We don't know if Deputy Tackett carries a police scanner. If we alert the department, he'll know and could warn the others. I'll let Levi know to pass the information to Dallas without going through 911 dispatch."

"We need to hurry," Parker said. "Tackett was heading to Mexico this afternoon, as soon as he collected Misty."

"Why would he take his girlfriend with a transport of captives?" Matt asked. "I would think he wouldn't want her to know what he was up to."

"Unless he was only leading her on with the intention of adding her to the collection of women they intend to sell." Parker swung up into his truck, started the engine and zigzagged past the emergency vehicles and out onto Main Street. He followed Trace's truck as the man flew through town.

It would only take ten minutes to get to the airport.

Parker prayed they wouldn't be too late to stop them.

ABBY FOUGHT AND won her effort to stay awake and not succumb to unconsciousness. She pushed and shoved Misty over to lie next to her in the trunk. She felt for a pulse, happy to find a strong one. It worried her that the woman had yet to wake.

As Abby lay in the dark, she tried to think, to come

up with a plan to get herself and now Misty out of the back of Sonny's trunk. She had to let Parker and Trace know who was behind the abductions before the women were flown to Mexico in Brandon Marshall's plane.

She'd been right to suspect the handsome deputy. He had to have been the man who'd lured the teens. His face looked completely innocent. A man a girl could trust.

Her mind flashed back to the men who'd been at the house when she'd tried to escape out the back door.

It made sense that their jailer was Roy Felton. Not many men were six feet four inches tall.

As for the man she'd run into when she'd tried to escape from the house through the kitchen door, she recalled he was a big guy with broad shoulders. Like a man who could've been a defensive lineman on a football team. The temporary tag was an important clue. William Dutton had been there that night.

Then there was the man in the white mask, wearing a tailored suit. She'd been intent on escape but was almost positive she'd seen a flash of silver hair. And he'd hurt his hand when she'd knocked him over.

At the real estate office, Brandon Marshall had winced when he shook hands with Parker. The pieces were all there. These were the men who'd kidnapped her and the others.

The good thing about being captured again was that the deputy would take her to where they were keeping the others. She'd escaped once; she could do it again. This time, she'd take the others with her.

Misty stirred and moaned.

"Hey," Abby touched her shoulder. "Misty, wake up."

"What? Where?" She tried to sit up and bumped her

head against the trunk lid. "What happened? Where are we?"

"Your boyfriend put us in the trunk. I suspect he's taking us to the airport to fly us to Mexico." Abby snorted. "And not for an all-inclusive vacation at a resort. Most likely we'll be delivered to a buyer."

"I don't understand," Misty said. "Why would Sonny do this?"

"Human trafficking is serious business and very lucrative," Abby said. "He's got this fancy car which I'm sure he couldn't afford on his deputy salary."

"He said he bought it used from his uncle," Misty said.

"Smells new to me," Abby said.

"He's going to sell us? But he's my boyfriend. I thought he loved me." She ended with a sob. "Human trafficking… Is that like the sex trade?"

"Yes," Abby said. "But it's not going to happen to us. We're going to get out of this."

Misty stopped sniffling and asked, "How?"

"I don't know. Feel around the inside of this trunk. Is there a release handle to open the lid from the inside? Also, if we can't find a way to get out, we have to be ready to make an escape when the lid is opened. Feel around for anything that can be used as a weapon."

"Okay," Misty said, her tone firming. The waitress wouldn't sit back and accept her fate; she was willing to fight to be free.

"There should be tire tools in here somewhere," Abby said.

"I think I'm lying on the compartment opening," Misty said. She scooted toward Abby and managed to lift the cover over the tools needed to change a tire.

Abby reached over Misty and felt the different shapes, picturing them in her mind. By feeling each tool, she was able to identify them, and her hand finally closed around a tire iron.

"What are you going to do with it?" Misty asked.

"I'm going to use it to fight my way out of here."

"Is there another?"

Abby weighed the tool in her hands. "There's usually only one in each vehicle."

"You should let me have it," Misty said, her voice hard. "I owe Sonny for almost choking me to death."

"He'll pay for his part in what these men have done."

The car slowed and turned, coming to a stop.

"Be ready," Abby whispered. She slid the tool beneath her shirt behind her.

"For what?" she asked.

"Anything," Abby said. "Mostly, be ready to run."

The driver's door opened and closed a moment later.

Abby held her breath, straining to hear footsteps approaching the trunk. She waited, the tire iron hidden beneath her.

Misty would get out first. Once she was on her feet, Abby would follow and whack Sonny in the head like he'd hit her. Hopefully, it would knock him out and they could make their escape.

Seconds went by, then minutes.

"Did he just leave us here?" Misty asked, keeping her voice quiet. "I should have known he was too good to be true."

"He had a lot of people fooled," Abby said. "He's been working with some other men in this operation. I just hope he's still alone when he opens the trunk."

"How did I not see this?" Misty said. "He talked

about going to Mexico. I had no idea he was trafficking women."

"We need to put the men responsible for this travesty into prison for a very long time. But we can't do that unless we find a way out." Abby scooted around until her head rested on Misty's leg. "I hope you don't mind. It's tight in here.

"Don't worry about it," Misty said. "Tell me what you want me to do."

"Just stay where you are for now," Abby said. "I want to see if I can fold the seats down." She planted her feet on the backs of the seats and pushed hard.

The seats didn't budge.

Cocking her legs, she kicked out as hard as she could. The seats held firm.

"Shh," Misty said. "I hear someone coming."

Abby scooted back into position and lay next to Misty. She wrapped her fingers around the tire iron that rested against her hip and thigh inside the leg of her jeans. She bunched her muscles, ready to fly out of the trunk as soon as an opportunity presented itself.

Voices sounded along with the footsteps, though they were too muffled to hear clearly.

A moment later, the trunk lid opened.

Abby looked around to get her bearings and look for an escape route. They were inside an aircraft hangar. A plane stood nearby with the steps lowered.

Her pulse quickened. This was it. They were preparing to take them to Mexico if Sonny's claim could be believed. He'd said he had a friend who would fly him there.

Sonny stood in front of the trunk with another man. The other man wore the white mask he'd worn at the

Golenski house. When he turned, Abby could see the silver hair and the tailored suit she'd seen Brandon Marshall wearing earlier. Beyond the two men was the wide-open door with bright Texas sunshine streaming through.

All Abby had to do was get past the doors.

Then again, she couldn't make her break until she located the other women. She could not leave them behind again.

She wished she had a tire iron for each of them. It would help give them more of a fighting chance against the two large men.

Another vehicle pulled into the hangar and a man got out, pulling a ski mask into place over his head. The broad shoulders and the shiny new car gave this one away. William Dutton had arrived.

"Get them on the plane," Marshall said. "We leave as soon as we're all on board. Good job getting our quota."

Sonny glanced into the trunk with no expression on his face. The nice guy smile was gone. The blue-gray eyes were more of a hard, steely gray. "Get out," he ordered.

"Sonny," Misty said. "Why are you doing this? Take me back home. I don't want to go to Mexico with you anymore."

"The choice is not yours." His voice was cold, unbending. "Now, get out. Both of you."

Misty climbed out of the trunk and stood in front of Sonny. "What you're doing is wrong," she said. "You don't have to go through with this."

Abby scooted toward the opening, careful to keep the tire iron out of sight as she moved. With the tire iron tucked into her back waistband and hidden beneath her shirt, she eased over the rim of the trunk and out onto her feet. When she straightened, she kept her back turned away from the men.

If they looked at her back, they would know something wasn't right.

"Move," Sonny ordered and shoved Misty toward the plane.

"Sonny, what's wrong with you?" Misty asked. "You're not like this. You're a good man. An officer of the law, sworn to protect."

The man in the white mask snorted. "Morals and integrity pale in comparison to cold, hard cash. Don't they, Sonny?"

The deputy's lip curled. "Especially when there's a lot of it."

"We're wasting time," Marshall said. "Get them on the plane with the others and drug them. I don't want any more slipups."

A tall figure appeared at the top of the stairs of the airplane.

"Roy, help get our last two guests on board. You know what to do." Marshall left Sonny and Roy to do the job and walked over to where Dutton was grabbing a suitcase from the trunk of his vehicle.

Abby knew she couldn't fight off four men with one tire iron. And from the bulge beneath Marshall's jacket, he was obviously armed.

Sonny had his gun out where she could see it. He turned to her and gave her a narrow-eyed glare. "Give me any trouble and I'll do to you what I did to her. Now, move."

If she wanted to get away, it had to be now, before Roy closed the distance between them. The trouble was that the other women were on board that aircraft. If the plane left the ground, there would be no going back.

Abby had to make sure that didn't happen. The tire iron would come in handy if she could manage to get into the cockpit and damage the controls and ground the plane. Then she could use the tire iron on the men.

She walked between Sonny and Misty toward the plane.

Roy came down to the bottom of the steps, grabbed Misty's arm and dragged her to the top. She looked over her shoulder at Abby before Roy pulled her inside.

Abby started up the stairs, trying to look normal when the tire iron was slipping lower.

"Move a little faster. We don't have all day," Sonny started to shove her from behind.

She turned to keep him from touching the metal, stumbled backward against the steps and the tire iron made a clunking sound.

Abby's heart skipped several beats. She coughed in an attempt to mask the sound and kept moving. When she reached the top of the stairs, Sonny shoved her again, sending her staggering into the plane.

What she saw made her gasp. Cara Jo, Rachel, Laura and Valentina were strapped to the plush leather seats, out cold. Roy held some kind of medical vial with a syringe stuck inside it. He pulled the plunger and drained the vial into the syringe and tossed the empty vial into a cup holder.

When he reached for Misty, she backed away.

"No," she said. "I won't fight you. Just don't drug me. Please."

Roy grabbed her arm and jammed the needle into her arm, injecting half of the liquid into her.

"Please, noooo." Misty slumped.

Roy, still holding onto her arm, eased her into a chair and turned toward Abby with the remainder of whatever evil was in the syringe.

It was now or never. Abby spun and shoved Sonny backward as hard as she could. He teetered on the top step, reached for her arm, missed and fell backward down the stairs.

Abby yanked the tire iron from her waistband and swung it at Roy's hand carrying the syringe. The loud crack of metal hitting bone preceded the launch of the syringe across the cabin. It crashed into a window and dropped to the floor.

Abby turned toward the cockpit and dove for the controls.

She only made it one step through the door before she was grabbed by her hair and yanked backward into Roy's chest.

With both hands, she raised the tire iron over the top of her head and slammed it into Roy's head. When she cocked her arms to do it again, Roy grabbed the tire iron on her upswing and grabbed it from her grip. Then he pulled her arms behind her and secured her wrists with a zip tie.

By that time, Sonny had made his way back up the stairs, his face a mottled red, an angry bruise on his cheek. He raised his arm across his chest.

Abby cringed, waiting for him to backhand her into the next county.

"Don't!" Brandon Marshall's booming voice arrested Sonny's hand in midmotion. "Don't damage the goods. Our customers pay top dollar if they're in good physical condition." He climbed the steps behind Sonny.

The deputy remained stiff in the doorway for another long moment.

"Save it," Marshall said, stepping past Sonny. "We need to leave before anyone figures out what's going on. You realize, we probably won't be coming back."

Sonny finally moved out of the doorway, his glare on Abby. "Being a deputy for barely more than minimum wage isn't worth putting on the uniform. After we're paid, I'm going to find me a little casita on the beach. There's nothing to keep me here."

"Or me." William Dutton entered the plane, pulling off the ski mask as he settled into one of the seats. "I'm tired of selling cars, barely making enough to pay salaries, commissions and overhead. I'm with Sonny. A casita on a beach is where I'm headed."

Roy grabbed Abby's arms and marched her to one of the chairs near the other women and forced her to sit.

"You won't get away with this. What you're doing is horribly wrong. How can you sleep at night?"

"Like a baby," Marshall said. He looked back at Roy. "Drug her."

Roy reached for the syringe that had flown across the cabin. He held it up and frowned. The syringe was empty, and the needle was bent. "That was the last of the drug," he said.

"Then can you at least slap some duct tape over her mouth?" Marshall said. "I don't want to hear a sound on this flight. But first, close the hatch. We need to get into the air."

He moved forward into the cockpit, settled into the pilot's seat and fired up the engines.

"Ain't got no duct tape," Roy muttered. He zip-tied her wrists to the armrests. "Start flappin' your gums and I'll use that tire iron on you in spite of what the boss says."

As the plane taxied out away from the hangar, Abby's heart hit the bottom of her belly. This was it. She'd failed to stop these men from ruining the lives of six women. When the plane left the ground, there wouldn't be a cavalry swooping in to save the day. They'd be sold into sex slavery, used and abused in some hovel. Maybe she'd get used to the drugs if they dulled the pain.

She wished she'd had a chance to get to know Parker better. She really liked him and there was a good chance she loved him.

Chapter Fourteen

Trace reached the turnoff to the Whiskey Gulch Municipal Airport and skidded around the corner, barely having slowed enough to make the turn.

Parker repeated the maneuver riding close on Trace's tail. He shot a glance at the runway, his heart in his throat, wondering if they were too late. He'd managed to open the flight app for Marshall's plane's tail number. The man had filed a flight plan from Whiskey Gulch to Monterrey, Mexico, scheduled to leave a few minutes ago.

They couldn't be too late. Abby would be on that plane. Parker wasn't ready or willing to end their relationship. It had only just begun, and he wanted many more years with her. He'd even admit to love at first sight and take a helluva lot of ribbing from the other members of the team. He didn't care as long as he had Abby.

While Trace headed for the gate, Parker rode along the fence paralleling the runway, searching for any sign of a plane. His breath held, and despair sank into every fiber of his being.

A flash of reflected light captured his attention. At the very end of the taxiway, a plane turned and started down the runway, picking up speed.

"No," Parker yelled. "You're not taking her." He yanked his steering wheel to the right and rammed his truck through the chain-link fence, bumped down into a ditch and back up onto the concrete runway, racing toward the plane coming straight at him.

Trace smashed through the gate and raced to catch up to the plane.

Parker wasn't sure how he could stop a plane with his truck, but he had to do something. They could not leave the ground.

He had to reach the plane before it reached its take-off speed. Not knowing how fast or soon that would be, he just had to get to the plane as quickly as he could.

Sixty…seventy…eighty miles per hour, he pushed the truck faster.

The plane sped down the runway without slowing.

Parker had to make a decision and fast. Did he play chicken and risk crashing into the aircraft, or did he dodge around it and watch it go airborne with Abby and five other women aboard? They'd be alive but disappear into a dark abyss of drugs, sex and abuse.

Parker's jaw set with determination. He would not let that plane leave the ground.

As he neared the point of no return, he slammed on his brakes and turned sideways across the runway, the truck's forward momentum sending him skidding ever closer to the aircraft.

He raised his arms to shield his face for the collision.

At the last moment, the pilot turned off the runway, down into a shallow ditch. Still going too fast to come to a complete halt, it rammed through the airport fence and rolled to a stop in a hayfield.

Parker raced after the plane with Trace not far behind.

Skidding to a halt twenty yards from the tail, Parker shifted into Park, grabbed the AR15 from the back seat and leaped down from his truck. He used the door for cover as he aimed at the top of the stairs ready to shoot.

The aircraft stairs were lowered. For a long moment, nothing happened. No one emerged from inside the aircraft, and no one shouted out a list of demands.

Suddenly, Abby appeared at the top of the stairs, her hands secured behind her back, the barrel of a handgun pressed to her temple by Sonny Tackett.

"We want safe passage for this airplane to Mexico, or this woman dies," he shouted.

"If that woman dies," Parker said, "You and your people die with her."

Trace parked several yards from where Parker stood. He and Matt reached for their rifles, got out and locked in on the deputy.

Sirens wailed in the distance.

"It's over, Sonny," Trace called out. "Release the hostages and your sentence will be lighter. You pay a lot higher price for murder."

"You hear that, Marshall? Dutton?" Trace shouted loud enough for the men inside to hear. "You aren't killers," Trace said. "Don't add murder to your sentence."

Another truck pulled up behind Parker's.

Parker didn't shift his focus for even a second.

"Sonny," Dallas called out. "You know that plane isn't going anywhere."

"That's right, Sonny," Parker added. "There's too much damage."

"Then get us another," Sonny said. "I'm not going down for this."

"You know that isn't possible, Sonny," Dallas said.

"There isn't going to be another plane. You're not going to Mexico. You're going to let Abby go and turn yourself in."

"No."

Brandon Marshall stepped up behind the former deputy. "It's over, Tackett. Put down your gun."

"No," Sonny said. "I'm going to Mexico. If we stay here, we go to jail."

"If you go to Mexico, the Mexican government will extradite you," Dallas said.

"They don't want our criminals," Levi said. "They have enough of their own. You'll be right back here with a heavier sentence."

"If you want to stand here and argue, leave me out of this." Marshall pushed past Sonny and Abby and descended the stairs, raising his hands as he walked toward Dallas.

"Dutton?" Parker called out.

"I'm coming," he said. "Don't shoot."

William Dutton pushed past Sonny and Abby. "Give it up," he said as he passed. "I didn't sign up for murder. Neither did you." Dutton descended the stairs and hurried toward the trucks, his hand held high.

Roy Felton appeared next. "I didn't sign up for murder, either. Take me to jail. It's easier than finding a job with a rap sheet hanging around your neck." He slipped by Sonny and hurried down the steps and marched up to Dallas with his hands held out, ready for her to cuff him. She pulled his hands behind his back and secured them with zip ties. Then she had him, Marshall and Dutton sit in the grass until transport arrived.

"That leaves you, Sonny," Trace said. "Let her go and give yourself up."

"No." Sonny shook his head. "I want that plane. If I don't get it, I start shooting, starting with her. And I have five more to choose from. So, what's it to be?"

"We can't get you a plane," Trace said. "Put down your weapon before someone gets hurt."

"You're not listening," Sonny said. "Maybe you will when I start shooting. I'll give to the count of three to get on your phone and call in favors from your rich friends. One…"

Parker looked down his scope, setting the cross-hairs across Sonny's face, just above Abby's head. If he took the shot, he could miss and hit Abby instead. If he didn't take the shot, Sonny would. At point-blank, he wouldn't miss.

"Two…" Sonny shouted.

Abby threw herself off the stairs.

Sonny aimed at her falling figure.

Parker took the shot, hitting Sonny square in the heart.

The deputy's knees buckled, and he tumbled down the stairs and lay at the bottom.

Parker, Levi, Trace and Matt rushed forward.

Parker knelt beside Abby and helped her to a sitting position. He pulled his pocketknife out and cut the zip tie. Then he gathered her in his arms and held her. She circled her arms around his neck and clung to him, her body shaking so hard her teeth chattered.

When the trembling subsided, she said, "I n-need to see the others."

A fire engine and three ambulances arrived.

He smiled and brushed a strand of her hair out of her face. "Let the professionals get them out of the plane first."

She nodded and leaned into him. "Just when I thought all was lost, the cavalry came through. Thank you."

"I died a thousand deaths between the time I realized you were gone and now." He pressed his forehead against hers.

She looked up and stared into his eyes. "How did you keep the plane from taking off?"

He drew in a breath and let it out. "You know those thousand deaths I was telling you about? That was 999 of them."

Trace laid a hand on Parker's shoulder. "He took a calculated risk and it paid off."

Matt stepped up behind Parker. "I've never seen a truck play chicken with an airplane."

Abby frowned. "Chicken?"

Parker pushed to his feet. "Let's get the medics to look you over after your spectacular fall. Then we can go back to the ranch and get some rest."

"I'll want to visit the hospital," she said as he helped her to her feet.

"We can make that happen," he said. He scooped her up into his arms and carried her to one of the ambulances for a quick once-over by an EMT.

By the time he declared her okay, the firefighters started bringing the other women out of the plane, one at a time.

Still heavily sedated, they slept through it all.

"Will they be all right?" Abby asked.

Trace nodded. "I spoke with one of the emergency medical technicians. He said the drugs should wear off in a couple hours. They're going to be okay."

"See?" Parker swung her up into his arms. "You kept your promise and brought help."

She shook her head. "The real heroes are you, the Outriders and Dallas."

"We wouldn't have known of their existence if you hadn't risked your life breaking out of the house and running through a thunderstorm to get help."

She wrapped her arm around his neck and smiled. "Oh, and don't forget the hogs."

He chuckled. "I'll never forget the hogs."

"And Brutus is a hero for saving me from them."

"And we won't forget Brutus's bravery." He settled her into the front seat of his pickup, leaned over and brushed a kiss across her lips and said, "When our grandchildren ask me if I think it was worth it to play chicken with an airplane, I'll tell them hell yeah. But I won't recommend they try it."

Epilogue

Two months later

"Thank you for letting us have his reunion here at the Whiskey Gulch Ranch," Abby said. "I was going to have it at our cottage in town, but it just wasn't big enough for all the Outriders, their gals, my fellow abductees and their families."

Rosalyn and Trace stood beside Abby on the porch looking out at the lawn, where Levi, Dallas, Matt and Aubrey were playing a rousing game of volleyball against Irish, Tessa, Becker and Olivia.

Laura Owens sat with Cara Jo Noble and Valentina Ramirez, giving them advice on how to prepare for college. She'd taken the teens under her wing and encouraged them to reach for the stars. She'd spent hours on the phone with Cara Jo, convincing her to get her GED and go on to a junior college to get her core courses and build her grade point average before applying to a four-year institution.

Valentina's mother sat with Rachel Pratt and her two small children on a blanket in the grass.

Rosalyn hugged Abby. "I want to thank you for getting married so quickly to our handsome Parker."

Abby's brow wrinkled. "Why?"

She grinned and looked up at her son. "Because you two committed so quickly, it reminded Trace and Lily that they had yet to set a date for their wedding."

Lily joined them on the porch. "We've decided to get married next month," she said, beaming up at Trace.

"It's going to be a challenge to make it happen so quickly," Rosalyn said. "But we will make it happen."

"We have to." Lily wrapped her arm around Trace's waist. "We can't wait any longer or I won't fit into a wedding dress."

Trace frowned down at her. "Why wouldn't you fit into a wedding dress?"

Lily pulled a white plastic stick out of her pocket and grinned.

Trace's eyes widened. "Are you?"

Lily nodded. "I am."

He grabbed her up and swung her around and then kissed her soundly. "We're going to have a baby," he shouted.

The volleyball game paused long enough for everyone to congratulate the couple.

Abby couldn't have been happier for Lily and Trace. She smiled at the glow in Lily's cheeks and sighed.

Parker slipped up behind her and pulled her against him. "You look happy."

Her smile broadened. "I am."

"You're not too sad about leaving your old school behind to move up to Whiskey Gulch?"

She shook her head. "Not at all. I'm happy to be with you and surrounded by all the members of your team. We have such wonderful friends who are more like family, and a lovely cottage just the right size for a growing family."

He cupped his hands over her still-flat belly. "Why didn't you say something when Trace and Lily made their announcement?"

She laid her hands over his. "They deserve the spotlight. They brought us all together and made this team a family. I'm just happy to know our child will have friends to play with. We are truly blessed."

"Yes, we are," Parker said. "I love you, Mrs. Shaw."

A wet nose bumped against Abby's leg. She reached down and scratched behind Brutus's ear. "I love you, Mr. Shaw, and Brutus, and Jasper."

* * * * *

THE LOST HART
TRIPLET

NICOLE HELM

For the savers.

Chapter One

The town of Wilde, Wyoming, was nothing like its name nor its nearest neighbor, Bent, which harbored centuries-old feuds and murderers and kidnappers and the like.

Wilde was small, quiet and *boring*. Aside from *two people* disappearing fifteen years ago which was clearly just a May-December romance leaving judgment behind, and a bank robbery in 1892 that many claimed was fictional, nothing ever happened in Wilde.

Until now.

At least, in Zaraleigh Hart's estimation.

Zara, because no one except her family was allowed to call her Zara*leigh*, for heaven's sake, watched her six employers with narrowed eyes. She didn't trust them, and she sure as heck didn't believe their cockamamie story about being brothers looking for the *simple* life.

The town—if one could call a tiny dot on the map surrounded by state parks and wildlife refuges and the Wind River Range of the Rockies, populated by only fifty people, many of them related, a *town*—had been abuzz since these six men had appeared six weeks ago. In the middle of winter. Ready to ranch.

Her ranch. Stolen out from under her by these…men. Who didn't *look or* act like any brothers she knew. Or ranchers, for that matter. They'd paid way over market price for the land and cattle—so much more than it was worth that her father simply hadn't been able to refuse their offer. And because of the outrageous amount, Dad had chosen to sell the ranch instead of passing the homestead down to her like he should have done.

But mostly Wildeans wanted to talk about the handsome, *single* out-of-towners, men who weren't related to any of their young daughters or nieces.

Zara didn't care about such frivolous, pointless nonsense. Zara wanted to know why they were *here*. And clearly lying. They weren't brothers in search of a simple life. For one, there was nothing simple about any of them. They were all tall and far too muscled. They all possessed a stillness and a wariness that made *her* nervous.

When she'd never been nervous a day in her life.

She'd helped them for over a month now, teaching them the ropes of how to run a ranch, even as they sank into the hard, uncompromising Wyoming winter—because they didn't know, of course. About ranching or real winters or *anything*.

Fortunately, they paid quite well for her tutoring, but a salary didn't earn trust.

Before they'd arrived, she'd called her cousin, a county deputy over in Bent, and he'd told her their backgrounds were clear.

Zara didn't believe it, but still, she taught them. Day in. Day out. Waiting for someone to slip up so she could figure out what their deal was.

They were quick learners. She'd give them that. They'd all taken to horseback riding easy as you please, except Dunne Thompson, who had some kind of injury which made getting up on the horse too difficult. They'd learned the lay of the land, the rhythms of ranch life. Quite frankly, Zara wasn't sure how much longer they'd keep her around— especially paying what they were paying.

But this was Hart land, and Zara was bound and determined to get it back once she figured out what these men were *really* up to.

Zara fingered the mane of the horse under her—they'd bought everything, down to Sam, her three-year-old mare. Her only saving grace was that she and Hazeleigh got to *rent* the dang cabin their great-grandpa had kicked the bucket in.

She looked at the men again. She understood men. Maybe she'd grown up in a house full of women, aside from Dad. Two sisters, identical because they were the Hart triplets. But she'd been the tomboy of the three girls. She liked ranching and sports and fighting.

These six weren't like the men she knew and had spent her life hanging out with. They were too...serious. Oh, they didn't all have the same personality. Six men were never *all* the same, but there was a guarded look in their eyes— which were all different shades and shapes—that matched.

Trauma could do that, she supposed. She figured hiding a body together or some such could too.

"All right, guys, you've got this side. I'm going to work from the other." She turned Sam around and ignored the offers to split up and help.

She didn't want their help or their proximity. They could work on fixing the fence from this side. She'd head several yards west and deal with the other broken section. Snow and ice wreaked havoc on a fence.

Zara eased Sam into a gallop and let the short ride clear her head. She was *almost* in a good mood when she pulled Sam to a stop. Until she saw Hazeleigh running toward her.

Zara sighed. She knew she should get down. Intercept Hazeleigh's wild run. Calm her sister down and tell her to take a breath.

Sometimes Zara felt like she was drowning under all the responsibilities left on her shoulders.

Hazeleigh came to a stop next to Sam, her hand immediately reaching out for purchase. She curled her fingers into Zara's pants leg.

"Stop. Don't."

"*Stop, don't* what?" Zara replied, resisting the urge to pull her leg away from Hazeleigh's grasp. "I was just going to fix the fence here."

Hazeleigh shook her head, dark hair whipping violently with the movement. "Don't."

Zara sighed at Hazeleigh's pale face, wide eyes and desperate pleas.

"Please, Haze, not another one of your 'feelings.'"

"Zee, really. Really. Something is wrong. You know I only say something when I can't get rid of it." She was grasping Zara's leg like it was a lifeline.

Zara hardly believed her sister could "feel" things. And sometimes her bad feelings came to nothing, so Zara felt confident in all that disbelief. Except when those bad feelings came to *something*, and someone—usually Zara herself—narrowly missed out on being hurt or humiliated.

"What am I supposed to do? *Not* fix the fence and let the cattle get out?" Zara swung off Sam so she could be identical eye to identical eye with her sister. Except no one ever got them confused. They were too different, no matter how alike they looked.

Right now, Hazeleigh was wearing an oversize coat she'd forgotten to button and was next to threadbare anyway. Like most of what Hazeleigh wore, it was a thrift-store find. She wore pants—not jeans, not ranch wear—but some kind of vintage trousers that reminded Zara of the old movies Hazeleigh liked to watch. Her dark hair was a swirling mass around her, likely having fallen out of some colorful, silken scarf or old-fashioned pins, depending on if she was working or not today.

Zara, on the other hand, was in jeans, a flannel shirt and a cowboy hat. She never left home in anything other than her cowboy boots. She kept her long dark hair pulled back in a tight braid at all times.

"Just…" Hazeleigh looked at the place where the fence post was angled too far to the right. She reached out and grabbed Zara's hand. "You need to get away from here. We need to get away from here."

Zara pulled her hand away. Frustration warring with sympathy. Love warring with disdain. "I can't ignore my job."

"Everything okay?" came another voice, a deeper voice.

Zara glared at Jake Thompson's approach. She glared at all six of them all the time, whether they deserved it or not, but there was something about Jake that made her always want to glare extra hard.

He was too…watchful. Especially of *her*. She didn't care for it. At all. So she glared.

And he always smiled.

Hazeleigh shrunk away a little as he approached. Zara watched Jake notice it and react accordingly. He kept his distance.

Unfortunately, she had to give him credit for that.

As much as she *wanted* to believe they were killers who'd buried a body in a shallow grave and run away to hide from their misdeeds, they never made her afraid. Not just because she had guts, but because they were polite, careful and ever *aware*.

Of Hazeleigh's skittishness. Of not cornering either of them or standing too close. Of their own height and breadth and strength.

Zara wished they were a little less *honorable* just so she'd have better reason to dislike them.

"Everything is just fine," Zara said to Jake firmly.

"I was following to give you a hand, but then your sister came running like a bat out of hell. Usually that doesn't mean things are fine," Jake replied, a small smile on his face. She supposed it was his attempt at a *kind* smile.

Zara was not a fan of all the ways he tried to be nice when she was trying to dislike him.

"Maybe, but it's also very much none of your business."

"Zara," Hazeleigh murmured in admonition. She never could stand to see anyone act *rude*.

Which meant she was in a near-constant state of scolding Zara, who was quite often rude on purpose.

"Go home," Zara said to her sister, trying to keep her tone gentle. "I have work to do." She went over to the fence post and gave it a yank.

"Please don't," Hazeleigh whispered, but she stayed back. As if she was afraid of the very ground Zara was on.

"Go home, Hazeleigh," Zara said under her breath, but firm and a little harsh because she could not have this conversation in front of Jake. She got the fence post free in no time. The post had rotted away, and rot was never a good thing.

"I think we'll need to repour the foundation here," Zara said to Jake, ignoring her sister's stubborn presence. "Higher, so the wood doesn't have as much contact with the soil. It rotted too quickly. It's just not old enough to warrant this decay."

Jake nodded. "Something strange around here. Look at the snow. It almost looks like there's some kind of sinkhole underneath."

Zara frowned. Yes, that's exactly what it looked like. She tried to think the last time her father and she had worked in this area, but it was before any major snowfall. There shouldn't be this much difference in the landscape.

"Could be the wind," she offered, even though that didn't make sense either. Why would the wind blow snow away from this one spot?

Jake frowned at the ground, and Zara had to frown at

it too. It was an odd place for a sinkhole. Not quite against the post or under the fence line but close enough to cause a problem.

"Maybe it's buried treasure." Jake grinned.

Zara had to fight very hard not to grin back. A ridiculous thought but kind of fun. "Maybe from that bank robbery back in 1892."

"You guys are really proud of that 130-year-old heist."

"The only thing interesting that's ever happened here," Zara said, trying to fight the feeling of easy camaraderie as they both grabbed short shovels from where Zara had packed them in the horse's saddle bag.

They wouldn't need to dig deep to get through the snow. The frozen ground might be an issue, but the other men could bring a post hole digger if necessary. Getting the fence back up was the most important thing.

They both began to clear the snow around where she'd removed the post. Once the snow was cleared, Jake dug in the hole left by the removed post. Zara knew she should too, but she couldn't stop looking at the strangely muddy ground next to where she stood. The grass hadn't grown back where the snow had accumulated less. Like someone had been digging just off the fence line.

She poked at it with her shovel, unable to ignore her curiosity. She didn't really think it was buried treasure, but it had to be something.

They needed to check before they poured more foundation here. Maybe something was causing the fence-post rot.

She jammed her shovel into the frozen patch. Not as frozen as it should be. She pulled out a chunk of dirt and then another. After a few scoops, her shovel hit something... strange. Not hard like an old cement foundation or anything of the like. Not frozen solid down below the surface. Hard but with an odd...soft give.

"Don't, don't, don't," Hazeleigh said desperately, covering her face with her hands. "Don't do it."

Zara looked at her sister. Dread curdled in her stomach, but how could she just ignore it? Maybe Hazeleigh's "feelings" had saved her from disaster once or twice, but what could be waiting in the earth that might harm her?

"Should we stop?" Jake asked, eyeing Hazeleigh balefully.

"No. She just… Ignore her. Here, I found something. Help me dig it out."

Jake nodded and moved closer to her. Too close. She could smell him. Soap and saddle leather. She could count the whiskers on his jawline that never seemed to fade no matter how often he shaved. She could see the glint of summer sky blue in his eyes. The sheer size of him, which oddly and unlike just about any other man she'd ever met, didn't make her want to challenge him.

And she did not care for her reaction to any of those things.

Jake let out a yelp of a curse, nearly falling backward as he scrambled away. She wanted to laugh at his reaction, tease him, but Hazeleigh's whispered *don't*s made her unable to come up with a smart remark.

"It's *you*," he said, looking at her like he'd seen a ghost.

Zara frowned, peering down into the hole Jake had made.

In an instant, her vision went gray. Because there was a face in the dirt.

One identical to hers.

JAKE MANAGED TO catch Zara before she tipped over like a tree that had just been felled. She was a sturdy woman, so it wasn't an easy catch.

Luckily he was strong enough to manage.

He looked back at the hole they'd dug. Had he really seen…?

Yeah, it was a face all right. Decaying a bit, but absolutely no doubt it looked exactly like the two women renting the cabin on the ranch. The two women standing right here.

"It's Amberleigh," Zara said. She sounded, for the first time in the six weeks he'd known her, rattled. She wasn't even standing on her own two feet. She was leaning on him as he held her upright.

A strange sensation, but one he didn't have time to analyze because there was a dead body buried on his property.

One who looked exactly like Zara and Hazeleigh.

"No," Hazeleigh was saying. Over and over again. "No, no."

Zara inhaled and exhaled noisily, then seemed to find her feet and took a step away from him. She wrapped her arms around herself as if that could hold her upright. "We need to… We have to…"

"Go on back to your cabin. I'll call the sheriff's department," Jake said. Though the dead body had surprised him, mostly because of how much it looked like their pretty ranch hand and her sister, it was hardly the first one he'd seen. Maybe he'd been optimistic enough to think he'd seen his last, but he'd get over his disappointment.

He didn't think these two women would be getting over this anytime soon.

"The police will want to talk to us," Zara said. She looked down at the ground like she wanted to look at the face again but couldn't bring herself to do it.

"Sure, but there's no reason you have to stand around here and wait." He put his hands on her shoulders. She stiffened but let him turn her away from the hole and toward her sister. Her *living* sister. "Go on."

Zara turned. Her chin came up, her eyes met his. "I'll stay with her."

Her. Meaning the dead body.

Hazeleigh reached out and grabbed Zara's hand. "We have to stay. And we should call Thomas… He'll handle it. Won't he?" Hazeleigh looked at Zara a little desperately.

Zara nodded faintly. Jake wasn't sure her eyes were really seeing anything. "Yes, I'll call Thomas," she said, her voice firm but tinny.

Shock. He'd seen a lot of that too. But Zara held firm as Hazeleigh began to cry quietly. Jake stood a few feet away, feeling at a loss.

Then instinct and habit kicked in. Maybe this was a ranch in the middle of nowhere, but he was a man who'd been trained to deal with too many disasters to name.

He sent a text to the guys explaining what had happened, warning them to stay back. As much as they could stay out of this, the better. He'd handle the police as much as possible.

Cops brought attention. Dead bodies brought *attention*. And that's what he and his "brothers" had come here to avoid.

But he couldn't rightly let Zara or her sister make the call, or stand here with another identical woman in the dirt. So, he called the sheriff's department himself. He spoke with a dispatcher, gave his details too many times to count, asked for the mysterious Thomas the sisters seemed to want and then settled in to wait.

It took too long. Hazeleigh was a mess by the time a lone cop got out of a marked car over by the main house. Zara stood firm, holding on to her sister, but it was the kind of firm that was just seconds away from breaking.

Jake watched the cop's approach. He was a middle-aged gentleman. Late forties maybe, tall with just the hint of a paunch. He wore a brown uniform and didn't seem to be any hurry.

Jake tried to keep the scowl off his face. He didn't like

cops on a good day. He knew it wasn't a *fair* feeling, but knowing and feeling were two separate things. But he immediately didn't like *this* cop and his lack of hurry.

"Zara. Hazeleigh," the deputy said, nodding at each of the women. He turned to Jake, suspicion in his eyes. "And you're one of the ranch owners?" he said with some distaste.

Mostly the town of Wilde had been friendly. But there were a few who weren't happy that Lee Hart had sold. And a few, mostly men, who put the blame for that unhappiness on the buyers' shoulders. Not the seller's.

"Jake Thompson." Jake had to beat back his desire to sneer at the man. He held out a hand instead and forced his mouth to curve. "Good to meet you. Wish it was under better circumstances."

The deputy nodded. "So, what's the problem?"

That was the thing about cops. They asked questions they knew the answers to. Hadn't he gotten a dispatch call? Didn't he *know* the problem?

Jake pointed at the hole, at just about the same time Zara did. Seemed neither of them felt like answering the question.

The cop stepped forward, peered into the hole, then stumbled back. "Holy hell," the cop said, his voice breaking. "It's…"

"Amberleigh," Zara finished for him. "Yes, Steven. Now, can we please get her out of the ground? Find out what…?" Zara's voice cracked, but she ruthlessly cleared her throat.

Jake had seen a lot of people do hard things in terrible circumstances. He'd seen acts of bravery and courage, failure and weakness. But Zara clearing her throat and saying the rest as she held on to Hazeleigh's shaking frame struck him as particularly poignant.

"We need to know what happened," she said firmly, her eyes on *Steven* the cop. "Where's Thomas?"

"This isn't his sector, Zara. Hell. Just… Okay." He took a deep breath, clearly rattled. "I didn't expect…"

"Steven," Zara said, her voice sharp. "Get it together."

The cop nodded and swallowed. He pulled his radio off his chest and began to mutter into it. Jake crossed to Zara and Hazeleigh. "Go home. I'll handle this."

"We should be here with her," Zara said, looking at the hole in the ground. They couldn't see the face from here, but Jake knew from experience Zara would see it in her mind's eye, probably forever.

Jake blew out a breath and put his hand on Zara's shoulder. A strong shoulder, but this was too much for anyone. "You can't do anything for her now except take care of yourselves." He nodded toward Hazeleigh.

Zara looked at her sister. A pale, shaking mess. She exhaled and nodded, care for her sister overriding the need to stay here and be strong.

"Come on, Haze," she said. "We should go home. We can't do anything here."

"I knew it was bad, Zara. I knew it was bad."

"I know. You were right," Zara said, turning Hazeleigh around, and they began to walk toward their cabin, horse forgotten. That was fine. Jake would take care of it.

He probably shouldn't. His job here, all six of their jobs here was to lay low. Avoid attention. Blend in.

A dead body on their property wasn't going to do that. Especially if he *handled* things for Zara and Hazeleigh.

"Jake?" Zara said, looking over her shoulder.

"Yeah?"

She gave him a firm nod. "Thanks," she said and then looked away, walking with Hazeleigh toward their cabin.

Yeah, he'd find a way to take care of it. That's all there was to it.

Chapter Two

Zara's head pounded after the phone call to her father. He'd refused to believe her, and she could hardly blame him for that. The police would verify the body tomorrow, and maybe that would convince him. Or maybe time would sink the truth into him. He needed time.

Zara didn't. Zara knew her own dead face looking up at her meant Amberleigh was dead, and there was no getting away from that.

But the part she couldn't work out, the part that didn't make sense, was Amberleigh being buried *here*. And if she looked just like Zara's reflection in the mirror and Hazeleigh's face when she wasn't drawn and pale, it meant she hadn't died when she'd run away at sixteen.

She'd died recently. And *here*.

It was something that sat in Zara's mind like an immovable stone. She ate supper with Hazeleigh in mutual silence, and then, when no one from the sheriff's department called or came by, they went to bed.

Zara didn't sleep and, based on the dark circles under Hazeleigh's eyes the next morning, she didn't think her sister had either.

"I've got to go check on the guys and make sure they did the chores," Zara said, feeling a mix of guilt and relief she had something to do. Somewhere to go. The cabin was too stuffy. Hazeleigh's grief was too…

Hazeleigh nodded vaguely. She had a mug in front of her but had never poured anything into it. Still she stared like it had all the answers. The little Christmas tree Hazeleigh had put in the middle of the kitchen table when she'd decorated for Christmas the day after Thanksgiving felt cheerful and so damn out of place.

"Haze…"

Hazeleigh shook her head, eyes filling with tears. "Why didn't I have a feeling before she was dead?"

Zara reached over and took Hazeleigh's hand. "It's not your fault. Honey, you put way too much stock in those feelings. Maybe you've got a sixth sense or something, but you can't save people from *murderers*. Amberleigh… She had to have been mixed-up in something."

"I saved you from that car accident."

"It was luck, Hazeleigh. Luck." Or a coincidence that Hazeleigh's desperate phone call a few years back had prompted her to pull off the road, and then yes, not be crushed by debris that had fallen onto the road in front of her seconds later. Luck, coincidence or some weird paranormal feeling, it didn't matter. She couldn't let Hazeleigh feel responsible for this.

Zara searched for the words. Comforting ones weren't easy for her, but this was so unfair. Hazeleigh couldn't control her flights of fancy, regardless of what they were, and Dad had… Dad had really done a number on her when Amberleigh had disappeared. Insisting Hazeleigh should be able to figure out where she'd gone, with her "feelings."

Just because life had been *boring* in Wilde didn't mean it wasn't without complications. Especially the family-ties kind.

"Maybe I should be the one to call Dad," Hazeleigh said, looking at her hands. "He hates me anyway."

"Dad doesn't hate you. He's a mean old jackass who

doesn't know how to process his feelings, but he doesn't *hate* you. Besides, I already called him. He didn't believe me."

Hazeleigh shook her head sadly. "He hates me. And Amberleigh's dead, so that's not going to change." By the time she got to the end of the sentence, her voice was just a squeak. "How can she be dead?"

"The cops will figure it out. They have to." Zara thought of Thomas. He was a good cop, but related to them, so he wouldn't be able to work on the case. Still, he'd be able to make sure it didn't fall through the cracks. "You know, the guys are doing pretty good on their own. I can skip chores and—"

"Don't. I know I seem fragile, and maybe I am a bit, but… I don't need to be sheltered from it." She clutched her hands into fists on the table in front of her. "I don't need a mother hen."

Zara wasn't so sure about that, but she was hardly going to argue over it. Maybe Hazeleigh needed some alone time. Zara would give it to her. For a half hour anyway. She'd just go find the guys and tell them she was taking the day off.

Normally it would kill her to ask for a day off, but she figured uncovering your dead identical-triplet's body buried on your family ranch was grounds for a day off.

She'd rather work through this strange mix of old grief— because truth be told, she'd already assumed her sister was dead or she would have come slinking back long ago—and guilt, because she *had* thought that and hadn't done anything about it.

Even knowing no one had ever been able to do a thing about Amberleigh. People thought *Zara* was stubborn, but she hadn't held a candle to her sister.

Who was dead.

Dead.

Zara closed her eyes against the heavy weight of it. It felt more real than it had when she'd simply believed it was true. More horrifying when she'd seen the evidence. She blew out a breath, gathering all her strength.

She wouldn't be emotional when she talked to the Thompson brothers. She'd be matter-of-fact. That's what this situation needed. Practicality. Sturdiness.

Hallmarks of who she was.

"Call if you need me," Zara said to Hazeleigh, shrugging on her coat and shoving her feet into her boots by the front door. She opened the door to find Thomas standing there, hand raised like he'd been about to knock. He was wearing his Bent County Sheriff's Department uniform.

That was not a good sign.

"Zara."

"Thomas. You…" She looked beyond him to a blonde woman standing there. She wasn't in a uniform, but that somehow made it worse.

"Zara, this is Detective Laurel Delaney-Carson. We've got a few questions for Hazeleigh."

Zara was about to step out of the doorway and let them in, but then what he said fully registered. She didn't move. "Why Hazeleigh?"

Thomas looked back at the detective. He didn't answer her question. "This is Zaraleigh. The other sister."

The woman smiled kindly, a mix of briskness and empathy that made Zara less inclined to hate her on sight.

"We're sorry to bother you so early, Zara. But the sooner we get started, the sooner we can find out what happened to Amberleigh."

"Why do you only want to talk to Hazeleigh? *I'm* the one who found her."

The detective pulled a notebook out of her coat pocket. "You and your employer, Jake Thompson?"

"Did I hear my name?"

Everyone on the porch slowly turned. And there he was. Striding up the yard, looking as he always did. Jeans, cowboy boots that were finally starting to look worn-in rather than brand-new. A cowboy hat that she hated to admit looked just right on him.

But this wasn't right. At all. "What are you doing here?"

"Just thought I'd bring by some breakfast," Jake said, smiling genially. As if he often…came into their cabin offering pastries, when he, in fact, *never* did. All the Thompsons gave their cabin a very wide berth.

But he was holding a white bakery bag, like he had brought breakfast. She studied his face skeptically, but his expression was all cheerful friendliness.

She didn't trust it for a minute.

"Mr. Thompson," the detective said. "I'm Detective Delaney-Carson." She held out her hand for a professional handshake. "I'm working the case about the dead body found on your property. I'll have some questions for you, but I'd like to talk to Hazeleigh Hart first. Perhaps you and Zara could wait out here with Deputy H—"

"No," Zara said, realizing with a start Jake had said the same thing in unison. She stared up at him, her eyebrows drawing together. What game was this guy playing?

JAKE WAS NO stranger to irritated females glaring at him. He'd had foster sisters once upon a time. They hadn't cared for him. He'd never been able to blame them for it, any more than he could blame Zara or the detective.

"It's procedure," Detective What's-her-names said. Firmly.

Zara opened her mouth, but Jake talked over her. Smoothly. Charmingly, if he did say so himself. "I'm sure it is, but Hazeleigh's pretty beat-up about this. Isn't she, Zara?"

"Of course. Understandably," Zara said, as if she was defending Hazeleigh to *him*. When he was trying to help.

Damn prickly woman.

"Understandably," Jake agreed gently. "She needs some support. Surely you can ask Hazeleigh your questions with Zara there to support her sister."

"I'm afraid I can't. I'll need to interview you all separately. It's absolutely necessary. I brought Thomas, though, because he's family. He can't be an active investigator on the case, but I thought a friendly face would help both of you feel more comfortable answering questions," the detective said pointedly to Zara and leaving him out of the equation.

Zara's gaze turned to this Thomas. A family member. Jake studied the tall, fair deputy. Not much of a family resemblance.

"We don't want to make this harder on any of you than it needs to be," the detective continued. "But we need to conduct an airtight investigation. So, if you two can promise to stay here, I'll take Thomas in and talk to Hazeleigh, so she'll have support."

She looked at Jake and then Zara, as if waiting for their agreement. He'd give her some credit for giving the illusion that they had any say in the matter.

Zara looked at the cop—her cousin, apparently. "I'm holding you to that, Thomas."

The cop looked a little hurt by Zara's guilt trip. "Come on, Zara. You know me."

Her frown turned into something else. Guilt or grief with a heavy dose of frustration. "Fine," she muttered.

She pushed past the cop and the detective and then him and marched her way through the front yard to a big tree that had a cracked, uneven concrete bench underneath.

Jake met the cop and detective's shrewd gazes but, in the end, decided not to say anything. He turned and followed Zara to the bench, the sound of the cops entering the cabin echoing in the quiet morning around them.

Jake stood in front of Zara. She sat, hands clenched around the edge of the bench, looking at her boots.

"Why are you here?" she asked, with just enough bitterness to make the lost look on her face less terrifying.

"We figured you'd want the day off, and your stubborn head wouldn't think to take it. I lost the coin toss to come tell you." The second half was a lie, but it suited his purposes. Keep his brothers out of it as much as he could.

She snorted. From his vantage point of looking at her bowed profile, she looked pissed and pale and exhausted but not exactly...wrecked. Like he'd maybe expected under the circumstances.

She turned that sharp brown gaze on him. "If you're looking for signs of a frantic female, you won't find it."

"I wasn't looking. I just... Your sister is dead."

Zara shrugged. "I've thought she was dead for years. It's awful to have it confirmed, but it's not exactly a shock. I didn't need...that kind of proof." She shuddered.

And didn't tell him to go away so he slid onto the bench next to her. Giving her as much space as he could on the small slab of concrete. "What's her story?"

"She ran away. When we were sixteen. Haven't heard from her since. She was..." Zara trailed off, something like a wince crossing her features. "It feels wrong to speak ill of the dead."

"Consider it giving me and my brothers the pertinent information to understand what's going on when we're inevitably all questioned."

She frowned at him. "Why would they question all of you? You were the only one with me."

"It's our land." And there'd be speculation. Investigation. When they could little afford this kind of attention.

"Ah," she said, shaking her head and giving a little laugh. "*That's* why you're here. You're worried you're going to be a suspect." She seemed to mull that over, looking at him skeptically. Then she let out a disgusted breath. "I want to think it's you. That'd be easy. But you could have kept us away from that spot. Beyond that, I saw how damn surprised you were. You thought it was me. You didn't know there was a third. Unless you're a really good actor. But that's not my place to decide. I'll tell the detective you thought it was me. You'll be in the clear because I know it wasn't you." She frowned at the cabin. "Why Hazeleigh first? *I* uncovered the body."

Like Zara, he looked back at the cabin. It was a valid question, and a concerning one. "She warned you. She didn't want you to dig there."

She shook her head. "They wouldn't know that. You were the only one who—" She jumped up, outraged. "You *told* them that."

He held up his hands and stayed seated so as not to give the impression he was fighting with her. "Zara, I answered the questions they asked when I made the call."

"You told them. You… This is all your fault. Go home, Jake. To *my* home that you stole from me, and stay the hell away from me and my family." She marched for the cabin, and no doubt she'd be in trouble for bursting in.

And no doubt he'd just screwed up his chance to make this less dramatic. To keep the attention far away from him and his brothers.

Who were really, *really* not going to be happy about the new developments.

Chapter Three

Zara stopped herself in the entry to the cabin. If she barged into the kitchen where she could hear the low tones of talking, it would complicate…everything.

But they couldn't honestly be in there with the thought *Hazeleigh* had something to do with it. She stood there, torn by indecision, breathing a little too heavily. She needed to get her temper, her anger under control before she went in there.

But that was hard for her on a good day.

After a long while, Thomas left the kitchen and saw her standing at the doorway. He smiled kindly. "Do you have time for some questions?"

She nodded.

"Hazeleigh went out back, into the garden. She said she was looking for the cat, but I think she needed some air. Some alone time."

Zara managed a nod. "Look, I can handle this questioning thing on my own. Will you stay with her?"

Thomas nodded, but he reached out and gave her shoulder a little squeeze. "She's not as fragile as you seem to think. She held up pretty well."

But "pretty well" wasn't good enough, was it? Zara stepped away from Thomas's hand and stepped into her own kitchen, feeling like a stranger. The detective had a small array of things spread out before her on the table in a neat, nearly anal fashion. Notebook, phone, two pens. All at the same angle.

The Christmas tree had been moved to the kitchen counter, and Hazeleigh's Christmas-themed mug sat in the sink as if she'd actually used it this morning.

The detective looked up at Zara and offered a kind smile. "Have a seat, Ms. Hart."

"Call me Zara," Zara muttered. It felt so formal to be called *Ms.*

"Do you want anything before we start?"

Zara shook her head. She just wanted this over with. She told herself not to be petty. They all wanted to get to the bottom of this. And the only way to do that was with clear, concise, *honest* answers.

But, oh, how she wished she could throw Jake Thompson under the bus.

The detective took a breath. "Before we start, I just want you to know, it's my job to find out the truth—regardless of what that truth is. I assume we're after the same thing, but I also know what it's like to have a sister you want to protect."

"Hazeleigh didn't kill our sister," Zara said firmly. It was the *truth.* The only truth.

"Why do you think you need to say that?" the detective asked, void of any inflection or any implication, but Zara felt them all the same.

"You interviewed her first when I was the one who uncovered the body. Well, Jake and I." She'd throw him a *little* under the bus. If only with the truth.

"I'm just here to ask questions."

Zara muttered an oath, then closed her eyes. "Sorry," she offered to the detective.

"No need to apologize. I've heard worse. Look, Zara, this is a trauma that you're going through, and it's going to have emotional responses. Especially this time of year. Emotions don't follow the rules. I'm not here to judge your emotions, *or* your sister's. I'm here to get to the bottom of the crime *and* to make sure we've built an airtight case when we do find out who did this. It's why Thomas can't be a bigger part of the investigation. It risks our credibility down the line. I won't risk anything on this case, I promise you that."

Zara frowned at the detective. She had to give the woman credit—she knew what to say to help… Zara couldn't say she felt better, but it eased some of those high-strung nerves. "Have you worked a lot of murders?"

"A lot? No. It is Bent County after all." She smiled kindly. "But this isn't my first murder case, no. So believe me when I say I need your cooperation and your honesty so we can make sure we get the person who did this and see them punished."

Zara nodded and swallowed. "Okay. How can I help?"

The detective tapped her phone. The home picture was of a smiling family. A Carson-Delaney family. Because she was one of the ones Bent had made such a stink about a few years back, because the Carsons and Delaneys were supposed to hate each other. A modern-day Hatfield and McCoy situation.

Apparently, now the enemies had two cute kids.

The detective swiped the picture away and brought up a recorder of some kind. "I'm going to take notes and record the conversation." She noted the date and time and Zara's full name, to Zara's distaste, and then looked up at Zara. Her gaze was frank but not unkind. "Let's start with how you found the body."

Zara went through the whole thing. She was honest, even when it came to Hazeleigh. The detective really made her feel like…well, like if she told the truth everything would be okay. The whole truth.

"She has these feelings," Zara said, unable to stop herself from wincing at the word. "She always has." Zara looked up at the detective imploringly. "She once saved me from a car accident. I know that sounds crazy, but she *does* get these feelings sometimes. Hazeleigh wouldn't hurt a fly. She wouldn't know *how*."

The detective smiled, and it was kind but…guarded. "It's good to have that kind of impression of your sister. And, I hope you understand that I'm not trying to be dismissive when I say feelings aren't evidence."

Zara sighed. No, she couldn't blame the detective for that.

"That's all I need from you and Hazeleigh today. Likely we'll have follow-up questions, either in person or by phone. We'll continue to interview those involved. Jake Thompson. The first officer on the scene. We'll wait for the coroner's report to give us an idea of when she died and other details that will help us come up with a timeline and some suspects." The detective began to pack up her items in a small bag. When she was finished, she held out a hand to Zara.

Zara shook it, a heavy weight in her stomach, but the detective held on. Gave her hand a squeeze.

"I will do everything in my power to find your sister's killer."

Zara managed a smile. "Thank you."

The detective dropped her hand, looked at the door in the kitchen, presumably the one Hazeleigh went out of. "Thomas was right when he told you she held up well." Her eyes returned to Zara's, frank and assessing. "But she's hiding something. I'd encourage her to tell me. Sooner rather than later."

Zara could only frown at the detective's retreating back.

Hazeleigh wasn't hiding anything. They didn't have secrets.

But that heavy weight didn't move, and for the first time in a very long time, Zara didn't know where to turn.

"You understand that this is a disaster, right?"

Jake lounged on the couch in the living room of the creaky old ranch house that was almost starting to feel like home. Not that Jake was well versed in what *homes* felt like, but if he thought back to his childhood dreaming of what one might be like, it would be a lot like this.

Spacious. Old. Newer little additions added on over the years in weird angles and uneven transitions between rooms.

It wasn't perfect or shiny or boring. So, yeah, he'd grown fond of the place.

But that didn't mean he'd found anything *easy* about the transition. Especially when Cal stood before him, legs spread, hands clasped behind his back, disapproving frown on his face.

Like they were back in training.

A dichotomy to that *homey* feel.

"Jake," Cal barked.

Jake sighed. Six weeks into their supposed new lives and Cal still acted like the commanding officer he wasn't supposed to be anymore.

"I didn't kill her and bury her on our property, so I don't see why you're lecturing me about it," Jake replied. He forced himself to remain relaxed, because they *weren't* in the military together anymore and he did not have to stand at attention to Cal or anyone else.

Truth be told, Jake was warming up to civilian life pretty quick. Cal…not so much.

"I guess you don't recall our mission when we were assigned here."

Jake shook his head, careful to keep his voice even instead of frustrated, because Cal thrived on frustration and dissent—in that, he thrived on stamping it out. It made him a hell of a commander.

Not such a great characteristic for a "brother."

"We're not on a *mission*, Cal. We're not on *assignment*. We've been hidden away. Stripped of all our ranks, responsibilities and connections. This is just supposed to be…life."

Cal's mouth firmed. He didn't like that reminder. That he wasn't in charge. That he didn't have a goal to accomplish other than fly under the radar.

Cal wasn't ready for all this *non*military life.

Jake might have felt sorry for him if he wasn't so worried. "Did you tell the boss?" he asked, infusing his voice and body with a casualness that was very much an act.

The boss. Major General Wilks, though they usually just referred to him as *the boss*, was their one and only connection to the old life. The life they'd had to leave because they were all marked men. Doomed to die if they didn't disappear.

So they'd come to the most out-of-the-way, boring place the boss could secure.

And somehow they'd stumbled upon a dead body. Not exactly the quiet life they were looking for.

Would the military make them move again? Erase these identities too? Start all over. *Again.* The idea made Jake… uncomfortable. At best.

"No, I haven't told him. Ideally, this all gets figured out in a few days and he's none the wiser, or doesn't know until the case is put to bed and we're squarely out of the spotlight." Cal didn't rake his hands through his hair or pace his frustration away. He stood there, military straight, completely immobile.

But Jake had been with Cal long enough to know that he *wanted* to do all those things. Would he ever let go and actually…let himself be normal again? With a little pang, Jake kind of doubted it.

"Look, maybe the cops ask a few questions, but whoever buried that body…" Jake suppressed a shudder at Zara's face in the dirt, unseeing and lifeless.

Amberleigh Hart. Not Zara. Hard to remember, even when there were two replicas of that same face walking around, that it wasn't Zara's body they'd found in the ground.

"Whoever did all this did it before we owned the land. They're not going to be looking at us too hard. It just doesn't make sen—"

His words were cut off by a firm, no-nonsense knock on the door. A *cop* knock. Cal gave Jake an eyebrows-raised look. One that clearly said "told you so."

Cal walked to the front door and opened it to the blonde detective. She studied Cal, sized him up quickly. Her smile was polite if distant. "Hello, I need to speak with Jake Thompson."

"And you are?"

"Detective Delaney-Carson. I just have a few questions for Mr. Thompson. To be asked of him. Alone," she said pointedly.

"Is he a suspect?" Cal demanded, point-blank.

The woman didn't flinch or bat an eye. She met Cal's glare with a bland one. "Everyone's a suspect right now. And you are?"

Cal's face went carefully blank, and no matter how smart this detective was, Jake was pretty sure he was the only one in the room who knew how much energy Cal was putting into that blankness.

"Cal Thompson."

The detective nodded. "One of the brothers." She turned her attention to Jake, behind Cal. "Is there somewhere we can speak alone?"

Jake nodded in assent, and with obvious reluctance, Cal stepped aside and let her enter. Jake jerked his chin toward the kitchen. "Follow me."

He led her into the small old kitchen and gestured for her to take a seat at the table Jake thought might be from the 1800s, it was so old and scarred. "Can I get you anything to drink?"

"No, this should be quick enough." She set her bag down on the kitchen table, pulled out a phone and a notebook. "No Christmas decorations?" she asked casually as she took a seat in a kitchen.

"Still in storage," Jake returned with the easy lie.

She didn't react. "I just need you to run through what you saw and did yesterday."

"To see if my story matches everyone else's?" he asked, standing.

She looked up at him with sharp brown eyes. She might be a little thing, but she wasn't a pushover. "To do my job, Mr. Thompson."

Jake sighed. "Call me Jake," he muttered. "I already ran through this when I called in what we found."

She nodded. "You did. Let's run through it again." She clicked a button on her phone, noted the date and time, and then asked him questions. She didn't ask him to sit. She didn't fill in any blanks. She just asked question after question.

And she didn't lie. It was quick. After he went through the ten minutes or so he'd been involved, the detective turned off the recording, closed her notebook and then studied him. Carefully. "Zara said that Hazeleigh gets these… feelings. Like premonitions," she said at very long length.

When the detective didn't ask a question after that statement, Jake shrugged. "Okay."

"You haven't had any experience with these…feelings?"

"Hazeleigh lives in that cabin with her sister, and that's the extent of what I know about her. I work with Zara on the day-to-day, but that doesn't exactly make us close. We've only been here six weeks. And you likely know Zara enough to know she didn't relish her father selling the ranch to us."

She nodded, then smiled and got to her feet. "Thank you for your time, Mr. Thompson."

"I'll walk you out," he said, feeling oddly…unsettled. Like that hadn't gone the way it should have. The feeling only intensified when they walked into the living room and Cal was still standing there, arms crossed.

The detective followed Jake to the door, pausing her exit as Jake held it open.

"It'd help a lot if you stay put for the time being. No trips or leaving the county without letting us know." She shrugged. "As a precaution." She turned to survey Cal. "That goes for all six of you, actually." Then she left.

The silence she left behind was…*heavy.*

A dull pounding started at the base of Jake's skull. He wasn't a suspect. Not seriously. *They* weren't, but they weren't exactly out of the woods and…they couldn't afford that kind of scrutiny.

"We're screwed," Cal said flatly. "I'm calling the boss."

"No. We're not." Jake looked at Cal. It was hard on a good day to talk Cal out of something, but this… He didn't want to be uprooted again. They'd worked this ranch for a month and Jake had let himself get…settled.

He wouldn't leave. Not on the damn boss's whim. For once *he* was going to have a say on where he went, where he *stayed*. He was too damn old to keep having someone else yank the strings of his life. "You like it here, don't you?"

Cal shook his head grimly. "It's not our call."

Which was as close to a yes as Cal was ever going to get. "But it could be our call." Jake wanted to reach out and shake Cal, but he kept his hands at his sides. "All we have to do is figure out who did this so it's all over before the boss gets wind."

"You're not a cop," Cal said, but there was just enough give in his voice Jake figured he was getting somewhere.

Jake grinned. "No, even better. I'm a soldier."

Chapter Four

When two uniformed cops returned to their cabin the next morning with a *search warrant*, Zara knew things were bad.

When they left the house with some of Hazeleigh's personal items, she knew things were catastrophic.

Hazeleigh's silent, unemotional accepting of it all was… beyond disconcerting. It scared Zara down to her bones. Hazeleigh was *always* emotional. About everything—kittens, Hallmark movies, the perfect piece of fudge.

But not the fact police had *seized* her belongings.

"I think I'll go in to work," Hazeleigh said, still sitting at the kitchen table staring at the door the cops had gone out of not fifteen minutes before. Christmas lights twinkled around the frame. "I'm falling behind and Mr. Field thinks he's *this* close to a breakthrough."

Hazeleigh worked as a research assistant for an eccentric old man who was determined to find out what had happened to the alleged gold stolen from the bank robbery back in 1892. A fool's errand, in Zara's estimation, but Hazeleigh liked losing herself in old newspapers and mysteries, and the crazy old man paid well.

"Mr. Field always thinks he's *this* close to a breakthrough," Zara replied.

Hazeleigh smiled faintly.

Zara wanted to shake her, but she was afraid Hazeleigh

would break apart. Dissolve. Or wind up buried in the ground just like Amberleigh.

"Is there something you're not telling me?" Zara asked, holding on so tight to the counter behind her she would no doubt have a hand cramp.

Hazeleigh's eyes widened. It might have been funny, the attempt at innocence, if innocence weren't absolutely imperative here.

"Haze."

Hazeleigh smiled. "Don't worry so much, Zara. Everything is fine. I hardly killed Amberleigh."

"I hardly think you did. But I don't like the thought that you're keeping things from me. That you're not taking this seriously."

Hazeleigh opened her mouth to respond, but the creak of a door and their father's gravelly voice calling out a greeting had them both flinching.

Hazeleigh jumped to her feet. "I'll just leave out the back."

"Hazeleigh."

She shook her head, grabbing her bag from where it hung off the back of her chair. "He won't want to see me, or if he does, it's only to be mean."

Zara couldn't argue with that, so she let Hazeleigh scurry out the back door. She huffed out a breath and held herself very still as her father entered the kitchen.

She forced a small, fake smile. "Dad, what are you doing here so early?"

He looked around the kitchen. The years had dug the lines into his face, the cigarettes he refused to give up had hewed his body down to a shade too skinny. Or maybe that was all the grief he held at arm's length. Or was it the alcoholism they all refused to acknowledge?

"Just you?" he asked.

"Hazeleigh went to work, which is where I need to be headed." But she didn't make a move to leave.

"I don't know how you live here with her. After yesterday, how you'd share a roof with her."

"Dad—"

"She could have found her all this time, and now Amberleigh is dead."

"She couldn't find her," Zara said firmly. Maybe Hazeleigh was uncharacteristically keeping something from her, but she hadn't been able to reach Amberleigh. Even if she could have reached their sister, what were the chances Amberleigh would have come home?

"I don't believe that."

"*I* do." Zara pinched the bridge of her nose. She'd always had to be the responsible one. Dad and Amberleigh fighting. Dad being too hard on Hazeleigh. And always Zara herself stepping in and getting things *accomplished*.

But she didn't know how to accomplish this, and it scared her more than anything. "We need to make arrangements." She wouldn't argue with him about Hazeleigh. It wasn't worth it. They had to focus on practicalities. "The detective said they won't be able to release the body for a few days yet, but we need to make arrangements."

"My daughter is dead."

My sister is dead. But she didn't say it. "Do you want me to handle things?"

He gave a curt nod. "All these people calling me. I don't want it. I can't even walk through town without someone saying something to me."

They're called condolences. It's called care. The town wants to grieve with you.

They'd walked down this road before. When Mom had died. Even then, Zara had spared his feelings. Taken on the responsibilities.

She'd been eight.

"I'll take care of it." It was what she could do, so she'd do it.

He looked around the cabin. "Don't know how you can live here. Work here."

"What other choice did I have?" Dad hadn't exactly offered to split the money he got for the sale.

"Keep the old ladies off my doorstep, huh?"

I love you too. This hurts too much. I don't know what to do. But she said nothing. After all, she'd had eighteen years to learn sentimentality wouldn't get her anywhere. "Dad?"

He looked back, and honestly, nothing had changed. Dad had been this way since Mom died, and Zara had stepped up to take up the slack. Why would Amberleigh's murder be any different?

But what she wouldn't do for a hug and a promise things would be okay.

"If you can't be nice to Hazeleigh, there's no point in you coming all the way out. Just call me if you need something."

He nodded. Unhurt. *People have to care about something besides themselves to be hurt.* "All right." He nodded and walked out. No goodbye. No comforting words. Just what he needed Zara to do.

So, she'd do it. All it would take was one call to Mrs. Vickers. She'd explain that Dad preferred their offers of grief to come through her. Mrs. Vickers would spread it around—the quilting club, the convenience store, the bank. Everyone would know.

And they wouldn't bring casseroles. They wouldn't ask if she needed any help. Zara Hart didn't need those things.

But she'd give Wildeans credit for one thing. They'd give her something her father hadn't.

A kind word. Maybe a hug.

As for everything else? Zara would take care of it the way she always did.

WHEN JAKE FINALLY found Zara that morning, she was in the horse stable, saddling up her horse like she was just… going to work today.

"I hope you know you don't have to do that."

She didn't look back at him as she fastened the saddle into place. "Do what? Saddle my horse? Kind of a requirement for riding her."

He didn't miss the way she said *my*. A not-so-subtle reminder she belonged here. And maybe a little dig that he didn't.

But he'd let it go because God know she was hurting. "Still mad at me?"

She let out a gusty sigh, and for a second, her shoulders slumped as if the weight of anger was just too much to bear. Then she straightened her shoulders and shook her head, staring at the horse's flank. "I couldn't lie to the detective. How can I expect you to?"

Which wasn't a no, exactly, but he'd take it.

Zara pushed past him and pulled her horse outside. Jake followed along, trying to work out how he was going to approach this. He needed to know what Zara and Hazeleigh had talked to the cops about, where the detective was leaning. He could approach Hazeleigh, but she could be skittish.

Zara seemed infinitely capable of…everything. Questions, certainly. But would the prickly woman offer him any information? Well, all he could do was try. "Landon said the cops were here. Early." He said it casually. As if he wasn't fishing for information.

Zara nodded in confirmation. "You gonna work today or just repeat what everyone already knows?"

He'd planned on focusing on the case rather than ranch work—there were five other people to take up the slack, but Zara was part of the case, wasn't she? "Sure, just let me get *my* horse."

She muttered something that sounded suspiciously like

"your horse my ass." But she waited, and when he led his own horse outside, she was sitting in the saddle. Her gaze was on the jagged mountains in the far distance, an odd yearning on her face that had something tightening in his gut.

He wasn't *blind*. He'd noticed she was attractive before. And she was different from her sister. Hazeleigh was pretty but skittish. Fragile.

Zara was strong and unafraid and… He studied her profile for a second as he settled himself in the saddle.

Today? None of her usual…vitality. She looked tired. Weighed down by the truly horrible situation she found herself in.

"You really don't have to work today," Jake said, trying to find some balance between gentle, which would put her back up, and dismissive, which might hurt her feelings. Not that she'd ever show it. "This is the kind of thing people take personal time for. Grievance time. You'd still be paid."

She squinted out over the rolling hills, the endless white of a snow-covered landscape, the blue sky, the puffy white clouds. All the way to those imposing mountains that had stood the test of time in a way Jake, who'd been born and bred in Pittsburgh, wasn't sure he'd ever understand. Or not be in awe of.

It was a bucolic picture. But more than that for her, no doubt. A home and legacy. Which were things he didn't know anything about—except that as a foster kid who'd never belonged anywhere but in the military, he envied that she had anything like it.

"This is my grievance time," she said, and the delivery was unemotional and quiet, but it landed with the effect of a sob. Something sharp and jagged twisted in his chest.

When she nudged her horse into a trot, he followed, saying nothing. But he was using the skills *she'd* taught him to ride the horse, and it felt like…something.

He'd never even had a dog. Animals were as foreign to him as *home*, but he liked the strange partnership between beast and man. The way the horse was a tool, but also a living, breathing thing, and they had to work together to get from one place to another.

He followed her, trusting where she'd lead and the speed she set their horses on. They rode for a while, the cold wind whipping at their faces. It wasn't a half-bad way to spend a morning, all in all. Something that shocked Jake just about every day he woke up here happy to start the day.

When she pulled her horse to a stop on the slope of a hill with a strange rock tower at the top rising out of the snow, Jake was no closer to knowing what they were doing. And when she just sat on her horse looking out at the land around them, he wondered if even she knew.

It was early enough that the moon was still a white ball, incongruous to the day sky. Zara stared at it like it might hand her an answer or two.

Jake didn't know how long they sat there. He'd waited in enough silences to know not to count the seconds. To simply find something to focus on, think about. To keep his eyes and ears open and wait without expectation.

A strand of hair had escaped her braid and danced in the wind and that was what he focused on while he waited.

Eventually, she blew out a breath, that stoic gaze faltering for a second. "They seized some of Hazeleigh's things."

He frowned over that information. "They have a warrant?"

She nodded. No matter how hard she worked to look unaffected, worry was in the set of her eyebrows. The purse of her lips.

Jake felt like he had to ask. "Is it possible…?"

Zara stiffened, scowled at him as she adjusted her grip on her reins. "Not even remotely."

Jake nodded, holding her accusing stare. "Who would want to hurt your sister? Either sister?"

She blinked. Then frowned down at her hands. "The detective asked me that, but Amberleigh wasn't here. I haven't seen or heard from her since we were sixteen. So how would I know on that score? And Hazeleigh? Everyone loves her."

He let silence settle in as she sat there and breathed, making no move to do any kind of work.

"They're not very forthcoming, are they?" he said, again working a casualness he didn't feel into the question. "All questions. No answers."

She finally turned her head to look at him. "Did they ask you questions?"

"A few. And gave me a warning not to go anywhere."

Her eyebrows rose. "Are you a suspect?"

"I believe the detective's exact words were everyone is."

Zara frowned over that. "Hazeleigh shouldn't be. And they don't treat me like one. Thomas says the detective is great, but... Why are they taking things of Hazeleigh's? Why are they focusing on her? She's as likely to kill someone as... I don't know, Mother Teresa."

"So why do you look so worried?"

"That detective? She said Hazeleigh is keeping something from her."

"Is she?"

Zara stared at him, as if deciding why they were having this conversation. She chewed on her bottom lip, which drew his gaze to her mouth. Which was *not* acceptable, so he looked out at the mountains again.

In the end, she didn't answer his question or keep talking about the case, like he'd hoped. She changed the subject.

"I might need to take the afternoon off. I'm handling all the funeral arrangements. I just had to...do something this morning. Get out here. Breathe."

"If you need any help with anything, let me know."

"Help?"

"Sure. It can't be easy to make those kinds of arrangements. I can make a phone call or pick up flowers or whatever funerals entail. To lighten the load."

"Lighten the load," she echoed, staring at him like he'd slapped her, all the while speaking a foreign language.

"Yeah. It's called being friendly. Or maybe around here you call it being neighborly. I'm sure you've got family, neighbors, friends. But we're right here, so if you need something, you only have to ask."

She just kept staring at him, eyes wide and arrested. Like he'd just admitted to murdering and burying her sister.

Then she did the most incomprehensible thing he'd ever seen.

She started sobbing.

Chapter Five

Zara couldn't say it was the worst moment of her life. She'd seen her sister dead beneath the earth. She'd witnessed her mother's slow, agonizing death from cancer when she'd been a child. There had been a lot of bad days, so this didn't rank.

But never had she burst into tears in front of…anyone. Especially a virtual stranger.

When has anyone ever offered to lighten the load?

Not in a very long time. She gave the reins a tug and turned Sam around, then urged him into a run. Back to the stables. Away from Jake.

It was a temporary escape. Jake would follow her, and knowing his type, would poke and prod until she explained her little outburst.

Quite frankly, she knew embarrassment was silly. He'd say what he kept saying. Her sister had died. She deserved some time off. Some time to grieve. Crying wasn't beyond the pale. Apparently that's what normal people did.

Zara didn't know how to be normal. And she didn't know how to deal with someone like Jake. Everyone in her life had pretty much always been there. Wilde didn't change, which meant *she* didn't change. At least in the eyes of the people who knew her.

But Jake didn't look at her quite the same way everyone else did. None of those Thompson brothers did.

So why are you focusing on Jake?

She reached the stables. She didn't have the time or energy to think about Jake. She swung off the horse. Unfortunately she couldn't just bolt because she had to take care of Sam.

The wind had dried most of her tears. No doubt she looked a little worse for the wear, but she'd be fine once Jake caught up. She'd shrug it off and move on with her day.

Far away from *him*.

She started to unsaddle Sam. She didn't get very far before Jake appeared and swung off his horse.

There was a natural grace in the movement, like he'd been doing it his whole life, even though she knew he hadn't been. God knows he'd been awkward and stiff when she'd first started teaching the brothers how to ride a horse. But Jake and Landon had taken to the horses easily and quicker than the other three who could ride.

Jake even wore the cowboy hat like he'd been born on a ranch, not raised in the city. Like he was a pro at changing himself into whatever he needed to be.

She frowned at him.

"Stop scowling at me. I didn't mean to make you cry."

"That's not why I'm frowning at you," she muttered, turning her attention back to her horse. "And *you* didn't make me cry. I was just…overwhelmed."

"Clearly."

"It's kind of you—" it sounded like an accusation, even to her own ears. She tried to soften her words "—to offer to help. It caught me off guard."

"You don't have to explain it away. I fully expect anyone to have a few crying jags while going through what you're going through."

Anyone. Not any *woman*. Well, he knew how to step carefully, didn't he?

But she realized this was all about…her issues. Because she'd been waiting for the censure she was used to. The rolled eyes and heavy sighs that her father would have given her.

Toughen up, Zara. One of you has to.

"I don't know why kindness would catch you off guard. Aren't small-town folk used to rallying around when the going gets tough, with all types of kindness?"

"Wilde does rally," Zara said, insulted on her small town's behalf. They did. It was just different for her. She was the strong one. "But you're not Wilde. You're just some guy who bought my..." She'd been about to say "legacy" in the snottiest way she could, but that hardly repaid his kindness. "...family's ranch."

"In spite of that, you've taught us how to do all this." He spread his arm around to encompass the whole ranch even though they were inside the stables.

"Sure, but you're pay—"

"Yes, I know we've paid you for it and well, but you are a good teacher," he said, sounding impatient and firm. "To six men who hadn't had to be *taught* anything in a long time. To six men who bought your birthright out from under you, without your say in the matter. You were hard on us, but fair. You didn't *have* to be. You even handled Dunne's silences and Landon's endless jokes. What I'm trying to say, Zara, is we appreciate what you did for us, and continue to do. If we can help you, we will. We're...friends."

Friends.

God, she could use a friend. One who offered to *do* things. Even if she'd never take him up on it, the idea that he might pick up a flower arrangement or make a call was...

Flattening.

Zara did not want to be flattened.

"I don't know what to say to that," she muttered, closing Sam's stable door and stepping away from the man standing too close as he did the same.

He studied her, those blue eyes a distraction all on their own. Then add the cowboy hat and stubborn jaw and dark stubble…

He smiled, and it was kind, but there was something more than kind that lurked in his eyes. She didn't want to know what it was.

"You say thanks. That's it."

She shifted on her feet, wholly nonplussed by the effect he had on her. "Fine. Thanks."

He chuckled, slapped her on the shoulder like they were *buddies*. Yes, she was quite used to *that* treatment from men.

But then his hand stayed there, gave her shoulder a little squeeze. She assumed that was the sort of sorry-your-sister-died-and-we-found-the-body gesture a man like Jake made.

But his hand…lingered. And Zara didn't have the first rightly clue what to do with *that*, and when she heard footsteps approaching, she only knew she had to step away from his hand.

When Thomas appeared in the stable entrance, she was glad she had.

"Sorry to interrupt," Thomas said, studying Jake with some suspicion. A suspicion Zara found she didn't care for.

But that was silly.

"We just need to go over the…site again. You guys can keep working. I'll act as go-between if we need anything else. I just wanted to let you know a few county guys would be out and about."

"Thanks," Zara said in unison with Jake. Because he was the property owner. Not her. It didn't just feel unfair in the moment. It felt wrong. Amberleigh pulled from the dirt—Hart dirt—but it wasn't even theirs anymore.

"I have to go to town. Talk to the Thompsons if you

need anything," she said, desperately working to keep the tears out of her voice.

She'd cried enough. Now it was time to get something accomplished.

ZARA SCURRIED OUT of the stables, leaving Jake standing there under the narrowed gaze of her cousin. Thomas Hart wasn't wearing his uniform this morning. He was dressed in jeans and a sweatshirt, a ball cap pulled low on his head.

Jake tried to push away his distaste for cops, because this was Zara's cousin, and he was clearly here not in any official capacity but in an attempt to make things easier for his cousins. Jake couldn't be hard on that.

Not when Zara had fallen apart at the smallest offer of help. Like no one ever reached out and did anything for her.

He rocked back on his heels when Thomas didn't disappear. "No autopsy reports yet?"

"No."

And, well, since he had a cop here, why not ask? "Any timeline on that?"

"Why? Worried you'll need to disappear?"

"I don't have anything to hide," Jake said, making his smile wide and maybe a little sarcastic. Especially since it was a lie. He had plenty to hide. Just none of it had to do with the dead woman on his property.

"Neither of those girls had any trouble before you and your brothers showed up."

Jake kept his voice mild, though his temper stirred. "Zara said she hadn't seen her sister since she was sixteen and ran away. Sounds like trouble enough."

Thomas didn't have a quick rejoinder for that.

"Look, you can keep trying to tie me to this, but I didn't know any of those women before I, along with my brothers, bought the place from their old man. We handled everything through brokers."

"And isn't that fishy?"

"Not where I'm from."

"Well, it is here. And that does bring up a pretty interesting question. Just where *are* you from? Because you and your brothers don't seem to be from anywhere."

"You really think I killed this girl I don't know anything about, buried her on my own property, then dug her up in front of her sisters?" Never let it be said that Jake didn't know how to sidestep a question he didn't intend to answer. Ever.

Thomas sighed, much like Zara had not that long ago. A slow sagging of the shoulders, regret, followed by shoring it all back up. "No, I don't really think that, but, boy, would it make my life a hell of a lot easier."

For the first time, Jake felt a glimmer of kindness toward the man. At least he could admit when he was wrong, much like Zara often did. "I can see the family resemblance. Zara can't lie either. The truth comes out in the same frustrated fashion."

Thomas slowly turned and fixed Jake with a speculative stare. "Just what kind of relationship do you have with my cousin?" He crossed his arms over his chest.

Jake tried not to scowl. So instead he half smiled. Maybe a little meanly. "Which one?"

Thomas sighed and looked up at the ceiling, filled with frustration and exhaustion. A look Jake remembered on quite a few foster parents' faces.

Too much work, this one.

But this was hardly about *him*.

"Look. Consider this a friendly warning. Zara isn't half as strong as she pretends to be. And Hazeleigh isn't half as weak as she pretends to be. Neither of them are as alone or defenseless as they might appear. So watch your step."

"They don't need defenses. Zara's been good to us when she didn't have any reason to be beyond a paycheck. I only want to repay her for that."

"Then stay out of the way of this investigation."

Jake kept his mouth firmly shut, because he wasn't so sure that was something he could do.

Thomas's phone rang and he frowned at the screen, immediately lifting it to his face. "What's up?" he answered.

He turned away from Jake quickly, but not before Jake saw the color in his face drain away. "You can't…" He took long strides out of the stables, but Jake followed. Silently, carefully. So Thomas wouldn't know he was within eavesdropping distance.

"Laurel," Thomas said. "Hazeleigh didn't kill anyone. I don't care what the evidence says."

Damn. They were going to arrest Hazeleigh. It would kill Zara. He glanced to where she'd gone. Her truck was still parked in front of the cabin, so she hadn't taken off yet. He'd need to stop her.

But he wanted to hear what else Thomas had to say.

"I know it's a conflict of interest if I arrest her, but I have to be there. She didn't do this. Surely we can put it—"

Thomas didn't speak, he just listened to whatever the detective said and then hung up.

Jake figured there was no point in pretending he didn't know what was going on. "Want me to go get Zara before she takes off?"

Thomas blew out a breath as he turned, somewhat incredulous that Jake was standing there. He looked like he was about to read Jake the riot act, then just slumped. "It'd be better coming from family."

"Nah, she's likely to kill the messenger." Bad choice of words. "She can punch me and not feel guilty about it later. You'll need to be with Hazeleigh, I suspect."

Thomas swore. "This is a mess," he muttered. "All right,

I'm going to meet the arresting cops over at Hazeleigh's work. Do everything you can to keep Zara here and not rushing down to the station. She'll only make matters worse. I'll call with lawyers I can recommend. Keep her here until I do."

"Got it."

"I sure hope you're her friend, Thompson. Because she's going to need one."

Chapter Six

Zara sat down at the kitchen table and made herself a list. They were almost out of milk. She supposed she needed to speak to the pastor at church. She didn't know how to plan a funeral, and she supposed she couldn't, really, until the body was released.

Body. Amberleigh.

She closed her eyes. Just for a second. Just to center herself. Find that well of strength she'd been building since she was a little girl. Because when there was no one else to be strong, it had to be her.

I can make a phone call or pick up flowers or whatever funerals entail. To lighten the load.

Jake had said that so sincerely. So offhandedly. As if it was just what people did. And maybe in his world that was the case. Zara wasn't sure she wanted to be part of that world. If she didn't handle everything, wouldn't that foundation of strength just dissolve away? Wouldn't she endlessly be leaning on people who would inevitably die, disappear, withdraw?

She stared at the little scrap of paper where she'd written *milk* and *church*.

Milk and *church*.

Suddenly those words didn't make any sense. A knock on her door even less sense, but it gave her something to do. She grabbed her keys and her phone. Whoever it was, she'd tell them she was on her way out.

Because she was. She had things to do.

She opened the front door and frowned at Jake standing there. "Are you following me around?" she asked, feeling... tired. Just completely exhausted by this constant parade of people.

"Actually, Thomas asked me to bring you some news."

She wanted to shut the door in his face. She didn't want news. She didn't want *Jake* to deliver it. "Why didn't he tell me himself?"

"He had to go... Listen, they're going to arrest Hazeleigh. He wanted to be there."

She appreciated the bluntness of it. Just rip off the bandage. Land the blow.

Arrest.

She laughed. The sound bubbled up and out of her. It was *insanity.*

Jake's eyebrows furrowed. "That wasn't a joke, Zara."

She shook her head. "No. Not at all." The laughter slowly morphed into something else. Something closer to panic and hysteria and she wasn't sure she could *breathe.* But if they were going to arrest Hazeleigh...

"I have to get to the fort. I have to be with her. Maybe I can—"

Jake stepped inside her cabin. *Her* cabin, blocking her way.

"Thomas asked me to keep you here," he said very seriously. All tall and imposing body, blocking her door. *Her door.*

She looked at him. It wasn't shock that rocked through her. That was too simple. It was a mix of everything. The grief. The fury. The surprise. The horror. It all rose up, tied together and turned into a blinding rage that had no target.

So, she made him one. She swung and he narrowly

grabbed her fist before it connected with his face. "Nice," he said, as if he was actually impressed.

"I *have* to get to Hazeleigh," she said between clenched teeth, trying to find her center of calm. That place inside her that always solved the problems, took control. Then she realized he was still holding her clenched fist.

She wrenched her hand out of his grasp. Her breath was coming in gasps and she supposed she should be grateful he'd stopped her before she could actually break his nose. It wasn't his fault… It wasn't…

She took two full steps back from him, lingering just a shade too close, like he'd physically stop her from leaving…or hug her if she fell apart again.

No, she wasn't going to fall apart. Couldn't let herself. Not again.

"I can't let her be alone."

"Thomas is going to be there. He said he'll call with a list of lawyers. Your cousin is going to look out for her."

"But she…" Zara swallowed. "You don't understand. Hazeleigh…" She couldn't say it. Couldn't tell him that her sister simply couldn't *handle* this.

"I've got something to show you."

"Jake—"

"Just follow me. Let me show you something, and then I'll drive you down to wherever they're holding Hazeleigh. Interfering isn't going to help. Don't you think Thomas knows what he's talking about?"

She tried to focus her scattered thinking. What was best for Hazeleigh? That's what she had to think about.

Not being arrested.

Could she beat the cops to Hazeleigh? Could she call and warn Hazeleigh? She knew Thomas would do what was best and right—within the *law*. But Zara didn't really care about the law when it came to her fragile, skittish sister. Ever since her last boyfriend had done a number on her, men in general had made her more uncomfortable than even her usual shy demeanor.

She jerked her chin to the door, a nonverbal sign she would follow him. Even though she had no plans to. He stepped outside and she locked up her cabin—something she wouldn't normally do, but with police crawling around happily arresting Hazeleigh, it seemed pretty imperative.

Jake started walking for the big house. Zara eyed her truck. How much space between them would she need?

"I wouldn't," he said blandly without even looking back at her.

Zara stopped where she was, keys clutched in her hand. "Or what?"

He turned and smiled at her, a little wolfishly. It felt a bit like they were in a Wild West standoff, ten paces apart, waiting to draw their weapons.

"I told Thomas I'd keep you here, so I intend to do it. I'd be honor bound to stop you from getting in your truck."

She narrowed her eyes, studied him, trying to figure out how she could metaphorically outdraw him. He was a big guy, but she'd seen him move around the past month. He could be quick when he wanted to be. He'd be stronger than her—that was just fact. She was sure she could get past him if she had the time to figure out *how*. But she didn't.

And there was something about the way he said "honor bound" that made her reluctant to test him—when she was usually happy to test anyone. Anywhere.

"Give her a call if it'll make you feel better, but I can't let you go anywhere right now. I can show you something that might…help."

"Help? How?"

He raised an eyebrow at her. A clear gesture that she needed to just do what he said if she wanted to find out.

Zara inhaled and exhaled, slowly, carefully. It was the

only way to make a decision when the world was falling apart around you. Breathe. Center. Focus.

She called Hazeleigh. First and foremost, she at least had to warn her sister what was coming. But when Hazeleigh answered, her voice was strained.

"I can't talk right now, Zee," Hazeleigh said, her voice faint.

"Haze, Thomas said they're going to arrest you. You need to—"

"Please don't worry about me. I can handle this."

Zara wanted to ask "since when," but she didn't say anything because Hazeleigh had already hung up.

Zara's fingers tightened around the phone. It took her long, ticking seconds to pull it away from her face. To accept the reality.

Hazeleigh didn't want her help. Oh sure, when Douglas had been harassing her, she'd needed help, but now that she was getting *arrested*, she could handle things.

Zara thought about what the detective had said. That Hazeleigh was hiding something. Hazeleigh was never hiding anything. Not from Zara. But…

"Come on, Zara," Jake said, a gentle note to his voice she wanted to soften against. So she did the opposite. Straightened her spine and leveled him with a cool glare.

"Fine. Lead the way." She'd go see what he had to show her, and it would give her time to come up with a plan.

JAKE WAS A little surprised when she actually followed him, walking across the long expanse between cabin and house. Despite her much shorter legs, she kept pace with him. She often did.

He'd half expected her to bolt for the truck and fight him. Half expected he'd be forced to stop her. But she'd sized him up and clearly decided she couldn't manage it.

That didn't mean he trusted her not to try it at some other

point. In fact, he wouldn't be surprised if she was just lulling him into complacency. She'd be disappointed. But he gave her credit for strategic thinking.

He'd have to be a little strategic here too. It wouldn't be easy, because Zara was no easy mark. She would question everything. Including his motives.

Complicated, that.

She moved onto the porch before him, reaching out to open the door. Then she stopped herself, something arresting and painful crossed over her face.

Then she stepped back.

For over a month this woman had taught him and his "brothers" to ranch, with steely glares and snappy commands but always a certain kind of fairness. A dry humor. There'd been a seriousness, a graveness to the way she taught them how to tend *her* land.

But he'd never seen the emotion slam into her in quite that fashion. Realizing this wasn't her home anymore.

For the first time, Jake deeply regretted everything that had brought them here.

She gestured at the door. "Guess I shouldn't go barging in. Who knows what six single men living together do in the privacy of their own home."

"Fantasizing about it a bit, huh?"

She let out a little huff of a laugh, like he'd hoped, but it didn't lighten the gravity on her face.

He opened the door, led her inside. She looked around like she was stepping into a dollhouse or a snow globe. Maybe a play set. Like it wasn't quite real.

"It's upstairs," he said, forcing himself to stop watching all her expressions, all her emotions. He'd brought her here to take her mind off Hazeleigh and it certainly looked like he'd succeeded.

She followed him up the stairs and he didn't look behind him as he strode through the narrow hallway. It struck him in the moment that she would have walked up and down this hallway as a child. A little girl.

Zara as a little girl was hard to imagine. He couldn't imagine her as anything but just the same, only smaller.

"No Christmas decorations?"

He found the lie he'd told the detective didn't roll off the tongue. "One of the things six single men living together don't really get around to doing." He stepped into his bedroom and, when she followed, closed the door behind him.

"Eyes closed for a second," he said.

Her eyebrows rose. "Is this where you kill me, laugh and say it was you all the time?"

He gave her a baleful glance. "If that's what you want to think." They stood in another kind of standoff and he waited. Since he kept all the things no one could ever find in the same place, he wasn't about to give her the ammunition.

He could have left her downstairs, but it was too likely one of his brothers would walk in and demand answers he wasn't planning on giving just yet.

After an interminable silence and refusal to blink on her part, she finally heaved out a sigh. "Fine. Whatever."

She turned and faced the door. He couldn't tell if she was closing her eyes, but as long as she was faced away, she wouldn't be able to see the intricate system of locks and codes that kept all his private information private.

He finished unlocking the door and opened the small walk-in closet to what he'd been working on the past few days. He slid his personal things to the side, hiding them behind a large bureau...which also hid things. He flipped over some of the pictures he wouldn't want her to have to see, on the big board of information he'd made.

"All right. You can look."

She turned and stepped over to where he stood. Her expression was skeptical and wary, but no, not afraid.

Either she trusted him in particular or she was too trusting in general. The latter made him feel fiercely protective. Which was funny since she was the type of woman who would be offended at the very thought.

She frowned at the board he'd been putting together. His very own nonmilitary military campaign. Maybe the cops would figure it out first, but that didn't mean he couldn't do his due diligence.

"What is…? You're investigating." Her dark eyebrows were drawn together, lines dug into her forehead. Her braid wasn't as tightly wound today, as if she hadn't had the energy to twist her hair into control.

She just stared. She reached out and touched the timeline he'd written out with what he knew.

He had blanks. Quite a few. She could probably fill a lot of them.

"I don't understand. How'd you put all this together?"

"Let's just say… I have a special set of skills."

"Or you've watched too many *CSI* television shows," she muttered, but her gaze took in everything. The timelines, the pictures he hadn't flipped over. "I asked the wrong question. *Why* did you put this all together?"

"None of this has sat right. I just thought if I tried to make sense of it, put the information together, I might be able to see something the cops don't."

She took that in, seemed to absorb the words as she scanned all the information on his makeshift board. Then she turned to him slowly, and it seemed she had a particularly difficult time dragging her gaze from the board.

But eventually she pinned him with one of her accusatory glares. "Why do you care? Don't tell me it's a kindness. Don't lie to me. Why would you go through all this trouble?"

He was getting a little tired of her casual accusations. "I didn't kill your sister."

She huffed out a frustrated breath. "I know that. But

you're hiding…something with all this." She waved at the board. "Why is everyone *hiding* something?"

And he found he wanted to tell her. All the truths he'd sworn to tell no one. He didn't know why. The way she impatiently and easily believed he didn't kill Amberleigh—even though she knew next to nothing about him. The way she seemed to march through life, being so sure of her place in it, even when her place had been uprooted.

How she wanted to swoop in and save Hazeleigh when there was no way to do it. That wouldn't stop her. He knew that.

But wanting something and doing something were two very different things.

"Let's just say it's in my best interest if there aren't a bunch of people poking around the Thompson brothers' lives. *Not* because we've done anything wrong. I know you suspect we did, or we're up to something. But it's nothing like that."

"Then what's it like?"

"I can't tell you that." He gestured at the board. "But the way I see it, we can work together because we have the same endgame in mind. You want to clear Hazeleigh. I want to get this taken care of and away from us. They've arrested Hazeleigh, and I think we both know she's no murderer. Which means someone has to figure out who is, because if the cops are focused on her, they aren't focused on what really happened."

Zara stared at the board again. She was faintly shaking her head back and forth, but she was thinking. Considering. He could see that easily enough.

So, he pressed. "I know you could fill in these blanks. So could people in town. So could some deeper research, but if we pool what you know and what I know about solving a problem, I think we can get Hazeleigh out of this mess without causing much of a fuss."

"That depends, doesn't it?"

"On what?"

"On who really killed Amberleigh. Because she didn't die out wherever she ran away to. She died here and recently." Zara shook her head. "Which means the chances of this being a stranger are low. And the chances of Hazeleigh hiding something, like the detective said, are high." She blew out a breath, still shaking her head. "Do you honestly think you can figure out who did this with…this?"

"Yeah, I do."

Chapter Seven

Zara knew a thing or two about false hope. About putting your faith into *words* and *promises*. Dad used to make those. Eventually she'd stopped believing and he'd stopped promising.

But she so desperately wanted to believe in *this*. It was work after all. Compiling the information. The evidence. The pictures. But a few were facedown against the board. She reached out to remove the magnet so she could flip them over.

"What are these?"

His hand flew out and stopped her. The gentleness of the way his fingers closed over hers at odds with the sudden, certain movement of his hand reaching out at all. He cleared his throat uncomfortably. "I got some pictures of the… scene of the crime. You don't want to see it again, Zara."

No, she supposed she didn't. She let her hand fall.

"How?"

"Best if you don't ask 'how' too much."

She truly didn't know what to do with this. *Any* of it. "I can't let Hazeleigh sit in jail. I can't…" He had put together all the facts he had about the case. Like a cop might. "We should show this to…" She trailed off, thinking of her cousin. Who was a good guy, but a cop. Someone who had to play by the rules.

Jake…wouldn't. She didn't buy his whole *innocent* routine exactly, though no matter how she tried to convince herself he was hiding something terrible, she couldn't quite believe that of him. She supposed women got fooled all the time by charming or even sometimes not-so-charming men who said they were harmless.

But that was it. She didn't think Jake was *harmless*. Certainly not that steely way he'd eyed her and very easily, gently and *seriously* warned her not to try and make a run for her truck. She didn't think he was even particularly honest all the time.

She just thought there was something…decent about him. He wasn't going to let bad things happen.

She sighed. She was going to be the woman who fell for "I've got a secret I can't tell you, but I swear it's for your own good."

And honestly, she was too tired to care. Here was someone offering something she wanted. An attempt at answers—that weren't the wrong ones like Hazeleigh being a murderer. Even if she *was* hiding something.

"So, what now?"

"You fill in some blanks for me. Then I'll take you down to talk to Hazeleigh, and you'll see if you can get her to tell you what she's hiding."

"And then what?"

"Those are today's steps. We get those tasks accomplished, then tomorrow, we'll work on next steps."

It sounded so reasonable. It sounded like action and a plan. So, she pointed at his timeline and started to fill it in for him.

"It was August when Amberleigh ran away. The summer we were sixteen. Right before school started."

"No one seems too keen on talking about *why*."

"No, they wouldn't." She wasn't. She could remember all too well the aftermath of what Amberleigh had done. She didn't want to bring it up now. Not when Amberleigh was dead. An unbidden image of her face in the ground had Zara closing her eyes in pain.

Yes, she thought her sister had been dead a long time, but that grief had never gone away. Now it was stronger, sharper, because there was no hope left.

Without hope, a person had to cling to hard work and the truth. So, she'd have to tell him. No matter what it made Jake think of Amberleigh.

"She disappeared the same day as a man twice her age. A man who was very well loved, very much respected and very married. It was a shock to everyone—not just that he'd have an illegal affair with a teenager, one of his daughter's friends, but that he'd then just up and leave town."

Jake frowned. "Isn't that the kind of thing people would love to gossip about?"

"Sure, when it was fresh. Not so gleeful when the girl they blamed is dead. Small towns aren't perfect, but Wilde loves its own. At least when they're murdered."

Jake seemed to think this over. He offered no commentary. Just wrote some things down on his board. "And this man isn't a suspect?"

"I suppose he is. We wouldn't know, would we? But no one's been able to find him. Either of them. My family tried to find Amberleigh, but we only had so many resources. The Phillips family was and is one of the richest families in town. I know Mr. Phillips's daughter spent years trying to track him down. Trying to figure out what happened. But he was never seen or heard from again. It's been ten years."

"And you never heard from or saw Amberleigh again?"

"No."

"What about Hazeleigh?"

"No." But a strange feeling skittered up her spine. Because the detective's words kept echoing in Zara's head. *But she's hiding something. I'd encourage her to tell me. Sooner rather than later.* And how unsurprised Hazeleigh seemed to be about being arrested, insisting on the phone she could handle it, when Hazeleigh was never known for her handling of anything.

She ran away, or avoided, or left Zara to handle it. Maybe that wasn't the fairest assessment of her sister, but she wasn't feeling particularly fair right now.

"Zara?"

Her first instinct was to push it away. To never speak word of her doubts. Certainly not to a stranger, but she couldn't stop looking at the board. The time and effort it had taken. Sure, he was doing it for himself—to get the cops away from sniffing around him and his brothers—but it was still time and effort.

"Hazeleigh never saw or talked to Amber that I know of."

"But you're wondering if she did without you knowing?"

"I really don't know. I never dreamed Hazeleigh was keeping something from me. Never in a million years, but the past day… It's all I can think." And it felt awful. Like a betrayal, but no amount of talking herself out of suspicion could make that little worm of a feeling go away.

"Well, maybe she'll tell you what it is now that she's in some serious trouble."

Zara managed a smile, though she knew it frayed at the edges. Because if Hazeleigh was keeping something from her, she was already in the serious trouble.

JAKE GOT ZARA to answer a few more questions he hadn't been able to surmise or pick up from town gossip. She looked like a ghost of herself, standing there in front of the board of information. Pale, still gripping her bag like it was a lifeline.

But she didn't fall apart. She didn't cry like she had this morning. She gave him the answers, a lot of time in a rather monotone voice, her gaze never leaving the board.

"Do you really think you can put all this together? I mean, I assume the police are working with the same information."

"I assume. Hopefully, if they are, they let Hazeleigh go as soon as possible. Unless they're barking up the Hazeleigh tree, one we both know is wrong, because it's convenient."

"Thomas might have to follow the letter of the law and allow Hazeleigh to be arrested, but he knows she's not a murderer. He won't just let them keep focusing on her."

"Unless he doesn't have a choice."

She frowned at that but didn't argue with him.

The door to his room burst open, and Landon stood there in nothing but a towel held around his waist, dripping wet.

"Jake, damn it, where the hell is the—oh." He cleared his throat, looked from Zara to Jake with some amusement, then grinned at Zara. "Well, hi."

Zara's eyebrows rose, but that was about her only reaction to a half-naked man standing in the doorway. Jake supposed he was lucky Landon had bothered with a towel.

"Where's the soap you were supposed to pick up this morning?" Landon asked, apparently having no qualms about dripping all over the floor or standing there in nothing but a towel.

"I haven't made it to town yet. I'm going out in a minute. Why don't you go put some pants on since there's a guest in our house?"

"Oh, I didn't mind," Zara said with just a little *too* much feeling and a sweet smile Landon's way to boot.

Which earned a grin from Landon and a scowl from Jake, though he couldn't say why it bothered him she should be…ogling.

"You can *go* now," Jake said pointedly at Landon.

"Touchy, touchy," Landon said with a grin Jake knew meant he would be getting razzed later. Landon finally turned and left, but Jake didn't watch him. He watched Zara *watch* him.

"Sorry about that," he grumbled, irritable for reasons he didn't want to analyze.

Zara was staring at the little puddle Landon had left behind. "The interruption or the strip show?"

"Both."

"I don't mind a show."

She had taken him off guard and so he could only stare at her, probably gaping a bit. She shrugged.

"You and your brothers aren't ogres, Jake. And, no matter what anyone might think, I *am* a woman. I enjoy a six-pack and impressive thighs."

"All right," he muttered, wanting as far out of this conversation as he could get. ASAP. He began closing up the board, locking up the closet.

"Nice shoulders are good too, and—"

"I said *all right*," he ground out, giving her a quelling glare.

She laughed. And it was hard to stay all tense and uncomfortable when she did. Not just because she was in the middle of something horrible and it was nice to be able to bring her some relief to that, but because she'd been pretty serious ever since they'd arrived. He knew she had a sense of humor. It usually came out cutting and snarky. But this was a sort of wicked delight.

"I'll drive you into town and see what's what at the police station. If they let you talk to Hazeleigh, I'll go run my errands, then pick you up when I'm finished. Sound good?"

She nodded. "I feel it's probably a waste of time to point out I could drive myself."

"Then it's just as equally a waste of time to point out I'm going to town anyway, and you might as well take an offer of help when it's made."

She stared at him for a second or two longer than was

comfortable. "All right," she murmured. Still staring at him, with dark brown eyes that…

He turned away abruptly. "So, let's get going."

She followed him out into the hallway. "How'd you pick your rooms?" she asked, and when he looked back at her, she was studying the upstairs. "Who got what?"

"We just walked through, picked what felt best suited to our needs. Dunne's downstairs because of his leg. Henry's in that outbuilding that has a bed, because he's a grumpy SOB. Then the last four of us are up here."

"Why did that room suit your needs?"

He shrugged, uncomfortable with the line of questioning but knowing her and life well enough not to show any discomfort. "I don't know. Had a nice view out the window."

They went down the stairs, Zara strangely silent behind him. When they reached the main floor he turned to look at her. "What?"

She inhaled, exhaled, still studying him in that way that made him want to fidget. When he'd been stared at and inspected and yelled at by so many superior officers and never so badly wanted to look away.

"It was mine," she said quietly. "So was that bureau in the closet. Let me guess. You have something you wouldn't want anyone to see hidden in that false bottom?"

It was such a shock, and he knew it shouldn't have been. But it had been a while since someone had gotten the best of him—and the last time had been an entire terrorist organization. Not a pretty rancher in small-town Wyoming.

Because yes, he had a few things hidden in that false bottom.

She sailed by him. This had once been her house and she knew the way after all. "We can talk about it on the way to the police department."

Chapter Eight

Zara savored the shocked look on Jake's face all the way to the police station. He was usually so…composed. She hadn't fully realized that. He did it with an ease and casualness that was easily mistaken as a happy-go-lucky kind of guy.

But there was a deeper current running under Jake's facade. Once she'd finally broken through it, she could look back and see all the ways he'd employed that facade.

And wasn't it disappointing that she was thinking more about that than Landon's impressive shoulders?

She sat in the passenger seat of the car and mostly kept her gaze on the windshield in front of her. But occasionally her gaze strayed to Jake's profile. He'd carefully hidden his shock and discomfort. His hand on the wheel was relaxed. His jaw wasn't tense and his shoulders lounged back against the driver's seat.

But there was something in his very, *very* intense gaze on the road ahead of him that Zara had the sneaking suspicion was all those *feelings* he was trying to hide.

"So. I guess you're not hiding any murder weapons in the false bottom."

His blue gaze flicked to hers, briefly, but there was a telling jerk of surprise in that almost-nothing move.

"No."

"But something?"

His gaze was back on the road, but his jaw had tensed some. "Sure. We all have secrets, don't we?"

She thought about the detective saying Hazeleigh was hiding something. Zara thought of her own life. Did she have secrets? Not the kind a person hid in false bottoms— at least, now that she didn't keep an adolescent journal full of ridiculously embarrassing thoughts she'd had the good sense to burn after Amberleigh had found it and read it aloud to her friends when they'd been thirteen.

But the man next to her—as helpful as he was being— certainly had bigger secrets than crushes, childish slights and pubescent, overemotional worries.

The kind of secrets he didn't want the *police* poking around.

Common sense told her she shouldn't trust him. Not a man so obviously trying to hide something. But underneath all that sense—she had a…gut feeling, her great-grandfather would have called it. It told her that while Jake might have secrets, he wasn't *dangerous*.

At least, not to her.

Jake pulled his truck into a parking space at the police station and dread iced her insides. She didn't want to handle this. She didn't want to face an *arrested* Hazeleigh. Or whatever her sister was hiding from her.

Worse, she didn't want to go in there only to be turned away. Would they even let her see Hazeleigh? Or would she be completely shut out?

Nothing like a situation with no good outcome.

Amberleigh's face in the dirt drifted into her mind and she squeezed her eyes shut in an effort to push it away.

She felt the gentle pressure of Jake's hand touching her arm through the sleeve of her coat.

"Do you want me to go in with you?"

She shook her head, though she didn't lean away from

his hand on her arm. It felt nice. Like something holding her up. Ballast.

Truth be told, she wanted some as she walked into the police station, but she had to be strong enough to do this on her own. "Thank you, but I feel like there might be some questions about why you drove me. Why you're getting involved. The kind of questions you're trying to avoid."

She opened her eyes, determined to be strong. In control. But Jake was staring at her with that *seriousness* she didn't know what to do with.

"I can handle a few questions," he said. Firmly. Certain. An offer of kindness at the cost of what he was trying to do.

It was a simple statement that landed with the strength of an avalanche. She'd thought earlier she didn't want to be flattened, but she was starting to wonder if she had a choice.

"I'll be fine," she managed to say. Because something about going in there with him as an anchor of sorts felt a lot more scary and dangerous than facing this herself. "Thanks. I'll text you if they won't let me see her." She got out of the truck and walked with purpose for the door.

She hesitated a moment before reaching out to open it. She glanced back, and he was sitting there. Watching her go in. Like he wouldn't leave until he was sure she was inside. Until he was certain she'd be able to do what she came for.

A lump formed in her throat. Old memories, being afraid, looking behind her, and no one being there. Because she was the strong one. The one who couldn't be afraid.

She cleared her throat and straightened her shoulders. Just because there was someone in that usual empty space didn't mean she could afford to be weak or afraid. She had to save Hazeleigh.

No one else would.

She stepped into the little entryway and waited to be buzzed in. She hadn't been in here for years. But back when they were sixteen, and Amberleigh had disappeared, she'd spent quite a bit of time in and out of the Bent County police station.

The receptionist smiled at her and offered a greeting, but the detective was walking down a staircase at the same time.

"Zara. Hi." She looked at the receptionist. "Sign in Zara Hart. No ID needed. I can confirm identity."

The receptionist nodded and pulled a clipboard toward her while the detective led Zara away.

"I guess you're here to see Hazeleigh."

"If I can."

Detective Delaney-Carson nodded, leading Zara up some stairs. "We can let you see her, but an officer will have to be in the room with you."

"Can it be Thomas?"

She smiled apologetically, and her eyes were kind. Not like so many of the officers they'd dealt with during Amberleigh's disappearance.

"I'm afraid not. Both because it'd be a conflict of interest and because he's on a call right now. He said he'd get you the name of some lawyers. I'd highly encourage you to find the right fit for you guys as soon as possible."

She led Zara down a hallway, another set of stairs. Then paused outside a gray metal door. She leaned in, her voice low and hushed.

"Thomas is adamant that your sister didn't do this. And I'm inclined to believe him. You might be his family, but he's a good cop and it doesn't feel like he's letting emotions cloud his instincts. But there is evidence against Hazeleigh. The kind we, as a police department, can't ignore. With evidence like that, we didn't have a choice in arresting her. But that doesn't mean, as the lead detective on this case, I won't keep looking for more evidence that proves a better theory."

Zara was slightly surprised at the detective's…kindness?

Belief in Thomas? She thought of Jake's board. Would he have more information that could help the detective prove Hazeleigh didn't do it?

But all of those questions faded away as everything the detective said fully penetrated. There was *evidence*. Whatever they'd taken out of the cabin with the search warrant. "What kind of evidence?"

The detective sighed. "I'm sorry. I can't give you that information. However, if Hazeleigh knows what we took or what it is, she can tell you."

It was a hint of sorts. To ask Hazeleigh about it. "Thank you, detective."

She smiled thinly. "Call me Laurel. And you don't have to be polite to the person making your sister's life harder. I can take a little resentment. Part and parcel with the job."

Zara looked at the doorway. Hazeleigh was in there. Her life definitely harder. But it wasn't Laurel's fault. "I think I'll save all my bad manners for whoever is responsible."

The detective opened the door and nodded to the officer in the corner. "This is Zara Hart, Ms. Hart's sister." As if it wasn't obvious by the whole identical-faces thing, but maybe it was procedure. "When she's done, have someone escort her back out."

The officer nodded.

"Zara, if there's anything you want to talk to me about afterward, feel free to ask an officer to bring you to my office. Or you can call me. You still have my card?"

Zara nodded. Laurel gave her a reassuring pat on the shoulder. "I'll leave you to it."

Zara turned to face her sister. She sat at a table. She had handcuffs on her narrow wrists, and she had her hands clasped tightly in front of her on the table.

Zara felt brittle. Like if she moved, she might tremble and fall into a million pieces.

Hazeleigh attempted a smile. It faltered at the edges.

"Everything is fine," she said, attempting a breezy tone that didn't fool Zara for a second.

"This is not fine," Zara managed. Her voice shook, hopefully with conviction and not fear. She moved to take the seat across from Hazeleigh.

"Well, not ideal. But fine enough. I just have to sit here for now, and that detective comes in every so often to ask me questions. I don't know what's going to happen next. But that's okay. She said Thomas can come in and talk to me too, when he's not busy."

"How is that okay? How is any of this okay?"

Hazeleigh reached forward, paused when the guard said "no touching" in a curt, no-nonsense order. Hazeleigh put her cuffed hands in her lap.

"The detective said they have evidence," Zara said, hoping if she supplied *some* information, any of this might start to make sense.

Hazeleigh's forehead puckered. "Yes. They found some things in my room, but they aren't mine. Well, some of it is. It's sort of complicated."

"What is it? How is it complicated? I'm in the dark here, Hazeleigh. Why are you keeping me there?" Was she just confused because of shock and tragedy? Or...

"They found a sweater with some blood on it, and because Amberleigh's body..." Hazeleigh swallowed, and her eyes flickered with pain and grief and something that looked altogether too close to guilt. "She was shot in the same place the blood was. I told them I'd never seen it, of course, but they think I'm lying because..."

"Because why?"

"It was in a trash bag. Under my mattress."

Zara was sure the room spun. Something echoed in her ears and a pressure built in her chest. *"What?"* she screeched. That wasn't just evidence. That was...damning. Hidden, bloody clothes.

Hazeleigh gave her a censuring look, and it was just as disorienting to have her sister be the calm, authoritative one while she panicked as it was to have Hazeleigh say a bloody sweater had been hidden under her mattress.

A shrill sound echoed through the room, and Zara nearly jumped a foot. She looked behind her at the guard. He'd answered his cell phone and was speaking in low tones.

Distracted.

Zara leaned forward. "What aren't you telling me?" she demanded in a whisper.

Hazeleigh whispered back, just as fervently. "Just let it be, okay? Everything is fine. Really. I'm safest right here."

"Safest?" As if her safety was in question. "Haze—"

"Leave it," Hazeleigh said. Firmly. As firm as she'd ever said anything to Zara. In their entire lives. "Don't go poking around looking for things. Let the detective handle it. She seems nice."

She seems nice. "She had you arrested for murder. *Murder*, Hazeleigh."

Hazeleigh leaned back with an odd coolness in her gaze Zara had never seen out of her sister. Not in their entire lives. "For my good. For yours. Let it be, Zaraleigh. Just let it be."

JAKE COMPLETED HIS errands for the house, did a little casual asking around about Amberleigh. Townspeople's theories on how she'd died, on why she'd run away. Why she'd come back recently, without telling her sisters. It helped to canvas opinions. Put them together and try to pull a thread of truth out of them.

He hadn't found the thread yet, but he was working on it.

When Zara texted him that she was finished at the police station, he was already in the parking lot. A few minutes later, she stepped outside, blinked at the bright afternoon sunshine and then started toward him.

She looked…shell-shocked. A soldier not quite sure what she'd just stumbled out of. Alive and still intact on the outside, but forever changed on the inside.

Jake himself had to blink away old images superimposing themselves on Zara. Bloody men stumbling through chaos, and Zara walking through the center of it all.

But half that vision wasn't true. *Just your brain playing tricks on you: one, two, three, four, five. You are safe and here: five, four, three, two, one.*

By the time she reached his truck, the coping mechanisms had settled him. Whatever leftover anxiety he felt she wouldn't see because she was wrapped up in her own.

She sat in the seat, clutching her purse, frowning at the windshield.

"Buckle up, and we'll head home."

She didn't say anything. Didn't even acknowledge he'd spoken.

"That bad, huh?"

When she still didn't acknowledge him, he reached over the middle console and her body and grabbed the seatbelt himself. He pulled it across her and clicked it into place.

She finally moved, turning her head to stare at him. And because he was leaning over, their faces were rather close. Close enough to count her eyelashes. To notice the faint freckles on her nose and an even fainter scar above her dark eyebrows. To find his mind rendered utterly blank by the depth of her brown eyes.

Which was shock enough he forced himself to ease back, desperate for a little distance from the heaviness of whatever emotion moved through him. Besides, there were more important things at hand. "So, you saw her?"

Zara nodded slowly. "Yes."

"Did she tell you anything helpful?"

"No. Not exactly. I…" Zara blew out a breath and seemed to get some inner grip on herself. The dazed look went away, the odd stillness turned into a wave of small movements. Purposefully unclasping her hands from the purse, sitting back in the seat, crossing her ankles and then uncrossing them as she leaned forward. "She told me to leave it be. To not go poking around looking for things. That she was *safest* there." Zara looked out at the police station building.

"Safe. That's an odd choice of words."

"I thought so too. Why would jail be safe?" She shook her head. "Laurel, the detective, said she's still looking beyond Hazeleigh, but the evidence was damning enough they had to bring her in."

Jake pulled out of the parking spot. "Well, that's better than her thinking it's Hazeleigh, I suppose. But what kind of evidence would be so damning?"

"A bloody sweater hidden in her room. Hazeleigh said it wasn't hers, but… How else would it get under her mattress?"

"Someone's framing her."

Zara's eyebrows drew even closer together, a deep line running across her forehead. He wanted to ask her about the scar there and knew now was especially not the time. He needed to focus. On the situation. Not on *her*.

"Who? How?" She shook her head. "Too many questions and none of it makes sense. She told me to leave it be. Not to poke into anything. But what would you do if your sibling told you not to do something?" she asked, turning to him. Her eyes so…vulnerable. An odd twist of events for Ms. Hard-Ass Cowgirl.

"I don't have sib—" He realized his mistake too late. She raised her eyebrows, and then a look close to triumph crossed her face.

Because she'd finally caught him in that lie she'd been so sure they'd been telling.

"I was adopted," he said before she could accuse him of

anything. It was always the story for when things didn't add up, and it wasn't so far from the truth as to be a lie. "When I was older, and they were. My brothers are my brothers, but it's different than identical triplets, I assume."

She frowned a little, that I-knew-it light fading from her eyes. "I suppose," she murmured, clearly not convinced. "But in *my* family, when you tell your sibling *not* to do something, it's like waving a red flag. Now it's all they want to do."

"So, you think she *wants* you to go poking around?" he asked, glad they had this to focus on rather than sibling talk.

"I'm not sure. Part of me thinks she was sincere, but she wasn't herself. She was acting like…"

"Like?"

"…me." Zara shook her head. "Strong and in control. The leader. That's always me."

Jake thought that seemed kind of sad. Reminded him a bit of Cal. Always a little separate from the pack. Always so determined to be strong, even when they could use some help. As if they didn't know how to handle a life where they weren't the leaders, charging through the fray, fighting all the enemies.

"You know, Thomas said something to me…" Jake figured telling her cousin had said she wasn't as strong as she acted wasn't the best way to get through to her, so he kept that part to himself. "Hazeleigh isn't as fragile as you think."

Zara shook her head. "No offense, but I think I know my identical sister a little bit better than a few dudes. She needs help, and I'm the only one who's going to do it."

"What about your father?"

She moved, strangely almost like a flinch. She seemed not to know what to say to that. "Listen, let's just head back to the ranch. I've got some things to do."

"Like what? Poke around where Hazeleigh told you not to?"

She shrugged as he pulled his truck out of the police station parking lot.

"It denotes a kind of guilt, doesn't it? Don't poke around. Leave things be. Why should I? Why shouldn't I know what happened to Amberleigh?"

"She said jail is the safest place for her. Maybe she's trying to protect you."

She bristled. "Well, I don't care if she is. If there's danger, then someone should figure it out to protect *her*."

"And that someone has to be you?"

"Apparently."

Jake frowned at the road. He didn't like the idea of Zara putting herself in danger, but he also knew the pointlessness of beating himself against the brick wall of someone who thought they had to be in charge of everything.

So, he'd just have to stick close. If she wanted to protect Hazeleigh, that was fine. But someone was damn well going to protect *her*.

"Okay. So, the cops already searched your place, but Hazeleigh doesn't want you poking around, which means there's more to find. Where would Hazeleigh hide something she didn't want you to poke around and find?"

"Work."

"So, let's go."

"Now? Jake, I really do appreciate your help, but I have my own truck. My own…two feet."

"'Course you do. But why only use two feet when four will get the job done faster?"

"It is on the way home anyway," she said with a nose wrinkle of distaste. "But I really don't need—"

"I didn't ask what you needed, Zara. I said we're going." And that was that.

Chapter Nine

It was a strange feeling in Zara's life to be railroaded by someone determined to help her. She didn't *like* it, because she didn't like anyone telling her what to do or deciding things about what she was going to do or whatever.

But it was hard to find a good argument when he wasn't taking over per se. He was mostly acting as chauffeur and what was wrong with that?

It felt like *something* should be, but she couldn't figure out whatever it was. So, she watched the world roll by. Back through Wilde. She instructed Jake to turn off before they got to the road that would lead them to the ranch.

He drove the back roads, following the small brown sign for Fort Dry. When he pulled into the park's lot, he stared dubiously at the sight before him.

Three small buildings huddled together, surrounded on three sides by a pretty white picket fence that Zara knew the park department painted every year. The landscape around the fort was nothing but flat snow-covered land, the mountains far off in the distance.

"This was a…fort?" Jake asked, sounding dubious.

"Someone inside will no doubt be quite happy to give you a history lesson, but yes. Fort Dry. It's a living-history thing. Hazeleigh works for the guy who runs it. She has a little office here, though she does most of her work at the library or at the cabin. But if she was hiding something, it'd be safest to hide it here."

But Zara didn't know what she'd be looking for. "I don't understand why she'd hide something from me. It makes *no* sense."

Jake's gave her shoulder a squeeze. "So let's go make sense of it."

Zara wasn't sure how to anticipate all those little touches. It seemed like second nature to him now. When for the past month he'd kept an easy distance. A *careful* distance.

But Jake had been there. Jake had been the first to dig up Amberleigh. She supposed that had to have been disorienting for him. Her and Hazeleigh's face in the dirt *and* right there in front of him.

"You don't have to…" She blew out a breath. She kept saying the same things to him, and yet, here they still were. No answers. Him still there.

Ballast.

"How about this? You stop telling me what I don't have to do, as I'm not at all afraid of saying the words *no* or *I'd rather not*. If I'm here, it's because I want to be. If I'm helping, it's because I want to be."

She wanted to ask him why, but she knew the answer, didn't she? He wanted to keep the cops off his proverbial doorstep. To hide whatever was in the false bottom of the bureau.

But that made *shoulder* touches a little unnecessary.

She marched forward, ignoring the odd pang inside her chest as Jake's hand slid off her shoulder. She bypassed the main building, hoping she'd avoid Mr. Field and anyone else so she wouldn't have to answer any questions or field any condolences.

But as she headed for the far building that housed Hazeleigh's office, Zara stopped on a dime. Even though the woman was dressed in historical clothing, a big, sweeping dress that went from her chin down to her toes, Zara recognized her immediately.

She also stopped dead in her tracks. And they stood there on the icy path staring at each other from a great distance.

Eventually, the woman broke the silence and the gap first.

Kate moved up to stand just a few feet away. "Zara. You… Um, hi."

Zara needed a minute to find her voice. "Kate. Hi."

"Hi."

They stared at each other in uncomfortable silence. Hazeleigh never mentioned Kate working here, though Zara knew it was true. Kate Phillips had become something they didn't talk about in their family. Just like Amberleigh.

Is that why Hazeleigh is hiding something from you? All those no-talk zones?

"I'm so sorry about Amberleigh," Kate said with feeling and kindness.

Years ago, Zara might have known what to do with it. Now, across a valley of accusations and bone-deep hurts, Zara didn't know what to say.

"The police came and asked me a few questions," Kate continued, standing there in clothes incongruous to the current time period, and yet Kate looked perfectly comfortable in them. She and Hazeleigh had always loved to dress up. "I told them everything I know."

Quite a few words, none of them kind, circled around Zara's brain. But Kate's gaze flicked to Jake behind Zara.

Zara had nearly forgotten about him. About why she was here. Because old hurts and pain had come back in the blink of an eye.

Apparently it was the week for that. "I just need to have a quick look around Hazeleigh's office."

Kate's gaze went from Jake back to Zara and she smiled thinly. "I was just locking it up. Mr. Field didn't want anyone messing with Hazeleigh's organization while she's…"

"In jail," Zara supplied for Kate. "Accused of murdering our sister."

Kate's face hardened. "Like I said, I told the police everything I know. I'm sure you believe my father did this."

"Gee, I wonder why."

"And I know my mother was cruel to you, so you have no reason to be kind to me, but I… I told them everything I've found out about Dad in the past few years. It doesn't amount to much, but I told them."

Zara knew her anger was aimed at the wrong person. She'd always known that. Easier to act out on when she was sixteen, a bit harder to hold on to these ten years later.

Kate turned on a heel. "Follow me. I'll unlock it for you."

Zara had no choice but to follow Kate into the small building. She glanced back at Jake, close at her heels, tall enough he had to duck to make it through the doors. Kate led them to the back of the building. She unlocked an unmarked door, stepped inside and flipped on a light.

She plunked the keys on the desk in the corner. "Return these to the front office when you're finished with them." Then she swept out of the room.

Well, there was one thing all those big skirts were good for. A dramatic exit.

Zara took a deep breath, studying the tidy desk. Where to begin?

"You failed to mention the old guy your sister ran away with was your best friend's dad," Jake said, and she didn't know what that note in his voice was. Only that it was something more than vaguely interested.

"How do you know she was my best friend?" Zara muttered, flipping through the notebook on Hazeleigh's desk.

"That kind of hurt isn't from a shallow, childhood friendship."

She set the notebook down. "No, I suppose not. But it doesn't matter."

He didn't say anything to that, which made it feel like it *did* matter. But how could it when Amberleigh was dead and Hazeleigh was in jail? And Kate hadn't been her friend for a very long time.

She opened the drawers in Hazeleigh's desk. She carefully and methodically searched. She read notes, flipped through files. But it was all about that ridiculously fake bank robbery. Nothing that might help Zara figure out why her sister thought she was *safest* in jail.

She moved to the other side, tugging open the much-bigger drawer. She pulled out a cardboard box. Newspaper clippings. Old pictures of the Wilde Bank.

And underneath all that, a wooden box.

She recognized that box. They each had one, hand carved by their great-grandfather. Given to them after he'd passed away. Zara's was in her room, one of the few knick-knacks on her shelf. Sometimes she passed by it and traced the *ZH* and reminded herself who she was and what she came from.

Maybe this was Hazeleigh's, Zara told herself, though she knew Hazeleigh kept hers on her nightstand at the cabin. Zara told herself she'd pick up the box, turn it around and the carved *HZ* would be on the front.

Her vision went a little dim around the corners as she reached out for it. Picked it up, turned it around. The weight and feel of it familiar.

But it's in the wrong place.

There was a Post-it stuck to the front, hiding the engraving that would tell her whose box it was.

She got the sense Jake had stopped looking and was watching what she was doing. Part of her didn't want to do it. Part of her wanted him to. But it was her hand that reached out, that peeled the Post-it away.

And just as she suspected, there was a delicate *AH* carved onto the front.

JAKE THOUGHT ZARA might actually faint. She swayed, but caught herself by grabbing the desk. He put his hand on her back to steady her.

There was something altogether too satisfying in the fact he seemed to be able to do that.

"That's Amberleigh's."

She nodded. "It was one of the few things she took with her."

"Took with her?" Jake asked. His heartbeat picked up a little bit. So they had found something. "You know that for sure?"

"I'm not sure I know anything for sure now. But it was one of her missing belongings. Some clothes. Any money she had. A diary. And this box."

She let out a shaky breath. She held the box like she was afraid to open it, and Jake couldn't blame her there.

"Why wouldn't the police have come to search here?"

She shook her head. "They might still. But Amberleigh was found on our property and plenty to search there. Bloody sweaters and the like."

"Are you going to take it?"

She chewed on her bottom lip, still staring at it. "I guess that depends." With trembling fingers, she lifted the lid. Jake peered over her shoulder.

There were letters inside. The top one was addressed to Hazeleigh. There was no return address.

Zara let out a huff of breath, like in pain. The kind of breath someone expels after a punch. "That's Amberleigh's handwriting."

"You're sure?"

She nodded jerkily. "Postmark is this year." She began to shake her head, vaguely at first but more insistent with each move. "This can't *be*. If she wrote letters to Hazeleigh, Hazeleigh would have told me. If Amberleigh was back, bringing her box and whatever else, Hazeleigh would have *told* me."

"Should we go to the detective? Show her this?" Jake asked gently.

She didn't stop shaking her head. "I have to know if…"

If it implicated Hazeleigh. Zara didn't want to believe anything bad of her sister, but he understood that if she had to…she'd hide it. She'd protect Hazeleigh, perhaps no matter what she'd done.

Jake didn't know how to feel about that, but he supposed in a way wasn't that what he and his *brothers* were doing? Lying and hiding…for the good of each other.

She didn't open the letter though. She closed the lid. "I need to read these but not here. It's already going to be sketchy enough we came here."

"Come on. Let's return those keys and get back to the ranch. We'll read through them together. Two sets of eyes will get through it quicker." He thought about offering up the rest of the guys, but he had a feeling he knew what Cal would say about all this *involvement*.

There was something else that had him holding back on that front, but he didn't want to contemplate it too much or too hard or remember the way Zara had grinned at a half-naked Landon.

He ground his teeth together and turned on a heel, exiting the building. "Which one's the front office?"

Zara pointed, then started walking for the building at the center. They walked across the snowy yard in silence. She hid the box inside her jacket, and Jake really didn't know how to feel about the fact more and more things were piling up to implicate Hazeleigh.

But he'd keep an open mind. They'd keep looking for evidence it was someone else. And if Zara had to face facts… Well, he'd help her. With whatever happened.

He looked around the yard. He wasn't sure where the

1800s-dressed woman had gone, but Zara led him to the center building. It was in a little better shape than the two around it. Honestly, they were kind of quaint, but it was the nothingness around the park that surprised him.

Who would build a fort here and why? What were they protecting here in the middle of nothing, with the mountains hovering in the distance? Had this area once drawn more people than it did now?

He stepped into the building after Zara, and suddenly his small, casual interest in history died. Immediately.

There were mannequins…everywhere. They were dressed in old-timey clothes, clearly arranged in scenes to depict life in the fort in the 1800s.

But the mannequins didn't have any *eyes*.

Jake stood struck frozen in place by the grotesque horror of the whole thing. Zara looked back at him, eyes questioning. "What's wrong?"

"Zara, I have faced down entire armies with tanks, grenades and sniper rifles pointed at me, and this is the most terrifying thing I've ever seen."

She turned slowly to face him fully, surprise registering in her expression. "You were in the military." She didn't say it like a question.

Well, he was 0-for-2 in the keeping-things-a-secret category today. And he didn't know what to say to that. There was no denying what he'd said. No easy adoption excuse. And even though the mannequins surrounding them didn't have *eyes*, he still felt like they were watching him.

Judging him.

"You all were in the military," she said with an odd kind of wonder in her voice. "It makes *so* much sense."

"Does it?" he muttered.

"I don't understand why it would be a secret."

"It's a difficult subject, that."

She nodded, as if it had dawned on her. That military included war and people didn't escape that unscathed. Maybe not in the way she might think, but it worked.

He eyed the mannequins warily. "Can we get the hell out of here?"

"I mean, I'm kind of enjoying watching you squirm in terror, but we've got things to do."

He trailed after her as she marched through the scenes of plastic, eyeless horror. "It's not terror," he muttered. But he supposed that's exactly what it was. He suppressed a shudder.

"Hi, Mr. Field," she greeted a small old man in a little room past all the mannequins. He hopped to his feet, hands fluttering about.

"Zaraleigh, oh my goodness. Please tell me this is all a misunderstanding."

Zaraleigh. It had legitimately never occurred to Jake that, of course, like her *triplet* sisters her name would end in *-leigh.*

The name didn't fit her at all, and it amused him beyond reason. Especially when she looked over her shoulder and glared at him. "Not a word," she muttered. Then she smiled at the old man fussing behind a giant desk piled high with magazines and who knew what all else.

"Hazeleigh didn't do anything wrong," she told the man firmly. "We're working with the detective to make sure she can come home soon. I just had to pick up some of her things. Kate gave me the keys and told me to return them to you." She held them out to him.

"Oh," the old man said. "Well, thank you, dear." He pocketed the keys and smiled blandly up at Zara. *Zaraleigh.* "I'm just so worried about the poor girl, but I suppose you've got everything handled."

"Of course I do," Zara said in a rote tone he'd heard her use a lot. And he realized in the moment that that rote tone wasn't confidence so much as an act.

Because everyone around her seemed to think she had it under control. When this was the kind of situation *no one* would be able to have under control.

"Take care, Mr. Field." She waved at him, then turned and led Jake back out through the museum.

"Zaraleigh," he whispered, to keep himself from thinking about the mannequins and the way their eyeless faces felt as though they were following him.

"I swear to God, Jake, if you ever call me that again, you won't have a tongue to call anyone anything."

"I appreciate the threat, really, but I think we both know you'd have a hard time de-tonguing me."

"All it would take is a sedative slipped into your coffee thermos and patience. Plus a really sharp knife."

He considered the rather detailed fantasy. He gave her a nod. "Impressive."

She made a noise, and her color had come back. She moved with purpose rather than in that shell-shocked way.

"We'll head to the ranch. Read those letters. Go from there." They reached his truck and climbed in. Zara remembered to buckle her own seatbelt this time, and she set the box on her lap, looking at it with trepidation.

He started the truck and backed out of the small parking lot. He began driving toward the ranch.

"Maybe I should read them myself," she said quietly. "That way if something happens, and someone asks you something, you won't know."

He flicked a glance to her briefly. She was staring at the box, tracing the *A* and *H* engraved on the front. She looked lost.

And in desperate need of someone to help her find the way.

"Better to do it quickly and work together to see what we can figure out. If the police start questioning me, I don't have to tell them the truth if it implicates Hazeleigh unfairly."

She looked up at him then. He could feel her gaze, but he kept his on the road. For safety. Not self-preservation.

"If they asked, you'd lie?"

He thought that over. Bit back the words that had popped into his head, unbidden. *If you asked me to.* "I'd lie about a lot of things, as long as it didn't put anyone in danger."

That was true. It was why he was in Wilde in the first place, wasn't it? Lies to protect the people most important to him.

What was a few more?

For her.

Chapter Ten

Zara wasn't sure what had happened. One minute, she was sitting in Jake's truck, clutching the box in her lap. The next moment, she was blinking her eyes open to a view of the house in front of her. A painful crick in her neck as she sat up straight with a start.

She blinked at the house, then at Jake in the driver's seat. He was playing on his phone, though he set it down when he realized she was awake and alert.

"I…fell asleep?" she asked, because she couldn't quite believe she'd just…dozed off. In the middle of the day. She glanced at the horizon. Well, late afternoon anyway.

"Adrenaline tends to run out, and then the crash."

He'd left the truck running with the heat on. Sat there with her. All the while, a good forty-five minutes had passed since they'd left the fort, and it was only a ten-minute drive from the ranch.

She didn't know what to *do* with him.

"I figure we should read those in my room," he said, nodding to the box that she was still clutching in her lap. "That way we can hide them quickly if we need to."

His room. *Her* room. She was still groggy from the sleep, and she supposed he was right about a crash. She felt like she'd swum out of some kind of bender. Only instead of alcohol it was worry and stress.

She loosened her grip, flexed her fingers and realized,

like her neck, they were cramped and aching. She knew if she went in there with him, with this box and these letters, she was letting him into something…complicated. Potentially dangerous even. Certainly the kind of trouble he and his brothers were hoping to avoid.

"You don't have to sink yourself into this any further. I can handle it on my own." She wanted to believe she could—*had* to. You couldn't *count* on help, even if it was nice to receive once in a while.

She didn't dare look at Jake. Something about telling him she could handle it felt like a lie—even though it wasn't—and she was afraid that would show on her face.

"I'm already in it," he said firmly and got out of the truck before she could say anything else.

Zara blew out a breath that felt all too much like relief. She shouldn't lean on him. She shouldn't depend on anyone's help, but she found herself getting out of the truck and following him into her childhood home.

The rest of the brothers should still be out doing ranch work, if they were following her task list without her around. She assumed they would be, but as the sun set, they'd come home. Maybe Landon had already seen her in Jake's room, and that would be a bit hard to explain, but twice in one day?

"Maybe I should find somewhere else," Zara said, keeping her voice low in case someone *was* home. "I wouldn't want to drag your brothers—"

He put his hand at the small of her back like he was guiding her deeper into the house—when she knew the way. In the dark with her eyes closed.

But that simple touch on her back was…*something*. A prickling heat she didn't know how to classify because that was not…normal.

"I'll handle my brothers," he said. As they reached the staircase, his hand fell away and she could *think* again.

"You'll handle everything?" she asked, climbing the stairs, looking over her shoulder at him following her up.

"No one can handle everything, Zara."

Which felt far more like censure than she knew he meant. She whipped her head around and stared straight ahead, marching perhaps with a little too much purpose to her—his—room.

Her fingers tensed around the box again and she stood in the middle of the room not sure how to proceed. She didn't want to sit on his bed. Where he slept. He'd made it, with a precision that had her remembering what he'd said back at the museum.

Military.

She supposed it might explain some things about the six men. About their secrecy. Their stillness.

She walked over to the window. There was an old chair, small and kind of rickety for a man of his size, situated facing out. Like he sat there and watched the sunset every night.

Just like she'd done every year of her life until the last month.

She looked outside now. Across the land she'd always been so sure she'd tend. Her heart. Her legacy. *Generations* of Harts had built this, and it wasn't hers any longer.

She looked down at the box in her hands. Amberleigh wasn't alive any longer. And it was altogether possible, no matter how impossible it seemed, that Hazeleigh was in some kind of unalterable trouble herself.

Zara needed to get started, but what she really wanted to do was lower herself into the chair and watch the sun slowly sink behind the mountains. The rays of light reaching beyond their craggy peaks, always seemingly *toward* her. Giving her their strength.

She was sitting in the chair before she fully understood it. And once she roused herself from looking at the sinking sun, she glanced at Jake. He stood leaning casually against the door he'd closed behind them. His hands were in his pockets, and though he studied her, it wasn't with the desire for her to get this rolling.

He was so *patient.* Hazeleigh had that kind of patience in her, but in Hazeleigh, it was a certain…separateness. Like she was living in her own world and didn't worry herself with the time in this one.

Zara had no doubt Jake was living in this very world, and that he was just waiting for her to be ready to take the next step.

So she needed to. She looked down at the box, forced herself to open it even though her hands shook. She pulled out the stack of letters and flipped through them, noting names and dates.

"They're all to Hazeleigh from Amberleigh," Zara managed, her voice rustier than she'd like it to be. "They go back to last year."

"Why don't you start at the beginning?" he suggested when she didn't move. Just sat there holding the stack of letters.

Why not? Because she was afraid of what was in them. Afraid of what she would have to do, prove, decide.

Which wasn't acceptable. Fear didn't change the situation in front of you. She should know.

She handed him the top half of the stack, and focused on her own stack rather than how he looked settling himself on his bed.

Where she'd once slept.

She pulled out the letter from the earliest postmarked envelope. The address on the front wasn't the house or the cabin, it was the fort. Hazeleigh had worked there since high school in some capacity, so Amberleigh would have known she could reach her there. Or someone there would know to get the letters to her.

Trying to keep her mind from engaging in the fact her dead sister had folded this paper up, stuck it in the envelope and sent it to her currently jailed sister, and Zara had never been the wiser.

So, she read.

Dear Hazie,
Merry almost-Christmas! Surprised to hear from me?
Believe me, I'm surprised to be writing! I could have
sent you an email or text I guess, but I knew you'd get
a kick out of a handwritten letter. (And people can
read emails and texts, can't they? But they'll never
know what I wrote you.)
Don't tell Dad. Don't tell Queen Zara. This is just
between you and me, Hazie. I know I can trust you.
And you know we can't trust them.
When can you get away? I want to see you!
Love,
Amberleigh

Queen Zara. Zara had always hated that nickname. Yes, she'd been bossier than she needed to be back then. Okay, always, probably even now, but sometimes being in charge meant being bossy. Especially when there was a ranch to run, a father to keep from falling too far into the bottle, and back then, trying to keep her grades up and...

She folded the letter back up and put it in the envelope and set it aside. She just had to read through them. Not defend herself to herself, or to a dead Amberleigh.

Dear Hazie,
I can't meet you until you promise me in writing that
you won't tell Zaraleigh.
Amberleigh

Much shorter that time around. And it didn't mention Dad. Just her. What had Hazeleigh's response said? How had Hazeleigh gotten a response to Amberleigh?

Zara flipped the envelope back to the front. "The return address on this one is a PO box in Harvey. That's only about two hours away." Had her sister been that close all along? Wouldn't that be impossible?

Zara had assumed she'd gotten the heck out of Wyoming, like she'd always wanted to. California or Seattle or New York City. Anything but craggy mountains and tiny western towns, she'd always said.

Zara had never understood how they were related, let alone shared the same face.

She flipped through the other envelopes, and though sometimes the PO box number changed, Harvey never did.

"All Harvey," Jake confirmed of his stack.

She looked up and he was studying her. "Zara..." He held up the letter he'd been reading. "This last letter..."

Her stomach sank. *Please no.*

"It seems to indicate Hazeleigh was meeting her. Routinely. Up till a month ago."

ZARA SQUEEZED HER eyes shut against what was a clear wave of pain. Jake wished he could take it away for her, but this was bad.

Really bad. The letter clearly spelled out where and when Hazeleigh and Amberleigh would meet. And the fact the letters stopped a month ago, which was probably way too close to when she'd died for comfort.

"She didn't *do* it, Jake."

"I believe you." He knew that looks could be deceiving, and that Hazeleigh's skittishness could have been a con in and of itself. But he also knew Zara, and his own gut instincts.

He also knew Zara *needed* him to believe her, so he simply would.

"I can't give this to the police. Not when they already have evidence against her. This is a nail in the coffin."

"Let's read through the rest of them," Jake said, keeping his voice even, calm. She was both, but he could sense if they didn't keep moving forward she might just shatter. "Maybe it gives some kind of clue. Something we can follow up on. Something that proves Hazeleigh wasn't involved, even if she was meeting Amberleigh."

Zara nodded and immediately pulled out another letter. She flew through them, so he did the same. He'd go over them again, add whatever details he could to the board, but for now they were just skimming for something that cleared Hazeleigh.

He didn't find anything of note. Just places and times to meet. And the recurring assertion Hazeleigh not tell anyone.

"Anything?"

When she didn't answer, he looked up. She had put away all the letters, stacked them again in the neat pile reminding him of Hazeleigh's ruthlessly organized desk. He handed her his stack. She added it to the pile, put them back into the box and closed the lid.

She stared at the box in her lap, still not speaking.

"Zara."

She inhaled deeply. "Nothing except the meetings. They've been meeting for almost a year…"

The "without telling me" was left unsaid but hung in the air just the same.

"I can't tell the police. Not yet. But…"

He waited as she wrestled with the weight of whatever it was she wanted to say.

"I don't know what to do," she finally finished, as if the words had to be pushed out with supreme effort.

Jake didn't either, but that was a pretty consistent place he'd found himself in. He'd learned how to cope and adapt. "Okay. This is what we know. Amberleigh had a PO box in Harvey. Amberleigh and Hazeleigh met at the Fish Inn, whatever *that* is, about once a month for a year." He didn't add the part where the meetings stopped around the same time Amberleigh was likely murdered. Without Hazeleigh saying anything to anyone.

Except for her "feeling" when she'd begged him and Zara not to dig in that spot. It was all too many coincidences not to wonder if Hazeleigh was the murderer, but at the same time, she hadn't really tried to stop him from digging. She'd been in distress, yes, but not physically trying to stop anything.

"Yes, we know all that," Zara agreed. "It's all bad news."

"Maybe." But he couldn't let her live in that bad-news space. "Maybe we just need more information. What if we go to Harvey?"

"Harvey? Like…the Fish Inn?"

"Yeah. We go. We ask around. Maybe someone saw them or overheard something."

"We?"

"Is it ever not going to surprise you that I'm going to work with you on this? We're after the same thing, remember?"

She stared at him for a very long time, her hands still tight around the box. And Jake found himself yet again *unnerved* by the way this woman looked at him, when he'd had foster parents look through him and superiors scream in his face and the enemy so close he could see the whites of his eyes, wishing him *dead*.

It had been easier in a strange way to deal with those things over the little glimmer of hope he saw in Zara's eyes.

"I'm sorry. I don't really know how not to be surprised by all…this," she said, waving her hand around the room as if to encompass everything. "Not because of you, just because… I'm the one who takes care of things around here. I have since my mother died. Problems with the ranch, struggles with the girls." She stared down at the box. "I thought I did a pretty good job all in all, and Amberleigh is dead and Hazeleigh is in jail."

"And you're working to get justice for both. I can tell you with certainty, Zara, not everybody does that. A lot of people leave you to the wolves, blood or no."

"Well, I'm sorry for that too, then. That you didn't have people who fought for you."

He shrugged, uncomfortable all the ways pieces of himself kept seeming to be uncovered. Unraveled. "I found them eventually." And he had. He'd learned how to stick up for people who needed help.

She stood, still gripping the box tight enough he thought the hinges on the lid might bend and the wood might splinter.

"I have to call the lawyer Thomas told me about."

"Call on the way."

"You want to go now?"

"Why not?"

"Your brothers…"

"There are five of them. They can handle the ranch and live without me for a day or two. And I hate to break it to you, but they're pretty adamant you don't come back to work until after there's a funeral. No matter what happens, you lost your sister. You deserve time off to deal with that."

"You guys are very kind, and I haven't been kind to y—"

"We're military men. We're used to drill sergeants and hard work. You made us feel right at home."

Her mouth almost curved and he was a little too desperate to make it stretch out all the way. "I'm doing this for my brothers and our life here, but I'm also doing it because you're not so bad to have as a friend."

She didn't smile. She almost looked pained.

So he went the opposite route. He grinned at her. "Zara-leigh." He hoped she'd scowl at him or make another de-tonguing threat. But she never quite went to plan, did she?

She moved forward and hugged him. A little bit awk-wardly, but it was a friendly, gratitude hug.

Might as well have shot him in the heart.

Chapter Eleven

Zara didn't know what possessed her. Except she didn't have the words to thank him. So she thought a simple hug would do the trick. Better than staring at those blue eyes and getting a little too lost in them.

Or so she'd thought. Turned out hugging a big, tall, hard *man* was not exactly the stuff apologies were made of. And a little more enjoyable than she felt comfortable admitting. She was a strong, independent cowgirl. Why the hell would it feel nice to lean on someone?

She pulled back and fought back a wave of embarrassment. "It's late. We could wait until the morning."

"You don't want to wait. You want answers. I'll grab a few things, some snacks, and then we'll head over to your cabin so you can too. Should we leave the letters here?"

"Let's bring them with."

He nodded.

"I can go get my things on my own. You don't have to…" She wondered if she'd ever be able to stop telling him all the things he didn't *have* to do, that he seemed to want to do or not mind doing.

He turned to look at her, then reached out and put his hand on her shoulder. It seemed to be his main way of giving comfort. His big, *big* hand on her shoulder. "Look, Hazeleigh saying she's safe in jail is a concern. You look exactly like her and the dead person. I'm not sure alone is what you should be right now."

Now he was worried about her *safety*. Oh, she was in so much trouble when this was over and she had some kind of terrible crush on him.

But this wasn't about her feelings, and it certainly wasn't anywhere close to being over. This was about getting Hazeleigh out of jail and figuring out the real murderer. Because someone *had* murdered Amberleigh and buried her on Hart land.

"Okay." What else was there to say? If they drove to Harvey and got some answers…maybe this *could* be over sooner rather than later.

He went to his closet, didn't unlock the part with the board and her bureau that had once hidden her secrets, but he grabbed a beat-up duffel and shoved a few things in it. He disappeared into the hallway to get some things out of the bathroom and then returned. All said and done, he'd packed up in under five minutes.

It was like an out-of-body experience. This couldn't really be her life. Something had happened a month ago. A break with reality. A rip in the fabric of time.

But when he was ready to go, it was her two feet that followed him out of the room and downstairs. Her reality, no matter how unreal it felt.

As they walked into the living room, voices wafted in from the kitchen area. A lot of low voices, talking and laughing and swearing irritably.

"Just got to pop in and tell them what's up," Jake said, already heading toward the kitchen.

Zara desperately wanted to sneak out the front door rather than face down how to explain all this. But it seemed wrong to duck away. Though she wished she had when five pairs of eyes were staring at her behind Jake with a kind of empathy she didn't understand. It was hard to not feel some guilt over the way she'd viewed them for over a month—as interlopers and enemies.

"We're headed out. Be gone a day or two."

"Day or two," Cal echoed incredulously, frowning at the bag in Jake's hand.

"Yeah, you guys can handle things for a day or two, can't you?"

"Sure. But where on earth are you going?" Cal demanded.

Zara hadn't been any kinder to Cal than she was to Jake or anyone else, but she understood Cal. He was clearly the leader of the group and Jake had just flipped the script. So he had demands. And anger.

"Just got a lead to check out," Jake said, wholly unbothered by the frown on Cal's face.

"Shouldn't you leave that to the police?" Brody offered casually, but there was a pointed look he gave Jake.

Which Jake clearly saw and ignored. "We will if it amounts to anything they can help us with. See you guys later."

He didn't wait around for any more questions or to assuage all the unsaid concerns very clear on his brothers' faces.

"They don't seem pleased," Zara said in a low voice, but Jake was propelling her into the living room, toward the front door, his hand on the small of her back again.

"They never seem pleased," Jake returned equitably. "Don't worry about it. Let's head over to the cabin."

Zara felt a bit like she was being led around on a leash. Which was a wholly new and strange feeling for her—so much so she didn't know how to fight it. So few people had ever *told* her what to do before, or decided on a course of action *for* her.

There was an odd relief in someone taking the reins.

Her phone rang as they approached the cabin and she

pulled it out. Wincing a little bit at the readout on her screen. "Hey, Dad."

"Z-sara."

He'd been drinking. She squeezed her eyes shut. "You okay?"

He swore at her, a filthy stream of words. She'd opened her mouth to cut them off, but the phone was plucked out of her hand before she could. Jake marched in front of her, presumably clicked End on the call and then dropped the phone into his coat pocket.

"No need for that," Jake said firmly, his jaw tight. He gestured to her door as a sign to have her unlock it.

Zara tried to process it all. She should probably be angry with him. He had no right to hang up on her father *for* her, or pocket her phone, or tell her what to do, or *help* her with this whole damn thing.

But no matter how she tried to stir up her own usual anger, she just thought…he'd defended her in a strange way. Protected her from having to deal with her father when he was acting like that.

But she did have to deal with it. "I should go check on him."

Jake eyed her, arms crossed over his chest almost casually. But there was a tension there. "Has interceding when he's drunk ever gone well for you?"

She supposed it shouldn't surprise her that Jake would see through the situation so easily. He seemed to see through everything, understand all sorts of things she'd never verbalized. And his question had her wilting, because no, she'd never been able to solve her father's issues. Least of all when he was drinking. "No."

"If you're worried about his welfare, call the cops. But don't put yourself in a position like that."

"Let me guess. You have experience with that too."

He laughed, but there was a bitterness in it she hadn't

heard from him before. "When it comes to the foibles of humans, there isn't a lot I haven't dealt with."

"I suppose you swoop in on your white horse every time?"

He studied her for a long while, something in his eyes as foreign to her as being led. "Not every time," he said with a gravity that made her heart beat just a little too fast.

She swallowed and fumbled with her keys, not meeting his gaze anymore. She really needed to stop that. Keep her wits about her—impossible when his eyes met hers. She jammed the key into the lock, but his hand came over hers before she twisted it.

"Wait," he ordered. "Something isn't right."

JAKE SUPPOSED, IN a way, it was like Hazeleigh's "feelings" as Zara had described them. He couldn't explain to her what was wrong, only that he had a sudden sensation that something was off.

There was a...smell in the air that didn't belong. An odd stillness to the air that should have been bustling with bird flight and breezes dancing through the...

Sand and desert and the bone-deep terror that nothing was going as it should. The faint sound of gunfire, the arid air making his eyes gritty and yet he couldn't blink. If he blinked...

"Jake?"

He started at Zara's voice, the current moment sliding back into focus. Her hand rested on his chest, and there was genuine concern all over her face.

He hadn't had a moment like that in a while. They'd been debriefed enough to know that certain...residual physical responses were normal. Nightmares, shakes, flashbacks. As long as they didn't interfere with his daily life, it was simply a...side effect, so to speak, of his military career.

They were rare, and he was rational, so he wasn't going to freak out about it.

But that didn't mean he was thrilled it had happened in front of Zara.

He cleared his throat. "Sorry."

Her hand fell off his chest, and he had the urge to grab it. Hold on to it. He didn't. He looked at the cabin critically. There wasn't anything off that he could see. But he didn't know the cabin as well as she did. "Does anything look out of place? Anything at all. Not just big things. Small, inconsequential things too."

She turned slowly, her concerned gaze changing to one of speculation as she studied her house. She turned in a slow circle, looking up and then down. She frowned at the pot of flowers on the porch. "It's been moved."

"Moved?"

She pointed at the depression of snow that made it clear the pot had moved an inch or two to the left. "Not by much. An animal searching for scraps could have done it. I could have done it, but it's definitely been moved and..."

"And?"

"I keep a spare key under that pot. We don't use it very often, because we don't lock up very often, but we keep it there when we do have to lock up. Which I have been, obviously."

"Does anyone know besides Hazeleigh?"

"I doubt it. Dad, maybe? But he doesn't come out here very often. He did come out the other day, but I really don't think he knew it was there. And if he's been..."

She didn't say it, but she didn't have to. He'd heard the muffled drunken tirade. The lack of surprise on Zara's face. A kind of exhausted acceptance as the color leached out of her face.

Yeah, he didn't have very many memories before the foster home, but that was one of them. He'd been too little to do anything about it then, so he'd be damned if he stood around and let it happen to someone now.

"Stay out here," he told Zara, putting his bag on the little rocking chair they had on the porch and digging around until he found his gun case. He unzipped it and pulled the revolver out. With quick efficient movements, keeping his body between the weapon and Zara's view of it, he loaded it. "I'll go in and make sure no one's in there."

"But why would anyone be in there? Why would *I* be in danger?"

He didn't know the answer to that. He only knew it was better to be safe than sorry. "I'm just going to check it out. Stay put. That's all you have to do." He pulled her phone out of his pocket and handed it to her.

Just in case.

She eyed the gun warily, but she didn't say anything as she took her phone. She pulled her keys out of her pocket and unlocked the door. He touched her arm with his free hand before she could turn the knob and open it.

"Just wait here," he said firmly, hoping she would listen. A few days ago, he knew she wouldn't have. She had been sure of her place in her little world and confident it was her role to march through it in charge.

Then they'd found Amberleigh buried in the ground.

He had never met Amberleigh, but even for him, it was a turning point. All of Cal's carefully instituted rules about boundaries and space had gone out the window. And Jake was too used to turning points not to go with the flow.

He moved into the cabin and did a sweep, mostly looking for evidence of someone or anything dangerous. He didn't see anything as he went through each room, every closet and possible hiding spot. He retraced his steps, checking a second time until he was satisfied the cabin was clear.

He returned to the porch and gestured for her to come

in. "It's clear, but I want you to look around and see if you notice anything I didn't."

He followed her as she walked through the cabin. He'd always thought she'd had a bit of a poker face, but today, she seemed to have lost the ability. Every emotion chased over her features. Worry, concern, self-doubt. He could practically hear her inner thoughts. *Was that chair really here? Or was it angled the other way?*

"Nothing's been moved," she said, hesitating in front of Hazeleigh's room. "But…" She trailed off and then inched forward, like she had to force herself to make the move.

Jake followed close behind, noticing that Hazeleigh's room was ruthlessly organized but still cozy and feminine, unlike Zara's room, which had been…utilitarian at best. And not particularly organized. It would definitely be easier to see if someone had messed with Hazeleigh's things.

She walked over to the nightstand next to Hazeleigh's bed. There was a box just like the one that had been in Hazeleigh's desk at the fort.

"It's backwards," Zara said, swallowing. "The initials should be facing the bed, but they're facing the wall. Like the pot, it could just be coincidence. The police searched her room after all."

But she reached forward and, with obvious trepidation, lifted the lid. Then she lifted the whole box and gave it a little shake. She turned it over and pushed something so the bottom popped open.

She peered in, then jumped back, the box falling onto the bed. She whirled to face him, her eyes squeezed shut.

"What is it?" Jake demanded, striding forward and looking into the box's false bottom himself. For supposedly innocent people, there were sure a lot of intricate hiding places.

There was a necklace in the bottom. With what looked like blood crusted in the chain.

"It was Amberleigh's," Zara whispered. "She…" She cleared her throat. "She came home with it one day. She never told anyone if she bought it or if someone gave it to her. But after she disappeared with Mr. Phillips, we always assumed…"

"We could call the police," Jake said carefully. "Maybe they would believe that someone had planted it. This Mr. Phillips…"

Zara eyed him. "I don't think I can deal in maybes. Not with Hazeleigh in jail and that being hidden in the false bottom the police wouldn't have originally searched."

He nodded. "Then we'll take it with us."

She nodded faintly, looking around Hazeleigh's room. "I think someone put this in here today, Jake. But that pot could have been moved by a million different things. This box could have been backwards for days. Maybe it's paranoia…"

"No, I agree with you. Something didn't feel right out there. I don't think we missed whoever put this here by very long."

"They expect the police to come search again. They must."

Jake nodded. "So let's get out of here. And do a little searching of our own."

Chapter Twelve

Zara grabbed a few things. Mostly things that no one would miss. She packed a travel toothbrush, a pair of jeans and a long-sleeved tee and flannel that wouldn't be missed out of the other pairs she had that all looked the same.

She mussed up her bed a little bit, so anyone would assume she'd slept in it, even though she didn't plan to tonight.

Because if someone put that bloody necklace in Hazeleigh's box, they expected the police to come back again.

She put said box, bloody necklace and all, in her bag.

Part of her felt like she was making a mistake. She should take it to the police and trust them. Thomas was a good police officer. Laurel seemed like an empathetic detective, and Zara knew Thomas looked up to the woman as a kind of mentor, which meant she had to be good at her job.

Zara should trust what she'd always been brought up to trust, but as she stepped into the living room, Jake was there. He still held the gun, though relaxed at his side rather than with that flinty-eyed stare he'd had when he'd pulled it out of his bag in the first place.

He stood there, tall and strong, looking through the window to the dark world outside.

She trusted him. More than her cousin. More than the detective. More than just about anyone.

She didn't know why. She couldn't begin to explain it.

Maybe it was something about the way he'd held that gun, or held her when she cried, or just kept offering to help.

She knew he'd had some sort of…flashback out there. His eyes had gone unfocused, his breathing had increased, and she'd just known he wasn't there with her. He was reliving something else.

Her heart had broken for him. And when she'd said his name, he'd come back.

She supposed it didn't mean anything. She didn't know anything about the military or what kind of scars it might leave with a person. How anyone dealt with them or how a soldier brought themselves back to the current world when lost in an old, painful one.

But she'd reached out and touched him, and he'd gotten to work. Protecting her. She wanted to make it about keeping his brothers out of trouble. She knew she should.

But it felt so much more personal than that the longer this went on, the more he was essentially lying for her.

"Ready?" he asked, without turning around. He'd sensed her or heard her and knew she was staring at him. She wondered how he did that, how Hazeleigh listened to "feelings." How anyone saw or sensed any more than the here and now.

But then she thought about the way she knew a calf would come or when the leaves would burst forth in spring. When she could smell rain or snow in the air. Because her life was attuned to the ranch, to her world. It was the same, all in all.

"Yes, I'm ready." Because she didn't know what was going on, but she knew her sister wasn't a murderer. And whoever *was* had spent some time framing Hazeleigh for it.

She'd made a promise to her mother, not that Mom had asked, that she'd protect her sisters. She couldn't protect them from Mom dying, but she could look out for them. Be a stand-in mother to them.

She had failed Amberleigh. She couldn't fail Hazeleigh too.

They walked out to Jake's truck and climbed in. The sunset had completely faded and stars winked above. They followed the moon out to the highway.

Jake didn't ask for directions. He just drove. A country station offered jovial drinking songs at low tones.

They said nothing for a very long time. She had forgotten to pay attention to the time, and instead counted the stars like she used to do when she'd been too worried to sleep.

"Someone's following us," Jake said quietly.

She started to whip her head around, but he let out a sharp "don't" and she stopped. Looking at him instead.

"We don't want them to know we know they're following us," he said. His voice was certain, his grip on the steering wheel still casual. His gaze flicked to the rear-view mirror. "Do you know anyone who drives a silver or gray Ford pickup?"

"I know a hundred people who drive that, Jake."

"Okay. Any cops?"

She thought about Thomas and the other cops she knew. "Not that I know of, but it's a pretty common vehicle around Wilde. Maybe it's a coincidence."

"Maybe," he agreed.

She didn't believe his agreement for a second.

She slowly moved her face to look forward again. Then she looked in the rearview mirror. She saw a pair of head-lights and maybe the slight glimmer that offered the color of the truck, but mostly his eyesight must have been much better than hers.

"So, what do we do?"

He didn't say anything at first. He was thinking it through, weighing options.

Because he didn't know what to do any more than she did.

"We shouldn't go to the Fish Inn if we're really being followed."

"Right, but we need to go somewhere convincing. If they're following, just following, they want to know where we're going," Jake said, mulling it over. "Somewhere two people might randomly drive to on a Wednesday night in December."

"We're going to pass through Bent in a little bit. There's not much there, but there is a saloon."

"A saloon," Jake said with the ghost of a smile. "You all take your Wild West very seriously."

It might have been a little funnier if they weren't being followed. But she still smiled. "Oh, you have no idea."

JAKE FOLLOWED ZARA's directions off the highway to the tiny town of Bent. Much like Wilde, there wasn't much to the town. A Main Street with a few of the basics, and at the end of that Main Street a…yes, saloon.

It looked like every saloon in every Western movie or TV show he'd ever seen. Wood siding and a walkway in front of it, a ramshackle overhang, hand-painted signs he couldn't quite make out in the dark and the odd glow of the neon signs—the only thing not very western about it.

Except one—a neon, centaur-like creature, half horse, half very busty woman, a blinking sack of gold hanging off her saddle. And the name of the bar in bright lights: Rightful Claim.

Jake pulled his truck to a park in the small gravel lot on the far side of the building. For a small town and a weekday night, there was a pretty full lot. They got out of the truck, and Jake watched the road for their followers.

"We'll go in and order a drink," Jake said, letting Zara lead the way to the front door. "After we order, you'll stay put inside and I'm going to come out and take a look around."

"Is that safe?" Zara asked, her footsteps echoing on the wood-planked walkway.

Jake didn't tell her he had his gun in his coat pocket. "I'll be careful."

She walked up to the entrance of the bar. They were actual swinging saloon doors. Jake followed Zara inside, watching as the pickup truck that had been following them drove down Main Street past the entrance. Jake tried to get a glimpse of the driver without being too obvious, but it was too dark.

Inside, rough-hewn wood planks made up the walls of the main area, high-top tables littered the room. Lining the doorway were pictures of the place over the years, a few photos including a signed one of country singer Daisy Delaney.

In the back was a long bar. Most of the stools pulled up to it were taken by men in heavy work coats. Two men tended said bar, both tattooed and bearded, laughing with each other and the patrons.

Jake put his hand at the small of Zara's back, propelling her forward. Her footsteps slowed, practically pushing back against his hand. "Uh, Jake. There's something I kind of forgot about when I suggested Bent and the saloon."

"Oh, yeah, what's that?" he asked, only half paying attention as he kept an eye behind them at the door, just in case the people or person following them was bold enough to follow them right into the bar.

"You know the detective? Laurel Delaney-Carson?"

"Yeah."

"One of those bartenders might be her husband. He owns the place."

Jake's head snapped forward again, taking in the two men behind the bar serving drinks. *Hell.* "Yeah, that might have been helpful information before we came inside." Still he didn't stop their forward movement. Best not to draw any attention. "Does he know who you are?"

"I don't know. It's possible. Thomas is good friends with their family, but I've never met them in a formal introduction way."

But if the detective brought any of her work home, it was possible the husband knew about the triplets who were his friend's cousins. One dead, one in jail and one right here.

"Stay behind me," Jake said quietly. "I'll order for both of us. Just try to look casual, but keep your head out of the bartenders' lines of vision as much as possible."

Zara nodded and fell back behind him a little bit as they finally approached the bar. Jake squeezed into a spot between taken stools, leaning his elbow on the bar and smiling at the bartender. "Can I get two beers? Whatever you've got in a bottle."

He didn't look back at Zara to make sure she was listening to him. That might bring attention to her too.

He fished a twenty out of his pocket and slid it across the bar as the bartender put two bottles out for him. He waited for the change, outwardly the most patient man alive. Inwardly, strung tighter than a drum.

He thought the bartender gave him a speculative, careful look, but Jake wasn't sure if it was simply because he was a new face in what was surely a small-town bar that didn't get many new faces, or because he recognized...something.

He pocketed the change, took the beers and then turned and gave Zara a little nudge. "Anywhere to sit?" he asked brightly.

"Yeah, looks like that table in the corner is free," she returned, and he was impressed with how casual she sounded. Her body was tense, but someone would have to be looking for that reaction to see it.

He hoped.

The table in the back hadn't been cleared since the previous guests had left, but they both took it anyway. Jake made sure Zara took the seat that kept her back to the bar.

She blew out a relieved breath when they sat down, but they were hardly out of hot water. He had to focus on the biggest threat at the moment—which wasn't the detective's husband figuring them out. It was who was following them. And why.

"I'm going to pretend to get a phone call and go outside. All you have to do is stay put and try to remain inconspicuous. I'll make sure the truck didn't stop around here to follow us any farther."

"What if they did stop around here to follow us farther?"

"Then we'll know, and I'll come back in and we'll decide what to do next. Okay?"

She was frowning, but she nodded, clutching the bottle of beer in front of her. "Okay."

He gave it another minute, then pulled his phone out of his pocket and pantomimed telling Zara he'd be back in a minute before he stood and weaved his way out of the bar. He didn't look back at the bartenders, no matter how much he wanted to. Didn't look back at Zara for a whole host of reasons he didn't want to identify.

He stepped outside, pretended to talk on his phone, all the while studying the dark world around him. The lights of the saloon were about the only ones on in all of Main Street. A building a ways down had some kind of security light on, but that was about it.

He walked toward the parking lot, still pretending to talk on his phone. He went to his truck, looking at every other one in the parking lot. A lot of them looked like the truck that had been following him, but if he touched the hood, they were cold and no one was in them.

He reached into his own truck, pretended to get something from the glove compartment, then made his way back to the saloon. Instead of heading toward the front though, he decided to make a quick walk around back to see if there was any more parking or an alley someone might have driven down.

He kept to the shadows. He tried to listen, but the voices and music from inside the bar wafted outside and it was hard to tell if the engine he heard was coming from behind the building or out on Main Street.

He slid his gun out of his pocket but kept it close to his side. In the back, there was a car idling. A silver Ford pickup.

Jake kept his back to the wall of the building and inched closer and closer, trying to get *some* glimpse of the man sitting in the driver's seat. He noted the license plate, committed the letters and numbers to memory. He couldn't make out any driver though.

Which put a little bit of a wrinkle into his plan.

So he'd have to come up with a new one.

Chapter Thirteen

Zara felt like every muscle in her body was tensed against her will. She kept her gaze trained straight ahead. Hung on the wall was a painting of a woman on a horse, leaning over and embracing a cowboy who was holding a bouquet of flowers behind his back.

It was a surprisingly sweet painting compared to some of the more rustic or bawdy decor. And if she thought about that, she could almost forget what Jake was outside doing.

Putting himself in danger. For her.

For himself and his brothers.

You really think so?

On and on, in circles. So she traced the flowers with her eyes, the purples and pinks. He was hiding them behind his leg. Would he give them to the woman? What would her reaction be? Why did he look a little too like Jake in her imagination, when the painting didn't look a thing like him?

Zara jumped a foot when someone behind her said her name. Her full name.

"Zaraleigh Hart."

The woman's voice was unfamiliar, and Zara was about to turn, but something sharp was being jammed into her back, *through* her coat, and she went immediately still.

The woman leaned over her, standing behind her and likely hiding her from view of anyone around them. Her voice was low in Zara's ear. "You're going to stand. Slowly.

Then you're going to head to the back and calmly follow signs to the women's bathroom."

Zara was terrified, but even shaken with fear, she didn't take well to orders. "If I don't?"

"Your friend outside won't know what hit him."

Zara's entire body went cold. "What do you mean?"

"Stand. Go to the bathroom."

Zara considered her options. She knew how to fight, but the woman clearly had a knife of some kind. Zara could stand up and yell and hopefully *someone* would help her.

But what about Jake? Outside, all alone? He wouldn't know what hit him. She couldn't... No, she couldn't let that happen.

She stood.

"Don't look back at me. Just turn and walk to the bathroom."

She did what the woman said, though she tried to see the woman out of her peripheral vision. But that sharp object jammed into her back again, and Zara stepped forward, weaving her way through the tables and people as the woman followed her, knife concealed by the woman's sleeve but definitely the sharp end breaking through the skin of Zara's back.

Zara glanced at the two men behind the bar as she passed. They were chatting and serving drinks, but as if he sensed he was being stared at, the one who'd served Jake looked up. The one she thought she recognized from the detective's phone.

She didn't look away. She didn't do anything. She just held his gaze, stared at him, *willing* him to see that something wasn't quite right.

He frowned vaguely, but someone must have called his name because he looked back to one of the patrons and smiled.

Zara weighed her options as she went into a little hallway that led to a back room. There was a men's bathroom, a women's bathroom and a swinging door she assumed went into a kitchen or storage room. There was also a little staircase that must have gone up to an apartment of some kind.

There weren't any people at the moment, but surely someone would come to go to the bathroom or emerge from those kitchen doors.

"See that door at the end of the hall? You're going to walk right out it. There's a truck waiting for you."

Zara studied the exit that likely led out behind the building. A truck waiting for her? That was not ideal. "And what about my friend?"

Out of the corner of her eye, Zara saw the woman *smirk*.

Which solved *that* for Zara. She knew how to fight. She'd learned in middle school the quickest way to get a boy to leave her or her sisters alone was to break his nose. If they were afraid of her, they didn't mess with Hazeleigh and Amberleigh so much.

This woman had a knife, but she wasn't much taller than Zara. It was hard to tell with all the loose-fitting black clothing she was wearing, but Zara thought she had the weight advantage on her.

She took a deep breath, remembered to keep her body loose so the woman wouldn't anticipate the blow, and then jerked her elbow up. She didn't get a full elbow to the chin before the woman jumped back, but between that and the glancing blow, she had enough space she could jump out of the knife's reach and whirl to face the woman.

She raised her fists, ready to fight her way out of this. The woman stood there with a sneer, holding the knife in one hand.

"You're going to regret that."

"You're going to regret trying to kidnap me." God, she hoped *that* was true. She eyed the entrance to the main part of the bar behind the woman. It was her best shot, because while she could run out the back door, she'd likely be running either into the dark or the truck the woman mentioned was waiting to take her away.

"What the hell do you want with me?"

"It's a shame you can't ask your sister." The woman flashed a nasty smile and then started advancing on Zara, knife pointed as if ready to do some damage.

Zara assumed the woman was referring to Amberleigh when she mentioned "sister," but what did she know? Maybe Hazeleigh was mixed up in *this* too.

Whatever this was.

Zara backed up, but knew she only had a few steps. If she kept backing up, she'd back right out the door and into whoever was waiting's hands.

She'd never fought with anyone wielding a knife, and she realized that while she'd never minded the threat of getting punched in the face, getting stabbed was a little more concerning.

"Things are going to go a lot better for you if you just follow orders."

Zara laughed. "I'm not stupid. Whatever you want from me is not *better* for me than getting far away from you."

"Suit yourself. We can fight. I'll win." She twirled the knife. "I do have this and all. But for taking up my valuable time…" She pulled a phone out of her pocket. "All it takes is one phone call to end your friend."

Zara kept her fists bunched and in front of her, but she eyed the phone. The woman could be lying, and Jake had been in the military. Maybe he could handle himself. He was out there looking for whoever had followed them.

Maybe she should trust him to take care of himself.

Put herself first. Get herself out of this. Then worry about all the rest, because this woman had a knife, and a phone that could apparently, possibly end Jake's life.

No, she really couldn't take a chance on that. Surely she

could survive being stabbed. It wasn't a gunshot after all. Even that was *survivable*, wasn't it? She'd been kicked by horses and cows and even a donkey once when she'd been very small and still learning the ins and outs of ranching with very little guidance from her father.

She wasn't a little girl anymore. So, she charged. Apparently it was surprising enough the woman *didn't* think to jab the knife into her stomach. The woman fell backward, the phone falling out of her hand.

Sadly, the knife didn't go with quite such ease, even as Zara landed on top of the woman. The woman reared back as if to use it, but Zara grabbed her arm and wrestled it away from her body. They tussled like that, Zara feeling a bit like she was in a calf-roping competition.

If only she had some rope.

She managed to put all her body weight on the arm holding the knife, but the woman rolled over with enough force Zara rolled across the floor, and the woman now had her arm free to stab.

They jumped to their feet at the same time. This time Zara was facing the exit, with the woman in front of her. Zara could easily bolt back into the bar.

She took a step back.

"I'm going to take real pleasure in hurting him," the woman said. "And you, eventually."

"If he doesn't hurt you first," Zara replied, hoping to God it was possible Jake could handle himself. Surely if *she* could, *he* would.

She took another step back, toward the bar and people and *help*.

What about that bloody necklace?

Help was just as dangerous as the woman with the knife, but one option she had a better chance of talking her way out of. Maybe. She took another step back and into a wall—

Or what she thought was a wall. When she looked over

her shoulder, she saw nothing but a man's broad chest. She looked up and realized it was one of the bartenders. He had his arms crossed over his chest and was eyeing the woman with the knife. "I called the cops."

The woman flicked a glance at the exit behind her, then made a run for it. Zara turned to face him.

The bartender studied her with concern. "You okay? Should I run after her?"

Zara couldn't look at him and his kind concern. The woman had run—without a phone now but she still had a knife. And she might be going after Jake. Jake was still out there.

"I have to go," Zara heard herself say, stepping away from the man. She started backing away, toward the exit where the woman had gone.

"You're one of Hart's cousins, aren't you?" The bartender held up his hands in a peace gesture as he moved toward her for every step she took back. "Laurel Delaney-Carson is my wife. She's working on a case for you, right? Why don't you come on upstairs? You can wait for the cops to get here. I called Thomas specifically. He lives just down the road, he should be here any minute."

Zara knew he was being kind. That he'd attempted to help her by calling Thomas. "I can't." She edged more and more for the door. She had to find Jake. They had to get out of here.

Maybe the woman with the knife was a problem, but so was the bloody necklace in her bag in Jake's truck. It pointed at too many things that made Hazeleigh guilty, and Jake guilty by association.

Zara made it to the door, pushed it open.

"They're just going to come after you. Those guys. The police." He said this sympathetically.

Zara nodded. He was probably right. But she couldn't let that stop her. "That phone on the floor was the woman's. Make sure the police know that. And could you tell Thomas not to follow us? I know he won't listen, but maybe if he understood I had to do this. That I'm not just... I *had* to do it. Tell him that."

"If you're scared, we can protect you here. You're among friends here. Hart is my daughter's godfather. I promise—"

She believed him. But that didn't change her reality. "I have to go." And she bolted.

JAKE HEARD THE FOOTSTEPS, too close and out of place with where he was crouched in the shadows. He had a mere second to whirl and react.

He blocked an arm that slashed down at him, holding a knife. He punched with the other arm, but the guy was big and muscled and mean, and the blow didn't seem to affect him.

The man stood facing him, a knife glinting in the faint glimmer of a streetlight a ways down the alley.

Jake adjusted the gun in his hand, lifted and aimed. "Looks like you brought a knife to a gunfight, friend."

"Quieter though," the man said, his nasty smile glinting in the sweep of far-off headlights. "You fire that gun at me you're going to have to answer a lot of questions from the cops."

The man was right, of course, but Jake had to pretend like that didn't matter to him. He shrugged. "I think I'll come out all right."

"You'd be surprised." The man laughed, edging closer, the knife still gripped and held out like it could trump a gun. "You don't know what you're dealing with."

Which was true. Clearly. This was getting more complicated by the minute. It made Jake even more leery of shooting. Made this all the more…precarious.

Someone clattered out of the back entrance of the bar. "Leave him," a woman said, running for the idling truck.

"Cops are on the way," the woman said on a hiss. "We'll come back for her later."

The man was momentarily distracted, and Jake could have shot him. Not to kill, just to wound, but the man wasn't wrong. It would bring up far, far too many questions and the kind of attention he and Zara couldn't afford.

So he charged instead. He could use the gun as a different weapon. Knock him down, get a good blow in. But the man held fast, going with the momentum rather than letting it knock him off his feet.

And the knife easily slashed down, into Jake's arm with a screaming bolt of pain.

Jake didn't react, kept the groan of pain deep within, didn't jerk away, though it was a hard-won fight with his body's reflexes. He did dodge the second swipe, then managed a decent blow against the guy's chin with the butt of the gun.

But the woman was screaming at the guy, and he retreated, running to the truck. Leaving Jake…dazed and struggling to tell his body to move. To chase.

He couldn't take them both unless he was willing to shoot, and he couldn't leave Zara behind. But surely he couldn't let them run. He couldn't…

The truck peeled out of the lot, sirens beginning to sound dimly. Another shadowy figure stumbled out of the back exit, but this time he knew it was Zara.

"We have to go," she said. "The cops are coming." She grabbed his arm and began pulling him in the opposite direction his assailant had gone. Each step was a jarring pain, but he simply accepted it. Like he'd always been taught to do.

She took his arm, stopping him as the streetlight revealed where the knife had slashed through his coat, shirt and arm. "Jake."

The horror in her voice was…strange. He didn't understand it. This was hardly the worst injury he'd suffered. He felt the gritty sand in his eyes, heard the distant echo of gunfire. Of explosions.

He blinked. *Not here. Not now.*

"I'm okay," he said through gritted teeth. It hurt. Damn it all to hell, it hurt. But he'd live. He began to pull her toward the truck this time. *Here. Now.* "Let's get out of here."

"You're hurt. You need a hospital." She stopped at the truck, looking up and down the road. "Maybe we should just tell the truth. Maybe…"

"Is that what you want to do, Zara?" he asked harshly.

She looked up at him with a pain in her eyes that twisted his gut. "I wish it was."

"Come on." He opened the driver's side door, but she snagged the keys as he pulled them from his pocket.

"I'm driving." And she hopped into the driver's seat.

Chapter Fourteen

Zara drove out of Bent, headlights off, slow and in the opposite direction the sirens had come from. When no lights flashed behind them for a good thirty minutes, Zara assumed the police had gone after their attackers for the time being, but they'd circle back to her and Jake soon enough.

She supposed it was the adrenaline wearing off when she began to shake. Still, she gripped the steering wheel as hard as she could and snuck a look at Jake.

With quick, efficient movements, he'd wrapped a bandana from the glove compartment around the horrible gash in his arm. Now he sat very still and said nothing as she drove toward the Fish Inn. It was their destination. That couldn't change.

He seemed unaffected, and yet she knew he was affected. There was something off about him. He wasn't *sharp*. Everything he did was careful and studied, but not *easy*.

And he didn't offer a plan. A course of action. He said nothing at all, which wasn't like him and might have scared her if she was a lesser woman. But she was a woman used to taking charge.

"We'll stick with the plan, but we'll get a room," Zara decided. Jake had been calling the shots, but he was hurt, and this was *her* deal. Amberleigh's bloody necklace. Hazeleigh in jail. *She* was the one in charge of keeping her sisters safe.

Not so great at your job these days, are you?

It seemed unfair the words would sound like her father's voice, when he'd never care enough to pass judgment on her lack of success.

"We'll need to clean you up and get some bandages." If that would work. Jake's wound looked like the kind of cut that needed stitches. "Maybe there's a doctor in town that could—"

"A bandage will do," he said with the same gritted teeth determination that made her wonder just what he'd seen in that military service of his. What he was seeing now. Back at her porch, he'd had some sort of flashback, if she had to guess. Was this the same?

He didn't offer that information up, and she didn't ask. She focused on driving. She focused on one foot in front of the other. It was the only way to get through anything.

When the sign for the Fish Inn came into view, Zara felt a relief she knew was disproportionate. They were hardly out of the woods, but she didn't think she could concentrate on what she needed to—Hazeleigh and the necklace and the framing—until Jake was…okay.

She drove around the parking lot, looking for the most out-of-the-way darkened spot. She didn't know if the cops would catch on enough to look for Jake's truck, way out here, but they had to be careful.

She parked in the back, in a darkened corner. They both got out of the truck and collected their bags before meeting at the front of the truck. She grabbed her hat and pulled it low on her head. She grabbed a hat from the back she assumed was his and handed it to him.

He settled it on his head, pulling his low like she had. In the dim light, he looked like a dangerous cowboy. Which should have been amusing since she'd been the one to teach him to ride a horse.

She didn't feel *amused.*

"Keys," Jake ordered. There was a strange note to his voice. A distance she didn't understand and didn't know how to parse. She frowned at him, but it was his truck, so she handed them over. She adjusted her bag on her shoulder. "Maybe I should carry your bag."

"It's a flesh wound on one arm. I'll survive," he said and began walking toward the hotel entrance.

Zara had to scurry to catch up to his certain, long-legged pace. When they stepped through the automatic doors, he slid his arm—his hurt arm—around her shoulders and smiled at the young woman behind the counter as they approached. "I don't suppose you have a room available. The wife and I didn't get nearly as far on our drive as we wanted to, and this is the first place I've seen to stay in miles."

The wife. Zara knew he was acting, but *wife* and *room* meant they'd be in the *same* room tonight and that wasn't exactly what she'd had in mind. Though she wasn't sure *what* she'd had in mind.

"We have a few rooms open," the woman said, typing something into her computer. "Just one night?"

"That should do it."

"I'll just need an ID and a credit card." Jake moved to pull his wallet out of his pocket, and she noticed the slight wince that he tried to hide behind the hat and his own stoic…whatever.

Zara turned her attention to the woman at the computer. "Do you have a first aid kit I could borrow? My *husband* here took a little tumble and needs some patching up."

The receptionist eyed Jake dubiously, and he smiled, a little glassy-eyed, as he handed the cards to her. "Clumsy me."

The woman took the cards, moved around copying the

license and running the card. She handed both back to Jake, including key cards with the room number written on the envelope they were inside of. She grabbed a small white box from underneath the counter and slid it to Zara.

"Thanks. Is it okay if I bring it back in the morning?"

"Sure. Your bill will be under the door in the morning too. Checkout by eleven."

"Thanks."

They turned and walked toward the elevator. Jake stumbled a little, and Zara's heart lurched as she reached out to steady him. Was he really that bad off?

He slumped against the wall until the elevator doors opened and they stepped inside. She opened her mouth to demand what was the matter, but he… He was himself again. Standing straight. Completely fine.

It hit her then. He'd been pretending to be drunk.

Well, it wasn't exactly inconspicuous, but hopefully it made the tumble and first aid kit seem a little less sketchy.

They walked to their room in utter silence, and Jake unlocked the door and held it open for her. She stepped inside the run-of-the-mill-if-a-little-dingy hotel room.

With one bed.

She stared at it for a moment too long. Silly to worry about *sleep* when there were much more pressing matters at hand. She turned to face him and fisted her hands on her hips. "Okay, take off your shirt."

JAKE KNEW WHAT she meant, but his mind went in a few other directions first. He was a little proud of himself for swallowing down "you first."

He raised an eyebrow, expecting her to wither a little. But she only lifted her chin. "Your arm needs to be bandaged, and I need to make sure you weren't cut anywhere else. We need to disinfect everything since you were rolling around in the back alley of a bar. And if you honestly think that I won't call a doctor because you're brushing it off like a scratch, you don't know me well enough yet."

It was probably wrong he liked that "yet" since it meant she planned for him to get to know her that well at some point.

So, he shrugged. He tossed his hat into a chair in the corner and untied the bandana he'd secured around the wound. It was soaked with blood, so he shoved it in his pocket rather than bloody up any of the hotel room. Then, ignoring the searing pain in his arm and some of the aches in his muscles from tussling, he shrugged out of his coat and then reached back and pulled his shirt off. He tossed them both on the chair. "Happy?"

She didn't say anything at first. She stood there looking very…prim and still. He might have said detached.

But her eyes wandered.

He grinned.

Which seemed to remind her of the task at hand. "Sit," she ordered, pointing at the bed.

The one bed.

He sat. She set the first aid kit the receptionist had given her next to him on the bed, then disappeared into the bathroom. She returned with a wet washcloth and some towels.

"Don't know that we should bloody up the hotel towels."

"I'll pay the fee," she returned. She took off her hat, then busied herself opening the kit and setting some things out, then examining his wound with a critical eye. There was some kind of antiseptic wipe in the kit and she opened it, using it to wipe away the drying blood.

She sighed, her breath brushing over his arm like its own caress. "Jake, this is bad. And I can see you've had worse, but that doesn't mean we can leave this unattended."

"A day or two, we head back to the ranch. Dunne can stitch me up."

"Because Dunne is a doctor?"

He shrugged. "Close enough."

Her frown deepened, but she continued to clean him up, using a few adhesive bandages. She used quick, economical movements that told him she'd done some cleaning and patching up of other people in her day.

"You really do just take care of everyone in your path, don't you?"

She flicked her gaze up to his for a startled moment, then frowned down at the supplies, grabbing some gauze. "You're helping me. You got stabbed helping me." She let out a shaky breath, the only sign of any distress. "I think I can slap on a few bandages."

She wrapped the gauze around the bandages, which was a smart move since the wound was so deep and every bit of pressure would help the healing process.

She smoothed some tape over the gauze into place, her face still tilted down so he could see only the crown of her head.

Her fingertips brushed across the scar right above where the man had slashed his arm. "Did you get these all in the military?"

He stiffened in spite of himself, even knowing it was more than likely she'd ask about his scars. He even had the lie prepared before he'd taken off his shirt.

But he found he couldn't quite commit to those lies. "Mostly. But I was a foster kid."

She lifted her head, that frown of confusion wrinkling her forehead. "What does that mean?"

"I survived a lot of injuries in the military between training and missions." The last mission had left the biggest ones on his leg, but he'd healed a lot better than Dunne. Still, the one on his shoulder she was touching hadn't had a thing to do with the military.

"But before that…you had injuries because you were a foster kid?"

He didn't have to answer her. He didn't *have* to let her push him into this conversation. A conversation he hadn't had with anyone since it had happened. Because he'd joined the military and his life had changed. Who he was to his marrow had inextricably changed.

But Zara and this little mission they were on had nothing to do with the military, and it made him feel a bit like that kid. He wasn't in control here. He was just a person, plopped down into a different life.

Not all that different from the foster homes. Except now he had a choice. A choice to stay. To build something. No one could kick him out or tell him what to do. No more missions he didn't volunteer for. No more rules.

There was only him.

And her.

"I was staying with this family when I was seventeen. They took in kids like me, about to age out, and tried to give them some kind of…something. They were good people." He owed them a lot. Even with everything that had happened. "They usually took girls, but they'd made an exception for me for whatever reason."

He looked down at his hands, then at her. Watching him. Interested. He wasn't used to someone being interested in old truths. Not when he was in the middle of living a lie.

"The mom had an ex-husband and he showed up one night. Drunk. Violent. He had this big hunting knife, and he was going after her, so I stepped in to stop him."

"Jake." She said it on a kind of gasp that didn't quite make sense to him. Sure, it had been a bad night. But he'd heard of worse nights. He was inexorably linked to five men with similar bad nights, bad childhoods that had led them to Team Breaker.

They'd all made something good out of it.

"That was very brave," she said. "I can't imagine… They must be proud of you. Of your service and—"

He shook his head and tried to hold back the bitter laugh. It shouldn't be bitter. It was just life. "Sent me back to the home the next day. The current husband thought it meant something it didn't. That I'd step in and risk my life like that. For his wife."

"Her husband." Zara bristled. "You mean your foster *father*."

He shrugged. "Whatever. It was a bad night, and he couldn't take it out on the ex, so he took it out on me. That's okay."

"It most certainly is not."

"I was seventeen, Zara. Practically an adult."

"Hardly."

"Because you were enjoying the childish, lack-of-responsibility life when you were seventeen? Or were you playing mother to your sisters who aren't any younger than you?"

She opened her mouth, but nothing came out. Because she might not have told him that point-blank, though it didn't take a genius to connect all her dots.

"Well, you're all patched up," she said, standing. She put away the first aid items. Then she grabbed his bag and set it on the bed next to him. "You should probably change your clothes."

"Probably," he returned. Standing. Best to let it all lie. They had bigger things to deal with than discussing their pasts.

It was just... For a moment, he'd felt that glimmer of being *human* that it felt like he'd lost as part of Team Breaker.

That was exactly why he couldn't entertain that feeling for too long. He was a liability.

He pulled some clothes out of his bag, then turned to watch her shrug off her coat.

She laid it over his discarded shirt on the chair. Which was when he saw the spots of red on the back of her blue T-shirt.

He swore and dropped his clothes. "*You're* bleeding." He stalked over to her, began to lift the back of her shirt. There were little scratches, pricks. She'd been *stabbed* and hadn't mentioned it.

She slapped at his hands, tried to turn to face him though he held her in place. "Stop that."

"Take off your shirt. *You're bleeding.*"

She slapped at him again. "I'm not going to take off my shirt in front of you."

He scowled at her, letting her go but not about to let *this* go. "Why not? You're wearing a bra, aren't you?"

Her cheeks went red again. "Of course I am."

"No offense, Zara, but I can't picture you wearing something lacy and see-through." Well, that was a lie. He could definitely picture it. He just meant he doubted his fantasy was based too much in reality. "It's no different than a bikini top."

"I would *never* wear a bikini."

He rolled his eyes. "Sit. Take off your shirt. Tit for tat, princess." That was a terrible choice of words.

She stood there, mutinous, like she was considering fighting him.

"You patched me up, and now I'm returning the favor. I can lift your shirt up and have this take twice as long, or you can stop being a baby and sit down and take your damn shirt off."

She sneered at him, plopped herself on the bed and then finally lifted the shirt over her head. She crossed her arms over her chest.

"It's a sports bra, for goodness' sake."

She glared at him. "So what?"

"So what? I could go to a gym and see a sea of women in a lot less than that and manage to contain my baser urges."

"Baser…" She made a choking sound as her cheeks kept getting redder and redder. "That's *not* what I meant."

"Then what did you mean?"

"I don't know. It's just…weird."

"Yeah, I'll apologize when I'm feeling less furious you've been hurt this entire time and didn't tell me."

"I forgot about it."

He scoffed. He pulled the bandages back out of the kit, and some antiseptic cream. He tried to rein in his temper, but the thought of her hurt… Hurt and not telling him. Taking care of *him* first.

Who had ever done that?

She had angled herself so her back was to him. There were little scratches, deeper gashes. Nothing as bad as he'd gotten on his arm, but certainly nothing you just *forgot* about.

"What the hell happened in there? I thought I was the only one dealing with a nutjob with a knife."

"It was a woman. She came up behind me. Put the knife to my back, told me to walk out the back door. I did at first, because…"

He sat down and used one of the towels to wipe down her wounds. "Because what?"

"She said you'd be dead if I didn't."

He stilled. And was glad her back was to him, because he had no doubt his usually carefully organized features had fallen lax in shock.

"But I figured maybe I should trust the military guy to take care of himself. But… Well, anyway. She didn't really hurt me, and the bartender came in and told her he'd called the cops. So she bolted."

It all came rushing back. Over the flashes of just surviving the man with the knife. The woman running out. *We'll come back for her later.*

He put some cream on his finger and gently rubbed it over the cuts. She jumped when the antiseptic touched her skin.

"Forgot about it, my butt," he muttered.

"It's *cold*. Not painful."

She held herself rigidly straight, arms still crossed over her chest as if she was guarding some sort of treasure. He'd been in the military too long, sharing barracks and showers and having nothing personal or private during and before his military service. It was hard to understand how different her childhood must have been.

He moved quicker, affixing bandages across all the cuts. He didn't let himself linger, or his eyes wander.

Okay, maybe once. But mostly he finished up everything quickly and stood. He grabbed her bag and handed it to her so she could put on a new shirt. She rummaged through it quickly and pulled the shirt over her head in a deft movement. He should have looked away, given her privacy, but it was all such a foreign concept.

"You have a scar on your shoulder too." He hadn't meant to say that out loud.

She finally met his gaze again. "Horse. Not human."

They stared at each other for a long while. He couldn't say why. He couldn't seem to bring himself to break the silence.

"I have the sneaking suspicion neither of us are very good at letting other people look out for us or work with us," she said finally.

His mouth curved. "Seems likely. But I think we're going to have to figure it out."

"The working-together thing."

"I meant both."

Chapter Fifteen

There was something about the way Jake held her gaze that made Zara want to run. Back to Bent. To the police. To Thomas. To whoever would get her far away from this… tight band around her lungs. This squeezing, unknown panic she didn't recognize, when she'd been very well versed in a lot of kinds of terror.

Fear was all the same, she supposed. It was something that had to be pushed aside in order to deal with the problem at hand. "These two people at the bar. They were following us. The woman mentioned my sister."

"Amberleigh or Hazeleigh?"

She let out a long, slow breath of relief. He wasn't going to push his odd…comment. "I'm not sure. It seemed like Amber. But… I can't be sure. I can't be sure of anything."

"Except they followed us. You, in particular. And wish us harm."

"Harm with knives? Why not shoot us?"

"The man I fought said something about being loud. Still, it was a risk to try and, what, kidnap you?"

Her. In particular. Not *them*. She tried to suppress a shudder.

"So, they're not exactly on a killing spree," Jake continued. "They want something from you. Something to do with Amberleigh."

"If they knew anything, they'd know I don't know *any-thing* about Amberleigh."

"But Hazeleigh did. She said she was safe in jail. Maybe these people were after her, and now they think you know what Hazeleigh knows." His eyebrows drew together. "So, they're after you." He swore and then grabbed her by the shoulders so suddenly she didn't know what to do but stare up at him. "You need to go back to Wilde. You need to go to Thomas or whoever. I'll handle this, but you need protection."

She tried to wiggle out of his grasp, but he held firm. His blue eyes serious and intense. So much so her first instinct was to simply agree with whatever orders he was doling out. But… "I can't do that. Everything I know makes it seem like Hazeleigh did this when I know she didn't."

"You just won't tell them what you know. I'll keep the necklace. I'll try to find these people, but—"

"We're in this together, Jake. You said that yourself. I'm not going to go hide away if you're not going to. Why should I?"

"Because *I* have experience with this."

"With hunting down murderers?" she scoffed.

He didn't falter. "More than less, Zara. Certainly far more than you."

"I am capable—"

"You are capable of everything." He gave her a little shake, frustration rippling from him in a way she'd never seen from him before. "I know that, but we're talking about someone out to *harm* you. Do you want to end up like Amberleigh?"

She had a flash of her sister, dead and buried in the dirt. Killed and discarded. Hazeleigh, pale and drawn in jail but certain she was safe there. Safe. Zara looked up at Jake. If she went back to Wilde and the police, she might be safe but Jake wouldn't be.

That felt…unendurable. That he'd be out here in danger when she was hiding. "You just said we needed to work together."

He touched her cheek. It was not…like anyone had ever touched her before. A gentleness, a reverence that had all the words and arguments in her brain simply fading away.

"I can't bear the thought of you getting hurt in this. Any more than you already have been. We'll still be working together if you go to the police. I'll still be trying to find the people who did this, and so will you. You'll just have better protection."

She wanted to reach up and touch his hand. Trace his fingers on her cheek and memorize how that fit and felt and reverberated through her. She didn't know what she was supposed to *do* with any of those wants, but they filtered through her mind like a to-do list.

Instead she only curled her hands into fists at her sides. Touching didn't seem like a reasonable response to him trying to get her out of the way. When this was her responsibility. "The only way I go to the police is if you go home."

He dropped his hands and stepped away, shoving his fingers through his hair as he turned his back to her. "Damn it, Zara."

"That's how it is," she said, terrified by all the things jangling inside of her that she didn't have the time to sort through, reason away. "Either we both retreat or we both see this through. This goes both ways, you know. The whole…" She swallowed at the tightness in her throat. It felt too much like fear to let the words go unsaid. "The whole seeing-you-get-hurt thing."

He slowly turned to face her, something like surprise or awe or anguish or all three on his face.

"So, the plan stays the way it is," Zara said firmly. She knew her voice was too high and squeaky, but she pretended she didn't notice. That she was the most in-charge person in the room. "In the morning, we go asking around. See if anyone saw Amberleigh and Hazeleigh together. Who they were with. We find the information we came for."

He gave a slight nod. "And what do we do until morning?"

There was something about the way he said "do" that had her thinking about the bed behind them. The *one* bed, and just them in this room, and the way he'd touched her face and... Well, the way he was staring at her now with all that intensity she realized he often *hid* that intensity, not that it was lacking.

Because he was an intense guy. A guy who always stepped in to protect, even when it got him hurt or kicked out of a nice foster house. He'd stepped in to help her when he'd owed her nothing. When to this very moment he owed her *nothing*.

Because it was who he was. It didn't have anything to do with her personally. He was just a...a...rescuer. She knew the type, wasn't *she* the same type? So... It was just...him out there doing the right thing because...

I can't bear the thought of you getting hurt in this.

When she wasn't used to people giving her much of a second thought at all unless it was "how is Zara going to handle everything?"

What would they do until morning? "Sleep?" she managed to croak. And she was quite sure she turned a furious shade of red when he only grinned.

"Is that a question?" Jake asked, amused by the possibility of what might be going on in her head. What with the blushing and squeaking.

"N-no. We should sleep." She swallowed. Hard. Then she turned toward the bed and stared at it. "We can... take turns."

"I think I can control my baser urges. Oh wait, you're not worried about that. So, what are you worried about?"

She scowled at him. "I don't know. It's just *weird*."

Jake shrugged. "I'm sorry. You have to understand, I don't have that same...'weird' lens. Growing up in foster care, my entire adult life in the military. Things aren't... your things. Space isn't your space. You learn to make do with whatever you've got." Which was a lot more truth than he probably needed to give her, but he didn't want her to think he was *trying* to make her uncomfortable.

Even if the discomfort did kind of amuse him.

"I'm sorry," she said softly. Eyes soft. Everything *soft*.

Which made everything inside of him twist in his own discomfort. Which was probably fair. "What's to be sorry about?"

"It sounds..."

He raised an eyebrow waiting for her response.

"Never mind. Let's just...go to sleep."

He wanted to argue, demand an answer and lots of other things he didn't fully understand churning around. But instead, he let it go.

They got ready for bed in silence. She crawled into the bed gingerly. She held herself very still, and though he didn't fully understand all of her concerns, he felt uncomfortable doing the thing she thought was "weird."

"I can sleep on the chair."

She frowned at him. "Oh, no. You can't make me feel bad and then play the noble guy."

"I didn't want to make you feel bad. I don't..."

"Just get in bed, for heaven's sake. And go to sleep." She rolled onto her side, tucked her hand under her pillow and resolutely closed her eyes.

He finally understood the idea of *weird*. Because now he knew what she looked like when she went to sleep at night. How she arranged her body, the different angles of her face when she was trying to sleep.

Knowing those things about Zara hit differently than when it was a foster brother or a fellow soldier. This was Zara, and knowing what she looked like curled up in bed…

Well, *hell*.

But he didn't have a choice now. He'd made her feel *bad*. He eased onto the bed, over the covers, wondering if it was enough of a barrier to negate the *weird*.

After a while of lying there, staring at the ceiling, she let out a gusty sigh and rolled over to face him.

"I'm exhausted, but I'll never sleep. Not when I don't understand anything that's going on. My mind will just run in circles until morning."

"So, talk out the circles. Think of it like counting sheep. Say all the possibilities until you're dead to the world."

His eyes had adjusted to the mostly dark, though a streak of streetlight pierced through the curtains and gave the room enough of a glow he could make out her features.

"Two people wanted to kidnap me. That we know."

"Yes."

"Hazeleigh thinks she's safer in jail, which means we can presume she's in danger. From these people? Are they the ones who killed Amberleigh?"

"I thought that at first, but it seems…if they killed Amberleigh, why wouldn't they just kill you too? You live on a rather isolated ranch, in that little cabin, with no real protection. And they're going through a lot of trouble to frame Hazeleigh…if they're the ones who killed Amberleigh."

"They think I know something, maybe? Some sort of information they need. But…for what?"

"The problem is, Amberleigh had a whole life away from Wilde that you don't know anything about. Now, she might have told Hazeleigh something. They might assume they told you too. But…"

"But if they want to silence me, they could have killed me when they killed Amberleigh. Hazeleigh too, for that matter."

"Maybe it's unconnected. Two separate things." But he didn't think so. He turned over everything they'd seen, been through today. What she was saying. "What if they *need* you?"

"What could they need from…?" Her eyes slowly widened as she seemed to come to the same conclusion he'd started to come to. "I look just like Amberleigh."

"I think they might need you to *be* Amberleigh for something."

She sat up suddenly, though she didn't leap from the bed. "Hazeleigh has to know. That's why she thought she'd be *safer* in jail. She knew they needed her for something. She was meeting with Amberleigh, so she probably knows what."

"She didn't tell you though."

"No, she won't. She'll consider it protecting me."

"Even if you tell her what's happened today?"

Zara took a breath, looked like she was going to say something but then just let out a slow breath.

"Ah, you won't tell her either."

"It's just… She'll worry."

He got up off the bed, too irritated with her to lie still next to her. "I mean, sure, risk your life so Hazeleigh doesn't *worry*."

"Well, don't get all angry about it."

"Angry about it?" She didn't know what angry *was*. "It's infuriating. I've spent the past ten years tethered to Cal, who does the same damn martyr stuff. You aren't the only one who can take care of things. You aren't the only one who has to suffer. I realize no one ever told you that, but you need to figure that out. All it ever does is make *you* and anyone who wants to help miserable."

"I'm not miserable."

"Aren't you?"

She looked so shocked by that, he pressed his advantage. "We're going back to Wilde. You're going to tell Hazeleigh what happened and make her tell you what they need a body double for, if they're the ones who killed Amberleigh."

He stood there feeling unaccountably angry with her and knowing it wasn't her fault. He had Cal issues. This wasn't about her.

Except in all the ways it was.

"You're right."

And because he was used to Cal's hardheaded refusal to listen to *anything*, he was taken wholly off guard. "I am?"

She laughed, a little sadly and got out of bed. "I don't know about going back to Wilde, but you're right. I take everything on my own shoulders because I've always had to. Or thought I did. But it sure seems like Hazeleigh did the same thing. I was upset because I thought they were keeping something from me on purpose. Because I was always the triplet who was all work and no fun, who wanted to follow the rules."

She flipped on the light. She looked exhausted, dark circles under her eyes.

"But your little…outburst makes me realize… maybe it's not leaving me out. Maybe Hazeleigh is trying to protect me. But that's the thing, Jake. When you love someone, you want to protect them. She's my sister. I've been playing mom to her since we were eight. Maybe even before that. We don't want each other to worry, because…that's part of loving someone. Not wanting them to hurt."

What she didn't say, but what hung in the air between them, was that he didn't understand because he didn't have a family.

Except he did. Maybe he hadn't grown up with one, and

maybe it had taken years to accept that he was stuck with the men of Team Breaker as his family, but they had become everyone who mattered to him.

And yeah, the infuriating part of Cal still playing leader after everything was that none of them wanted Cal worrying over them. They didn't want him stressing himself out over them, because they didn't want that challenge for him. Their brother.

And Jake didn't want it for Zara either. To think she had to handle this hard thing on her own.

"So, what do you want to do, Zara?" he asked, feeling tired and pummeled…a familiar feeling. Because he didn't know how to make this right for her.

Before she could answer his question, a hard knock sounded on the door.

Chapter Sixteen

Zara looked at Jake, who looked at her. Who would be knocking on their door in the middle of the night?

"Don't move," Jake said in a whisper. She didn't know where he'd stowed it, but suddenly the gun was back in his hand. He moved for the door, silently and like…someone else. He put on a mask or a costume and became someone else entirely.

She supposed it should concern her, but mostly she just felt safe. Like someone had her back. Someone saw through all her tough acts and heavy burdens and just…picked them up with her. Because…

The "because" was still a little too murky.

He was looking out the peephole. "It's your cousin," Jake said, clearly as confused as she was. "He's not in his uniform."

"Damn it, Zara." Thomas's strained voice came through the door. "I know you're in there. I came alone. Off duty. Let me in."

Jake looked back at her. Like it was her choice and he'd follow it either way. She supposed, since it was her family, it had to be her choice.

She didn't know the right one to make. But that had never allowed her the choice *not* to make the decision.

"Do you really think he's alone?"

Jake nodded.

"All right. Let him in."

Jake put the gun away first. An interesting detail, since she had no doubt Thomas would be carrying, even if he *was* off duty.

Thomas stepped in when Jake opened the door, then let it close behind him. He eyed Jake with skepticism and some very faintly veiled animosity before he turned his gaze to Zara.

"What the *hell* are you doing?"

Zara crossed her arms over her chest. Much as she might want Thomas's help or to confide in someone who might know more about the case than she did, she knew where his loyalties lay. That badge. Whether he was wearing it or not. "Maybe it's best if I don't answer that."

Thomas raked his hands through his hair. "I am not here as a cop. I am here as your cousin."

"Is there a difference? As I recall, you *arrested* Hazeleigh."

"You know *I* didn't. There is evidence against her and—"

Zara turned away from him. The fact he could still defend Hazeleigh being in a *cell*. "You should go."

"I have to talk to you. *Alone*."

She didn't have to look to know he'd be glaring pointedly at Jake. "Jake stays," Zara said firmly. "*Jake* has helped. I can't say the same for you." She knew it wasn't fair, but she was afraid if she wasn't a little unfair and mean to Thomas, she'd end up confiding in him and getting Hazeleigh into even deeper trouble.

There was a tense silence, and Zara stared at the rumpled bed. Jake had been angry with her. For wanting to do this all on her own. He'd called her a martyr and she couldn't say he was *wrong*, just that she'd never been given the opportunity to be anything but.

Until now. And not just with Jake. Could she trust Thomas? Ask for help? Let someone else shoulder the burdens?

She looked back at Jake. Because she didn't know what to do and she'd never had someone to help in that department.

She wanted someone to help in that department now and again.

Jake gave her a little nod. "It's okay. I'll take a look around the hotel. See if anyone else has followed us. I'll be back in fifteen."

When she gave her own nod in return, he slid out the door, leaving her alone with her cousin. She couldn't look at Thomas. It hurt too much. If she'd ever been forced to ask for help, Thomas was the one she would have asked.

And he'd been complicit in Hazeleigh being arrested.

"Hazeleigh told me you might be here," he said after a few quiet moments.

Zara whirled on him. "What?"

"I told her you'd up and disappeared and asked her if she knew anything about that. She was worried, Zara. Clearly, she's in danger and now you are too."

Danger, yes, and Hazeleigh apparently knew where she'd go. Which meant Hazeleigh knew Zara would have found the letters.

Which wasn't surprising. They were triplets and lived together. They understood each other, even when they didn't act the same. But if Hazeleigh knew enough to know she was in danger, to be worried about Zara, it meant she knew way more than she was letting on. Not just to the police, but to Zara too.

"What else did she tell you?"

"Not much. I'm here because of you, Zara. You shouldn't be here at all, let alone with that *guy*. Jake Thompson isn't who he says he is. I haven't figured out who he *is*, but not who he says."

Zara knew that, didn't she? Jake had all but admitted it to her. She figured it had something to do with his military service. But none of it had to do with *this*. "Maybe not, but he doesn't have anything to do with Amberleigh. Why are you focusing on him when you should be focusing on who actually killed Amberleigh? Hazeleigh didn't. Jake didn't."

"Can you be sure of that? That Jake doesn't connect to this?"

"Yes. More than sure. I trust Jake, Thomas. I'd trust him with my life."

"Look, if this is…personal…"

The face Thomas made might have been comical if Hazeleigh wasn't in jail. If Amberleigh wasn't dead.

"This isn't about Jake. It's about getting Hazeleigh out of jail. It's about finding out who killed my sister. *Jake* is helping because…because he's a good friend."

"Helping and investigating is the police's job."

"As long as Hazeleigh is in jail, they suck at it."

"Laurel believes me." He tapped his fist to his chest. "She knows Hazeleigh didn't do it. We're looking for the real killer. I told you that. She told you that."

"And what have you got?"

"Since Grady told me—and Laurel—everything he saw at the bar, we've got the two people who attacked you and Jake to go on."

Grady must be the bartender who'd helped her. The detective's husband. Which was good, all in all, if the cops were looking for people who'd attacked them. It would be harder for her would-be kidnappers to get to her. She hoped.

"Laurel is looking into this," Thomas continued. "She won't be far behind, and no, I didn't tell her anything about coming here or Hazeleigh telling me you'd be here. I'm just saying, she's smart. She's going to put it together."

"Well, when she does, maybe you can arrest the people who attacked me instead of my sister."

He groaned in frustration. "Do you really think I want Hazeleigh in jail?"

"No, I don't." She swallowed down the wave of guilt. "But I think if the evidence points to her being guilty, you'd let it happen. It's your job to let it happen."

"It's my job to help enforce the truth."

She felt sorry for him, even though she wanted to harden her heart against it. He was in an impossible situation. She knew how hard he'd worked to become a cop. How much it meant to him. Now he was being torn between what he'd dedicated his life to and his family.

"Go enforce the truth then, Thomas," she said, trying to firm her voice against the way it wanted to shake with emotion. "Leave me be. Some of us put family above all else. If that isn't you, you can go."

He looked at her a bit like she'd shot him, but Zara didn't have time to feel guilty about that. The door opened and Jake slid back inside in absolute silence. But he immediately crossed to her, and she could tell no matter how stoic he tried to act, he was a bit rattled.

"You've got to get out of here," Jake said, taking her arm and already moving her toward the door.

She dug her heels in out of reflex. "What? Why?"

"The two people from the bar are out there in the parking lot. They are not alone."

JAKE GRABBED ZARA'S bag with his free hand and shoved it at Thomas. "Get her out of here. I'll create a diversion."

"No," Zara said, still trying to wriggle out of his grasp.

He held firm. "You need to get somewhere safe. We know they want you. I don't plan on letting them get you."

"Explain that," Thomas ordered.

"It's noth—"

"The theory we're working on is that they need Zara for something," Jake interrupted, not about to let Zara play it off like it was nothing. Not when she'd been *stabbed* in the back in a kidnap attempt. "Like impersonating Amberleigh, maybe." Jake understood Zara's reticence to trust Thomas, but in the current circumstance, he was her best shot at getting out of here in one piece *and* getting somewhere safe. Maybe to a jail cell like her sister.

"Why would they need that?" Thomas asked.

"*That* we don't know. But they wanted to kidnap Zara, not kill her. At least right now. Hazeleigh feels safer in a cell than at home. The common denominator isn't what they know. If Hazeleigh has much more information about Amberleigh's past than Zara does, the commonality is the face."

"All I need to do is call someone in," Thomas said. "You can identify the woman who attacked you and so can Grady. We'll arrest her and see what she knows. It doesn't have to be all dark-alley schemes."

"I'm not dealing with the police," Zara said, crossing her arms over her chest. She gave a sideways look at her bag that Jake sure hoped Thomas didn't catch on to. Because that bloody necklace in Zara's bag was a big problem.

"I know you're ticked Hazeleigh is in jail, but the police can and will help. We will *help*. And do the right thing. If you'd stop playing at vigilante, we can figure this out."

"Oh, can we?"

"Call the cops if you have to," Jake interrupted. "Do what you've got to do, but she has to be out of here. I can take her or you can."

"Do I get a say?" Zara asked, dangerously casual.

"No," he said in unison with Thomas. Then they both winced, as if they'd realized at the same time they'd made a grave tactical error.

"So, to be clear, you plan on carting me around like a *child* while I let the big, strong men handle things?"

"Zaraleigh—"

She sent Thomas a cutting look.

"They are after *you*," Jake said, trying to keep his fury and worry leashed. "It's not about men and women. It's not about anything except the fact they want *you* and we are trying to keep that from happening."

Zara finally tugged hard enough he let go of her arm. "They want me." She seemed to consider that as she crossed to the window. She looked out for a while and Jake had to battle against the impatience to get her far away from those people downstairs.

Eventually she turned to face him and Thomas. "Why not let them have me? It would answer our questions. I'd just…do whatever they asked. Then we'd know what they want me for."

Jake laughed. Thomas sputtered. Then they both said the same thing at the same time.

"No."

"And," Zara continued as if this was somehow a plausible or reasonable course of action. "Thomas and his cops can arrest them for kidnapping me after. Not only does it give us answers, but also it puts them in jail."

"I can already have her arrested for assault. I don't need your kidnapping plan."

"Jake said there's more than just the woman. A whole group of people who might have answers about what happened to Amberleigh. Don't we want all of them?"

"Not if it puts you in danger," Jake said before Thomas could.

She stood there, looking angry and frustrated, but she didn't keep arguing. She wasn't the kind of woman who beat her head against a brick wall.

She was the kind of woman who figured her way up and around it.

"Fine," Zara said. "Call your cops. Arrest the woman and just the woman." She shrugged. "I have to go to the bathroom." She turned and disappeared into the bathroom, the lock clicking shut.

"I don't trust her for a second," Thomas muttered. "There's not a window or a way out in there, is there?"

"No."

"Good. Keep an eye on her." Thomas pulled his phone out of his pocket and stepped into the hallway, free hand on the butt of the weapon he clearly wore under his coat.

Jake watched the bathroom door. There weren't any other exits *in* the bathroom, but he didn't trust her either. He had a very bad feeling he knew just what she was up to.

And that he'd go along with it, simply because she was going to ask him to.

She poked her head out of the bathroom, looking around the room, likely for Thomas. "He gone?"

"Just out in the hallway."

She gave a sharp nod. "Okay, here's the plan."

Chapter Seventeen

"I'm not going to get in the way of him arresting her, if that's why you're scowling," Zara said, moving over to her bag.

"Oh, good. So there is some reasonable part to your plan?"

He sounded sarcastic, so she glared at him. "But that leaves how many people out there who presumably want to get their hands on me? Or my face anyway?"

"Four. And I'll be damned if I'm going to let that happen. Sorry."

"It'd be easier. Quicker." Frustrating to be thwarted by do-gooder men, but she'd deal. She didn't exactly *want* to be kidnapped, but much like back at the bar, she realized she was willing to do a lot of things she didn't want to in order to get to the bottom of this. "We'll follow them instead."

"Follow them," he repeated, as if it was just as insane as letting herself be kidnapped.

She checked on the bloody necklace. Still there. Still a problem. She thought about handing it over to Thomas. He was here in an unofficial capacity.

But he was calling the cops in. He wasn't bending any rules. He was just getting in the way. She zipped her bag and turned to face Jake. "They followed us. Why can't we follow them?"

"Because they're potential murderers?"

"There's also potentially more of them out there? All after me maybe? Or Hazeleigh? We don't know, and the cops keep focusing on one little thing at a time. Them arresting the *one* woman who tried to kidnap me does nothing."

Jake didn't say anything to that, and she knew it wasn't for lack of *trying* to come up with something to say. It was just he had to know she was right.

"You'll tell Thomas that you're taking me back to Wilde to keep me away from these folks. Keep playing up the macho, I-know-better-than-the-little-girl act, and he'll eat it up."

"That's not what that was," he returned, scowling. "I'm very aware you can take care of yourself. On a ranch. In life. But we're talking about murderers here. We're talking about the very real possibility you get hurt. *Again*."

"If I get hurt in the process, at least I did something to help."

"And if you're dead in the process?"

"How do I just go around knowing someone killed my sister? Knowing someone wants Hazeleigh to take the fall for that? The police haven't gotten as far as we have."

"Because they don't have all the information."

"Are you suggesting we give them all the information?"

He inhaled. "No. But… Thomas seems to want to help."

"By the book. The book sucks."

His mouth curved just a little bit. "You would have made a decent addition to Team Breaker, Zara."

"What's Team Breaker?"

"Something I really shouldn't have mentioned. There are things you don't know about me."

He said it so seriously. Holding her gaze. As if there was something *bad* about that, something to apologize for.

But she'd meant what she'd said to Thomas. She trusted this man with her life. "Wow. So surprising, Jake," she said with a roll of her eyes in an attempt to take some tension out of the room. "However will I cope?"

His mouth quirked again. "So, we say I'm taking you back to Wilde. We follow whoever scatters when the police come. And then what?"

"We see where they go. We see if it gives us answers."

"And if it doesn't?"

She searched for a next step. For *something*. But she came up empty. She shrugged, hating that she felt lost all over again. It seemed every time she latched on to the next step, things got murkier and murkier. "I don't know."

He nodded like that was okay, but before he could say anything, Thomas stepped back into the room.

"I've got a couple county deputies responding, and Laurel is going to come question the woman. We'll need to bring you into the station to give a statement."

"I'll take her back to Wilde," Jake said, his gaze never leaving hers. "You can trust me."

He was lying, for her. And though he was saying those words *to* Thomas, he was saying them while looking into *her* eyes.

"Straight to the station. No detours. If you don't arrive in twenty minutes, I'll be coming after you myself."

Zara forced herself to look away from Jake and to her cousin. She hated breaking his trust like this, but she hated Hazeleigh in jail and being framed more. "Can I run home real quick and check on things at the ranch? It'll only add on another twenty or so."

"Have one of the Thompson brothers do it," Thomas replied. "Twenty minutes. Now, I'm going to stay here and watch our friends from the window until one of our marked cars arrive. You two get to the station. Tw—"

"Twenty minutes. We got it." Zara headed for the door, Jake opening it for her.

"Be safe," Thomas said, so seriously she had to fight away the jolt of guilt. But maybe when this was all over, he'd understand. She sure hoped he would.

She managed a wan smile and left the room, Jake close behind her. Once again they were silent on the elevator ride down. They stepped out into the hall. Zara didn't see anyone, but as they turned the corner to the back exit, suddenly she was being pushed, nudged, led and then cornered behind a big potted plant next to the elevators.

It was the strangest thing because Jake was basically pressing her up against the wall. With his *body*.

She should probably ask him what he was doing, but no sound came out of her mouth. His face was hovering over hers. Close. Way, way too close.

"Just don't say anything for a few minutes," he whispered, his breath fluttering over her mouth.

Her *mouth*.

A strange need to giggle rose up inside of her. Which made *no* sense. Except his mouth was just…there. Really, really close to hers. Wasn't that funny?

Except his eyes were so very blue and he positively blocked out the entire rest of the world with the sheer size of him and this…this…*feeling*. The kind she usually avoided, because *feelings* led to more responsibility, more people to take care of.

And yet Jake was never someone who added responsibility to her shoulders, was he?

"That detective just walked in," he whispered.

The *detective*. The problem at hand. Hazeleigh in jail and Amberleigh dead.

"How'd she get here so fast?" Zara started to turn her head to look, but Jake shifted, angling his body, his mouth moving closer to hers.

His *mouth*.

"Look, I'm sorry, but this is about the only thing I can think of."

Before she could ask him what that meant, his mouth was on hers.

JAKE KEPT THINKING there had to be another way to do this, but in the end, there wasn't. That detective was striding down the hall, and while she *might* take a second look at two people making out in the hallway, she likely had more important things on her mind.

Nor would she expect two people running around trying to solve a murder to have time for hallway make-out sessions.

But that meant he was kissing Zara. And as much as it was a ruse to avoid the detective's attention, his mouth was on her mouth and he couldn't seem to resist falling into a *real* kiss.

He didn't have to cover her cheek with his hand to angle her face better. He didn't have to indulge in the feel of her lips, her body pressed to his. He didn't have to taste her and torture himself with that new carnal knowledge.

He shouldn't have forgotten where they were or what they were doing for ticking seconds, where it seemed to be only them and this.

He certainly shouldn't be thinking of possibilities. Of what he wanted. If he was someone else, what he wanted might matter. If he was someone else…

But he wasn't. He pulled himself back. He hadn't been sent to Wilde to build a life, even if that's what he wanted to do. He'd been sent to Wilde to hide. He'd never be able to tell her why, and he was already risking too much just by being here.

He stayed close but fully pulled his mouth from hers. She blinked up at him, mouth slightly agape. Dark eyes wide and, well, certainly not angry or offended.

A strange panic settled over him. A flustered feeling he thought he'd eradicated from his life after that first foster home didn't work out.

"That was just a…" There was a word he was searching for. Somewhere inside of his melted brain. He cleared his throat. "I figured she wouldn't look too closely at two people making out in the hallway. What with the danger and death and all."

Zara didn't move. Didn't say a word. And they couldn't stay here with cops on their way, and the group outside being able to leave at any second.

"We have to go." He took her by the arm and started pulling her toward the door. Still, she said nothing, but she followed.

He stopped at the door, studying the dark parking lot out the glass of the back door. He didn't see anyone from this angle, but they still had to be careful.

He didn't drop her hand. He kept her close. As his heart beat painfully from every emotion that kiss had stirred up, he forced his brain to focus on the mission.

Because the mission was keeping her safe, and that was everything.

They walked to his truck, sticking to the shadows. Jake heard low voices. He moved, keeping Zara behind him, acting as a physical barrier between her and where he thought the voices were coming from. The group he'd spotted on his first perusal was standing in the same place, though now one of the trucks they were standing next to was running.

He didn't have to tell Zara they needed to be utterly silent. They inched toward his truck, keeping each footfall absolutely silent. When they reached his truck, he used his key to manually unlock the driver's side door. The group was a good ways away, but it would only take one to see his dome light go on.

He put his mouth next to Zara's ear. "We're going to

stand here and not get in until they leave. We'll watch which way their headlights go and follow at a good distance. We have to be careful and stay far enough back they won't notice someone following them in the middle of the night, in the middle of nowhere."

She nodded. He could feel the brush of her hair against his jaw. He had the overpowering need to bundle her up, shove her in the truck, take her back to the ranch and lock her in her cabin so he could take care of this himself.

She'd never go for it. He understood that, but it didn't mean he could get rid of the impulse to take care of this *for* her.

Sirens sounded in the distance and Zara jerked a little bit. Jake gave her hand a squeeze. Reassurance. A reminder to stay still and quiet.

Connection.

The group in the front lot looked around, clearly a little worried about the source and reason for those sirens. Coming closer. Jake held himself very still, again keeping Zara behind him so if they *did* make him out in the shadows, they didn't see her.

Three men got into the running truck and began to pull away. The two people left tried to get into the cab, but the truck screeched away without them. Jake could hear their muttered curses as they began to run. Maybe toward a car of their own.

But they were stopped, just before they were out of Jake's line of sight, by Laurel and Thomas. The man tried to punch Thomas, and Zara gasped, so Jake squeezed her hand tighter as a reminder to be quiet.

Laurel had the woman in handcuffs as a police cruiser with lights and sirens on pulled into the front lot and then out of view.

Enough commotion Jake thought they could get going

and hopefully catch up with the truck—that clearly left the would-be kidnappers behind on purpose.

He opened the door, pushed Zara inside. She quickly scurried over the driver's side to the passenger seat. He hopped in and immediately turned the ignition. He didn't peel out. He drove slowly and carefully behind the hotel.

"They took a right out of the lot, yeah?"

"Yeah," Zara agreed. She pulled her phone out. "We can't go around front." She pulled up a map as Jake eased his truck toward the street connected to the back lot. "Take a left here. We can circle around. Hopefully catch up."

"Got it."

"Why did that truck of guys leave them behind?" she asked before telling him to take another left.

"Buys them time. But it certainly points to a bigger operation." He slid her a look. "We could leave it to the police."

She stared straight ahead. "I can't."

"Understood." He followed the rest of her directions back to the highway. It was the middle of the night in the middle of nowhere. He had to be…beyond careful.

He pulled onto the highway—a deserted two-laner, the kind of nothing road he was still getting used to after over a month of living in Wyoming. In the far distance, he could just make out the taillights of a truck like the one that had pulled out of the hotel.

He couldn't be sure it was the same truck, but everything was so deserted it was unlikely to be anyone else.

Zara said nothing, and Jake couldn't think of anything to say. Not even to ask her what she thought they were going to do once the men in the truck stopped wherever they were going to stop.

He could take on three men. He'd done it before. But he was worried wherever they were headed would have more. He shifted, pulled his phone out of his pocket and shot off a quick text to all five men back at the ranch.

Track me. SOS means backup.

Maybe he shouldn't involve them, but… He couldn't keep living his life tethered to a military he couldn't be a part of anymore. At some point, he had to have his own life. Even if it had been made up for him by the military.

This was his life now. *Their* life now. Why couldn't they still do some good with it?

He kept driving, watching the taillights. He didn't know this area well, but he was pretty sure that truck could drive down this highway for hours on end and not really end up anywhere. Eventually they'd need gas. Food. Sleep.

But for now, he just followed through pitch-black night.

"I have one non-danger-related question," Zara said after a while.

"Okay."

She was quiet for a long moment while he waited. When she spoke, it was in a rush.

"I get the whole kiss-so-she-wouldn't-look-too-closely-at-us thing, but I'm not sure she was looking closely enough you had to put your tongue in my mouth."

He choked even though there was nothing in his mouth. "Sorry," he managed to croak through a coughing fit.

"I'm not looking for an apology," she said, sounding irritated with him.

"What are you looking for?"

"An explanation."

"Of why I kissed you?"

She sighed heavily, like *he* was the one not making any sense. "You're hot, Jake."

"O…kay?"

"Hot guys don't generally kiss me. I realize you were playing a part and all, but you didn't have to get *that* into it—"

"Hold on a sec. Do you think you're…not hot?"

"I mean, I can be cute like…when I brush my hair, and maybe put on non-ranch clothes, but those days are few and far between."

He didn't dare take his eyes off the truck lights so far ahead of them, so easily lost. But he shook his head and tried to put what he felt into his voice if not into his expression. "Zara, you're beautiful. Hair brushed or not."

She was quiet again. When she finally spoke, it was softly. And with that rare hint of being off-kilter. "I don't know what to say to that."

"I don't think you have to say anything."

"It's just Amberleigh was always the attractive one, and Hazeleigh the pretty one."

He wasn't sure he'd ever guess all the twists and turns her mind made. "You all look alike."

"Sure, but they try. You know, makeup and dresses and brushed hair." She waved a hand in the air in front of her. "I've known all the same people my whole life. They have all looked at me the same way my whole life. I guess I see myself the way they see me, and you see me differently… kind of. So I don't understand you. You don't need anything from me."

"Am I supposed to?"

"That's the part I don't understand. I don't have people like that in my life. You're here and doing all this and *kissing me* really well and I don't know how to reconcile all that."

"Well, as long as I'm kissing well."

She sighed. "I'm glad you think this is *so* funny."

"I'm not making it a joke. It's not a joke. I just…" He stared at the taillights. At that symbol of all the danger they were walking into. All the involvement he was supposed to avoid but hadn't been able to because it was…*her*.

There'd been something about *her* since he'd walked onto that ranch and she'd scowled at all of them. So furious they'd bought *her* ranch. But teaching them anyway. Taking care of everything anyway, because that's who she was.

He'd held back because he was supposed to. Because the military dictated it. Well, he was tired of it.

"I like you, Zara. I care about you. I'm attracted to you. I *want* to help you, because it's right. But more than that, because I don't like seeing you hurting."

He couldn't look at her, no matter how badly he wanted to. Those taillights were his only focus right now. But he couldn't stop himself. He gave her a quick once-over.

In the dark, he couldn't make out every nuance of her expression. He could only tell she held herself very still. Like she always did when she wasn't quite sure what road to go down next.

But that was the beauty of Zara. She never stayed there long. She made a choice, and she followed that road until the next choice. No waffling. No wondering. Just forward movement.

That he understood.

"Zara?"

"I don't see the taillights anymore," she said, her voice sounding very far away.

Which was just as well, since she was right. The lights had disappeared. Somewhere up ahead, the truck had pulled off the highway.

Chapter Eighteen

Zara didn't know why her eyes were all teary, why her throat felt tight. Why she couldn't seem to think beyond his words.

I like you, Zara. I care about you. I'm attracted to you. I want *to help you because it's right. But more than that, because I don't like seeing you hurting.*

That list…

Of course someone would feel all those things for her while she was trying to solve her sister's murder while her other sister was in jail. A bloody necklace in her bag. The timing made far more sense than the man.

Beautiful. No one had called her beautiful in her entire life, even on the rare occasion when she had pointed out that she had the same face as Amberleigh and Hazeleigh who were considered far more *feminine* and *desirable* than rough-and-tumble Zara had ever been.

What a bizarre thing to think about when real danger lay ahead.

"Look out for turnoffs on your side. I'll watch for them on mine. They weren't more than a mile head of us, so if we don't see anything for a mile, we'll flip around and try again until we find an option," Jake said.

He was different again. Serious. Focused. Like he could just fold up everything they'd been talking about and set it aside.

She supposed that really was the only option. So, she focused on the dark world around them and watched for a turnoff. She also thought about where they'd been driving. They were still in Bent County, but there weren't really any towns out this way. A few older ranches and some rich-folk spreads—usually vacation homes. A strange area for a bunch of people who'd possibly killed her sister.

Except it was isolated. Though she could think of more isolated spots. Better places to hide a murder. But Amberleigh had been buried on the Hart ranch. What sense did that make?

None of this made any sense.

"There," Zara said, pointing at a gravel turnoff.

Jake slowed his truck and pulled off the highway onto the gravel shoulder. He turned off his headlights and they both looked down the gravel road for signs of lights or life. Nothing Zara could make out in the dark.

Jake reached into the backseat and rummaged around in his bag. He pulled out a flashlight, and though she didn't see it, she had no doubt he had his gun somewhere on him.

"Stay put."

"Jake—" She had the strangest impulse to reach out and hold on to him. Keep him here in the truck where it was safe.

But was anywhere safe?

Jake met her gaze and smiled. "Just stay put for one minute. Just one. Promise."

She nodded, unable to voice any response. She believed his promises. That he thought she was beautiful. That he cared. She didn't know why she believed all that, only that she felt it in her bones.

So, she waited and watched carefully as his flashlight bobbed outside the truck. She didn't know what he was looking for—what she thought they might find, following these people connected to her would-be kidnappers. She supposed like every step so far, there was no way of knowing until they found it.

They.

He'd kissed her. Not just a distraction kiss. In that moment afterward, when he'd stared at her in a kind of shock, he'd seemed just as taken aback as she had been. It was a comfort, in some ways, to know he wasn't at all certain what *this* was.

Maybe uncertainty wasn't such a bad thing. Maybe it was okay to take things one second at a time before making the next choice.

After a minute and not much longer, he got back in the car. "They definitely went down this lane. There's fresh tire marks in the snow. Deep, not iced over or windswept."

"Should we go down it?"

"We follow down this isolated gravel road, even with our headlights off, we're asking for trouble. Bring up that map of yours."

She pulled out her phone and the map of the area. Jake studied it. "No other roads lead down there. Do you have any idea what's back there?"

Zara squinted into the absolute country dark. The area seemed vaguely familiar to her, but she couldn't put her finger on why. *Killroy Lane.* "I feel like I've been here before, but I don't know why. If it doesn't connect to any other roads, it's likely a drive back to a ranch or a house."

"We could walk it," Jake mused. "Still dangerous but less conspicuous. Problem is, it seems pretty long. We could be walking till daylight, and we don't know if we'll have cover."

Zara kept staring out the window, willing herself to remember why this all felt familiar. Something random. When her life was never random. She had the ranch and she had…

"Wait." She squinted into the dark. "When you were out there, did you see a mailbox?"

"Yeah. It was weird. Like a circle."

"Like a golf ball?"

"Oh, yeah. I guess so." He nodded. "Yeah, a golf ball."

Pieces started to domino in her head. It still didn't make sense, but she knew where she was. She reached out and clutched his arm. "I *know* that mailbox. I've been here. There's a house at the end of the road."

"Whose house?"

"This guy Hazeleigh dated. It was…last year I guess? This is his family's, like, summer home or something. If I'm remembering right, they don't live here full-time. He had a pool party, and Hazeleigh brought me along even though I repeatedly told her anyone who had a *pool* in Wyoming needed their head examined. But Hazeleigh doesn't really like to drive very far away, so she wanted me to go with her."

Jake was frowning. "When did Hazeleigh stop seeing him?"

"Right before last Christmas. He didn't take it well either. He called her constantly. Showed up at our house a few times. I chewed him out, even had Thomas go talk to him. The harassment stopped a few days after that, and I sort of forgot about it. Haze has never had the best taste in guys."

Zaraleigh looked at Jake. It seemed important to put it out there. "Amberleigh's first letter. It said it was almost Christmas. So, he stopped bothering her right around the time Amberleigh's letters started."

JAKE DIDN'T KNOW what to make of Zara's story. Except that he'd like to march down the lane and pop the guy one for harassing poor, skittish Hazeleigh and making Zara play protector yet again.

Of course, maybe he was *why* Hazeleigh was skittish.

Still, the timing fit too well with everything else they were trying to figure out. Amberleigh was the center. "Is there any way this guy had anything to do with Amberleigh running away back when you were teenagers?"

Zara frowned, clearly trying to comb back through years of memories. "I don't know how he would have. His family is from the county but not from Wilde. He's a doctor and Hazeleigh met him when she took Mr. Field into the emergency room one day when he was having heart troubles. The doctor asked her out, then they dated for…six months, tops. She liked him but said he was too intense."

Zara let out a breath of frustration. "It seems like it should connect, but I don't understand how. What would the letters have to do with Hazeleigh breaking up with this guy? And he wasn't one of those guys who got in the truck. He's a *doctor*. He wouldn't be loitering in a hotel parking lot in the middle of the night. He fancies himself *very* sophisticated, and he is a bit of a big fish in a small pond."

Exactly the type who would *hire* people to do their dirty work in Jake's estimation.

"So, he harassed Hazeleigh for weeks. Then the letters from Amberleigh start and his bothering you guys stops."

"I don't know, Jake. I did sic the police on him. Maybe that's what it really took. Maybe it's a coincidence."

Normally he'd agree with Zara, and he knew it was a possibility. But too much coincidence usually meant something else going on. Even if it wasn't something Jake could untangle. "What's this guy's name?"

"Douglas Nichols. *Dr.* Douglas Nichols." She rolled her eyes, clearly not a fan of the guy. "He works at Bent County Hospital."

Jake looked him up on his phone, but his signal was too weak for the results to come up quickly enough. He muttered a curse under his breath. "Someone needs to ask

Hazeleigh about it. About him, specifically. And the timing with the letters from Amberleigh."

"Well, we did tell Thomas we were going to the station." Zara glanced at the clock on the dash. Way more than twenty minutes had passed. "He likely has since sent out someone to look for us."

Jake glanced out the window, toward the gravel road. He saw the faintest flash of light. It might have been nothing. A falling star. A reflection of something else.

But it looked like the flare of a match.

Jake reached over and gently pushed Zara's head down, so if someone was out there, they wouldn't be able to see her. *Or shoot her.* "Get down."

"What is it?"

He felt the flashback creeping in. Shattered images in his mind, but he also knew he didn't have time for that right now. In a moment like this, he had to use the coping mechanisms he'd learned to separate the two things in his mind.

Because this was too important. Zara was too important.

The flare of a match in Syria. The flare of a match here in Wyoming. Two different moments. Two different situations. But he had to protect people in both.

He kept his hand gently resting on Zara's head. Both to keep her down, away from the windows, and to keep himself tethered to the moment. Zara. Wyoming. Here. Now.

There was an odd *pop* sound, and the slight jerk of the truck.

Someone had shot out a tire.

He didn't understand. He'd just been outside and hadn't heard or seen anything. Now there were people shooting out their tires? And he'd *felt* her jerk right along with the truck, so he wasn't in full flashback, leaving reality behind.

"Okay, Zara, listen to me. I once took down five men who very much wanted to kill me. All on my own. Without a gun. I tell you that so you understand. So, you don't argue with what I'm about to say. You just agree. Because I've done stuff like this before. Okay?"

"I'm going to hate this."

"Yeah, no doubt. I'm going to go out there. I'm going to fight whoever is out there, debilitate them. While I'm doing that, I want you to run."

"Jake—"

"You kind of know where we are. You have the best chance of running somewhere safe, somewhere away from this place. You call Thomas. You tell him everything. This doctor. The bloody necklace. Everything. We don't have time to argue. I just need you to go the minute I start fighting them."

"They have *guns*."

"Someone does, yes. But it's dark, and I know how to fight in the dark. I can do this, Zara." But he knew that no matter how skilled he was, it only took a moment. He fished his phone out of his pocket and shoved it at her. "If something happens, hit send on this text."

"I can't take your phone. How will we contact each—" Another pop, another jerk of the tire.

"We can't drive now. The tires are shot. Someone's likely getting closer." Someone or ones. "Can you shoot a gun?"

"Of course."

Thank God for ranch women. "There's one in the glove compartment. Grab it just in case. Then run. Trust me. You trust me, right?"

Her head nodded under his hand.

"When I close the door, count to thirty, then run." He eased the door open and listened to the night around them. He eased it closed with a quiet *snick* that seemed to echo loudly. He used the truck as a shield as he moved, trying to figure out where the shooter was coming from and how many men he might be up against.

He heard the crunch of snow in front of him, but on Zara's side.

He shoved his hands in his pockets. He found a stray screw he'd shoved into his coat pocket back at the ranch yesterday. He gave it a toss. Then he crouched down and listened as the footsteps pivoted and then headed for where the screw had landed.

So far, just one set of footsteps. Jake listened hard for anyone else close by but didn't hear anything. So when the man came around the back of the truck, Jake lunged and knocked him down. Thankfully, the big gun the man had been holding fell with a soft *plop* out of his hands and into the snow.

Jake couldn't listen for Zara. He could only hope she'd followed his instructions as he fought the man underneath him. They both grappled, punched and tried to grab the gun the man had dropped.

The guy got a decent gut punch in, but that only ticked Jake off. He landed a hard, sudden jab to the temple, knocking the guy out. Jake gave it a second, made sure the guy stayed limp and it wasn't an act.

When he was certain he'd incapacitated the man, he got up and grabbed the dropped gun. Now he had a weapon. He didn't know how long he'd have with the guy knocked out, but at least Jake was the one with the gun now. A barrier between the house and any other men that might come and Zara, running in the opposite direction.

He moved toward the gravel road, surprised to find no one else approaching. No flashes of light. No signs of life. Where had that *one* guy come from? Maybe Jake shouldn't have knocked him out and gotten some answers instead.

But there'd be answers down that road if he went down it. If Zara had listened, had run away and called Thomas, she'd have help. Maybe it was worth the risk to see if he could get her some answers.

He took a step down the road. It was pitch-black. He could only feel his way as he moved through the snow. He could only listen to the muffled sounds of a winter country night.

Maybe he should turn back. Find Zara. Make sure she was okay. She was the priority, wasn't she? Above answers. Above everything. It was cold and snowy and...

He realized someone was there in the dark with him too late. So late he didn't even have time to fight off the sudden jab of metal to his back.

"Drop it," a low voice growled.

It was always the wrong move to worry about someone else. To put someone else's well-being above your own. It led to mistakes. Just like this one.

Still, it was only one guy. Jake just had to play it right. So he didn't wince, barely even scowled. He slowly raised his hands, though he didn't drop his gun. Not just yet. Someone who could move that quietly, that stealthily had to have seen combat. "Former military too, huh?" he asked, trying to sound relaxed and casual.

"I wouldn't worry about it if I were you." The gun jabbed into his back. "Drop the gun and state your business."

His *business*? "I was lost. Looking at the map in my car and your guy blew out my tires."

"Not my guy." He jabbed the gun harder into Jake's back. "Drop your weapon."

Reluctantly, Jake lowered and placed the gun carefully on the snow. Not *his* guy. Was the gunman lying, or were there two dangerous groups out here?

"What were you doing out here?"

"Just driving, man."

The gunman scoffed. "Maybe you're a cop."

Jake laughed. "I don't think so. Pretty sure the cops want me."

"Why'd you stop in front of this guy's house?"

"This a house? I just stopped. Figured out I was lost when I hadn't seen a town in a while. Pulled to the side of the road. Got my map out—"

"You mean the lady you were with got her map out."

This time Jake couldn't control his body. It stiffened against his will at the mention of Zara.

"You've been following us since the motel," the gunman said. "We don't like being followed."

So this was one of the guys from the parking lot. "Don't know what you're talking about."

"Well, since we had someone following you, I'd think you would. You can tell your doctor friend that his sad attempts at turning this around on us aren't going to go the way he thinks. Well, if I let you tell him anything."

The doctor? This guy thought he was connected to the doctor? He wasn't sure if it was better to go along or disabuse him of the notion or something else entirely. But if they were ever going to find out the real truth, Jake was going to have to take some chances.

"Not here about the doctor," Jake said, trying to match the way this man spoke. Prove they were one and the same. "I'm here about the dead woman."

"Don't know if you're playing dumb, or you think I am, but the doctor's got everything to do with the dead woman. Don't let him tell you otherwise, bud. Because I'm not taking the fall for him. I wouldn't even let you take the fall for him after what he did to Amberleigh. Of course, I could always kill you and let him take the fall for both."

Surely this guy didn't mean the doctor had killed Amberleigh. He just meant… Well, if Hazeleigh was being framed, maybe this guy was too.

Headlights appeared on the highway. A truck pulled up behind his. Two men got out. They killed the engine but left the lights on.

Nothing good could happen in the dark, but Jake had a bad feeling with these three guys, the light would be even worse.

Chapter Nineteen

Zara had listened to Jake's instructions.

At first.

She'd gotten out of the car, run in the opposite direction of the doctor's house as Jake grappled with some guy. She'd trusted him to handle it, no matter how it made her throat tight and her nerves jangle like little live wires all over her body.

But when she'd pulled out her phone to call Thomas, she realized she'd lost all cell service somewhere along the way. In order to find some, she'd have to retrace her steps. She could keep going, but she'd easily get lost and there was *nothing* around here except snow. Back to the highway was her best bet.

So she'd turned around and started moving slowly and carefully, back toward the truck where she knew she had at least one bar to get a phone call or text through to Thomas.

Thomas would be looking for them anyway. She held on to that. Still, she knew she needed to make contact so he knew *where* to look. She'd led Jake into something she shouldn't have, and that was on her shoulders. No matter how willingly he'd followed.

Then there'd been headlights, and she'd taken a dive into the ditch on the other side of the highway than they'd been parked on. She'd peeked up over the cold ground and watched two men get out of a truck and stride toward…

Now that there were headlights, she could see. Jake's truck's shot-out tires. The stupid golf ball mailbox. The gravel road.

And Jake. With a gun in his back. Two more men with guns approaching.

He'd said he'd once fought off *five* men when he'd been unarmed, and he wasn't the kind of guy to make up or exaggerate war stories. He was the kind who didn't have to.

Maybe she should trust that he could handle it.

But she couldn't *stand* it. Him standing there because of her. Three guns pointed at him. No matter how relaxed he looked.

She tightened her grip—not on her cell phone, but on the gun she'd gotten out of the glove compartment. Now that she had light and could see what was going on, she had a chance to help. Maybe Jake *could* fight off three men with guns while he had none, but she had one. She could give him a hand.

She only had a second, she knew. Once one shot went off, hell would break loose, and quite possibly these men would begin to shoot too. But if she could get two quick shots and disarm two of the men, then trust Jake to take out the third on his own, maybe they could get out of this.

The first and most important target was the man with the gun jabbed into Jake's back. She tested the weight of her gun, glad it was close to the kind of gun she was used to shooting. She had so little margin for error.

But in the wild world of things she didn't know, there were a few things she trusted herself with infinitely. Cows and ranching, mostly, but she also knew how to shoot a gun with pinpoint precision because she'd always wanted to be able to protect her family out there in the middle of nowhere and she'd known Dad wouldn't always be reliable in a dangerous situation.

She took a deep breath and steadied herself. She focused

on the arm the man was holding his gun with. She'd aim for his arm, then the man on Jake's right's leg. She'd hope and pray he could take out the one on his left on his own.

She counted her breaths, tried to find a stillness, even with her nerves strung far too tightly.

One, two.

One, two.

She pulled the trigger once. Moved slightly. Twice. She couldn't pay attention to the results. She had to shoot and duck.

And pray.

It was a quick prayer, just *please, please, please,* before she popped up and looked at the scene below.

Three men slumped on the ground, and Jake standing over them. He looked like he was speaking to them, maybe. Zara adjusted her grip on the gun and then began to move forward.

When she approached the men, Jake frowned at her. "You were supposed to run."

She shrugged. "I ran. Then I came back."

He shook his head, then looked back down at the men on the ground. He'd collected all of their weapons. One was passed out cold, one was writhing around holding his leg, and the other looked straight at Jake, a furious scowl on his face.

"This guy says the doctor is trying to pin Amberleigh's murder on *him*," Jake said, pointing the gun at the scowling man.

"Why would Douglas have killed Amberleigh? They didn't even know each other."

"That's the part he's remaining a little too tight-lipped about," Jake said.

"I don't have to tell you anything. Either of you. Kill me if you want. I'm dead either way."

Zara wasn't sure what swept over her. A surge of fury

so bright and potent it took over everything. Reason. Compassion. What was right and wrong. *Amberleigh* was dead. She didn't have a choice—hadn't had one, as far as Zara could tell.

Why did this guy get one? "I don't plan on killing you," she said, her grip on the gun so tight it hurt. She eyed the man, aimed her gun between his legs. "Just causing some damage."

She didn't miss the way Jake's eyebrows winged up—surprise, maybe even some discomfort. But he stood behind her. Backing her up.

"You shoot me, you'll either miss or kill me."

"That's funny, I didn't miss or kill you when I was back there. I'm *much* closer now." To prove it—and her impeccable aim—she shot at the grass, between his legs, without hitting anything. But close enough to scare the life out of him.

He scrambled back on a high-pitched scream. "Okay, okay," he said his voice quite a few octaves higher than it had been. He brought one hand to his ear, as if it was in pain.

Zara was so furious she barely noticed the dull echo of the very loud gunshot in her ears. "Tell me what happened. Now."

"Amberleigh was working the doctor over a little bit, and since she knew he'd been dating one of you, all she had to do was pretend to be her. He had some access to things we needed. So it worked out."

"Worked out?"

"Drugs," Jake said flatly. "Amberleigh was pretending to be Hazeleigh and conning the doctor out of drugs. Or prescriptions. So you could sell them, I assume?"

The man shrugged. "So what? How the hell else am I supposed to make a living around here?"

"Amberleigh…worked with you?" Zara said, because

it still didn't fully make sense to her. "To get and sell the drugs?"

"You guys gonna turn me over to the cops or what?"

Zara looked over at Jake. She honestly didn't know how to sort through all of this.

"Seems like you'd have just as much reason to kill Amberleigh as the doctor."

"Are you kidding? Do you know how much money I made off of Amberleigh? Girl could talk a prescription pad or case of tranqs out of just about anyone. As far as I'm concerned, that doctor owes me now. That's why we're here. If you two hadn't started interfering."

"He owes you because my sister made you *money*?" Zara didn't realize she'd aimed the gun again at first. She only saw red, only felt a well of grief and rage. But Jake's hand gently rested over hers on the gun.

"We should get out of here," he said in low tones.

"You can't leave me to his guys," the man yelled.

Jake shrugged and began to pull Zara away. He also pried her fingers off the gun and took it.

"Who taught you to shoot like that?" he murmured as they began to walk.

"No one. I just practiced. Jake…"

He shook his head as if in some kind of amazement. "I think I'm in love with you. Come on." He pulled her back into the dark and began to run. "We have to get out of here. We just walked into something far more complicated than we anticipated, and gunshots are going to lead to—" he stopped suddenly "—people coming. From both sides." He blew out a breath. "All right. Stick with me. Don't say a word."

He began to run again, her hand secure in his. She knew he was keeping his pace slower because of her, so she tried to increase her speed without being too loud. She let him lead her through the dark, because words like *love* were rattling around in her head along with more complications than they'd anticipated. Of course that love comment was a figure of speech...not...real.

They crested a snowy, rolling hill and there were lights in the distance. A house. The house.

Jake stopped her on a dime. He held her close. "I see two guards on the front. I think there are more. We've got a couple men behind us, but they're being more careful."

"So what do we do?"

"There's something due east. A fence or a...something. I can't quite make it out. But we're going to very slowly, very quietly move toward it. Hold my hand the whole way there, and if I give you a push, you run for it. No matter what. Got it?"

"Yeah." His hand slid down her arm to grasp her hand, fingers interlaced as he began to move. The pace was excruciatingly slow, but he was paying more attention to the house than their progress.

Rightfully so, if there were people closing in on them.

They reached whatever Jake had seen. A pillar of some kind that attached to a wrought iron fence. But the pillar was tall and thick and could hide both of them. Jake gave her hand a tug, pulling her into a squatting position against the brick.

"Can I have my phone back?"

She pulled it out of her pocket and handed it to him. He cursed quietly. "There's no service down here."

Zara thought about that text he'd asked her to send only if something went wrong. She leaned close to him, careful to keep her voice at a whisper. "I feel like I should tell you something."

"What's that?"

"I sent the SOS text to your brothers before you even got out of the car."

He was so still. Like, he didn't even take a breath.

But then he let out a long, slow exhale. "Well."

"I'm sorry."

"No, no, it's…fine. We're in a hell of a jam. If you couldn't get through to Thomas, they're the next best thing."

But he didn't sound certain about that. Of course, he didn't sound…upset either. Though it was hard to tell when they were speaking in hushed whispers. "You're not mad?"

"No, I think we're going to need the backup."

"Your…brothers."

"We were a military team. I'm not supposed to tell anyone that. No one is supposed to know anything about our past."

"Because…"

"Because we're terrorist targets if anyone ever finds us."

Terrorist targets. She blinked. "That sounds…bad." Which was a lame comment, but she didn't know what else to say to terrorist targets.

"Yeah, it does, doesn't it?" He sighed heavily. "Our histories, our identities were wiped so what was left of the terrorist organization we took down couldn't find us. We got new identities, a ranch in the middle of nowhere and presumably a place we could just disappear since the screwup was the military's fault."

Zara swallowed. She didn't know what to make of that. A terrorist target. Hiding in small-town Wyoming. She certainly believed he was the kind of man who'd taken out terrorist organizations, but to land here…

"So, it's all a lie. Jake Thompson is a lie?"

He made an odd noise. Not quite a sigh, not a grunt of pain. "Everything I've told you about my life is true, Zara. Foster care. Maybe I wasn't adopted into the guys' families, but we became each other's family. They are my brothers, and we all just want…to build a normal life. You can hate me for that. God knows, I'd get it."

"I don't hate you," Zara said quietly. She was still wrapping her brain around what he'd said. Here in the dark and cold. How could she hate him? "Why did you tell me?"

"I don't know. I shouldn't have. Cal will kill me if he ever finds out. We could be yanked if it ever got back to the man in charge of relocating us."

"Yanked. You mean…leave?"

"I'm not leaving. I'm not having another home ripped from me."

He said it with such vehemence, she believed him. And she believed him about the foster homes and the terrorist target no matter how crazy it all sounded, because he just… He made sense. Somehow. To her.

Except he was holding her hand. He'd said he *cared* about her and thought she was beautiful. So, she did the only thing she could think of.

She leaned her head on his shoulder and waited for the next step.

Chapter Twenty

Telling Zara what and who he was—no matter how few details—should have bothered Jake more than it did. But it was like a weight off his shoulders. When she leaned her head on his shoulder, it was like every step he'd ever taken in his life had led him right here.

Except he had to get them both out of this in one piece.

So, now his brothers-in-arms would show up, and if they got themselves too wrapped up in this, the boss would pull the plug. And Jake knew without a shadow of a doubt, he'd fight a reassignment. They wouldn't take him from this new life. They wouldn't take him from Zara.

But that'd be a lot easier to make happen if he could extract them all from this problem before the police got mixed up in it. Which meant he had to stop thinking about Zara and, worst of all, himself.

He needed to focus on the task at hand. "Do we believe that guy? That the doctor killed Amberleigh?"

"It makes sense… I guess. I don't know why Amberleigh would have been involved in drugs. Selling or getting or whatever. She ran away from home, sure, but she could have come home. We would have taken care of her."

Jake didn't say anything to that. He might not have had a real family, but some of his brothers had. And had purposefully left them behind—choosing possible death to having to go back and face them.

Sometimes going home was a lot more complicated than if people would take care of you or not.

But there was a second part to all this. Not just Amberleigh's murder, but someone trying to pin it on Hazeleigh. "Zara, would that doctor know you guys kept a key to your cabin under that plant on the porch?"

She was quiet for a moment, perhaps both surprised by the question but also considering. "I doubt it. We don't tell anyone about the key. He might have seen Hazeleigh use it, but then wouldn't he have used it when he was harassing Hazeleigh?"

"Are you so sure he didn't?" Jake asked gently. Because Zara hadn't noticed someone had been in her cabin before he had. Couldn't the doctor have been in there, messing with things the sisters didn't notice?

"He could have done it like that guy said, and he could be the one trying to pin it on Hazeleigh. It makes a twisted kind of sense, doesn't it?" Her hand shook in his—cold or adrenaline wearing off or just exhaustion. He pulled her close, for warmth, for comfort.

She leaned into him, so he adjusted them into a sitting position, leaning against the pillar. It gave them cover on one side and a line of sight on the other. Hard to sneak up on them this way. Now he just needed a way out of this.

He played over everything that had happened. "The drug guy—his two men who came as backup had followed us from the hotel."

"So, they're part of the group that wanted to kidnap me?"

"Unless there's a third group. But if Amberleigh was impersonating Hazeleigh to get the drugs…maybe they wanted you to do the same."

"Like hell I would."

"I assume that's why they felt the need to kidnap."

Zara let out a long, shuddering breath. "Douglas killed Amberleigh. Because he thought she was Hazeleigh? Because he figured out what she was doing? I don't understand how someone could…could…"

"I've killed people, Zara."

She stiffened, but then she shook her head. "It's different. It's different when you're in the military."

"Maybe. And it never set…well. You convince yourself you're doing it for the good of other people not losing their lives, but it weighs on you. Or I should say, it weighs on some people. The point I'm trying to make is, killing doesn't bother some people. It makes them feel important or powerful. And the whys of that don't have anything to do with Amberleigh. They have everything to do with Douglas."

"I guess." She rested her head on his shoulder, her body leaning closer to his. She sighed again when he wrapped his arm around her shoulders.

"Not quite what I expected to find."

Jake had the presence of mind to clap his hand over Zara's mouth, muffling the scream of surprise she made at Cal's unexpected voice.

"It's just Cal," he murmured into her ear. She nodded against his hand, and he released her and got to his feet. "You made good time," Jake said. He ignored Cal's comment.

"Not going to lie, we were on our way the minute you said to wait for an SOS," Landon said.

Jake realized they must all be there, hidden in various shadows. Because if there was one thing Team Breaker knew how to do, it was disappear.

"Dunne's taking care of those guys you took out at the road." That came from Brody. "We loaded them into the truck and he'll dump them not far from the hospital. Then he'll come back and pick us up."

"Hopefully we're done by then," Cal continued. "What's the status?"

Jake didn't care for Cal's tone of voice. Disapproving and controlling. He didn't have time to fight Cal for the upper hand, and he needed Cal's help and expertise. So he just pretended he didn't feel the undercurrents. "We have two problems here," Jake said.

Zara stood, putting her hand on his back. A bodily move of support, as if she felt or heard the undercurrents, and was backing him over Cal.

He didn't have time for petty infighting, but he couldn't deny it felt good to have Zara supporting him.

"If the information we have is correct, the man who lives in this house is the one who killed Zara's sister. And might even be the one trying to frame Hazeleigh for the murder. But we've got another group out here. One Amberleigh was working for. From what we can tell, they want Zara so they can use her identical face in whatever scheme they had going with Amberleigh. On the positive side, they're also after the doctor."

"Sounds complicated," Landon offered.

"Those are just the parts we're aware of," Jake said, knowing it wouldn't particularly help his case with Cal. But still, they had to have eyes wide open going into this.

"This all sounds like a job for the police," Cal said in that I'm-the-leader voice that had worked in Syrian deserts and Iraqi hotspots but not so much here. Now. "We'll get you guys out, tow Jake's truck and leave it to them."

That wasn't going to work for Jake.

ZARA HELD HER BREATH. It was certainly an option. One that would keep them all out of trouble and danger—or at least bigger trouble.

"But…" She swallowed. She didn't feel right bringing all these guys into it. Guys who were apparently terrorist targets. But didn't that mean they could handle this? Didn't Jake sticking with her through this entire thing mean she should see it through to the end? "What if we call the police and they don't find anything to exonerate Hazeleigh? The police won't listen to the word of a drug dealer."

"You don't have to be here, Cal," Jake said, and his tone was *frigid*. It made Zara want to shiver. Instead, she pressed her hand to his back.

But he continued to speak to Cal. "We're not a team anymore. Feel free to head home," Jake said, a challenge laced with hurt, though Zara wondered if anyone noticed aside from her.

There was a long, tense silence.

"What's the plan?" one of the men who wasn't Cal asked. She couldn't make them all out in the dark. She recognized Cal's weighty, authoritative voice and Landon's joking, ease-the-tension quips, but Brody and Henry sounded the same to her here in the dark.

"We have two objectives. First and foremost, keep Zara away from the group that wanted to kidnap her. There were two other men who arrived here before us. I don't know where they are or what they're doing, but they're here somewhere. They might be after the doctor in the moment, but they'd take her in a heartbeat."

"So we'll take Zara out," Cal said.

"No. You won't take me out." Maybe if she had nothing to offer, she could understand. But everything Jake had been talking about had given her an idea. "I have the same face. You might be able to use me. I could…convince Douglas that I'm Hazeleigh. Maybe. And then maybe he'd confess or something, and I could record it on my phone. Or… I don't know. Maybe there's a better plan, but you need to keep me around in case you can use me. I'll take the risk."

"No. You won't," Jake returned firmly. "We'll take the risks."

"I understand you know how to do this, that you have experience with…missions or whatever. I get it. But she's my sister. All these people around here, whoever they're with, whatever they're doing, they hurt my sisters in *some* way. I have to do everything I can to make sure they pay for that."

"She knows about missions," Cal muttered disgustedly.

Jake clearly ignored the comment. "We could use her," he said reluctantly. "But no taped confessions. No…going in there trying to convince him you're Hazeleigh."

"The other group is ticked at the doctor too?" Brody or Henry asked.

"Yes. We could do an Op B," Jake returned.

"What's an Op B?" Zara asked.

But he didn't answer. Jake turned away from her and when he spoke, she realized it was at his brothers, leaving her completely out of it. Maybe not meaning to, but they'd changed into what she assumed was some kind of military mode and she couldn't follow all the acronyms and code words they seemed to be using.

But they hadn't sent her away. She held on to that.

"We stay at a distance. Pretend we have Hazeleigh. In the dark, far away, Zara won't have to really pretend. He'll just assume we have Hazeleigh."

"Even though Hazeleigh's in jail? If he's obsessed with her, surely he knows her whereabouts."

"Maybe, but I think we can fast talk our way around that." Jake turned to her in the dark. "You won't do anything or say anything. You're basically a prop. If things go sideways, your only objective is to—"

"Run," she finished for him. "And what would have happened if I had run the last time you told me to?"

"I would have been fine. It just would have…taken a little longer."

"Well, time is of the essence because you know Thomas also has someone looking for us now."

"Would it really be so bad if the police showed up?" Cal asked.

"Not…too bad. But there's a slight problem." Jake explained the bloody necklace, and Zara winced as Cal swore harshly.

"Maybe we made a few miscalculations," Jake offered.

"Maybe?" Cal returned incredulously.

"But no one would even be looking at Douglas if we hadn't. So, sometimes miscalculations work out. You should know that better than anyone. And if we can prove Douglas had *something* to do with it, we can explain the necklace away and they will be more inclined to believe us rather than try Hazeleigh for murder."

"All right. Well, if you're taking the lead on this, organize the teams."

Even in the dark, Zara could tell Jake was a little taken aback by Cal's acquiescence of decision making. But he recovered quickly.

"Brody and Henry, you'll scout out the perimeter. We need a guard head count, an idea of the security measures on the—"

He stopped talking abruptly and then grabbed her fiercely. She had a sense there was some kind of communication going on between the men—though she couldn't hear or see anything.

Then there was a beam of light. It was pointed straight at Zara, and she winced and threw up her arms to shield her eyes from the painfully bright and surprising light.

Then she was being shoved. Hard. Her eyes flew open, but it was dark again and she couldn't see. The shove was hard enough she fell to the ground.

She lay there, not sure what to do in the dark with muffled grunts and thudding sounds of punches landing around her. The flashlight had fallen to the ground, so she could only see the occasional pair of boots come into view in that beam of light.

She began to inch toward it on her hands and knees, not

wanting to draw any attention to herself. If she could get the flashlight, she could see what was going on. She could help.

Someone tripped over her and fell to the ground with a crash and a yelp of surprised pain, likely landing at an odd angle or hurting themselves trying to stop the fall. It didn't *sound* like one of Jake's brothers, but in the dark, she couldn't be sure.

She kept moving, got to within an arm's reach of the flashlight. She could see two men fighting to the side. She reached out to grab the flashlight, to try to hopefully point it more toward them so she could make out who was who, but right before she managed to get her fingers around the flashlight, someone pulled her roughly to her feet.

She was about to fight with everything she had, but she sagged with relief when she realized it was Jake. But he held her strangely. Not roughly, but with one arm around her midsection and in front of him, like he was holding her against her will, though he wasn't. Like he was using her as a shield when *that* would never happen.

"Sorry," he whispered, and then pressed the barrel of his gun to her temple.

"Come a step closer," Jake said, his voice loud and clear, and Zara realized he was speaking to someone else. "And your boss is going to be pretty mad at you."

A man all in black, now holding the flashlight in one hand and a high-powered-looking gun in the other, was facing off with Jake. But Jake held her in front of him, the gun to her temple.

It was a very strange, uncomfortable feeling, but he kept his hold on her gentle, and while that steadied her some, she knew it didn't look great to the security guard that had to believe this was Hazeleigh.

The security guard studied Jake in the flashlight beam. "Let's everyone just stay calm," the guard said carefully.

"Get your boss out here. *Now*," Jake returned, his voice gravelly and cold. "He has five minutes."

Chapter Twenty-One

Jake had been in a lot of terrible situations but few matched having to hold a gun to Zara's head and pretend like he might kill her. Knowing he had to make it realistic.

Luckily, the guard seemed to believe him. He'd backed slowly away, toward the house.

His brothers had scattered after taking care of the other two guards who had snuck up on them. Jake still wasn't sure if they were the doctor's guards or members of the other guy's little drug gang, but it didn't matter. They'd taken care of them.

Now they needed the doctor.

Maybe the plan hadn't been fully fleshed out, but Jake trusted each of his brothers to do what was right. Necessary.

For the briefest moment, he rested his cheek against the top of Zara's head. He didn't dare put the gun down. He wasn't sure he'd be able to bring it back up, and here in the dark, it was too easy to be caught off guard.

"You need to take my hair down," Zara whispered.

"Huh?"

"My hair should be down. I'll look more like Hazeleigh if my hair is down. If I can have five seconds to take the coat off and tie it around my waist—"

"It's freezing out here."

"That'll add to it. Me shivering and uncomfortable. Hazeleigh isn't big on jeans, but it'll be more like her if I have the coat tied around my waist. Hair down. Just pull the band out and undo the braid."

She was likely right. She'd certainly know better than him. It worried him, the time it would take, but he didn't have time to waver then. "Okay. Quickly. Take off the coat and I'll handle the hair."

She shrugged out of the coat, and he pulled the band out of the braid while she tied the coat around her waist. Her hair stayed wound together so he had to quickly unravel the twisted strands while still holding the gun close enough to her head it didn't look like he was about to let her go.

Light flooded on from the house. Jake forced himself not to flinch or close his eyes in instinctual response.

They were now swathed in it. The whole front yard practically bright as day. It wouldn't help them with pretending Zara was Hazeleigh, but for now, they had to stick with the plan. Jake looked around quickly. He saw two men lying on the ground—neither were Jake's brothers, so they had to be either more security for the doctor or the group that wanted drugs.

The guard from before stepped back out of the house, followed by a tall man with sandy-blond hair.

"I suppose for a couple of thugs, you think this is very impressive."

"You must be Douglas Nichols."

"Dr. Nichols," the man corrected. "It'll do well for you to remember I'm a *doctor*, with unlimited connections and resources. Whatever your sad little group is trying to do will only get you in trouble. The police *are* on their way."

"Are they?" Jake returned, as if he was unbothered, though the police being on their way definitely put a wrench in his plans. Maybe they'd look closer at Douglas because of this, but maybe they'd find that bloody necklace in his truck and draw all the wrong conclusions. "Then we better hurry this up. You'll be taking the blame for Amberleigh Hart's murder or you'll have another murder on your doorstep that I'll make sure the police take a real hard look at you for, *Doctor.*"

The man scoffed.

"I don't know why you think I'd care what a careless group of drug-addicted criminals would do to that woman."

Jake had a beat to think, to pivot. He looked at Zara in disgust. "I thought you told me he cared about you."

"I… He did. I thought he did. Maybe Zara was right."

Jake was impressed by how different Zara managed to sound. Uncertain and stuttering, as though she was both afraid and another person entirely. The skittish Hazeleigh.

"Hazeleigh is in jail," Douglas said flatly. "I'm not a moron."

"Zara took my spot," Zara blurted.

The doctor blinked at that, and Jake had to fight to keep his own surprise out of his expression.

"When they were coming to arrest me," Zara continued, still speaking in that breathier, more halting pattern of speech. "We switched places. She didn't think I'd make it in jail. You know how protective she is."

"You've been…pretending to be Zara," the doctor said, clearly trying to sound like he didn't believe her, but there was enough speculation in his gaze it was obvious he wasn't convinced one way or another.

Zara nodded. "I've done all her chores. Gone to visit Zara in jail. One of those men who bought our ranch was even helping me look for who killed Amberleigh, thinking I was Zara. Zara's really the only one who knows me well enough to tell. Well, and you, of course."

Jake had to angle himself so his face was hidden behind Zara's head because he wanted to laugh. She was laying it on a little thick, but the doctor seemed to be eating it up, and that's all that mattered.

"Come here."

Zara stepped forward, but Jake's grip tightened, and though it pained him, he jabbed the gun tighter against her temple. "Uh-uh. You give me what I want first," Jake said, shifting so he could glare at the doctor again.

Douglas sighed heavily. Dramatically. "What you really want are drugs. The woman currently in jail will take the fall for the murder. That doesn't matter any. We'll set that aside." He said it without pause. Just a man issuing orders, like Jake would automatically follow.

"I know your little friend was more interested in the prescriptions, but that's simply far too easy to trace back to me, which I tried to tell her. It's really her own fault she wouldn't just listen."

"You killed her because she wouldn't listen?"

"I killed her because she was a duplicitous, argumentative, piece of trash who thought she was better than me and my beloved." He said all of that with a pleasant smile, but his hand had curled into a fist. "Now, let Hazeleigh go and we'll come to some sort of deal. The police *are* on their way, so time is wasting."

"Let me go," Zara said under her breath.

"Over my dead body," Jake muttered right back.

"We're going to hide," Jake said firmly to Douglas. "You're going to get rid of the cops. *Then* we can talk."

"You will not be issuing orders. Now. Men?" Douglas snapped his fingers and the man next to him used some kind of two-way com unit. But all the response was static.

Then Cal, Brody and Landon stepped into the light.

"Sorry, buddy," Landon said with a grin. "I think we took care of your *men*."

ZARA THOUGHT SHE should feel some kind of relief. Surely Jake and his brothers could take care of a doctor and one security guard. And Douglas had confessed. Out loud. In front of all of them.

But the tension inside of her only wound tighter. Because while Jake's brothers had moved into the light, Jake hadn't moved. He didn't put the gun down. They were still playing a game, and as long as they were playing it, everyone was in danger.

The guard with Douglas had a gun. Zara couldn't tell if it was pointed at any of the brothers in particular or if he was just ready to shoot at wherever the threat came from.

Each of Jake's brothers had a gun—most looked like the guns Jake had picked off the drug dealer before the brothers had arrived.

"Face it, Doc," Jake said. "You're surrounded. You've confessed to murder. Have your man put down his weapon. Maybe we'll wait for the cops after all."

"Oh yes. The police will believe a band of drug-dealing thugs who held Hazeleigh Hart at gunpoint over an upstanding doctor with a spotless reputation," Douglas said, disdain and condescension dripping from every word. "You can't beat me. I thought of every possibility. There is no way anyone can pin Amberleigh's murder on me."

"That a fact?" Jake returned. "Anybody get it?"

Cal held up a phone, and though it was tinny and far away and she could only hear muffled words, she realized it was video. Video of Douglas admitting to the murder without any provocation.

Zara looked away from the video to Douglas. She wanted to see the realization dawn on him that he'd been caught. That he'd done it to himself.

But she saw something grim and dangerous in his expression. Like when he'd been outside their cabin and she'd threatened to call the cops. He hadn't hurt them. He'd just pounded on the door and demanded to see Hazeleigh, and Zara had determined he was harmless.

But he'd killed Amberleigh, so that couldn't be. She looked down at his hand and realized he was slowly pulling something from behind his back. There was only one thing it could be.

"Gun. Gun! He's got a—"

Jake practically threw her to the ground at just about the same time a shot exploded around them. The fall to the ground jarred her, and it took a moment to regain her wits and get back up. She whirled around to where Douglas had been.

Henry held him now. The doctor struggled against him, but it was no use. Henry was bigger, stronger. Brody had the guard. Zara whirled to see if Cal had been hit.

But Cal was standing, still holding the phone out like he was showing it to everyone. There was a frozen look of pure, undiluted shock slackening his features.

Because Jake was crumpled on the ground in front of him.

Zara's heart simply stopped. "No." She lurched toward him, and by the time she got there, Cal had gathered his wits enough to be kneeling next to him, rolling him over.

Zara barely heard the sound of anguish that came out of her own mouth. He'd been shot. Cal immediately put his hands over the bleeding wound on Jake's stomach.

"No, no, no." Zara fell to the ground next to him. She touched his face. "Jake."

"I'll be fine," he muttered, but his eyes were closed and his words were slurred and *pain* radiated from him.

But he was alive. Talking. Writhing in pain. "Jake..." She didn't know what to say or do. "Please."

Someone tried to nudge her out of the way, but she slapped at them. She couldn't leave him. She couldn't... "Jake. Jake." She didn't know what to say. She wanted to demand he open his eyes. Demand he be fine. Yell at him for being a jackass. *A hero.*

"Zara, get out of the way. Dunne can help, but you need to move. You have to give him room to work."

It took a few more seconds for the words—Cal's words—to actually penetrate her brain. She stopped fighting the arms that pulled her away, as she realized Dunne was in fact there, already pressing something to that awful bleeding hole in Jake's abdomen. He had a bag or something. Medical supplies. He was going to make it okay. He *had* to make it okay.

Cal was the one who had dragged her away.

"It's going to be alright," Cal said roughly. "Dunne has experience with this."

Because they'd each been hurt before. To war before. Together. A team. *Brothers.*

But Jake had moved to save Cal. To take the bullet instead.

"I can hold his hand. I can talk to him. I can—"

"Just give Dunne room to work."

She whirled at Cal as a tide of anger and fear swept up and over any last vestiges of reason. "Why'd you let him do it?" she demanded, tears pouring down her face no matter how she tried to restrain them. She pushed at Cal. "You shouldn't have let him jump in front of you."

Cal didn't say anything. He stood there with that same frozen shock on his face as from before.

Zara couldn't stand to look at him any longer. As far as she was concerned, this was half his fault.

But only half. She looked around the yard and found the other half. She stormed over to where Henry held a still-struggling Douglas. She marched right up to him, the need to hurt him so very potent she didn't even question it.

"You're not Hazeleigh," he said with disgust as she approached. "You lying—"

She punched him. Hard as she could, right in the throat where she knew it would do a decent amount of painful damage.

"You will rot in jail and hell for what you did to my sisters and Jake."

She could tell he wanted to respond, but he was still too busy gasping for air. She wanted to punch him again. Take one of the guns from Henry or Brody and shoot him. Kill him like he'd killed Amberleigh.

But she only stood there as the red haze of fury and fear began to drain out of her, into a numbness.

That's when she heard the sirens. Sirens. Help. God, they needed help. She started to run toward them. Cal did too, and beat her to where an ambulance had parked behind two Bent County Sheriff's Department cruisers.

"He's been shot," Cal was saying as he led an EMT over to where Dunne was still working on Jake.

Jake, still as death. She moved for him again, but someone grabbed her arm. She whirled, ready to punch and fight her way out of whoever's grasp. But it was Thomas. Still not in uniform.

She dropped her bunched fist. She couldn't read his expression. "Let me go."

"Give them room to work," he said flatly.

Why was everyone telling her to give them room? Jake needed someone. Someone to hold his hand. Someone to tell him… She didn't know, but she couldn't stand this. "I need to be with him."

"I'll drive you to the hospital."

"But you have work here."

He shook his head. "I can't be on this case, Zara. I'm only here because of you." He tugged her arm. She wanted to shake it off, but they were moving Jake onto a stretcher. The low murmurings were nonsense to her. She didn't know any medical terms.

Dunne moved with the EMTs, talking to them in serious tones. And he got into the ambulance as they loaded the stretcher, so Jake wasn't alone. He was with his brother.

Thomas pulled her arm again. "Come on. We'll follow."

So she walked with him to his car. His personal car because he wasn't acting as sheriff's deputy here. He was here as her cousin. He'd come because...

Well, likely because she'd lied to him. In a way that might get him in trouble with his job. She closed her eyes, too many emotions battling for prominence, so she just felt like she'd hit a brick wall. Impenetrable. Heavy.

"You lied to me," he said after a long while of following the ambulance, his eyes on the road ahead of them.

"Yes," she said and felt guilty despite herself. "Now we know who killed Amberleigh. You're welcome." And Jake had been shot trying to save his brother. His brother who had only been there because Zara had gotten Jake all mixed up in this.

She'd figured he was something like invincible. He could fight men off with weapons and pretend to hold a gun to her head. He could help her—when no one else in her life had ever really helped. Ever really just *been* there.

But he couldn't let his brother get shot.

She closed her eyes against the wave of pain. When the car stopped, she opened her eyes and saw the hospital entrance. She didn't know what she felt. She didn't know how to *bear* any of this. But she wanted to do it alone.

Alone was what she should have been all along. "I don't need you to come in with me."

Thomas looked at her, a mix of hurt and something else in his gaze. He shook his head. "Maybe you don't, Zaraleigh, but it's about time people stopped listening to what you say you don't need."

In a different moment, she might have been offended enough to yell at him, but he parked the car and took her by the arm as though she wasn't strong enough to walk on her own.

She swallowed at the lump in her throat and had to admit

to herself that Thomas knew where to go a lot better than she did. He took her to a waiting room where Jake's brothers were sitting or standing in various positions.

"Any news?" she asked. Any of them. All of them.

Cal shook his head. He was staring at his hands. Clearly he'd been cleaned up a little bit, but there were still traces of blood there.

Jake's blood.

It hurt, but something about the way Thomas was still holding her arm reminded her that hurt wasn't all about anger. Anger was easier, certainly. A safer place to hurt, but it wasn't…right.

"I need to apologize for what I said to you back there," she managed to say to Cal.

He laughed, bitterly, and shook his head. "Why?"

"It's not your fault he jumped in front of you. He would have jumped in front of anyone. That's…who he is." The lump in her throat seemed insurmountable, but she forced the words out. "He saves people."

That didn't seem to ease the guilt Cal clearly held on his own shoulders, but he feigned a smile anyway. "You're right about that."

A nurse bustled in and surveyed the group. "Are any of you Jake Thompson's immediate family?"

Cal stood, and all the other brothers waited. Because Cal was their leader, even in this. "I'm his brother."

"All right. Come with me."

Cal followed the nurse.

And Zara could only wait.

Chapter Twenty-Two

Zara was numb. No one at the hospital would tell her anything, and Cal didn't come back before Laurel showed up and pulled her aside.

"We're going to need a formal statement. Dr. Nichols already has lawyers crawling all over the station, so the sooner we do this the better."

Lawyers. "But he did it. He admitted to doing it on video."

"Yes, and Mr. Thompson handed his phone over to the police officers at the scene, but we still need to make this case airtight. I want a statement from you, but let's find somewhere a little private."

Laurel took her arm like Thomas had.

"I'll text you if there are any updates," Thomas said. Even though he didn't need to stay. He didn't *need* to do any of this. He was doing it because they were family.

Zara felt shamed for lying to him, even knowing they'd had to do it. Shamed that she hadn't leaned on him in the beginning of all this when maybe she should have trusted him.

Too late now.

Laurel led her out of the waiting room and into the main lobby of the hospital. She found a bench in a little alcove. They sat down, practically hip to hip.

"We'll start back at the hotel. I want you to tell me everything from there until Thomas drove you to the hospital. No detail is too small."

Zara swallowed and nodded. It felt like so much pressure, and instead of Jake sitting next to her, holding her hand, she was alone. He was in an ICU room…

Getting help. He was getting *help*. She had to remind herself of that.

She took a deep breath and tried to remember everything. Arriving at the hotel. Their plan. Zara recounted it all, but when she got to Thomas showing up… "I don't want Thomas to get into any trouble. He was trying to do the right thing, really. We lied to him and—"

"It's imperative you tell me the whole truth, Zara, but I have a confession to make that might make you feel better about Thomas keeping some things from me." Laurel shifted on the bench. "I saw you. You and Jake in the hallway at the hotel. Kissing."

Zara's mouth dropped. "What?"

"It was a valiant effort to hide in plain sight, but I'm a detective. I pay attention to details. What boots a person wears, the way they hold themselves when they're trying to hide something. And a million other things that made you two instantly recognizable."

"But you didn't…" Zara tried to work through it. Laurel had recognized them, but she hadn't stopped them. "You let us go."

"Yes, I did."

"Why?"

"Because… I believe in law and order. I believe in investigating by the book because I have to build a case. I have to make sure the right outcome follows solving a crime. But I also know what it's like to have the law be in your way. To need to go around it to keep the people you love safe, or find the truth. I wasn't about to stop you from finding that."

Zara didn't know what to say.

"So, no. Thomas won't be in trouble for not telling us he'd found you guys."

"Detective… Laurel… He killed her. Douglas *killed* Amberleigh. He can't get away with it."

Laurel reached out and patted Zara's hand. "We will do everything in our power to make sure he doesn't. The fact of the matter is, I don't believe in a perfect crime. I believe we would have figured this out…eventually. But it would have taken a long time. Dr. Nichols definitely covered his tracks, and you and Jake interfering the way you did allowed us to connect him to everything a lot quicker than we would have, and the video confession tightens the case considerably. I can't say you did the *right* thing, because you could have let Thomas and me in on some of this, but you didn't do the *wrong* thing either. Now, tell me the rest."

Zara went through all of it, only choking up when she got to the part where Jake had been shot. Shot protecting his brother.

Laurel's hand patted hers again, and this time stayed on top. "I know it's hard watching someone you love get hurt. I've been through that a time or two myself, or been the one getting hurt. You've been through a lot of hurts. It's okay to…let yourself feel all that. No one expects you to power through losing your sister and watching your boyfriend get shot."

Love. Boyfriend. They'd kissed. Once. For fake reasons. And yet…*love* felt exactly right. But there were more people she loved involved in this.

"My sister?"

"Hazeleigh is in the process of being released. She's having a friend pick her up since you're otherwise detained." Noting Zara's discomfort, she looked through her notes. "Friend's name is Kate Phillips?"

Zara nodded. Kate would be good for Hazeleigh. Calm and good at taking care. Something Zara wasn't good at.

Laurel asked a few more questions, noted everything down. Recorded some things. Zara was exhausted by the time Laurel was satisfied, and she hadn't realized she'd dozed off until her phone buzzed.

She jolted awake and looked up. Instead of Laurel sitting on the bench with her, it was Thomas.

"Laurel thought it best to let you sleep."

Zara nodded, then her phone buzzed again and she pawed at her pocket. She opened the text message from Cal.

Awake. Okay. I'll sneak you in.

Zara hopped to her feet. "Cal said he can sneak me in."

Thomas took her arm as she began to walk back to the waiting room. She frowned at him. "I can walk, you know."

"You can walk, sure. You can lean too."

She stared at him a long time. "I'm sorry. That we lied to you. I really am. I just thought it was the only way."

"I'm sorry you thought it was the only way, Zara."

Zara didn't know what to say to that, so she decided she'd go ahead and get better at leaning, and she let Thomas hold on to her while they walked back to the waiting room.

WHEN JAKE WOKE UP, groggy and fuzzy-headed, he thought he was back in a military hospital in the Middle East. Cal was here, after all, looking guilty and furious at once.

But he wasn't in his military uniform or even his civilian, desert clothes. He was dressed in ranch clothes. Because they were in Wyoming.

"Zara." His voice came out a croak with no real enunciation, but Cal seemed to understand.

"She's on her way."

Jake let out a breath and relaxed into the bed. He managed to swallow some of the rustiness in his voice away. "Going to live then, I guess?"

"Looks like. Going to have to take it easy for a while. Clean shot and all, but it'll take a while to heal."

Cal didn't give anything away in his voice, but Jake knew it wouldn't set well with him that Jake had risked his life over him. "Had to do it, you know."

"You really didn't."

"I was the only reason you were there. You couldn't go down because you'd taken the video. Because I needed your help."

"Would have preferred it."

Jake let out a little laugh, but even with the drug haze, he could feel the pain. "You need your head examined, Cal."

"Maybe."

They lapsed into a silence, but it had weight.

"Let me guess," Jake offered. "The boss wants to pull us."

Cal said nothing but eventually nodded.

Jake shook his head. "I'm not going. I'm not. They can't force me. It was their screwup that led us here. I'm not losing this." *I'm not losing her.*

"That's what I told him."

Jake had been ready to rail at Cal, but that stopped him. "What?"

"What? I watched Zara—Zara Hart, who I saw get kicked in the shoulder by one of the cows and not cry—sob all over your sorry ass. Then take a chunk out of me because she was so upset that you'd been hurt. She was *inconsolable.* I don't know anything about love, but I suppose if it's real, that's it."

Jake shifted uncomfortably. *Love.* It was a big, scary word that kept cropping up.

"So, I told the boss that you'd done more for our case by helping a local girl than us pretending to be six related loners could. That you were the one who thought we should get involved so people take us at face value and ask fewer questions. I told him it worked. You'd be hailed a hero, and people would stop looking into our backgrounds."

"I can't imagine he took that very well."

"Not at first, but when I told him you had a local girl-friend, he warmed to the idea."

"Huh?"

"Oh, he said getting married to a local was a great idea. Connects you to the community, lends credibility to our backstory. He was all for it."

"Married?" Jake practically squeaked.

Cal chuckled. "Well, you're well enough to know that's a terrifying thought, but we're staying put, Jake. I'll fight the boss on that. I promise you that."

"I don't need your penance, Cal."

"Maybe not, but you've got it."

Something caught both their attention, and they looked over at the door. Zara was standing there.

"Sorry to interrupt. Dunne showed me the way."

Cal shook his head. "No interruption. I'll wait outside." And he was gone in mere seconds.

Leaving Zara and Jake alone. Her hair was a mess, her clothes still wet and dirty from all the running around in the snow. But she was whole and in one piece and *beautiful*.

"You're okay," she said in a squeaky voice he could hardly reconcile with the Zara he knew.

"I told you I was."

She smiled faintly, finally moving across the room. She looked down at him, brushed her fingers across his fore-head. "You're an idiot," she said, tears in her eyes.

"Yeah." He reached up and found her hand with his. "Going to have to get used to my idiocy."

Something flickered in her eyes that had Jake realizing she might have heard… "I don't know how much you heard of what Cal said, but—"

"We should probably go on a few dates before we decide

if we want to get married," she said seriously, but there was mischief in his eyes.

Jake laughed. Winced. Sighed. "Come here." He gave her arm a little tug.

She looked a little uncertain, but with extraordinary care, she slid into the bed next to him, still holding his hand and managing to avoid all the machines hooked up to him. She rested her head on his shoulder.

And everything inside of him eased. He lifted his hand, drew it down her tangled mess of hair. Despite the gun-shot-wound discomfort and his exhaustion, something right washed over him. Exactly right.

Her. Here. Them.

"How's Hazeleigh?"

She sighed. "She went home with Kate. I'll have to go to her, but I needed to see you first." She rested her hand on his chest, gingerly. "Are you sure you're okay?"

"Going to be a bit of a healing process, but I've survived worse." Which reminded him that he'd…told her. Everything. "Listen, about what I told you back there…"

She lifted her head so she could look him in the eye. "I won't tell anyone. Ever," she said so seriously. A vow. "You're just Jake Thompson from…"

She knew his secret and would keep it. He knew she'd keep it, no matter what. So there was only the truth. "Pittsburgh."

She seemed to think this over. "A long way from Wyoming."

"Yeah, just a nomad looking for somewhere to belong."

Her brown eyes were suspiciously shiny, but no tears fell. "You belong here, Jake. That I'm certain of."

So was he, but that didn't mean things were easy. "Your land, your ranch. You love—"

"I do," she said, cutting him off. "I can't say I'm joyful

about not owning Hart land, but the fact it's keeping you and your brothers safe? That's worth it to me."

Which didn't sit right at all. "You shouldn't always be the one taking care of everyone."

She studied his face, and it was like she understood him down to his soul. She knew his secrets. The things he didn't talk about. Somehow, she understood him. All of him, when he was certain no one would—or could—after all he'd been through.

"Some people take care," she said softly. She pointed to where he'd been shot. "Some people save. It's not so different really. And not as much of a sacrifice when you're doing what's right. For people you care about."

He didn't speak at first. He couldn't. Something had banded around his lungs, tight and squeezing. A depth of emotion he'd need more time to sort through, but there was a basic truth to *all* of this.

"I don't need a few dates to know that what I feel for you is big. Important. And that I don't want to let you go."

She studied him. Dark eyes so serious. Then, very carefully, she pressed her mouth to his. She sighed against his mouth. "I think that's a good place to start," she murmured.

Then she laid her head on his shoulder, hand on his chest.

A very good place to start.

Epilogue

When Zara got home, it was practically midafternoon, even though it felt like it should be the middle of the night. Thomas dropped her off and offered to stay with her, but she sent him on his way so she could be alone.

She had talked to Hazeleigh briefly on the phone, and her sister seemed content to stay at Kate's. Zara knew she should want to see her sister. Maybe even go over to Kate's and confront her. They had so much to talk about, but Zara needed…time. Strength.

She had to be strong for Hazeleigh and she just didn't feel very strong. So, she let the days stretch out. She talked to Jake on the phone, visited once the hospital allowed non-family, texted her sister, did ranch chores with the stoic Thompson brothers. On Christmas Eve, she went to her aunt and uncle's house in Bent, visited briefly with her father.

She'd taken Jake a Christmas Eve dinner, and he'd joked it was their first date when they ate it together in his hospital room.

Hazeleigh kept her distance.

So when Christmas dawned, bright and snowy, Zara decided enough was enough. She got up and dressed, determined to drive out to Kate's, even if it was too early, and demand to see Hazeleigh.

But when she stepped into the living room, the tree was

glowing, even though she'd had the lights unplugged for days. Hazeleigh was sitting at the foot of the tree, looking at the lights. Until she turned her face to Zara.

She managed a small smile. "Merry Christmas."

Zara knew she should demand to know…a million things, but instead, when Hazeleigh got to her feet, she simply crossed the room and hugged her sister. They held on to each other for a long time.

"I'm sorry I stayed away," Hazeleigh said after a while, her voice squeaky. "I just…couldn't face it all. I couldn't come here knowing Douglas had been in there. Planting evidence against me." She shuddered. "A murderer."

"He's in jail now. I talked to Laurel yesterday and she's very pleased with the way the evidence is shaping up."

Hazeleigh nodded and tried to smile, but Zara knew it was fake. And because she did, she couldn't help herself from stepping back. From asking what she promised herself she wouldn't. "Why didn't you tell me? About Amberleigh being back?"

Hazeleigh sighed, then collapsed onto the couch. "I couldn't face you either. Because… Oh, Zara. I knew Amber was mixed up in some bad things. Right from the get-go. She was… I just knew she was lying to me. But I thought if I didn't tell you, if I tried to help her on my own, I might be able to get through to her. You two would have just fought, but I thought I could…fix it."

Zara was quiet. She didn't know what to say to that. It was the truth, but it still hurt because Hazeleigh had never lied to her before.

"I thought it was the group she was with. She told me how dangerous they were. How they'd killed some dealer of theirs who hadn't held up their end of the bargain. She was… She liked it, though, Zee. I couldn't believe it then.

Didn't want to. But she liked doing bad things. She didn't deserve Douglas…"

Zara reached out—something she wasn't sure she would have been able to do if Jake hadn't shown her how easy it could be. She closed her hand over Hazeleigh's. "Don't blame yourself."

Hazeleigh looked down at their joined hands. A tear slid down her cheek. "She died pretending to be me."

"Yes, but that wasn't your choice. And it wasn't your choice to have Douglas be a murderer. You were the pawn, Haze. Not the cause." She grabbed her by the chin so Hazeleigh had to look her in the eye. "It's not your fault."

"Maybe not, but I feel like I'm always the pawn. I'm tired of it."

Zara didn't know what to say. It didn't seem right to tell Hazeleigh it was her choice what to be—pawn or in charge of her own life. So she simply sat in silence and held her sister's hand.

They both sighed at the same time and leaned their heads together, still holding hands. They'd lost the other piece of themselves, but they still had each other.

"I love you, Hazeleigh."

"I love you too."

They were quiet a long time, sitting on the couch, looking at the tree.

"How's Jake?" Hazeleigh asked after a long while.

"Healing well. He should be home tomorrow." Tomorrow. Today was Christmas, but Jake wouldn't be celebrating it in the hospital. She thought of the house, devoid of all Christmas decorations, and how much joy Hazeleigh always got out of decorating.

"I have an idea." She got to her feet and grinned at Hazeleigh. "How about we go be Christmas elves?"

"You *hate* Christmas decorating."

"No, I hate Christmas putting away. There's a difference. Come on." She grabbed Hazeleigh's arm.

A few hours later, after what Zara figured *might* constitute breaking and entering, the house they'd grown up in glowed with Christmas magic.

She stepped back to admire her handiwork. Then looked at her sister.

Hazeleigh was grinning. Color was back in her cheeks. Yeah, this had been a good idea. Even if the guys didn't appreciate it, Hazeleigh did.

"We should get going if we want to be gone before they get back," Zara said. The sun was setting, and the guys should be coming back in from the field soon. Someone would be at the hospital, but they had been taking turns staying with Jake during visitor hours. But Jake had told her not to come today, to spend Christmas with Hazeleigh and any other family she wanted to see.

She hadn't argued, but now she thought…she'd head out to the hospital anyway. Because who she really wanted to see was him. But before she could articulate any of that, the door opened.

Well, she'd face the brothers first, she supposed.

"Merry Christ…" She trailed off as Hazeleigh finished because, while four of the brothers had stepped inside, she was shocked to see Jake was standing in the center of them.

"Well, you two have been busy," Landon said with a grin. "Did you break into our house?"

But Zara barely heard him. Jake was *here*.

"They let me go a little early," he said, as if he too wasn't paying attention to anyone but her.

He was on two feet, standing on his own, and she hadn't realized until this moment how much worry she'd still been carrying about his recovery. But him being home…

She crossed the room and threw her arms around him.

His came around hers. She was careful not to squeeze, not wanting to hurt him. But… "You're home," she whispered into his shoulder.

"Yeah, I am."

* * * * *

MILLS & BOON

THE HEART OF ROMANCE

A ROMANCE FOR EVERY READER

MODERN

Prepare to be swept off your feet by sophisticated, sexy and seductive heroes, in some of the world's most glamourous and romantic locations, where power and passion collide.

HISTORICAL

Escape with historical heroes from time gone by. Whether your passion is for wicked Regency Rakes, muscled Vikings or rugged Highlanders, awaken the romance of the past.

MEDICAL

Set your pulse racing with dedicated, delectable doctors in the high-pressure world of medicine, where emotions run high and passion, comfort and love are the best medicine.

True Love

Celebrate true love with tender stories of heartfelt romance, from the rush of falling in love to the joy a new baby can bring, and a focus on the emotional heart of a relationship.

Desire

Indulge in secrets and scandal, intense drama and plenty of sizzling hot action with powerful and passionate heroes who have it all: wealth, status, good looks…everything but the right woman.

HEROES

Experience all the excitement of a gripping thriller, with an intense romance at its heart. Resourceful, true-to-life women and strong, fearless men face danger and desire - a killer combination!

To see which titles are coming soon, please visit

millsandboon.co.uk/nextmonth

LET'S TALK
Romance

For exclusive extracts, competitions
and special offers, find us online:

- facebook.com/millsandboon
- @MillsandBoon
- @MillsandBoonUK

Get in touch on 01413 063232

For all the latest titles coming soon, visit
millsandboon.co.uk/nextmonth

JOIN US ON SOCIAL MEDIA!

Stay up to date with our latest releases, author news and gossip, special offers and discounts, and all the behind-the-scenes action from Mills & Boon...

 @millsandboon

 @millsandboonuk

 facebook.com/millsandboon

 @millsandboonuk

It might just be true love...

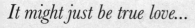

GET YOUR ROMANCE FIX!

Get the latest romance news,
exclusive author interviews, story
extracts and much more!

MILLS & BOON
MEDICAL
Pulse-Racing Passion

Set your pulse racing with dedicated, delectable doctors in the high-pressure world of medicine, where emotions run high and passion, comfort and love are the best medicine.